FUKU

Kitten Tales

2

Konami Kanata

CONTENTS

FUKU
FUKU

Will FukuFuku Be a Star?!

FUKU FUKU

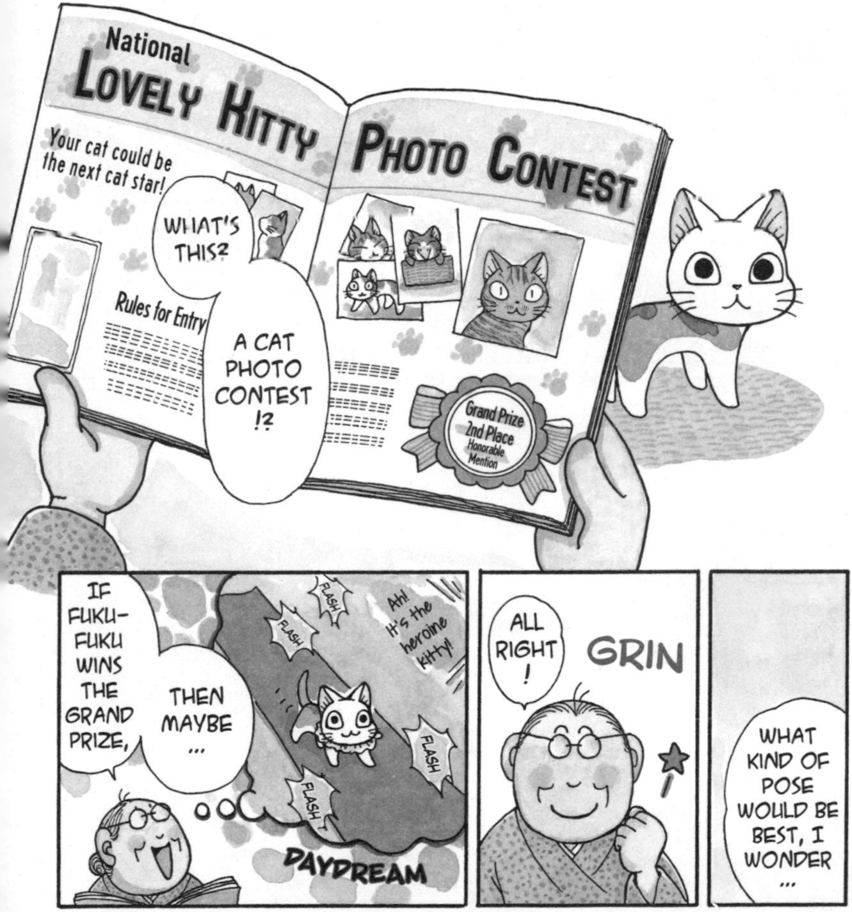
National
LOVELY KITTY PHOTO CONTEST
Your cat could be the next cat star!
Rules for Entry
Grand Prize
2nd Place
Honorable Mention
WHAT'S THIS?
A CAT PHOTO CONTEST!?
IF FUKU-FUKU WINS THE GRAND PRIZE,
THEN MAYBE...
FLASH
FLASH
FLASH
FLASH
Ah! It's the heroine kitty!
DAYDREAM
ALL RIGHT!
GRIN
WHAT KIND OF POSE WOULD BE BEST, I WONDER...

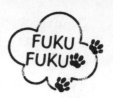

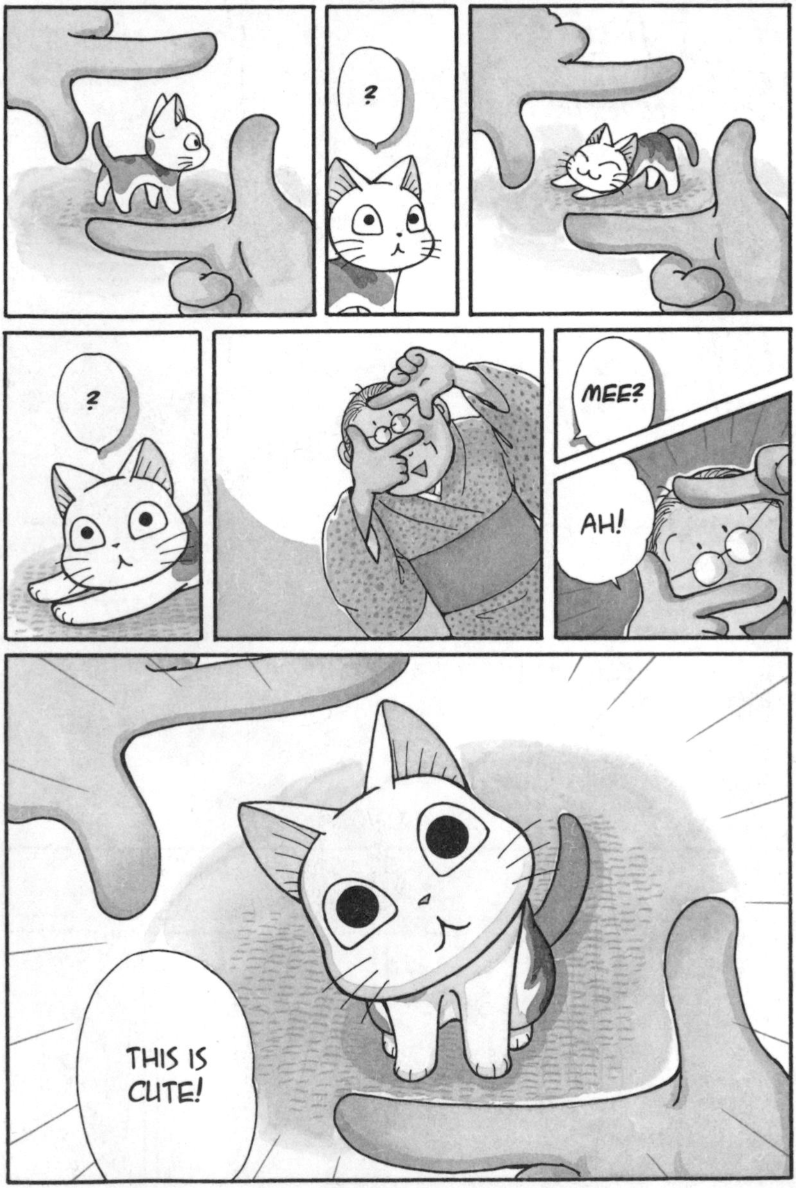
?
?
MEE?
AH!
THIS IS CUTE!

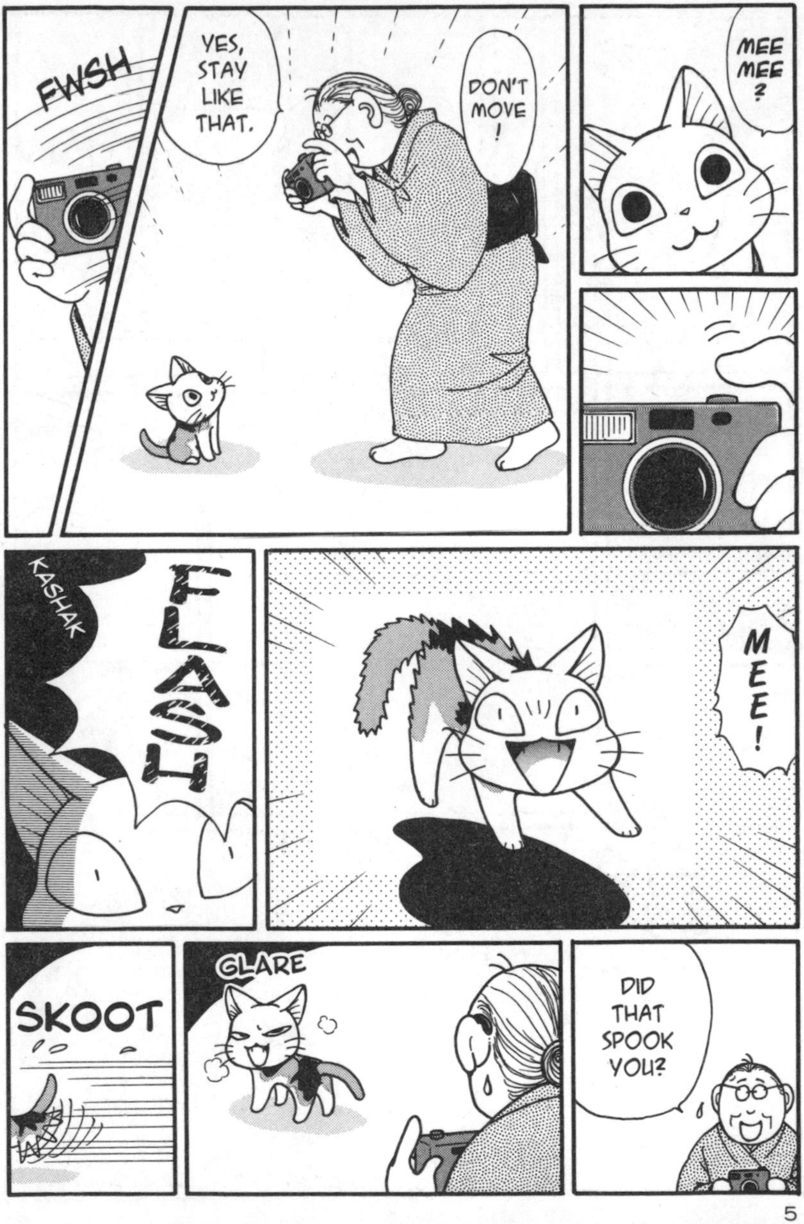
FWSH
YES, STAY LIKE THAT.
DON'T MOVE!
MEE MEE?
KASHAK
FLASH
MEE!
SKOOT
GLARE
DID THAT SPOOK YOU?

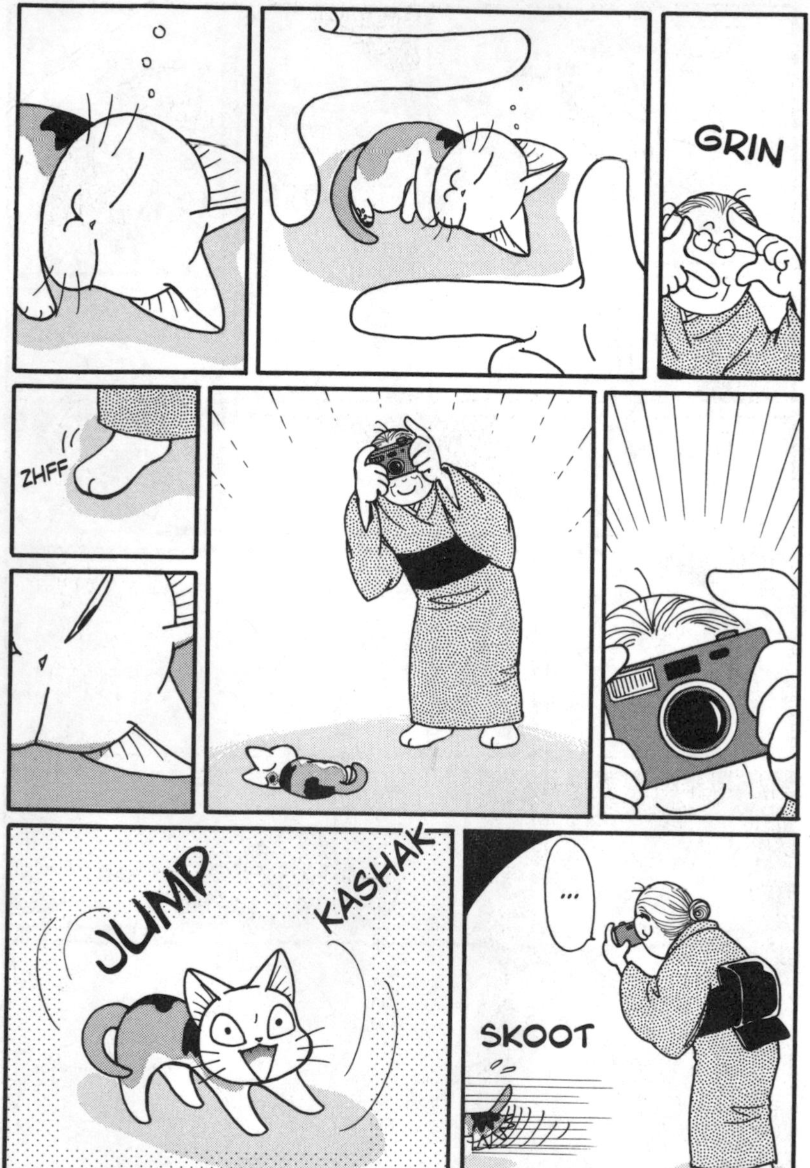
GRIN
ZHFF
JUMP
KASHAK
...
SKOOT

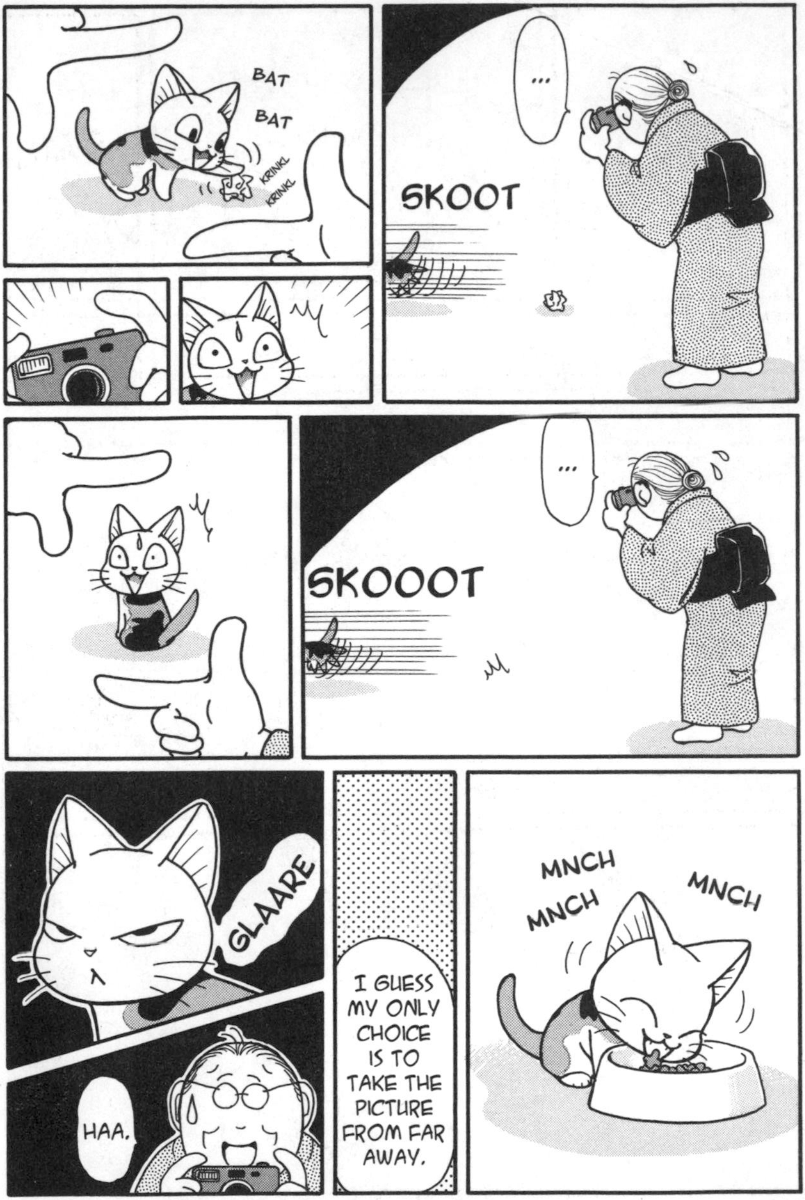
BAT
BAT
KRINKL
KRINKL
...
SKOOT
...
SKOOOT
GLAARE
HAA.
I GUESS MY ONLY CHOICE IS TO TAKE THE PICTURE FROM FAR AWAY.
MNCH
MNCH
MNCH

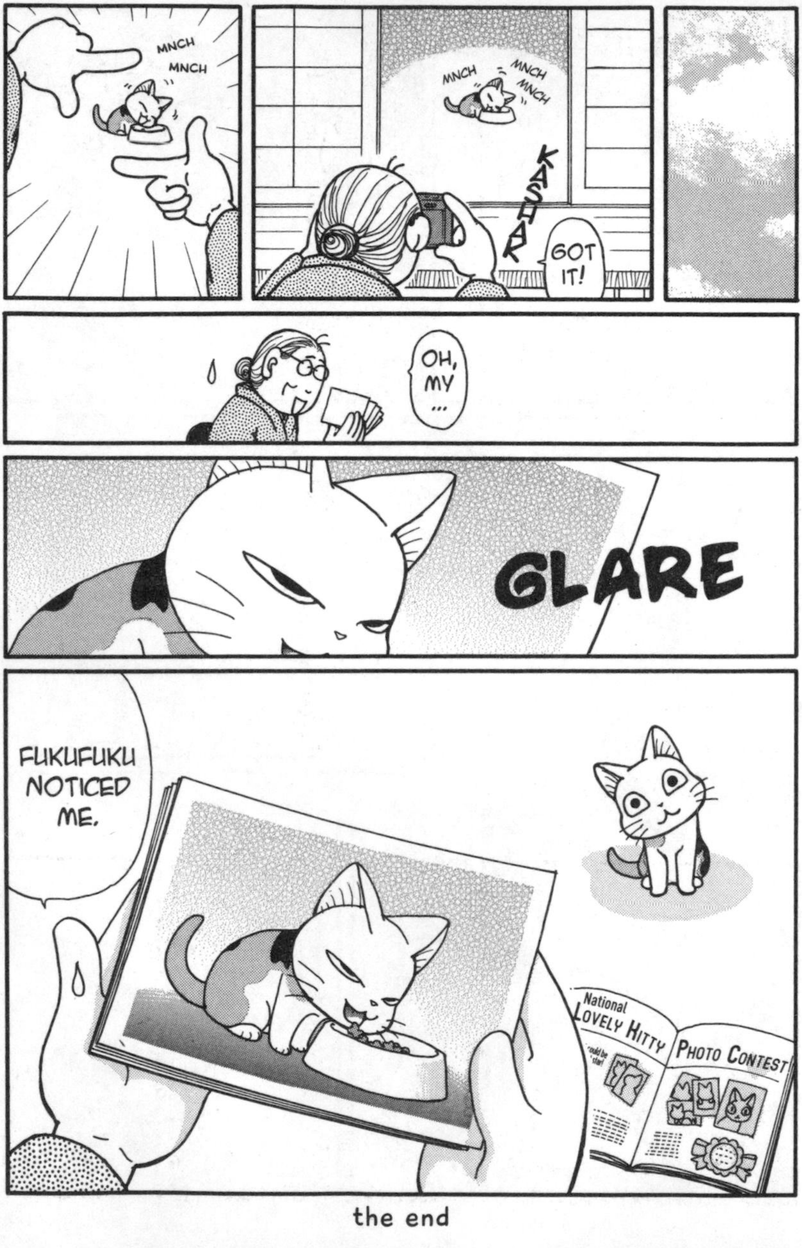
MNCH
MNCH
MNCH
MNCH
MNCH
KASHAR
GOT IT!
OH, MY ...
GLARE
FUKUFUKU NOTICED ME.
National
LOVELY HITTY
PHOTO CONTEST

the end

Kitten in the Gap

FUKU FUKU

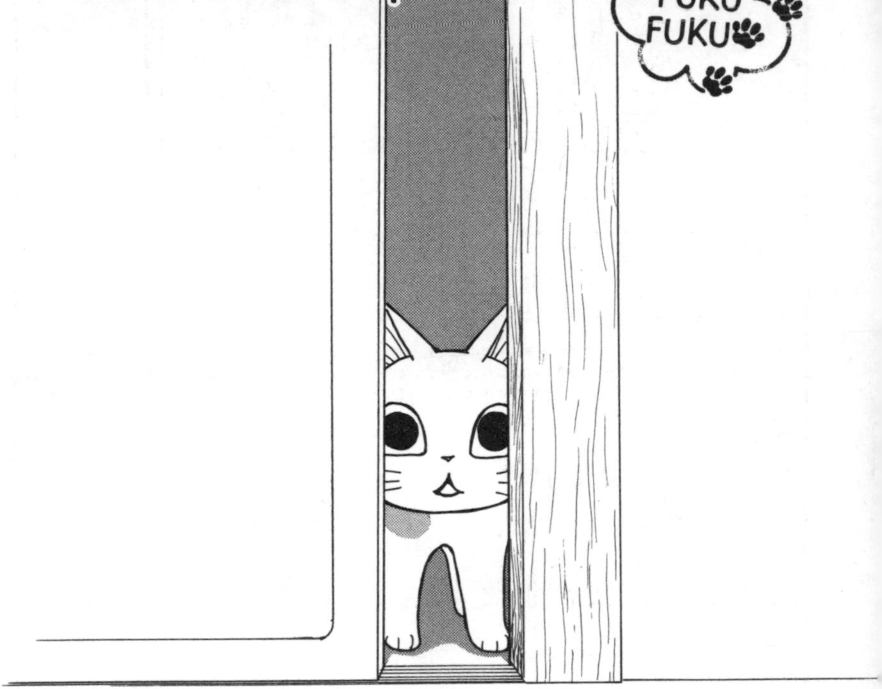

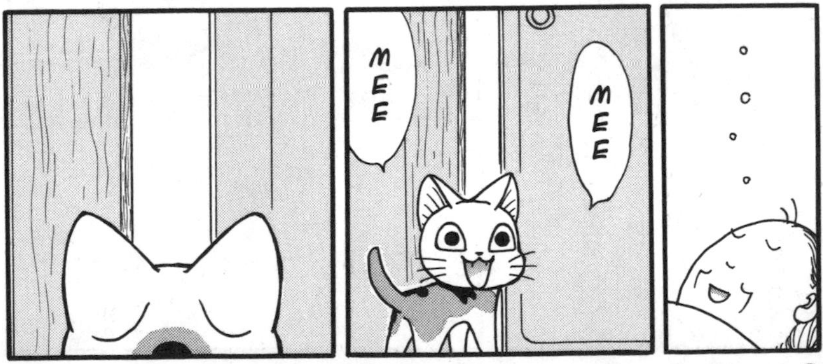
MEE
MEE

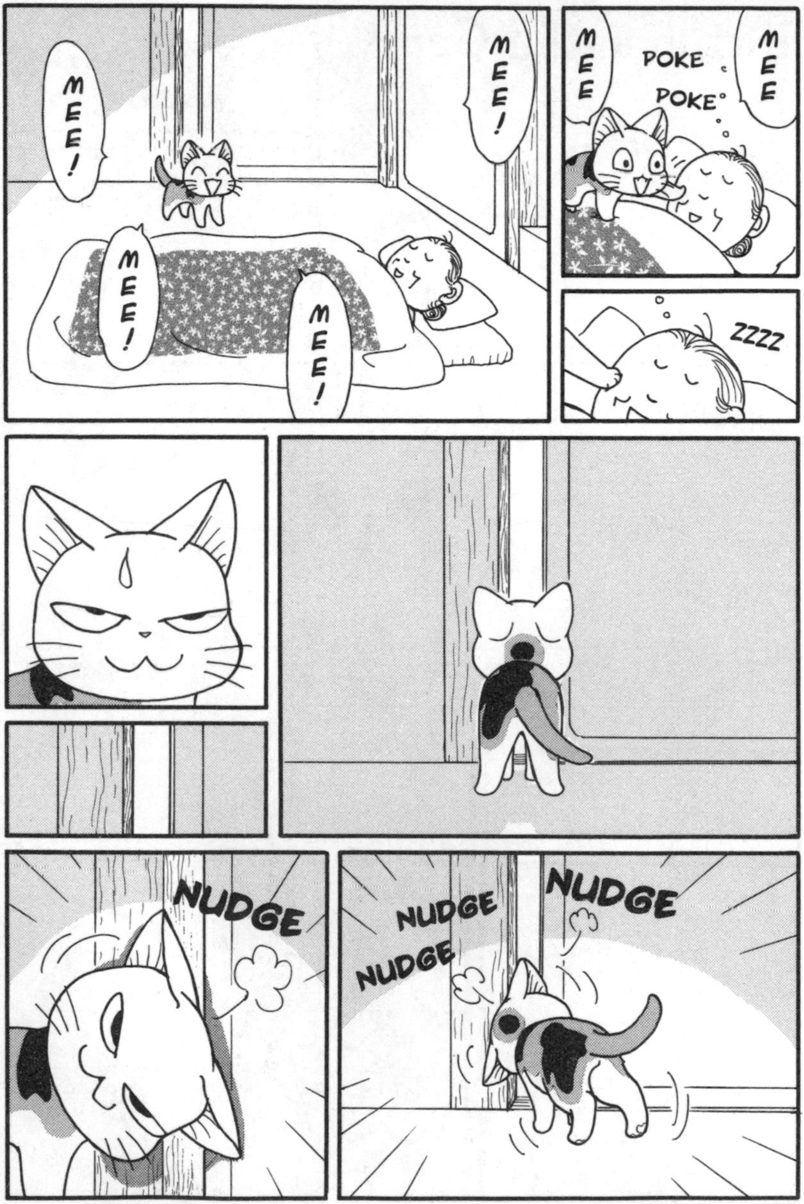
MEE!
MEE!
MEE!
MEE!
MEE
POKE
POKE
MEE
ZZZZ
NUDGE
NUDGE
NUDGE
NUDGE

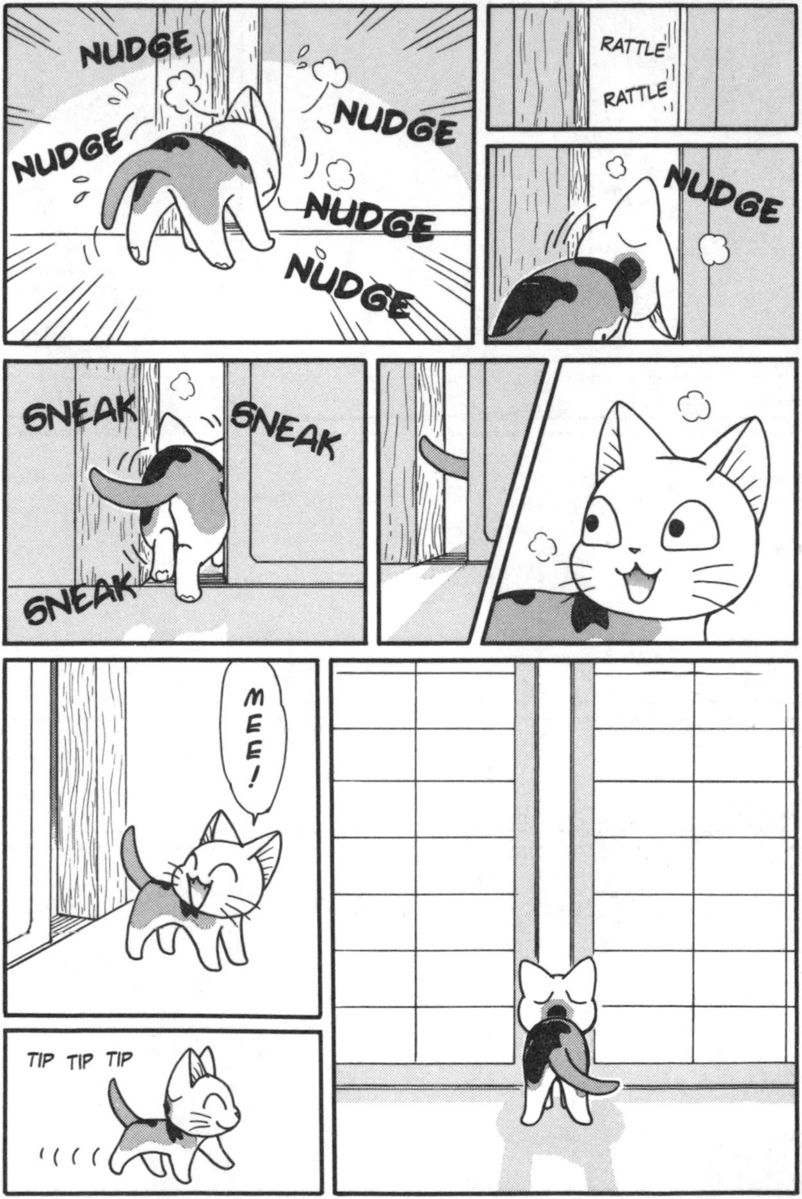
NUDGE
NUDGE
NUDGE
NUDGE
NUDGE
RATTLE
RATTLE
NUDGE
SNEAK
SNEAK
SNEAK
MEE!
TIP TIP TIP

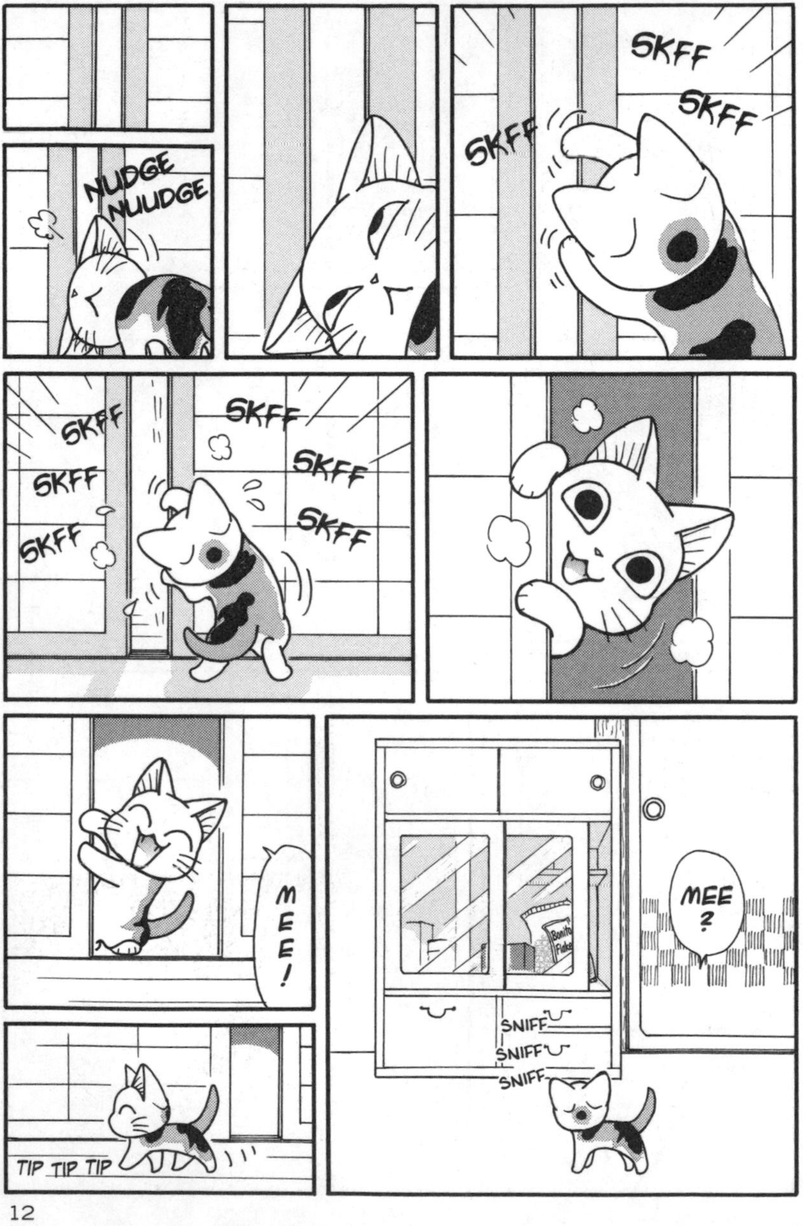
NUDGE
NUUDGE
SKFF
SKFF
SKFF
SKFF
SKFF
SKFF
SKFF
SKFF
SKFF
MEE!
TIP TIP TIP
Bonito Flakes
MEE?
SNIFF
SNIFF
SNIFF

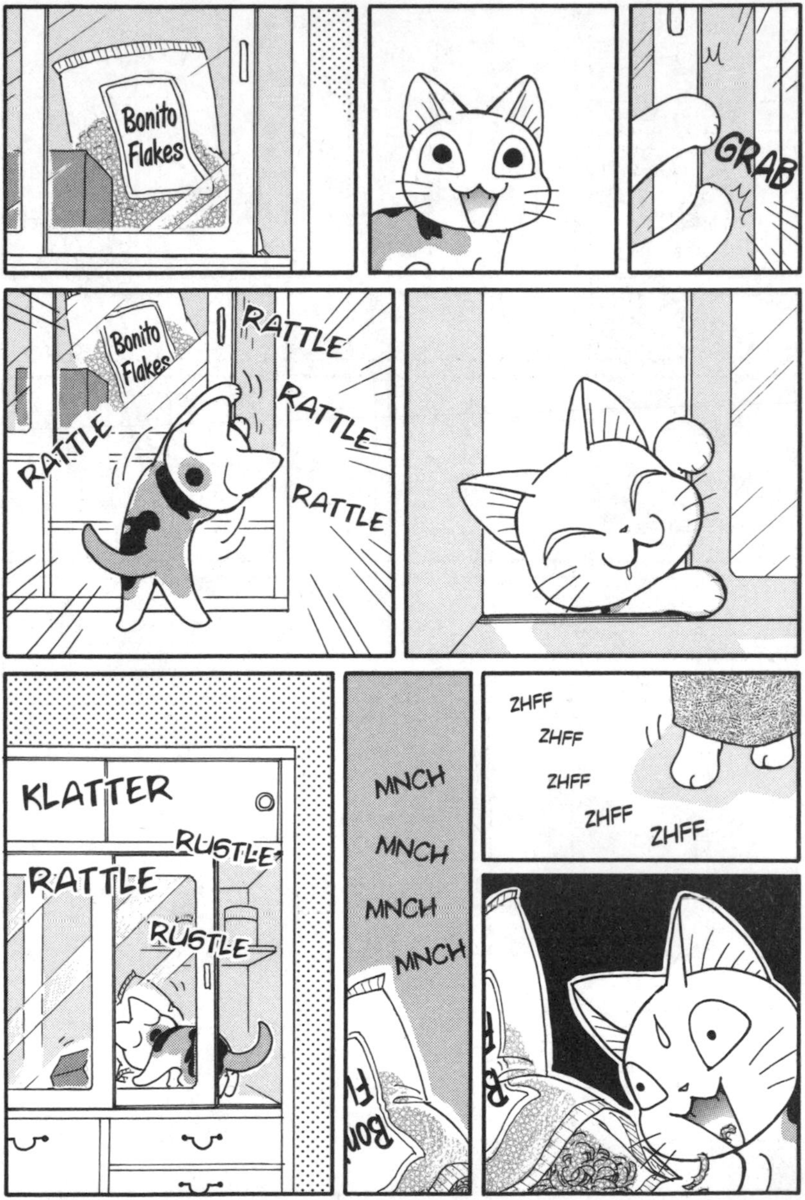
Bonito Flakes
GRAB
Bonito Flakes
RATTLE
RATTLE
RATTLE
RATTLE
KLATTER
RUSTLE
RATTLE
RUSTLE
MNCH
MNCH
MNCH
MNCH
ZHFF
ZHFF
ZHFF
ZHFF
ZHFF

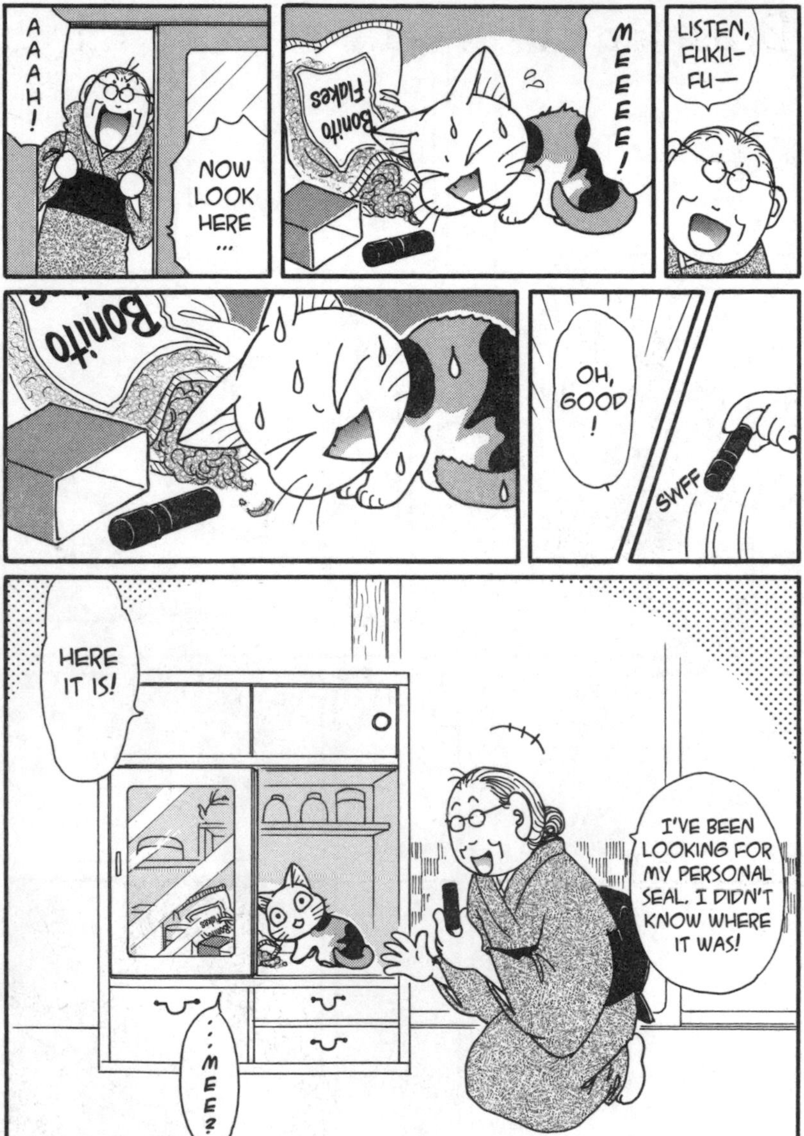
AAAAH!
NOW LOOK HERE...
Bonito Flakes
MEEEEE!
LISTEN, FUKU-FU—
Bonito
OH, GOOD!
SWFF
HERE IT IS!
I'VE BEEN LOOKING FOR MY PERSONAL SEAL. I DIDN'T KNOW WHERE IT WAS!
...MEE?

the end

Brushing FukuFuku

FUKU FUKU

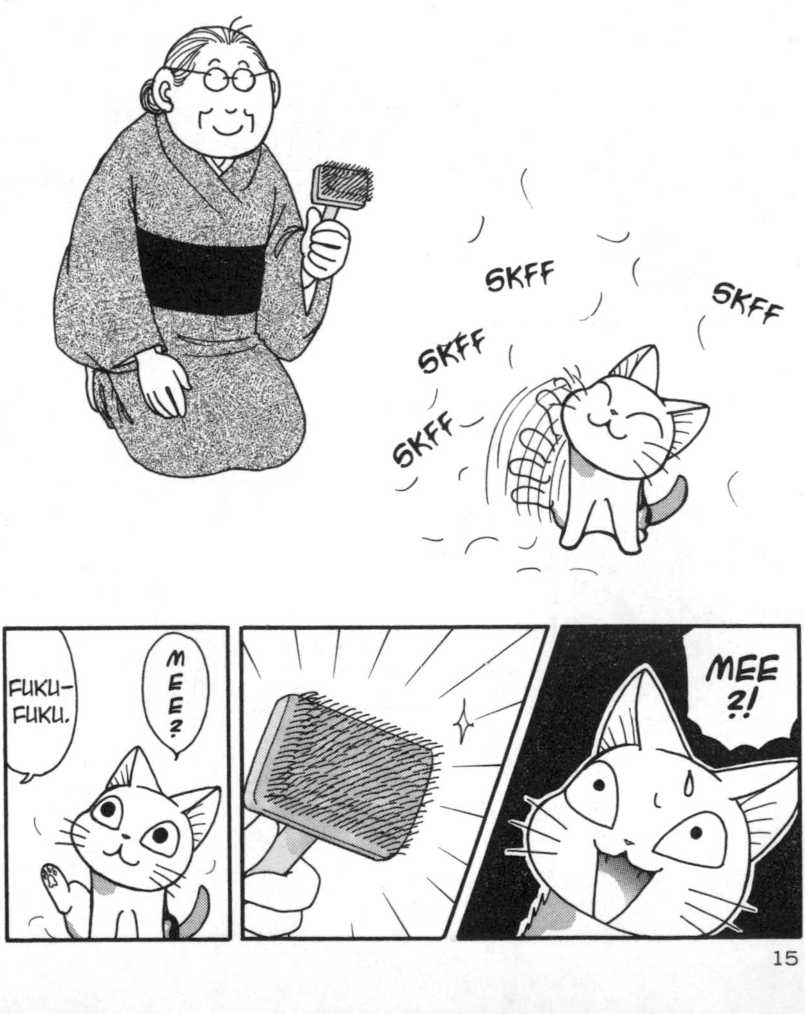

SKFF
SKFF
SKFF
SKFF
FUKU-FUKU.
MEE?
MEE ?!

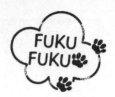

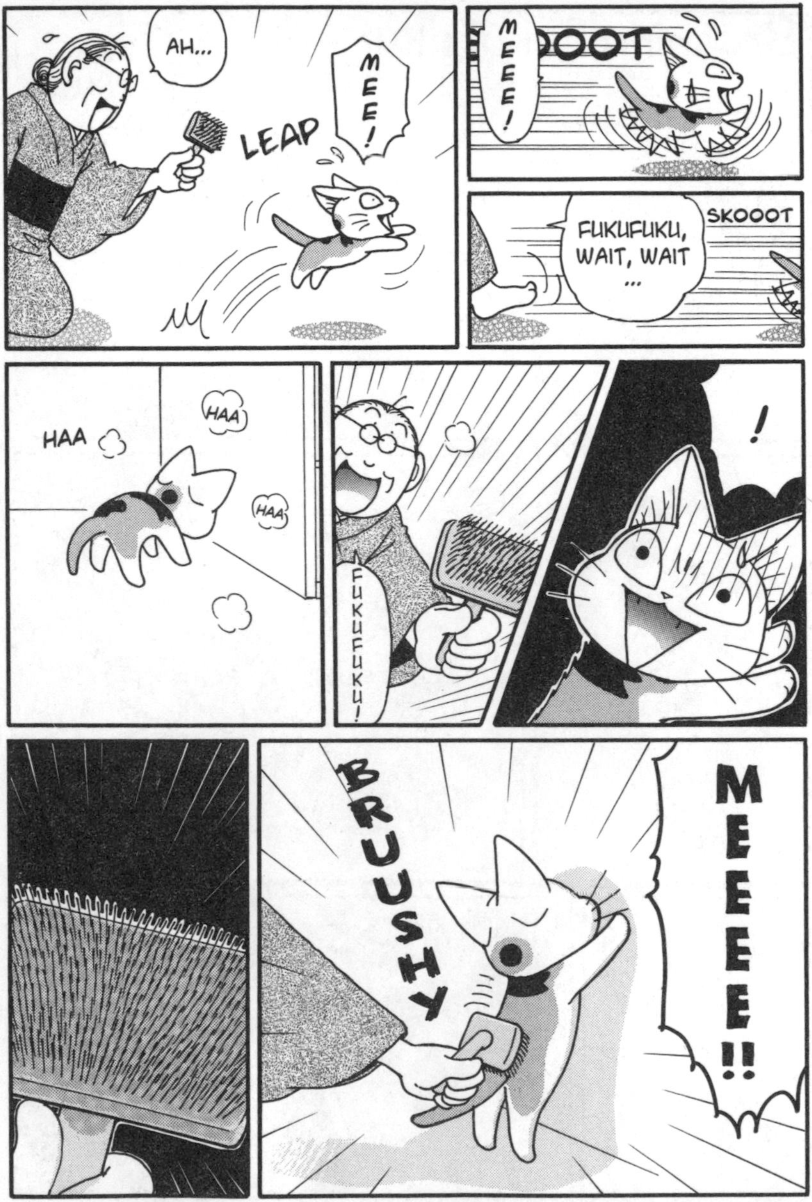
AH...
LEAP
MEEE!
MEEE!
OOOT
FUKUFUKU, WAIT, WAIT ...
SKOOOT
HAA
HAA
HAA
FUKUFUKU!
!
BRUUSHY
MEEEE!!

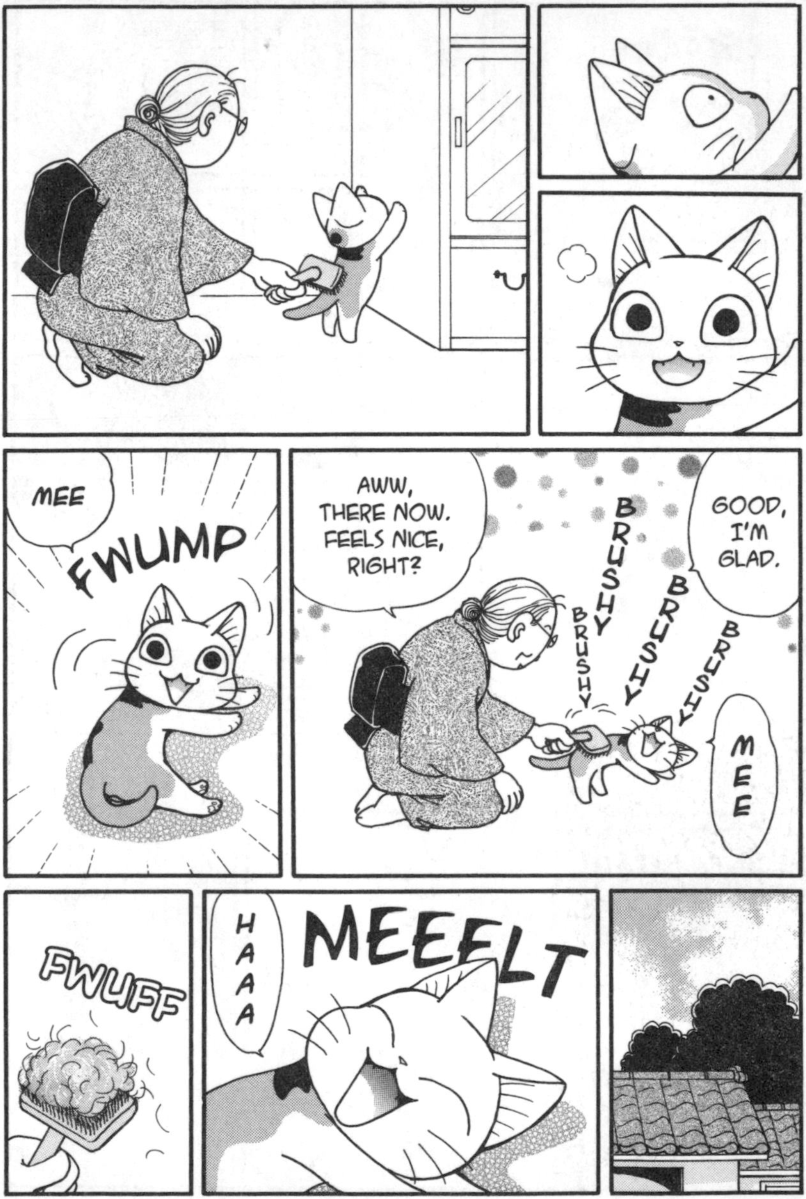
MEE
FWUMP
AWW, THERE NOW. FEELS NICE, RIGHT?
BRUSHY
BRUSHY
BRUSHY
BRUSHY
GOOD, I'M GLAD.
MEE
FWUFF
HAAAA
MEEELT

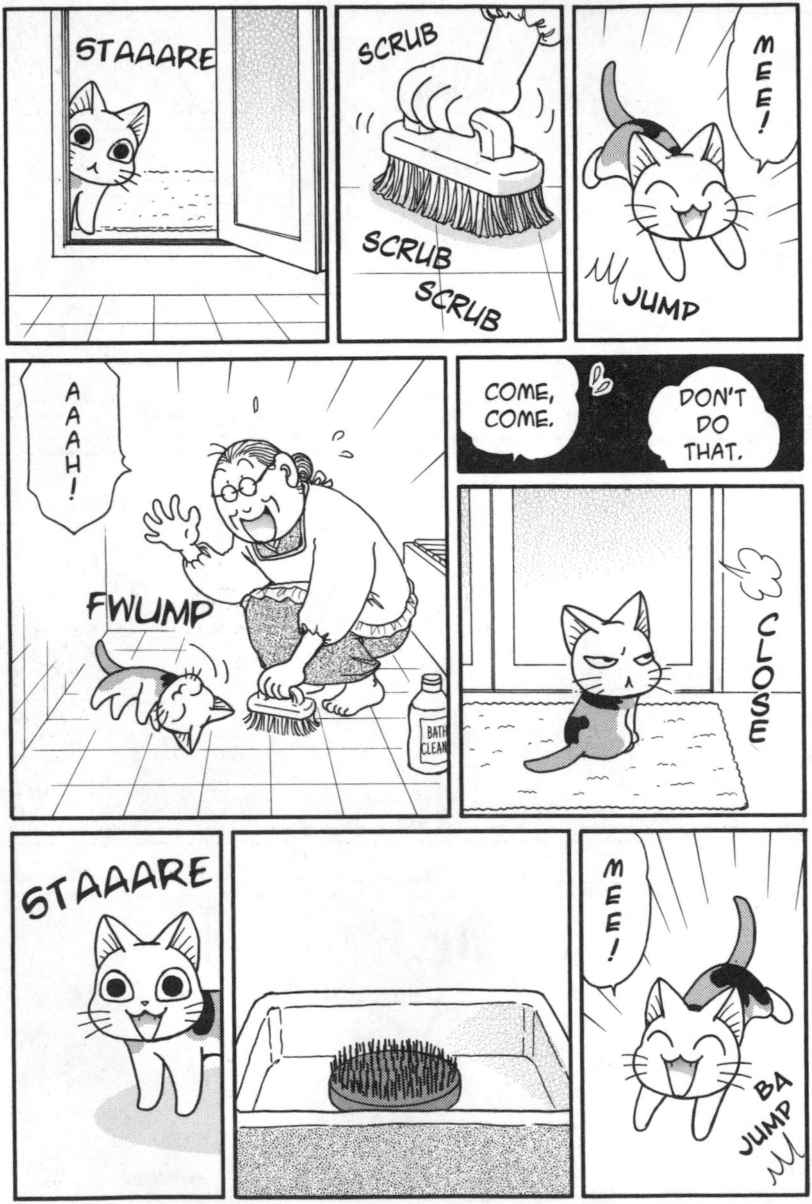
STAAARE
SCRUB
SCRUB
SCRUB
MEE!
JUMP
AAAH!
FWUMP
BATH CLEAN
COME, COME.
DON'T DO THAT.
CLOSE
STAAARE
MEE!
BA JUMP

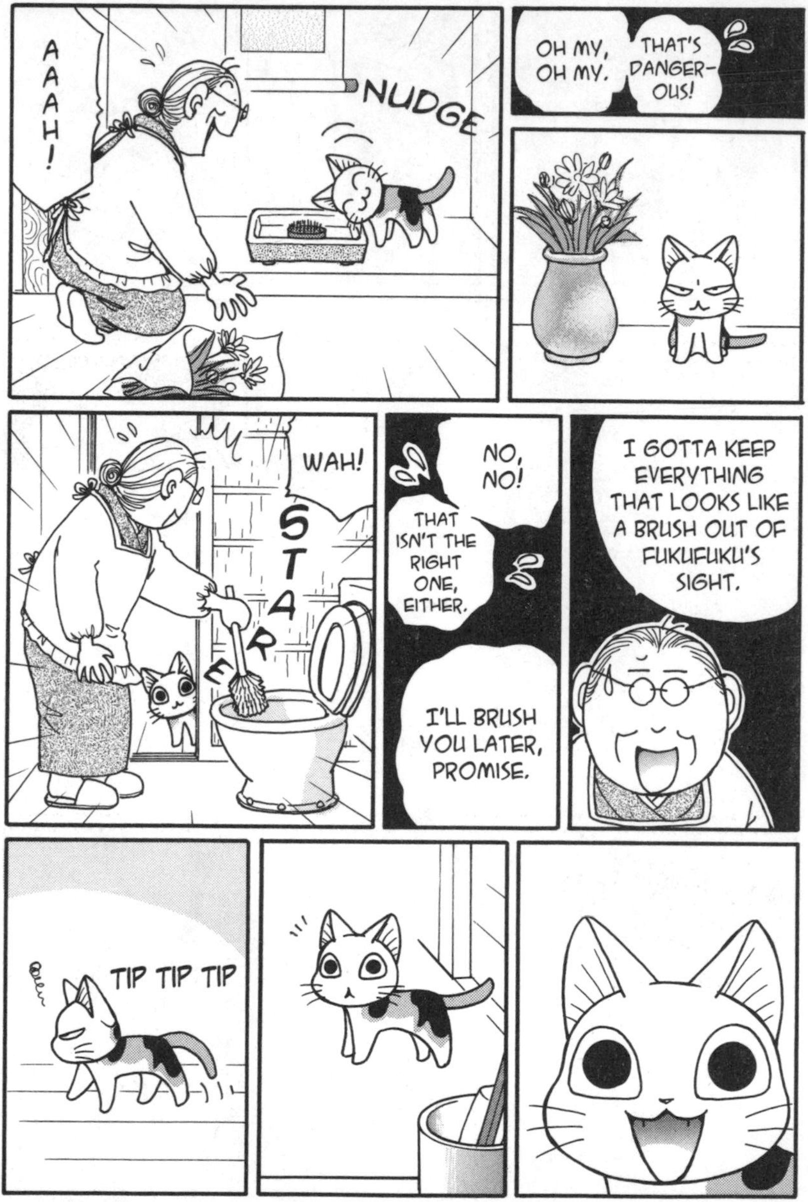
AAAH!
NUDGE
OH MY, OH MY.
THAT'S DANGER-OUS!
WAH!
STARE
NO, NO!
THAT ISN'T THE RIGHT ONE, EITHER.
I'LL BRUSH YOU LATER, PROMISE.
I GOTTA KEEP EVERYTHING THAT LOOKS LIKE A BRUSH OUT OF FUKUFUKU'S SIGHT.
TIP TIP TIP

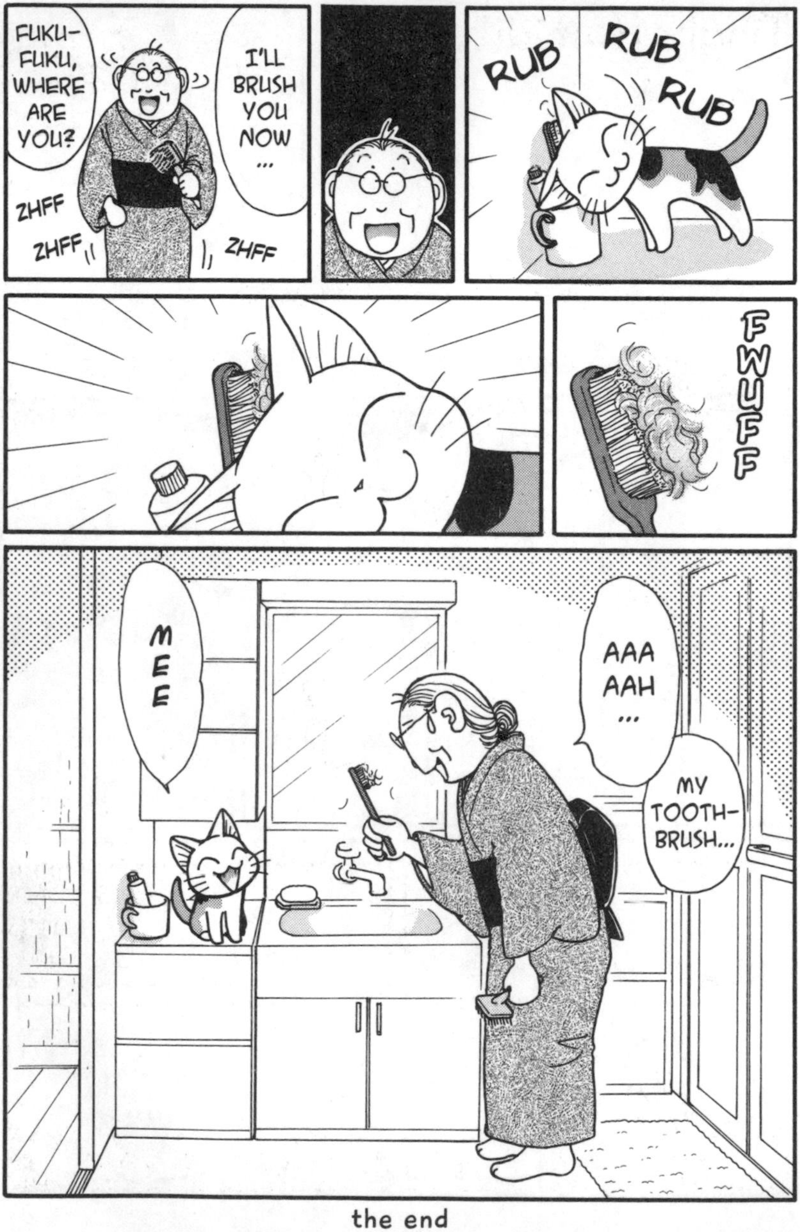
FUKU-FUKU, WHERE ARE YOU?
I'LL BRUSH YOU NOW ...
ZHFF
ZHFF
ZHFF
RUB
RUB
RUB
FWUFF
MEE
AAA AAH ...
MY TOOTH-BRUSH...

the end

Tingly Humidity

FUKU FUKU

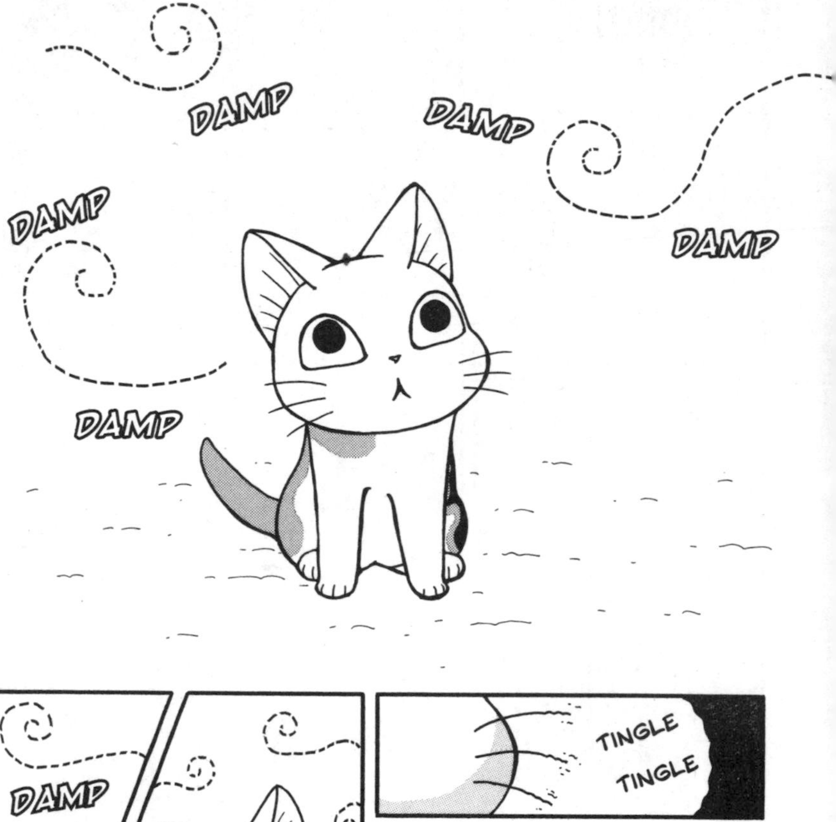
DAMP
DAMP
DAMP
DAMP
DAMP

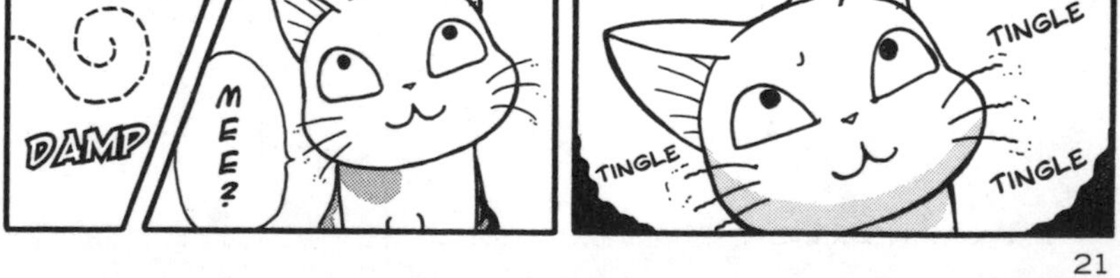
DAMP
DAMP
MEE?
TINGLE
TINGLE
TINGLE
TINGLE
TINGLE

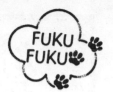

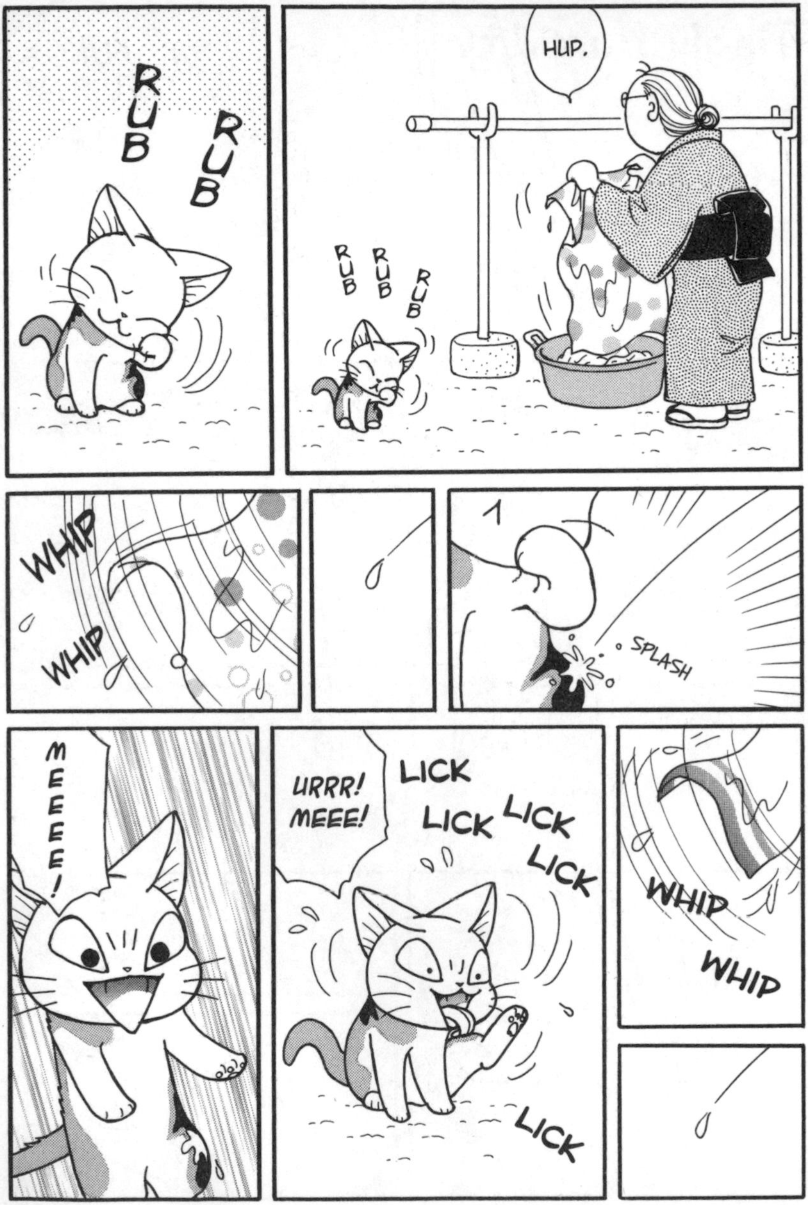
RUB
RUB
HUP.
RUB
RUB
RUB
WHIP
WHIP
SPLASH
MEEEEE!
URRR! MEEE!
LICK
LICK
LICK
LICK
LICK
WHIP
WHIP

!
JUMP
SHPP
SPTT
FRRMEEE
HUP.
TIP TIP TIP
GLOOOM
SWOOP
SWOOOP
TPP TPP TPP
MEE ?
TINGLE

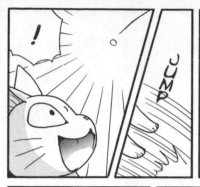

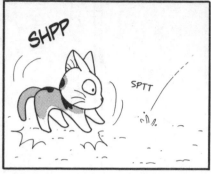

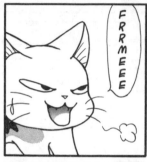

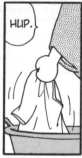

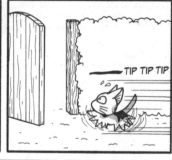

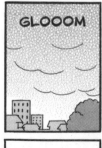

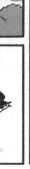

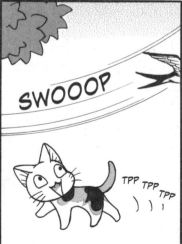

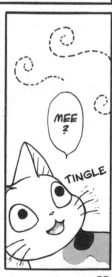

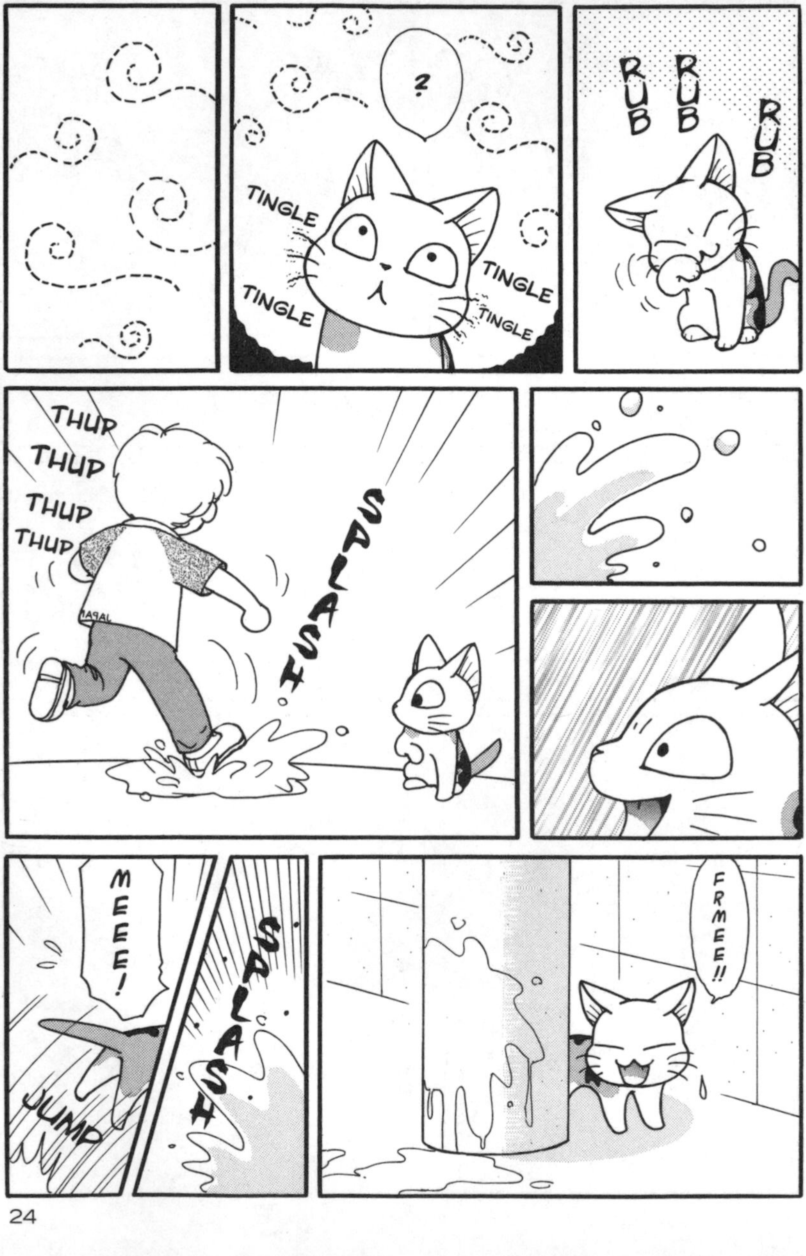
?
TINGLE
TINGLE
TINGLE
TINGLE
RUB
RUB
RUB
THUP
THUP
THUP
THUP
JAPAN
SPLASH
MEEE!
JUMP
SPLASH
FRMEEE!!

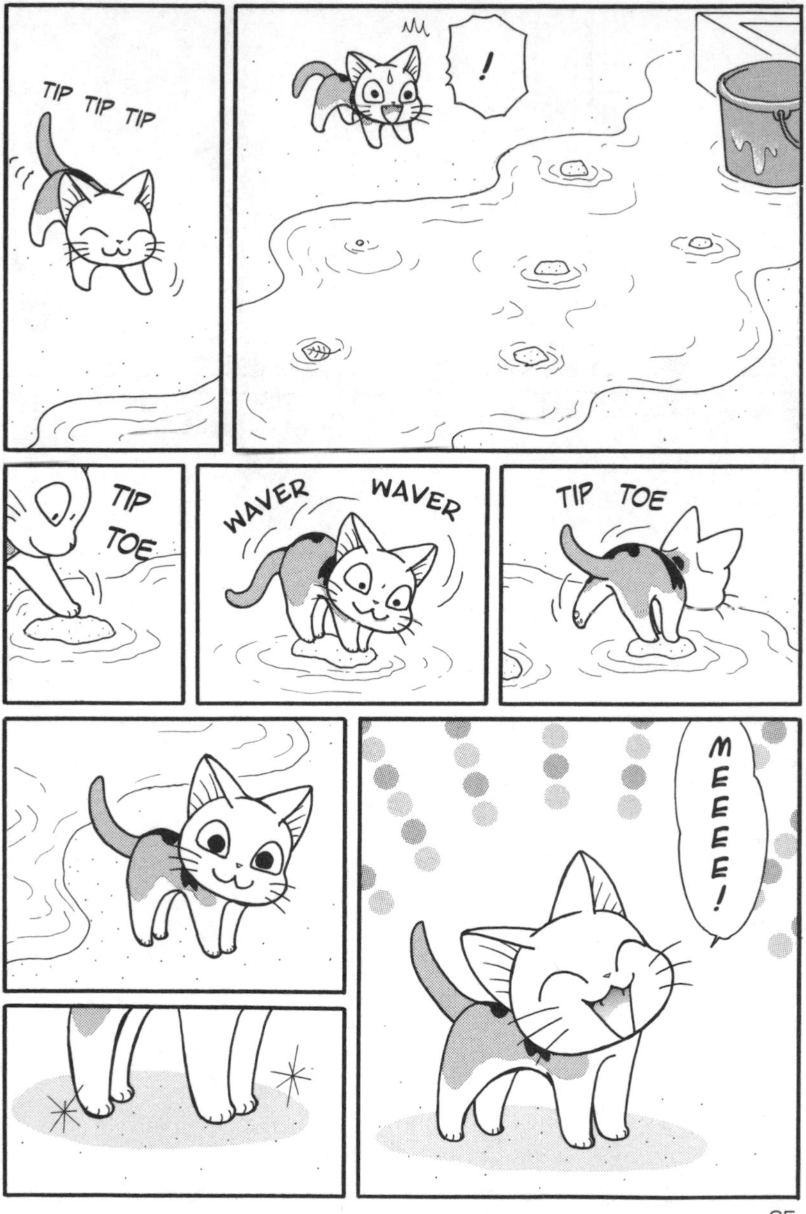
TIP TIP TIP
!
TIP TOE
WAVER WAVER
TIP TOE
MEEEE!

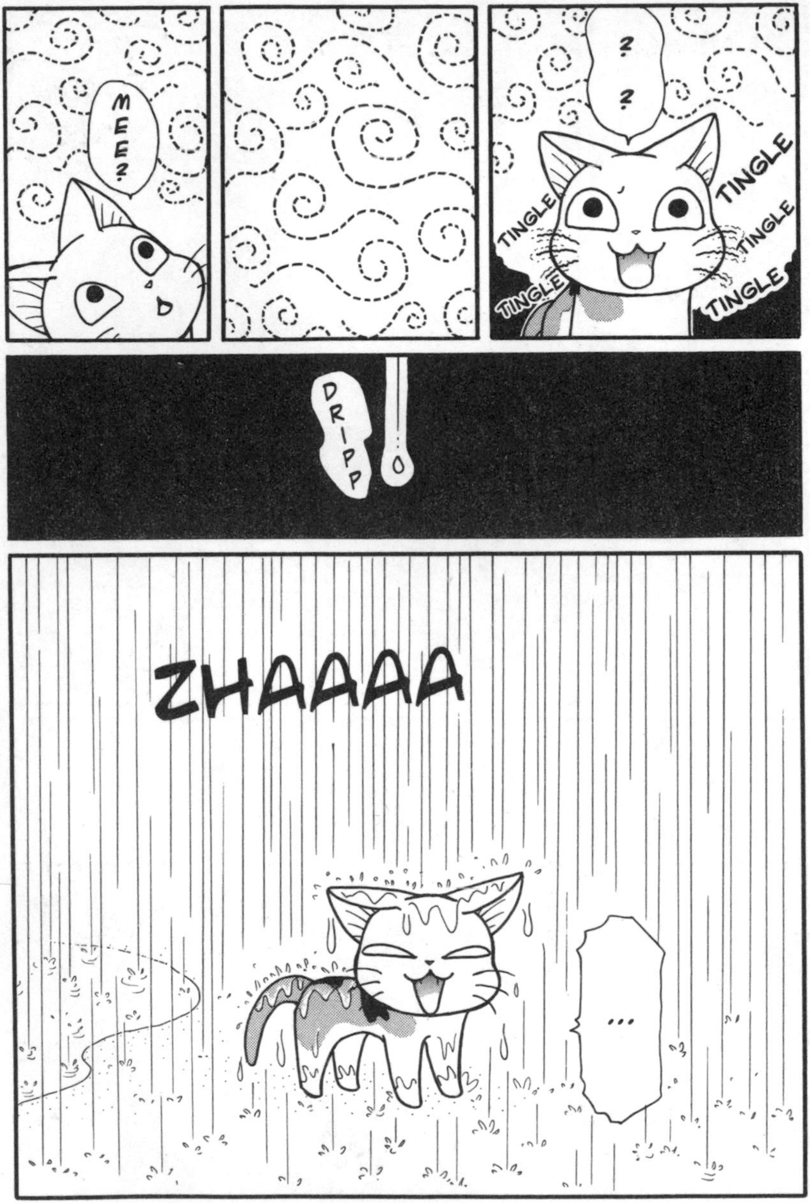
MEE?
? ?
TINGLE
TINGLE
TINGLE
TINGLE
TINGLE
DRIPP
ZHAAAA
...

the end

Summer Star Festival

FUKU FUKU

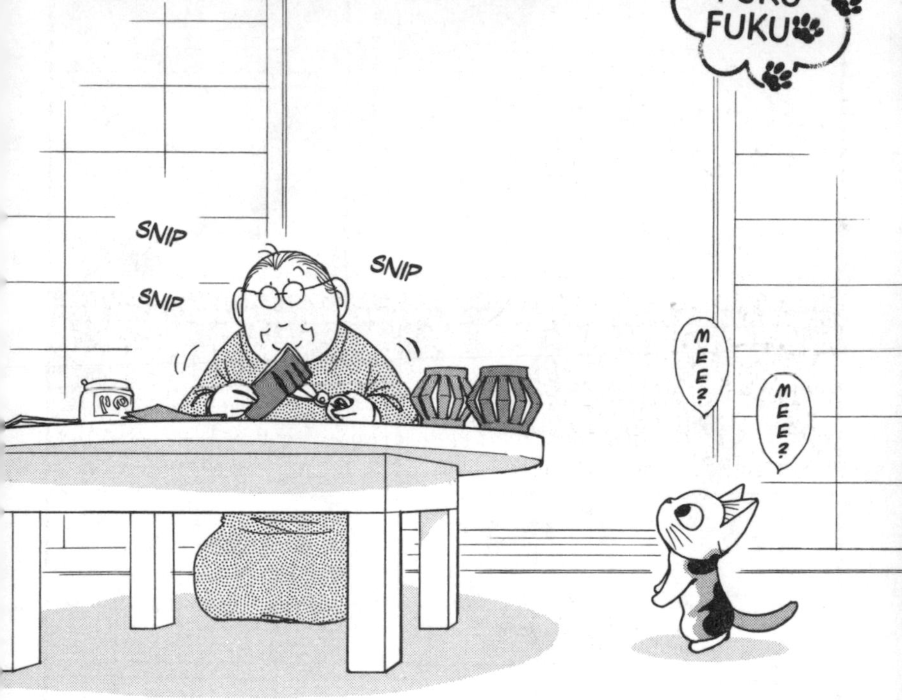
SNIP
SNIP
SNIP
MEE?
MEE?

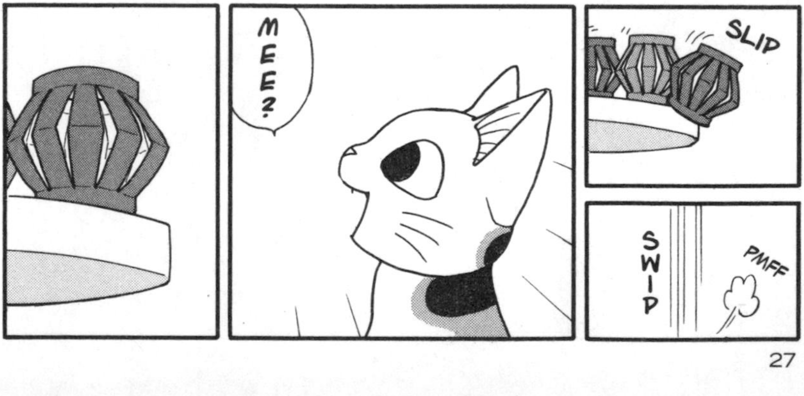
MEE?
SLIP
SWIP
PMFF

WOOOOW!
SKASH
MEE
MEE MEE!
HM?
OH, DEAR.
ZHFF
MEE!
SWAP
SWAP
SWAP
MEE!

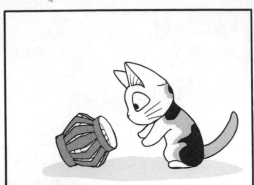

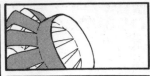

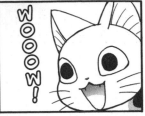

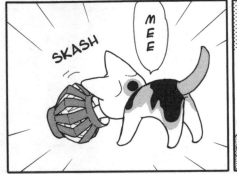

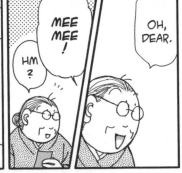

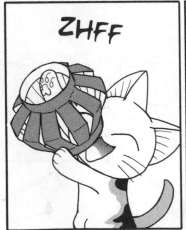

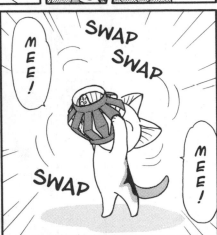

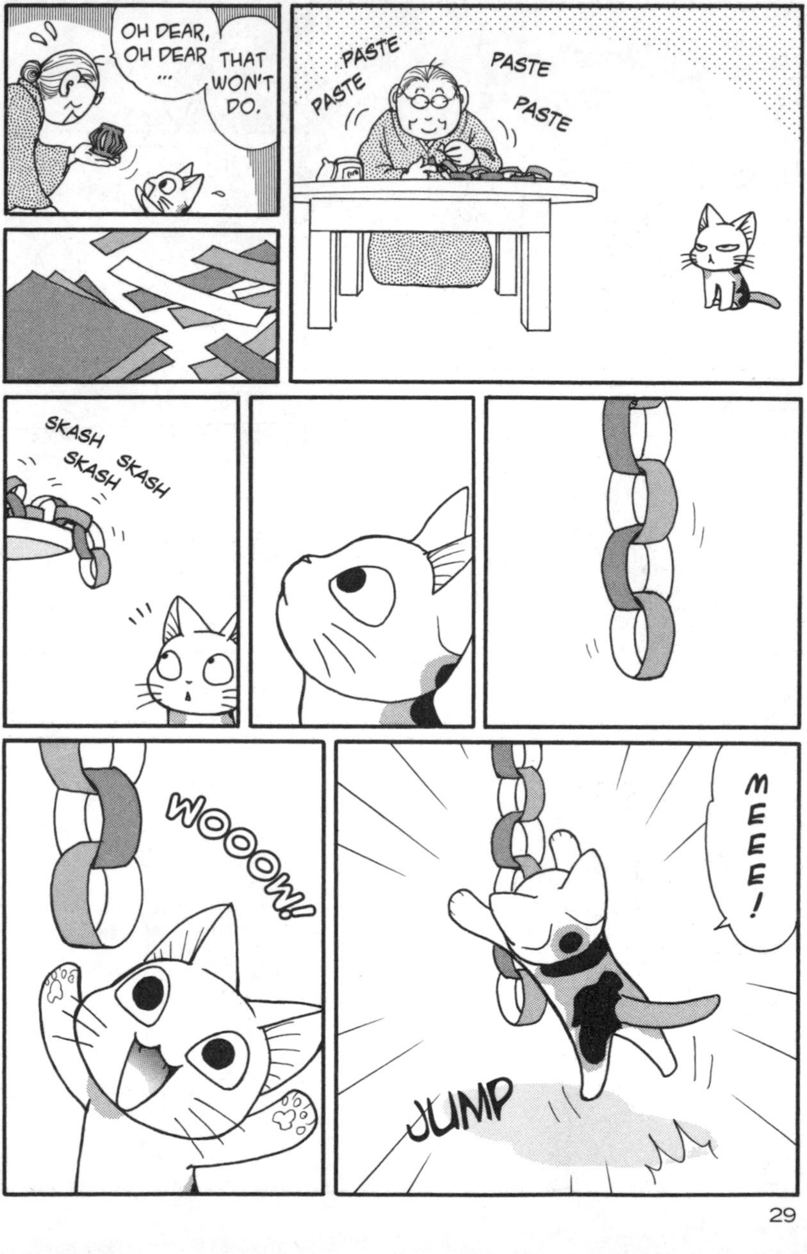
OH DEAR, OH DEAR ...
THAT WON'T DO.
PASTE
PASTE
PASTE
PASTE
SKASH
SKASH
SKASH
WOOOW!
MEEE!
JUMP

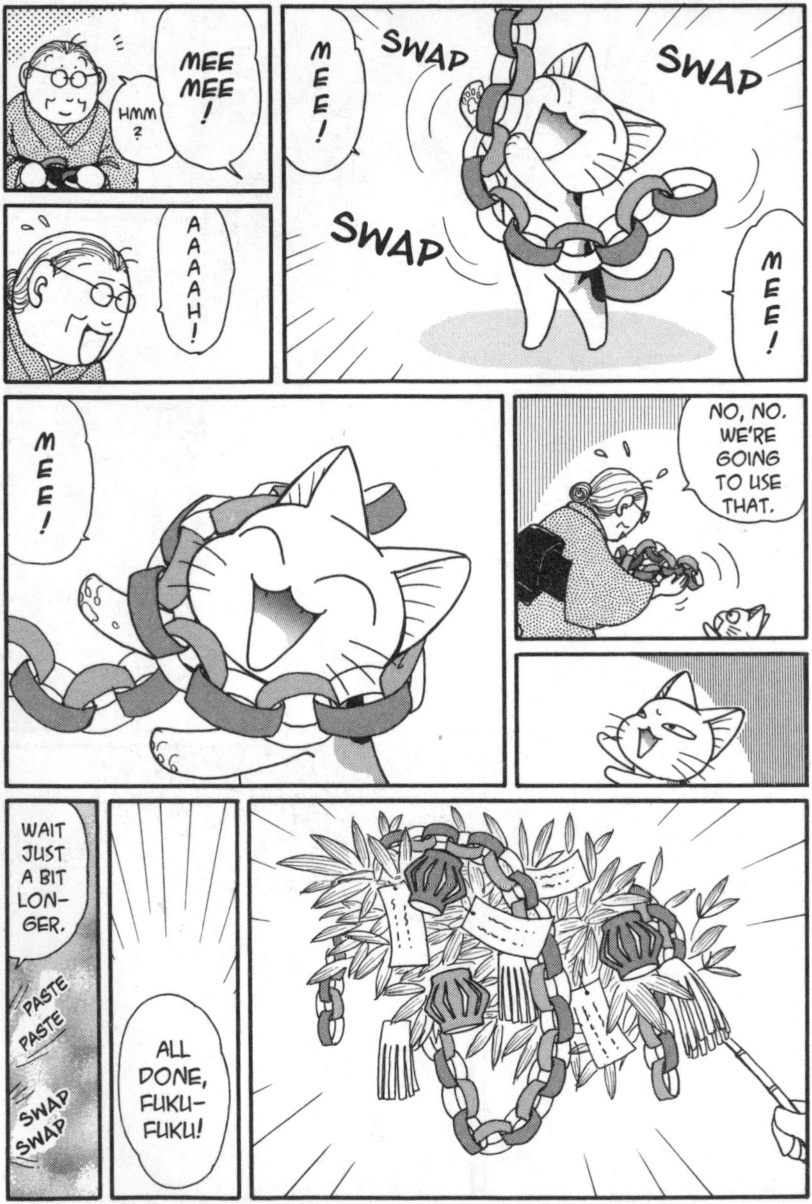
MEE MEE!
HMM?
AAAAAH!
MEE!
SWAP
SWAP
SWAP
MEE!
MEE!
NO, NO. WE'RE GOING TO USE THAT.
WAIT JUST A BIT LONGER.
PASTE PASTE
SWAP SWAP
ALL DONE, FUKU-FUKU!

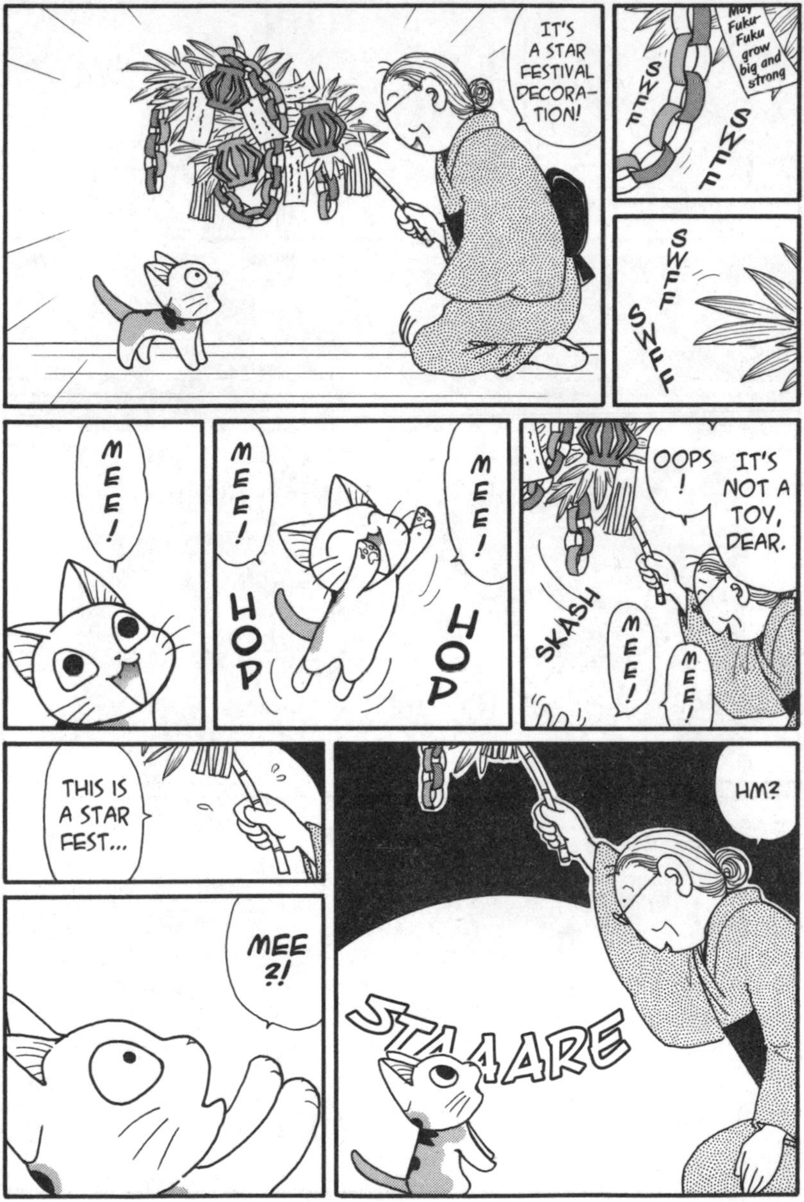
IT'S A STAR FESTIVAL DECORA-TION!
May Fuku-Fuku grow big and strong
SWFF
SWFF
SWFF
SWFF
MEE!
MEE!
HOP
HOP
MEE!
OOPS!
IT'S NOT A TOY, DEAR.
SKASH
MEE!
MEE!
THIS IS A STAR FEST...
MEE?!
HM?
STAAARE

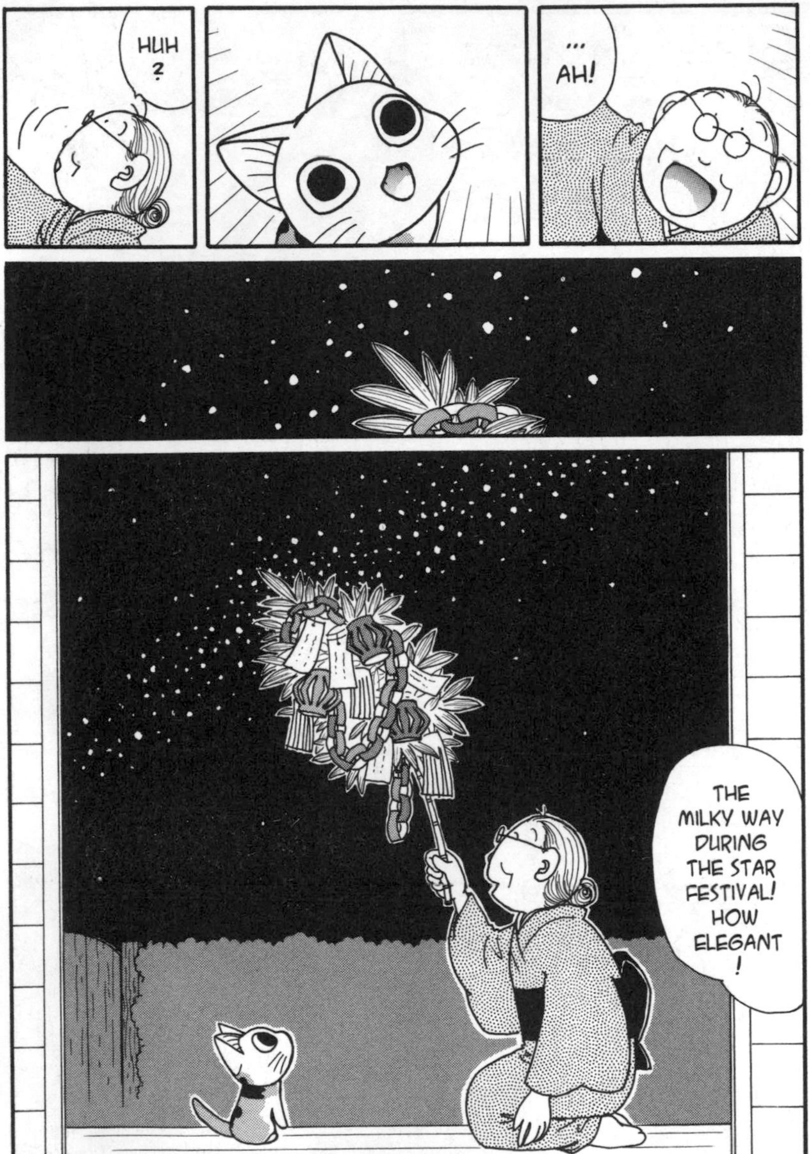
HUH ?
... AH!
THE MILKY WAY DURING THE STAR FESTIVAL! HOW ELEGANT !

the end

Green Growing Things

FUKU FUKU

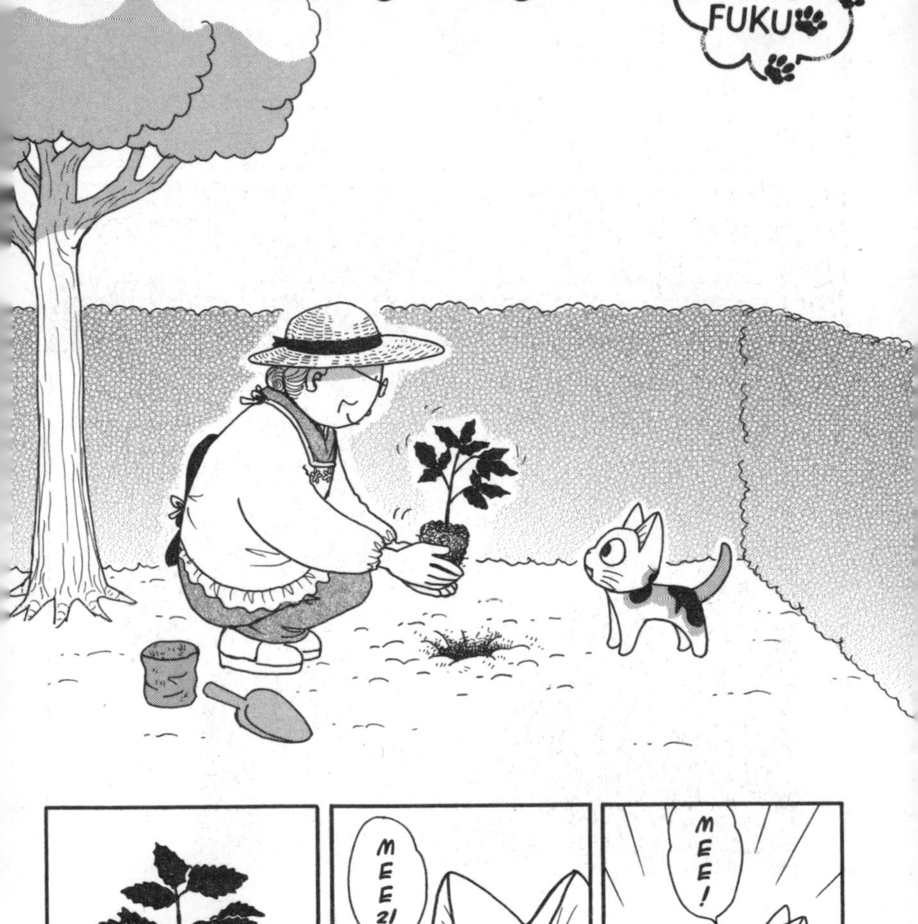

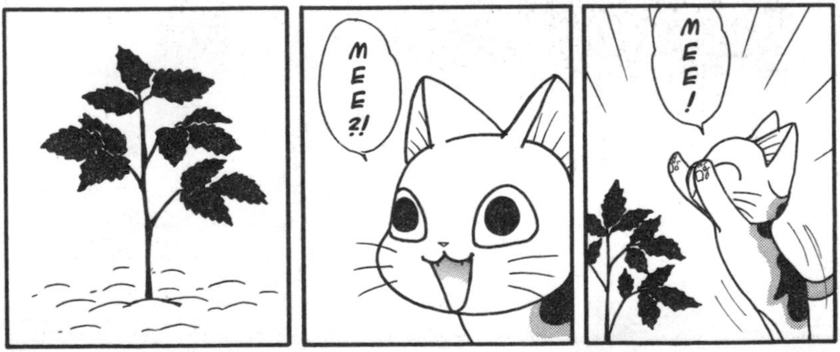
MEE?!
MEE!

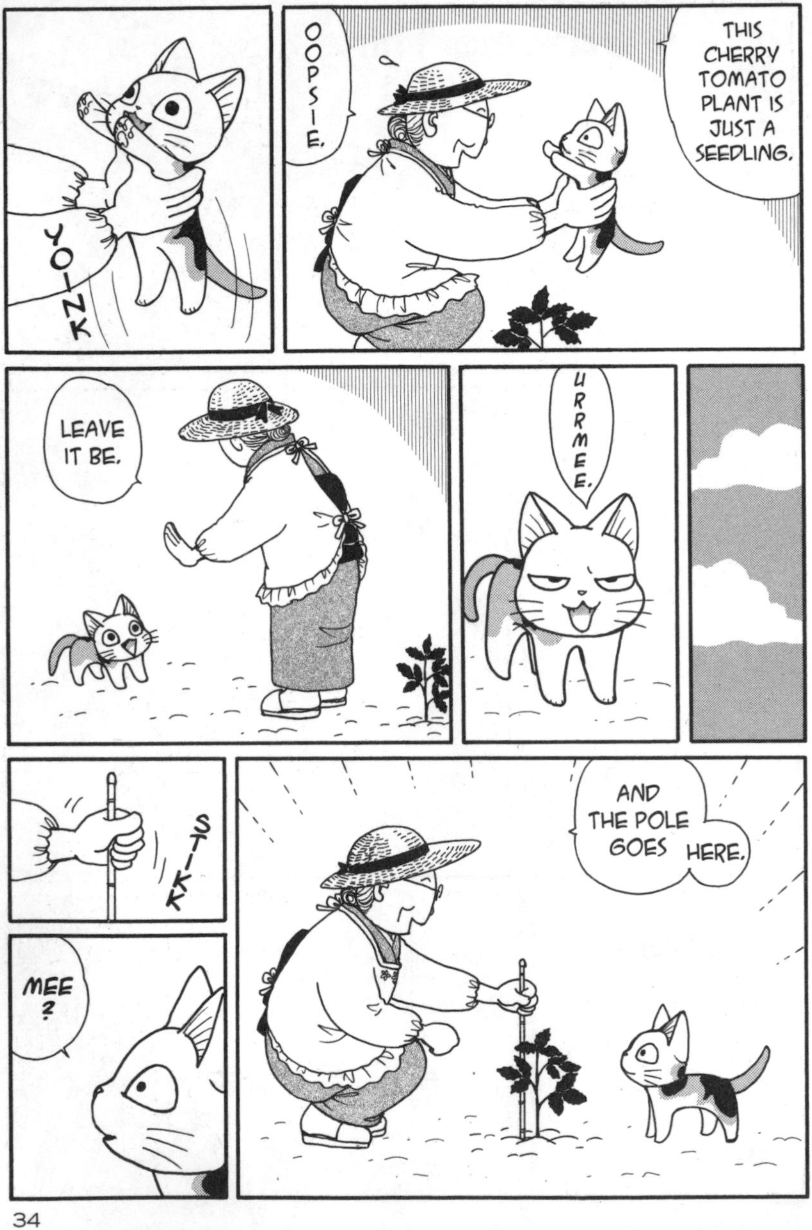
YO-INK
OOPSIE.
THIS CHERRY TOMATO PLANT IS JUST A SEEDLING.
LEAVE IT BE.
URRMEE.
STIKK
MEE?
AND THE POLE GOES HERE.

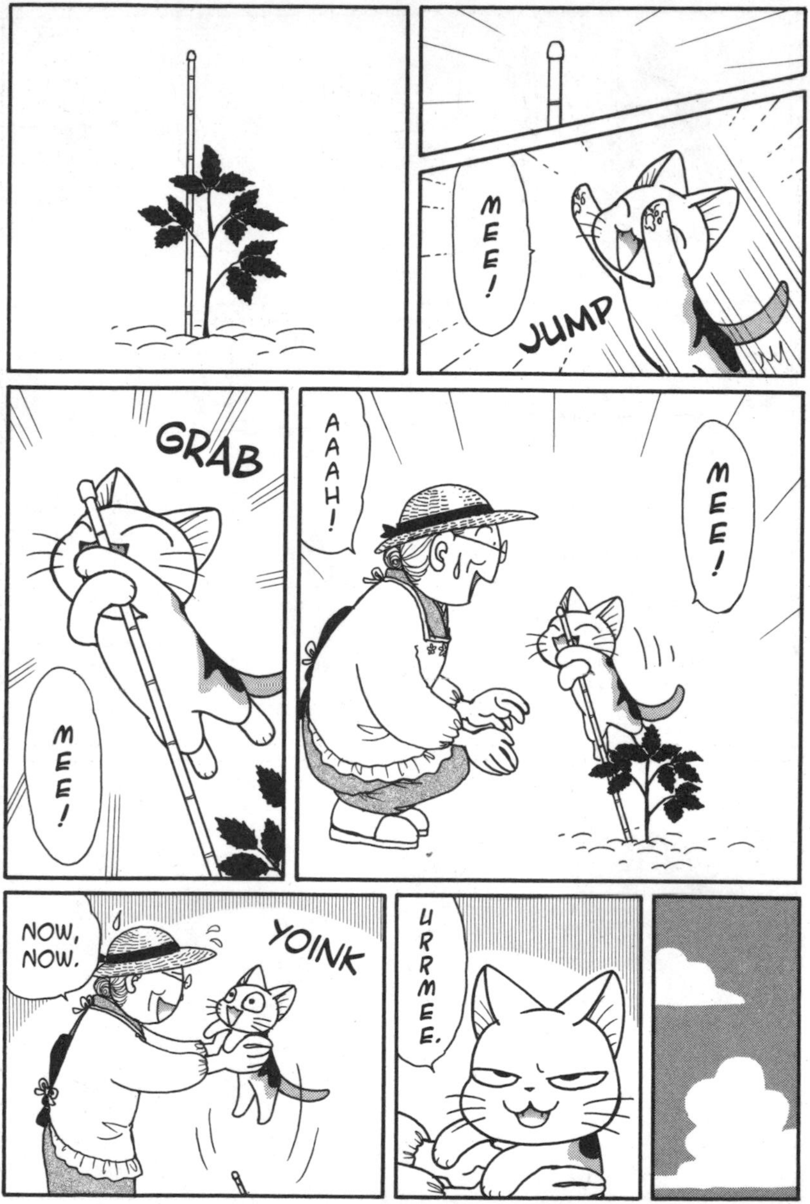
MEE!
JUMP
GRAB
MEE!
AAAAH!
MEE!
NOW, NOW.
YOINK
URRMEE.

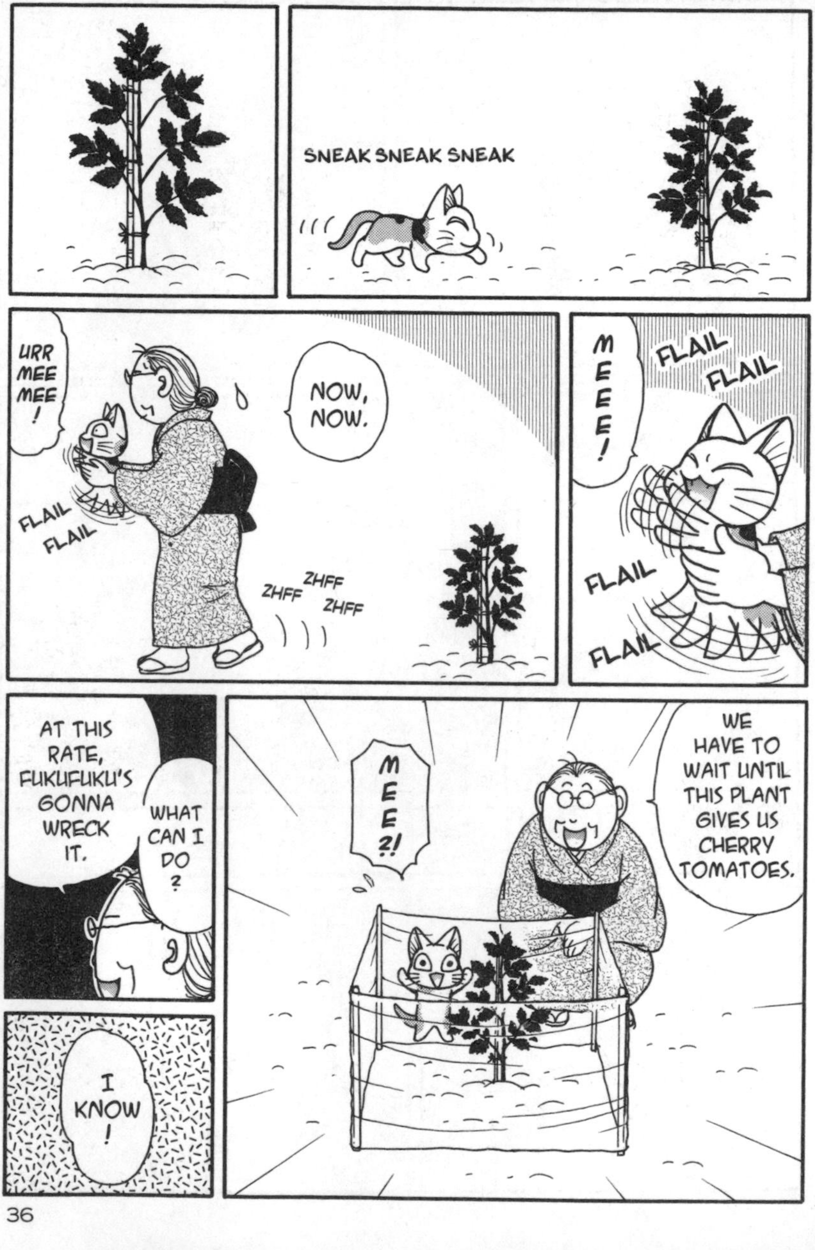
SNEAK SNEAK SNEAK
URR MEE MEE!
FLAIL FLAIL
NOW, NOW.
ZHFF ZHFF ZHFF
MEEE!
FLAIL FLAIL
FLAIL
FLAIL
AT THIS RATE, FUKUFUKU'S GONNA WRECK IT.
WHAT CAN I DO?
I KNOW!
MEE?!
WE HAVE TO WAIT UNTIL THIS PLANT GIVES US CHERRY TOMATOES.

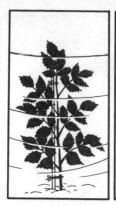

BE PATIENT, FUKU-FUKU.

ZHAA

ZHAA

PATIENCE, PATIENCE, FUKUFUKU.

JUST A BIT LONGER, FUKUFUKU.

SPARKLE

IT'S READY !

37

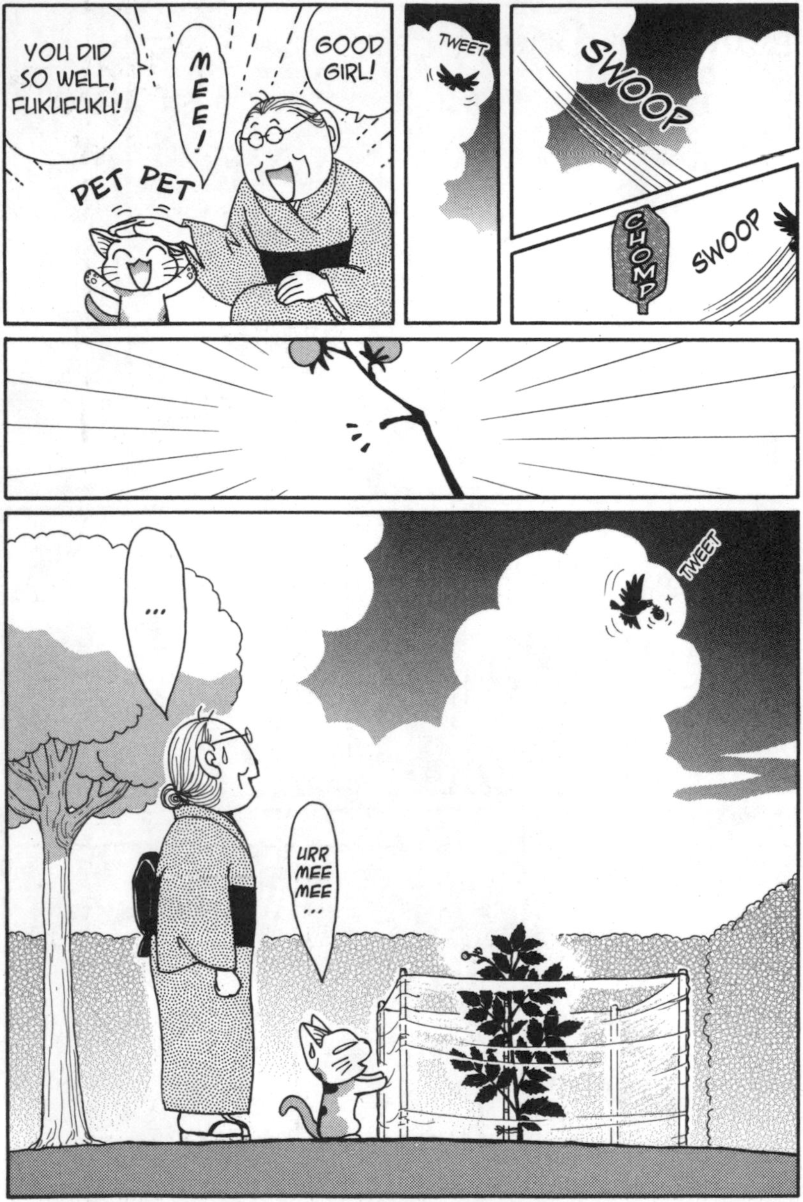
YOU DID SO WELL, FUKUFUKU!
MEE!
GOOD GIRL!
PET PET
TWEET
SWOOP
CHOMP
SWOOP
...
TWEET
URR MEE MEE ...

the end

Summer Cold Scare

FUKU FUKU

SHRED
SHRED
SHRED

TIP TIP TIP
Supe
SKAASH
MEE!
OH, DEAR.

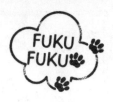

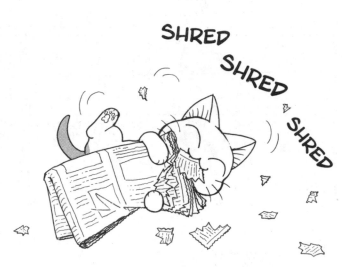

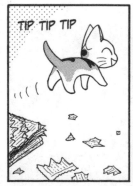

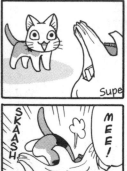

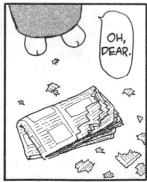

FUKUFUKU, YOU'RE SUCH A RASCAL.

BUT...

THAT'S PROOF THAT YOU'RE HEALTHY!

SNFF SNFF

TIP TIP TIP

AH AAH...

CHOO

HUH?

FUKU-FUKU...

KCHOO!

KCHOO!

KCHOO!

OH... OH NO!

A SUMMER COLD?!

40

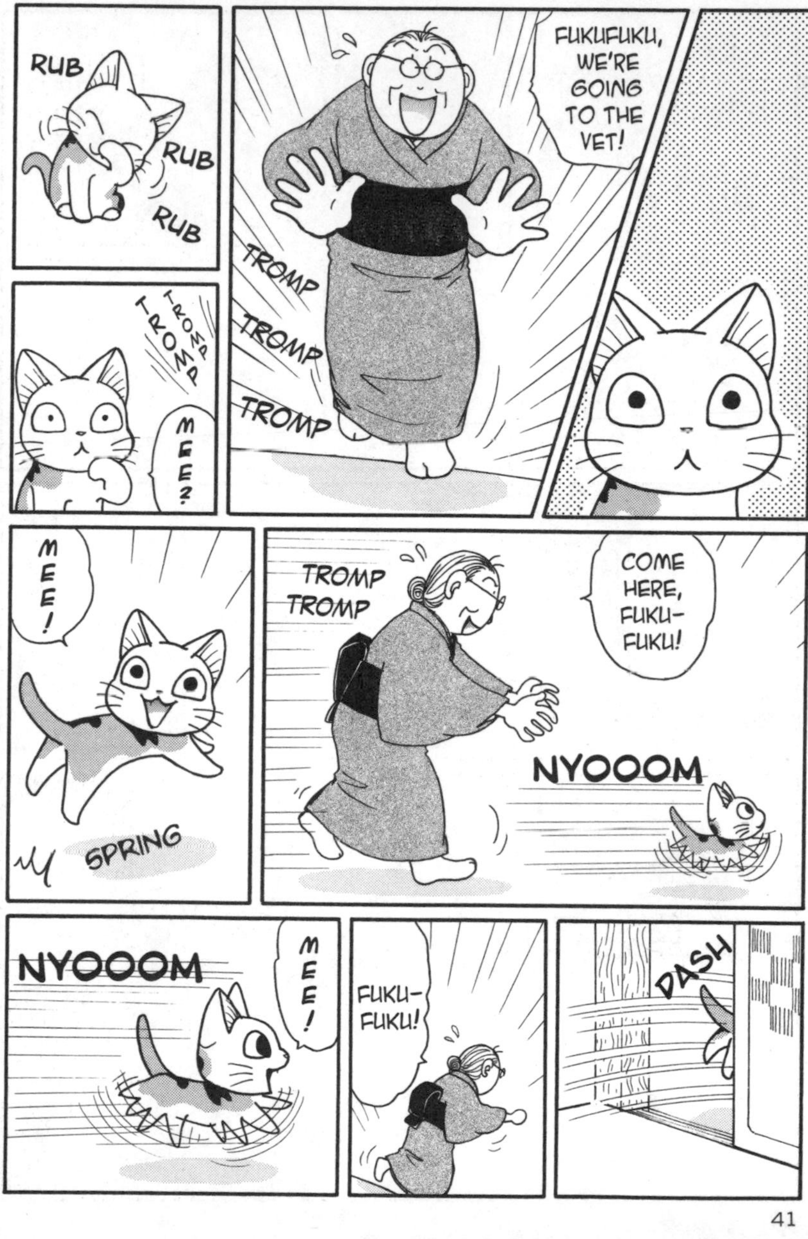
RUB
RUB
RUB
FUKUFUKU, WE'RE GOING TO THE VET!
TROMP
TROMP
TROMP
TROMP TROMP
MEE?
MEE!
SPRING
TROMP TROMP
COME HERE, FUKU-FUKU!
NYOOOM
NYOOOM
MEE!
FUKU-FUKU!
DASH

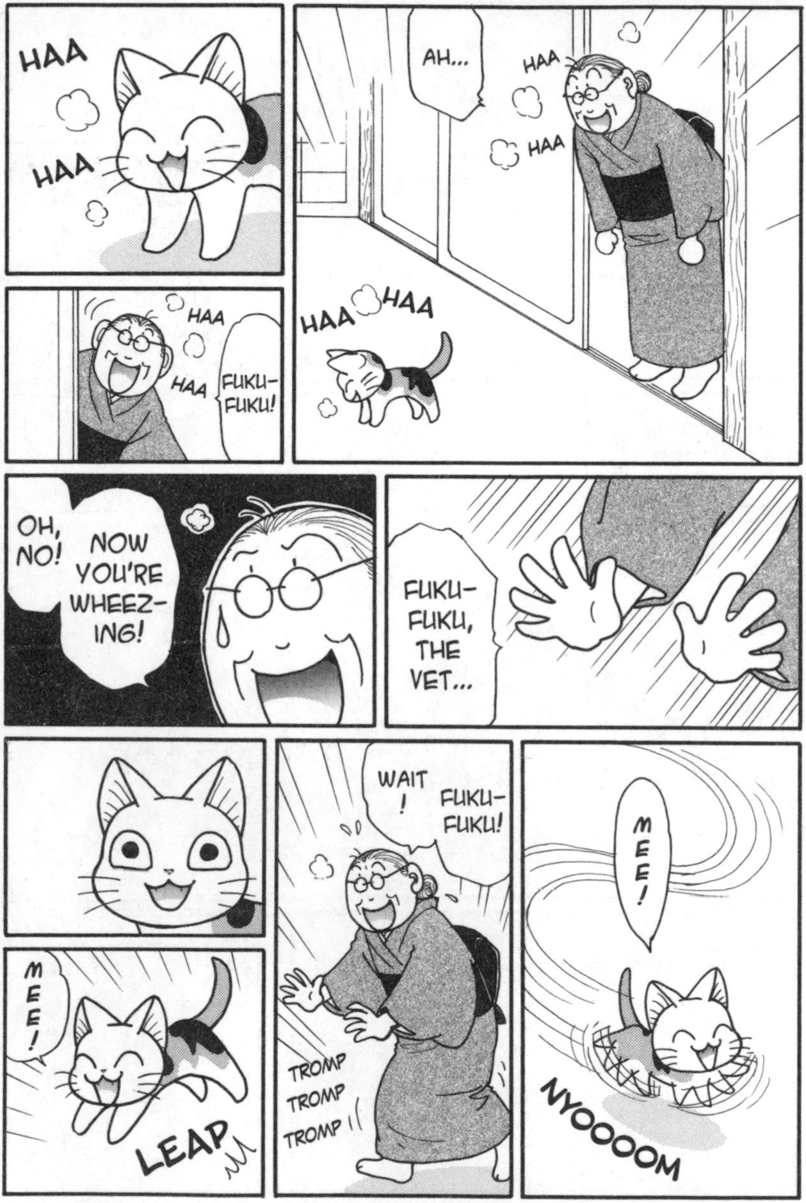
HAA
HAA
AH...
HAA
HAA
HAA HAA
HAA
HAA
FUKU-FUKU!
OH, NO!
NOW YOU'RE WHEEZ-ING!
FUKU-FUKU, THE VET...
MEE!
LEAP
WAIT!
FUKU-FUKU!
TROMP
TROMP
TROMP
MEE!
NYOOOOM

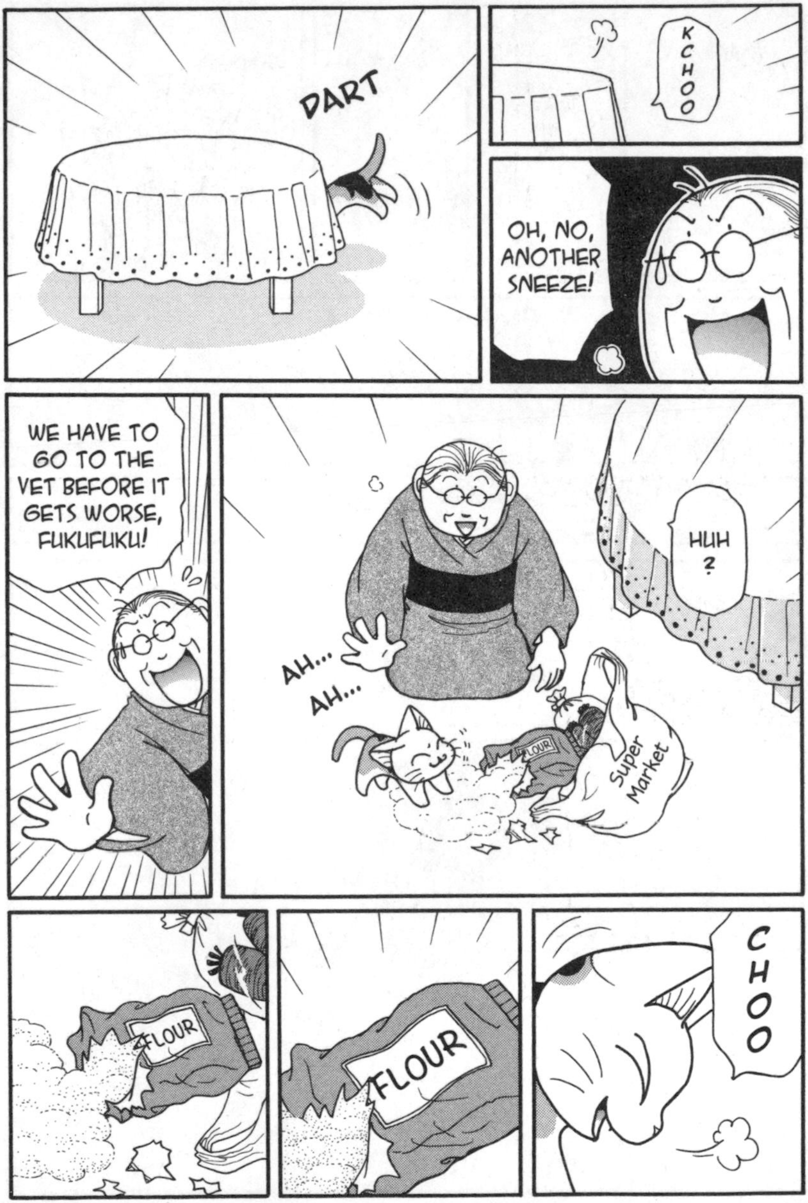

DART
KCHOO
OH, NO, ANOTHER SNEEZE!
WE HAVE TO GO TO THE VET BEFORE IT GETS WORSE, FUKUFUKU!
AH... AH...
FLOUR
Super Market
HUH?
FLOUR
FLOUR
CHOO

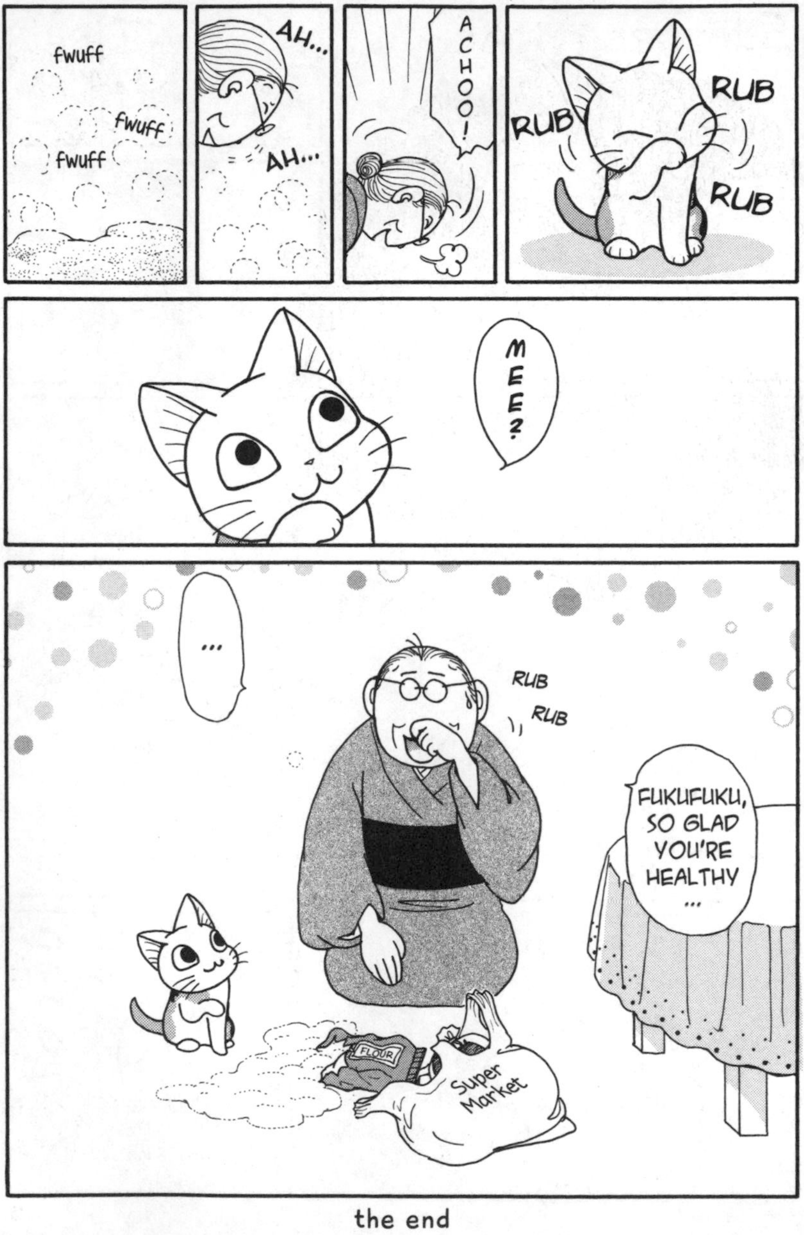
fwuff
fwuff
fwuff
AH...
AH...
ACHOO!
RUB
RUB
RUB
MEE?
...
RUB
RUB
FUKUFUKU, SO GLAD YOU'RE HEALTHY ...
FLOUR
Super Market

the end

Summer Fright

FUKU FUKU

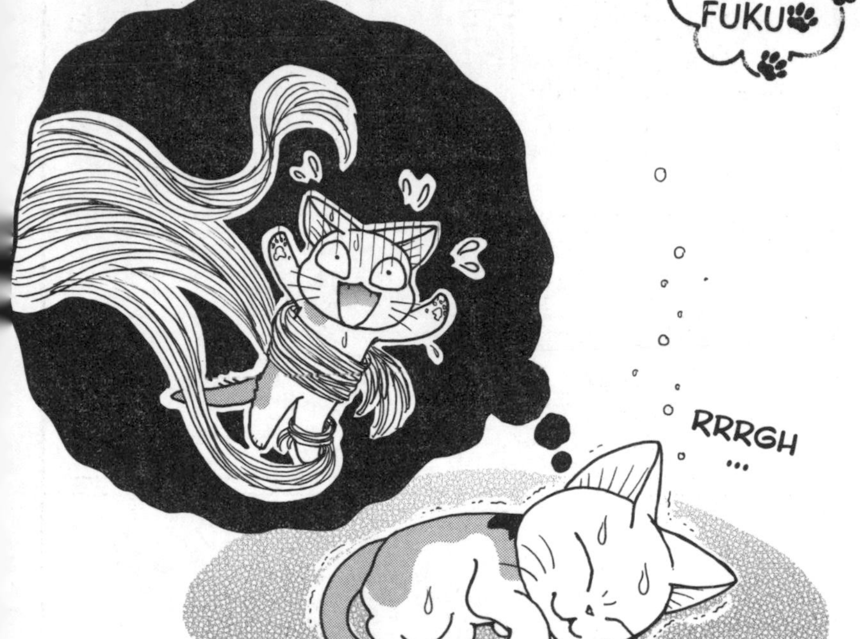
RRRGH
...

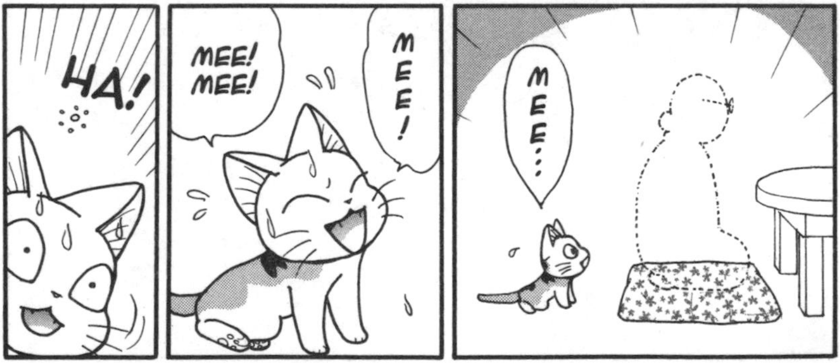
HA!
MEE! MEE!
MEE!
MEE...

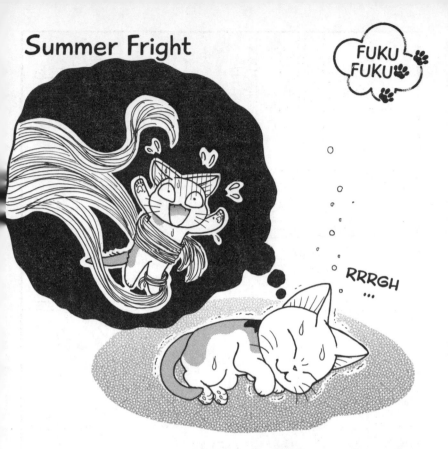

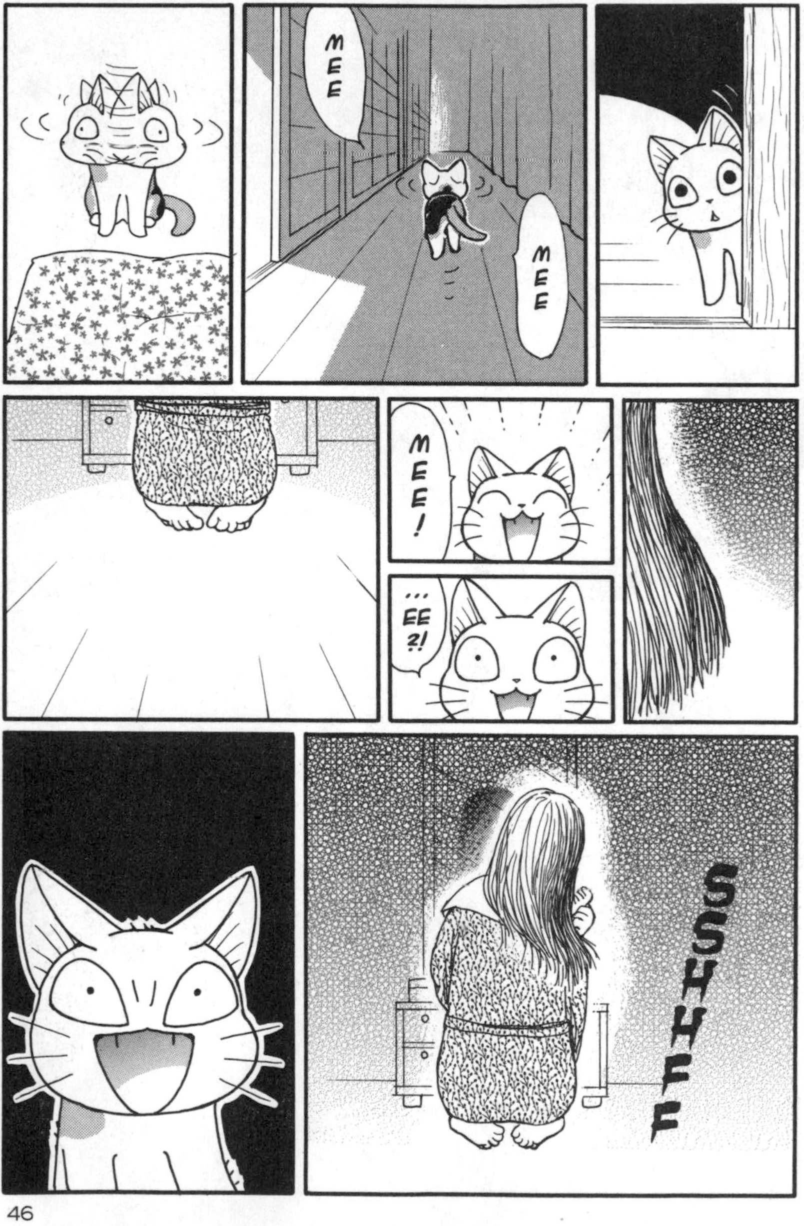
MEE
MEE
MEE!
...EE?!
SSHHFF

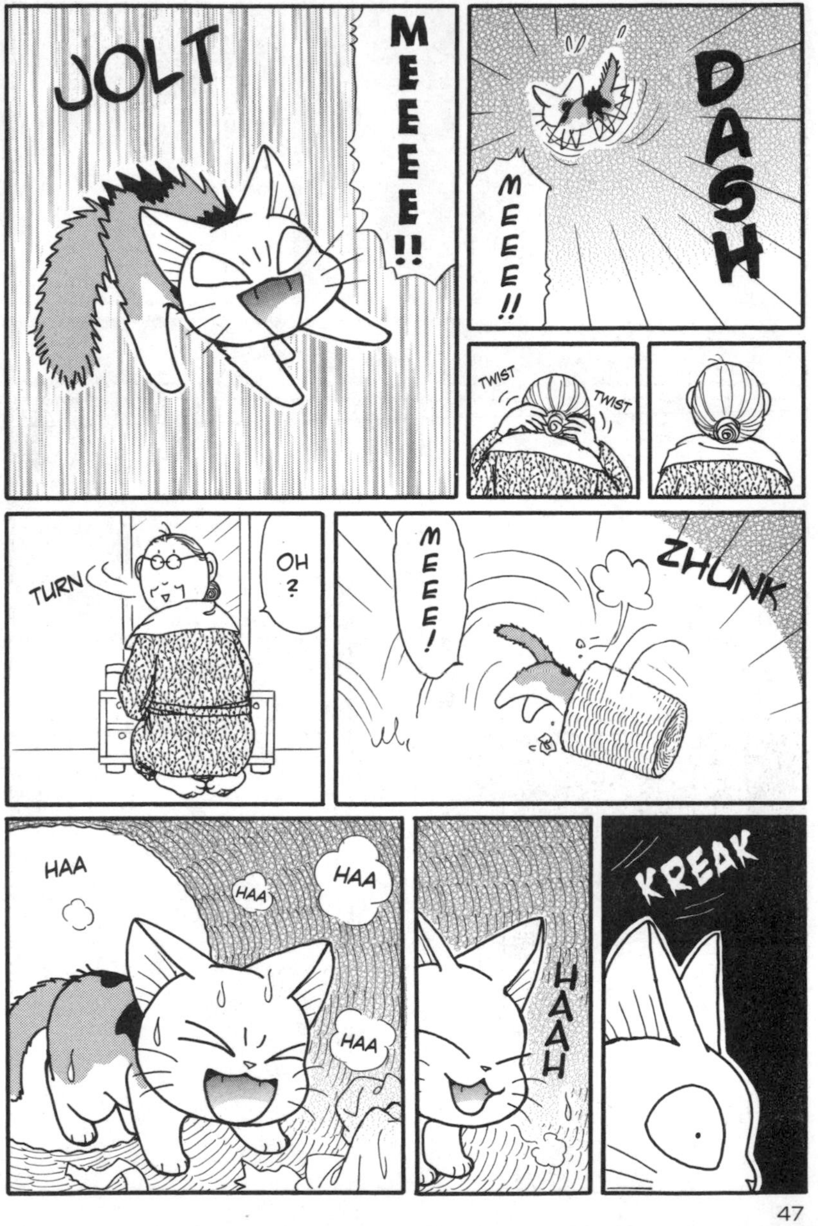
JOLT
MEEEE!!
MEEEE!!
DASH
TWIST
TWIST
TURN
OH?
MEEEE!
ZHUNK
HAA
HAA
HAA
HAA
HAAAH
KREAK

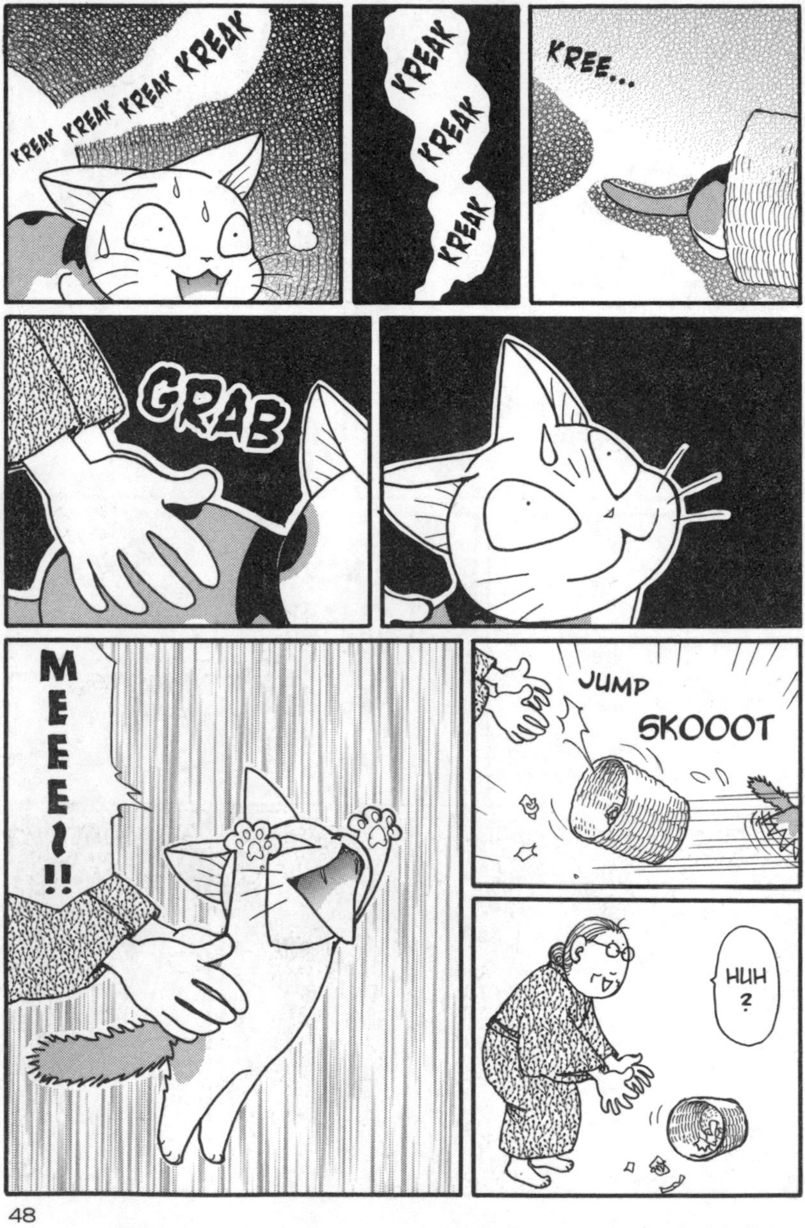
KREAK KREAK KREAK KREAK
KREAK
KREAK
KREAK
KREE...
GRAB
MEEE~!!
JUMP
SKOOOT
HUH?

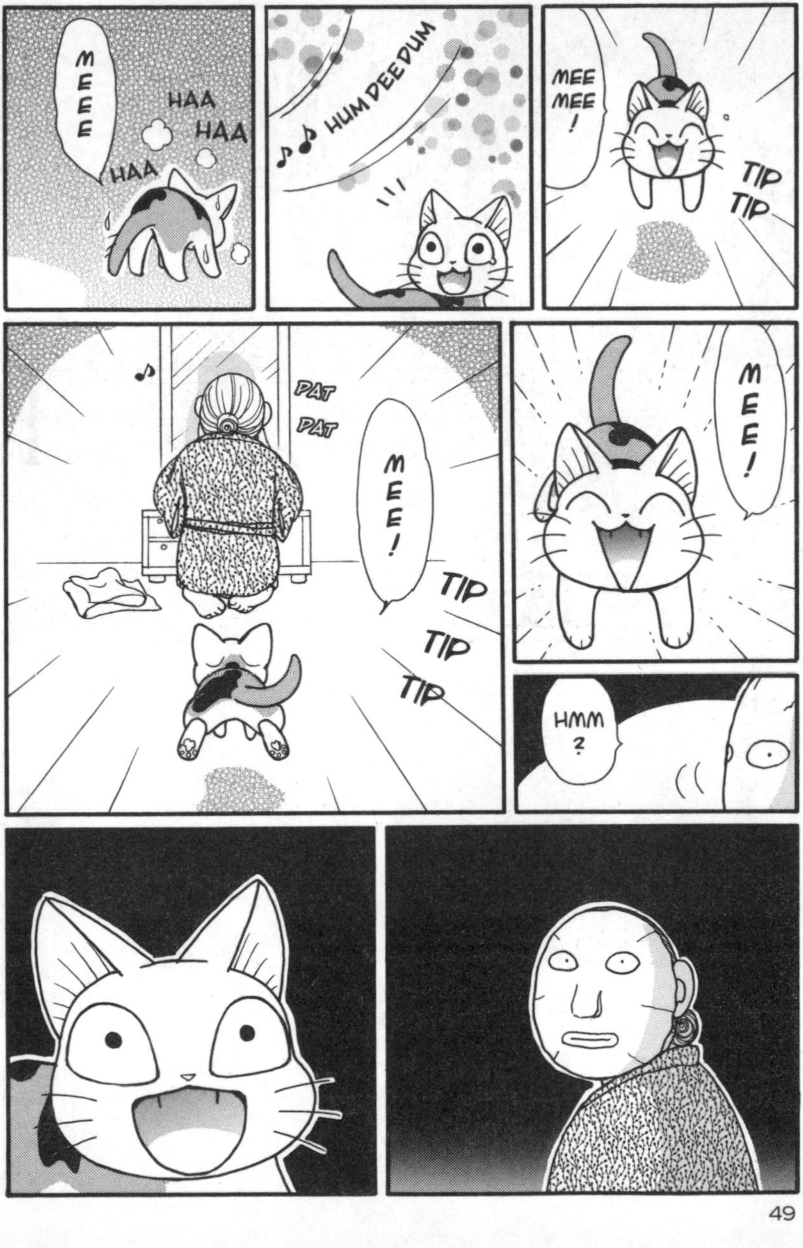
MEE MEE!
TIP TIP
♪♪ HUM DEE DUM
MEEE
HAA HAA
HAA
MEE!
HMM?
♪
PAT PAT
MEE!
TIP
TIP
TIP

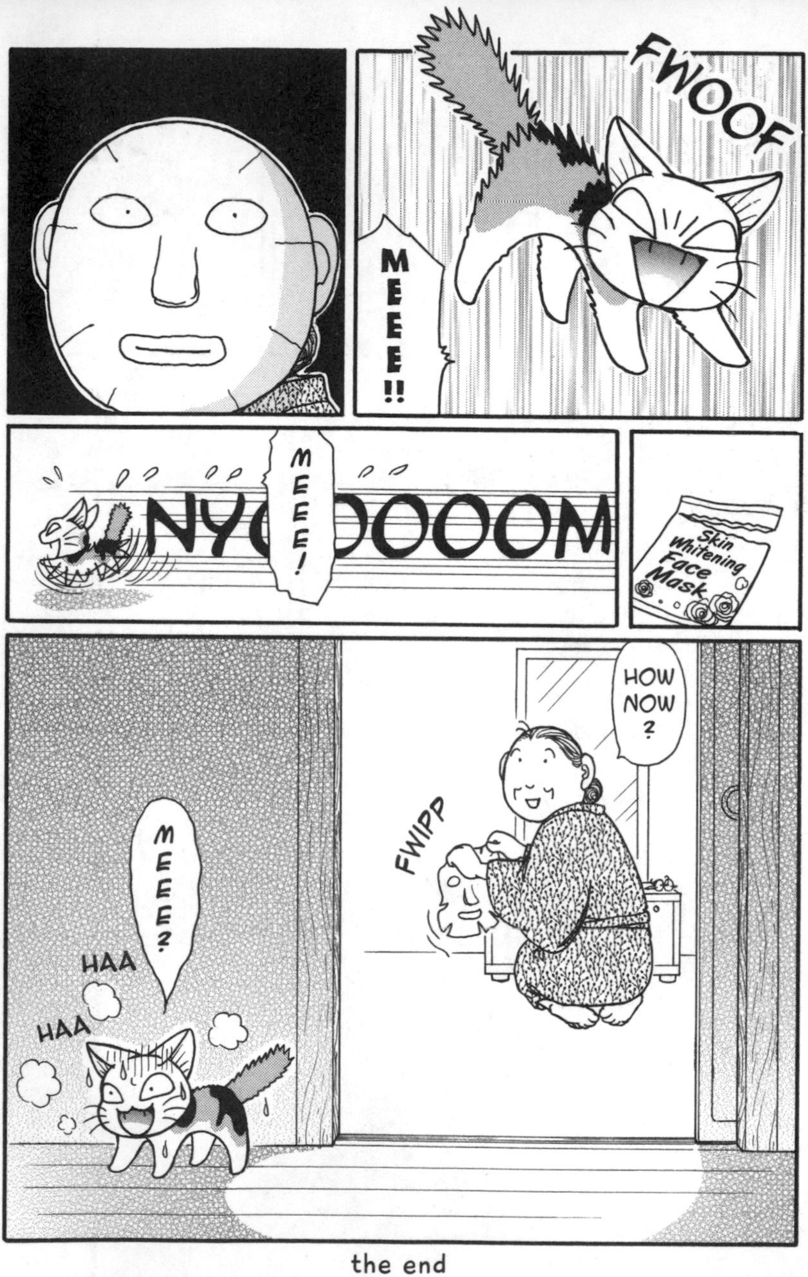
FWOOF
MEEEE!!
NYOOOOOM
MEEEE!
Skin Whitening Face Mask
HOW NOW?
FWIPP
MEEEE?
HAA
HAA

the end

FUKU
FUKU

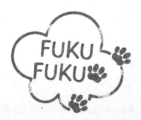

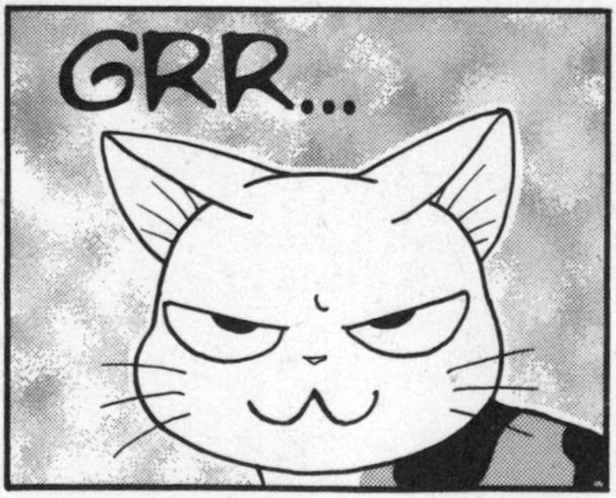
GRR...

Night Walk

FUKU FUKU

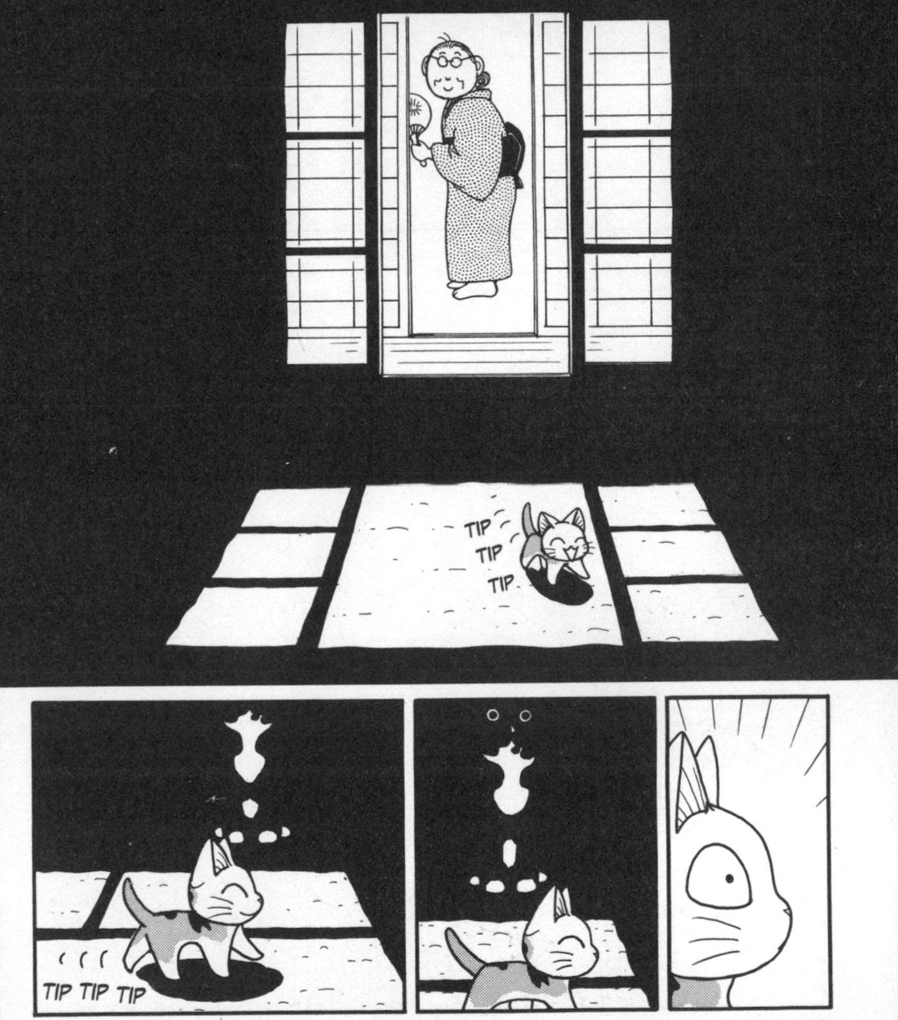
TIP
TIP
TIP
TIP TIP TIP

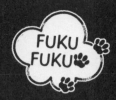

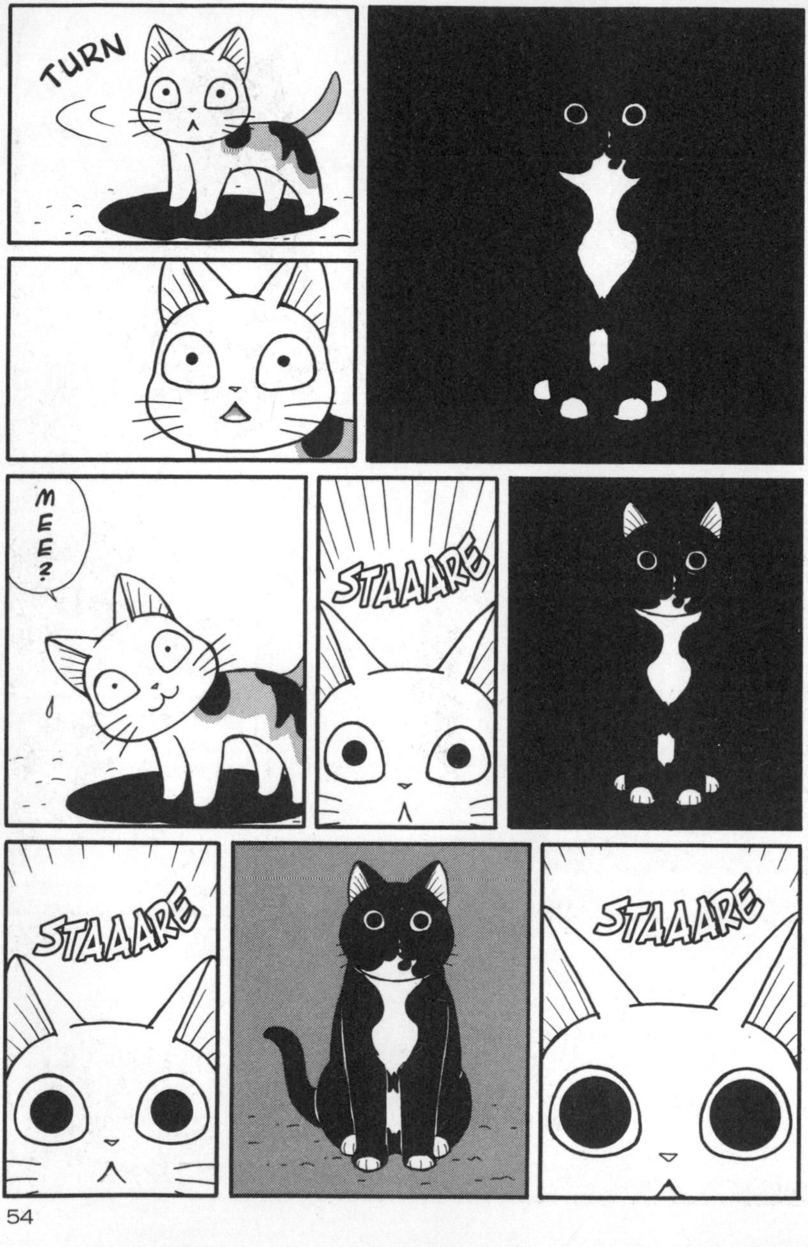
TURN
MEE?
STAAARE
STAAARE
STAAARE

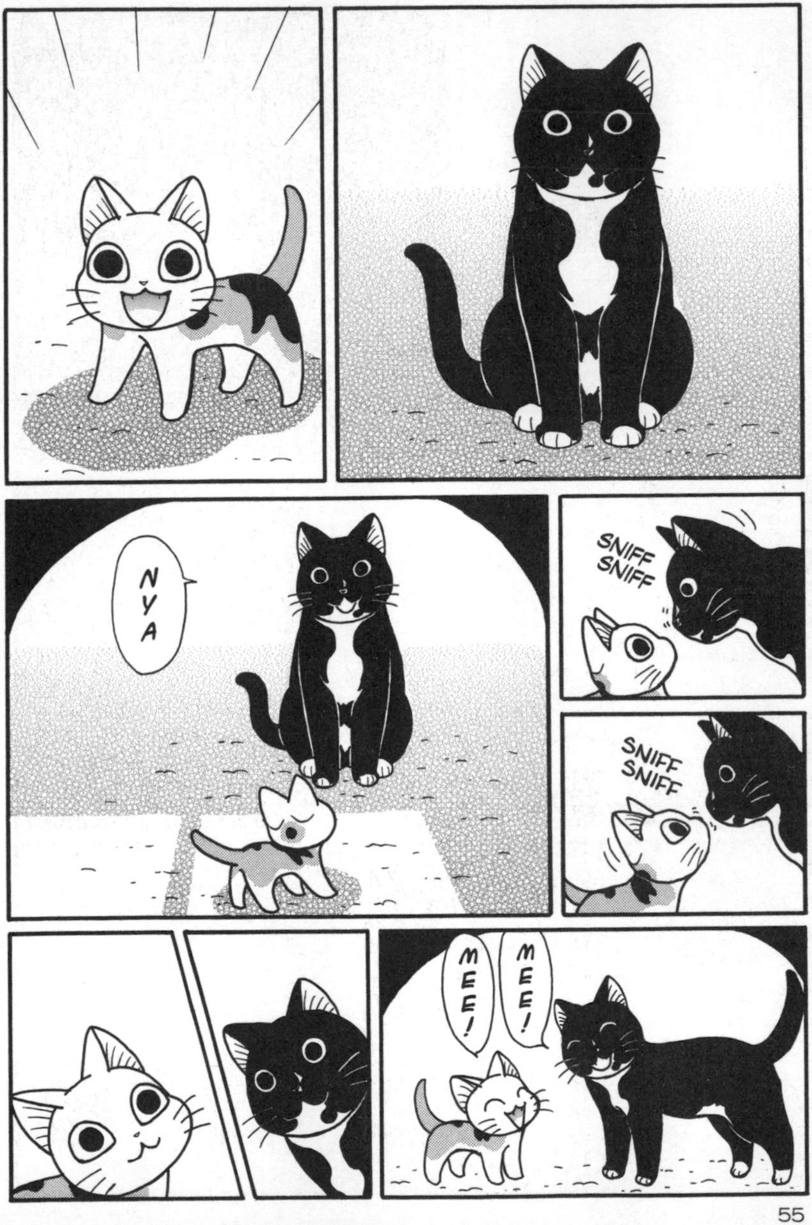
NYA
SNIFF SNIFF
SNIFF SNIFF
MEE!
MEE!

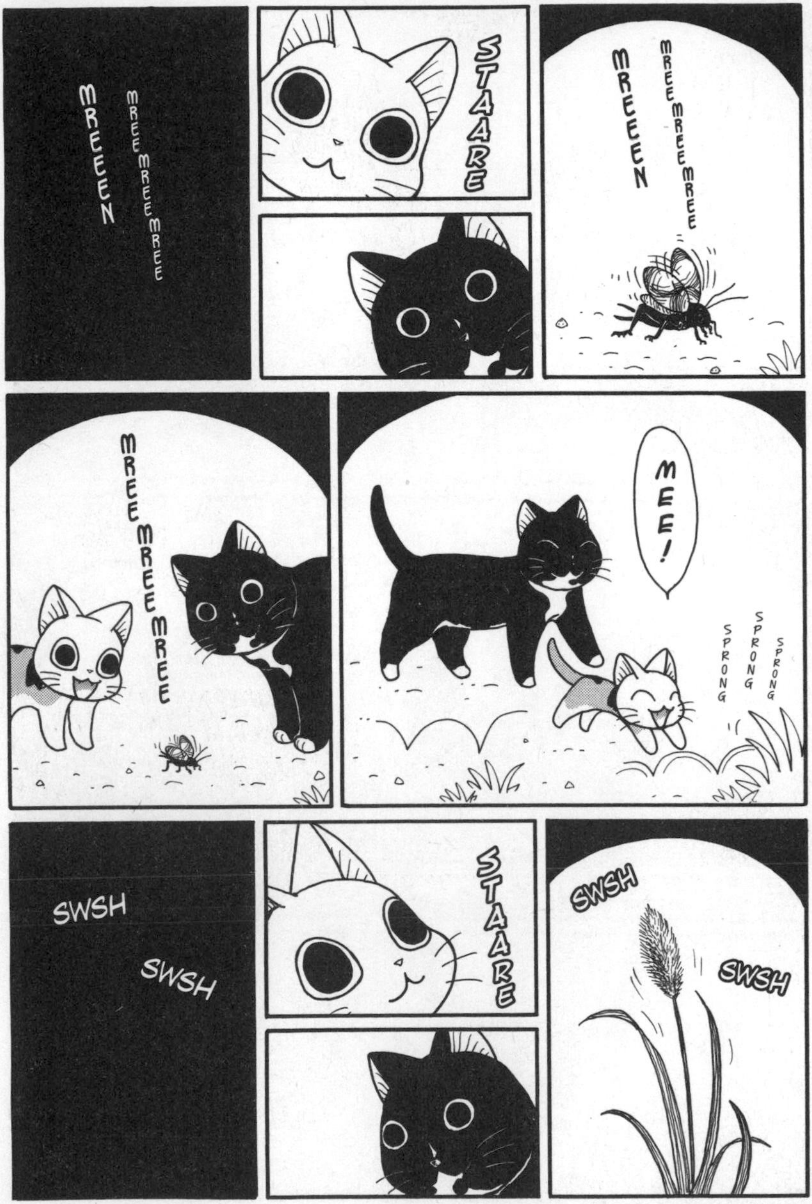
MREEEN
MREE MREE MREE
STAARE
MREEEN
MREE MREE MREE
MREE MREE MREE
MEE!
SPRONG
SPRONG
SPRONG
SWSH
SWSH
STAARE
SWSH
SWSH

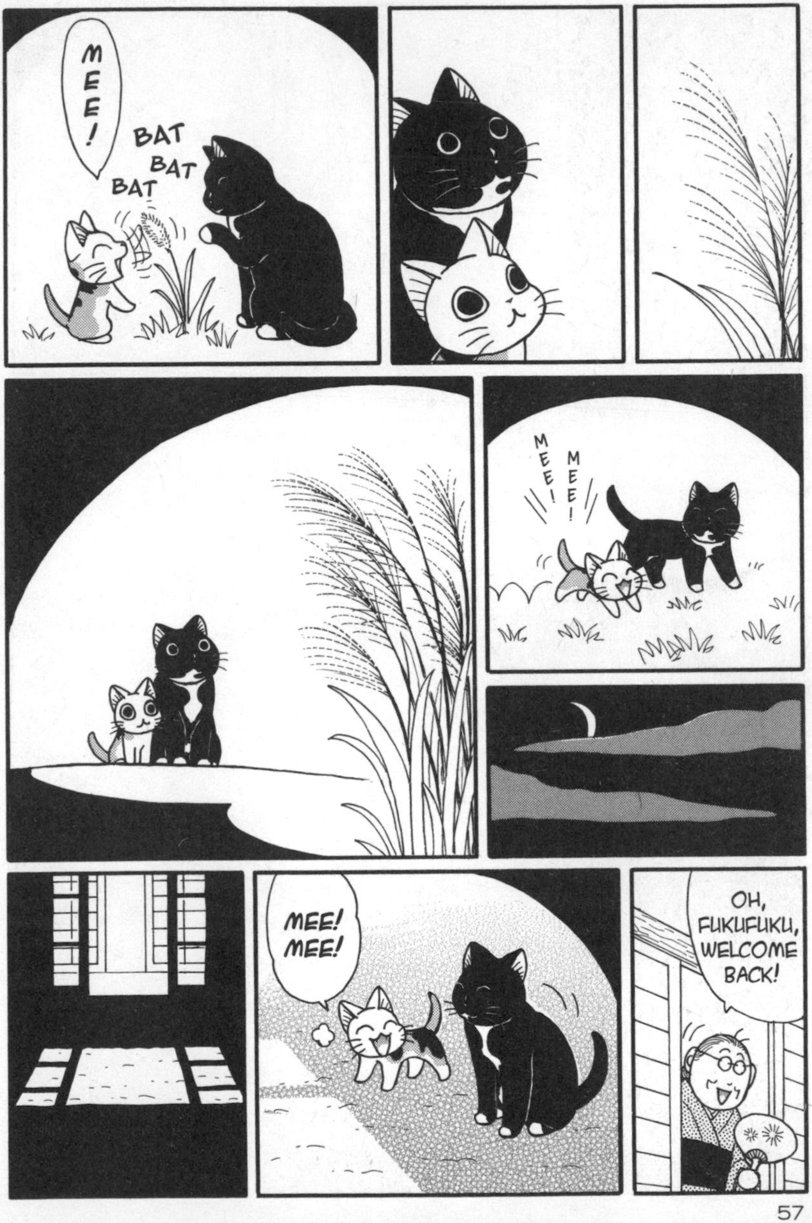
MEE!
BAT
BAT
BAT
MEE!
MEE!
MEE! MEE!
OH, FUKUFUKU, WELCOME BACK!

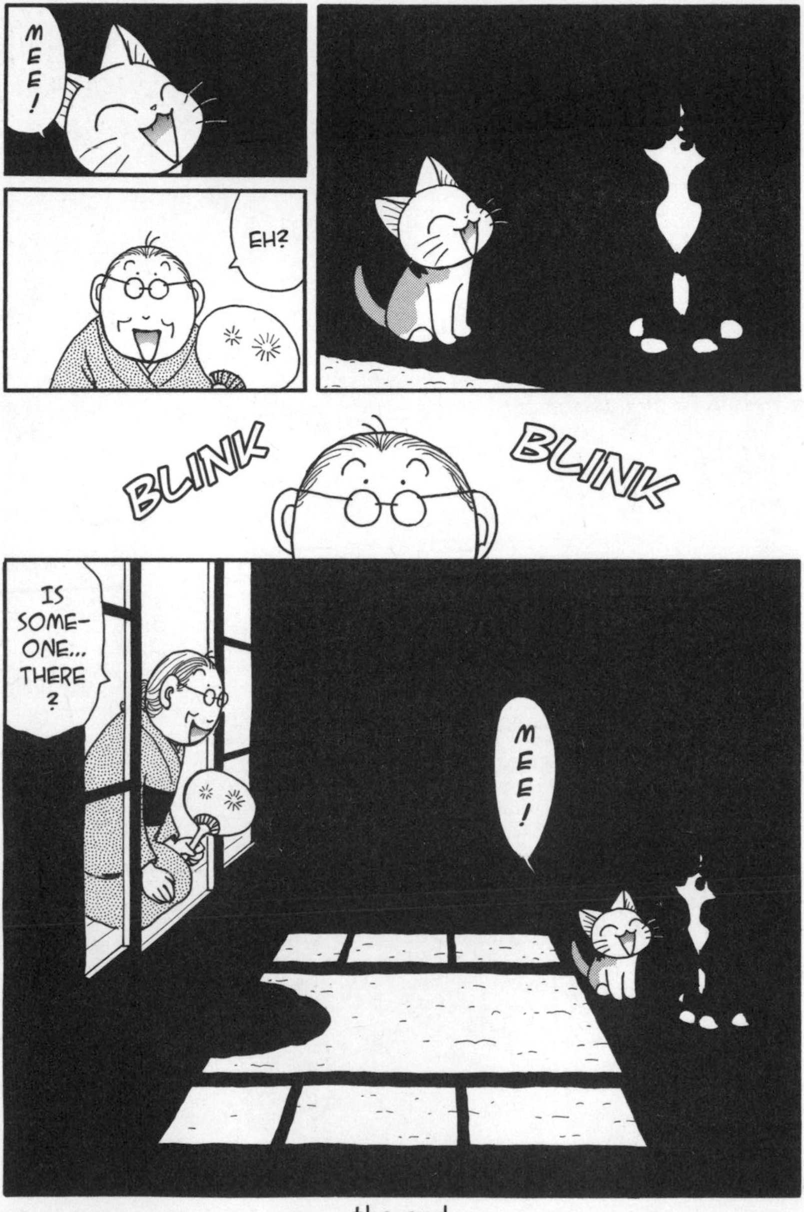
MEE!
EH?
BLINK
BLINK
IS SOMEONE... THERE?
MEE!

the end

Strong Winds

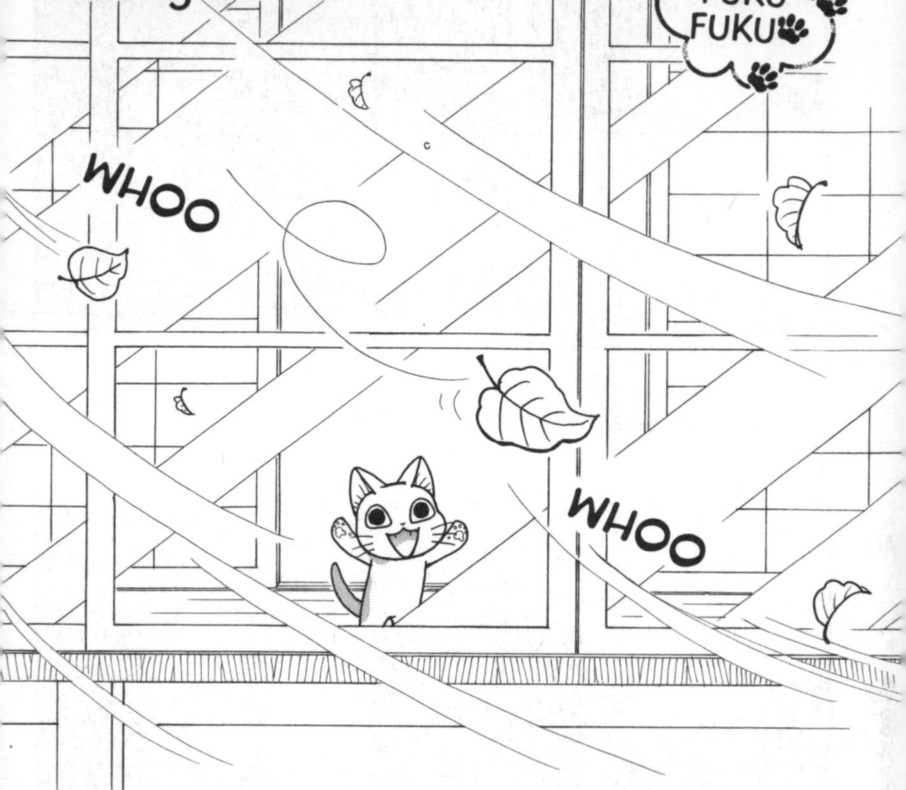
FUKU FUKU
WHOO
WHOO

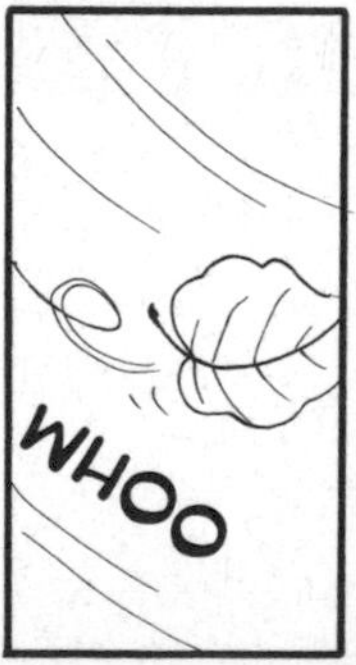
WHOO

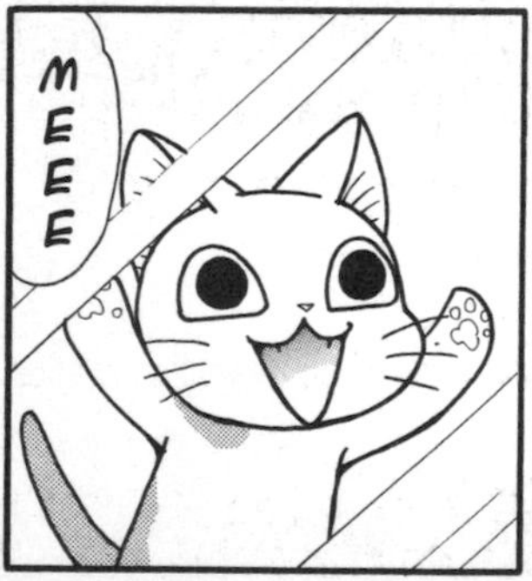
MEEE

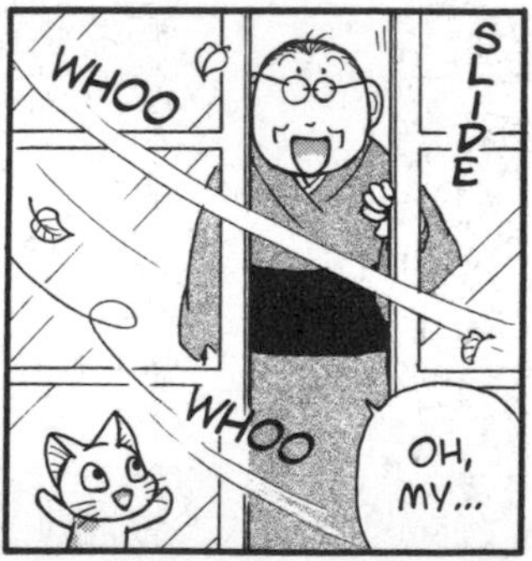
WHOO
SLIDE
WHOO
OH, MY...

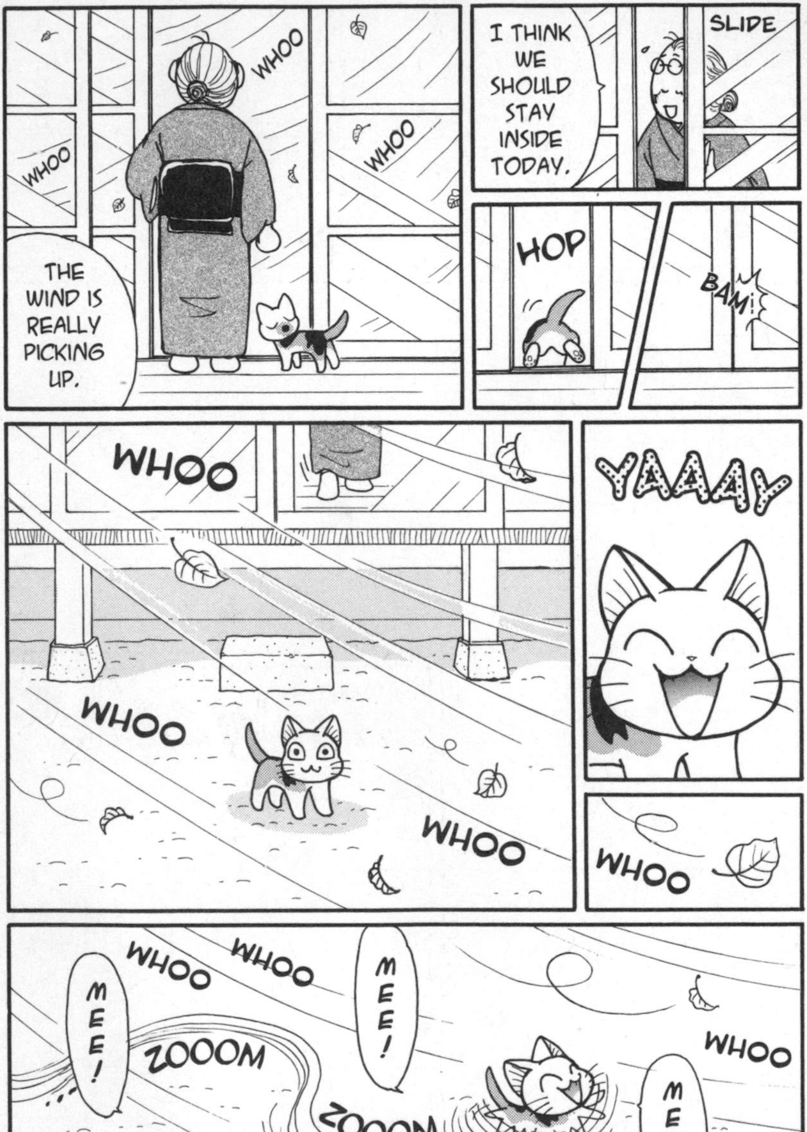
WHOO
WHOO
WHOO
THE WIND IS REALLY PICKING UP.
I THINK WE SHOULD STAY INSIDE TODAY.
SLIDE
HOP
BAM!
WHOO
WHOO
WHOO
YAAAY
WHOO
WHOO
WHOO
MEE!
MEE!
ZOOOM
ZOOOM
WHOO
MEE!

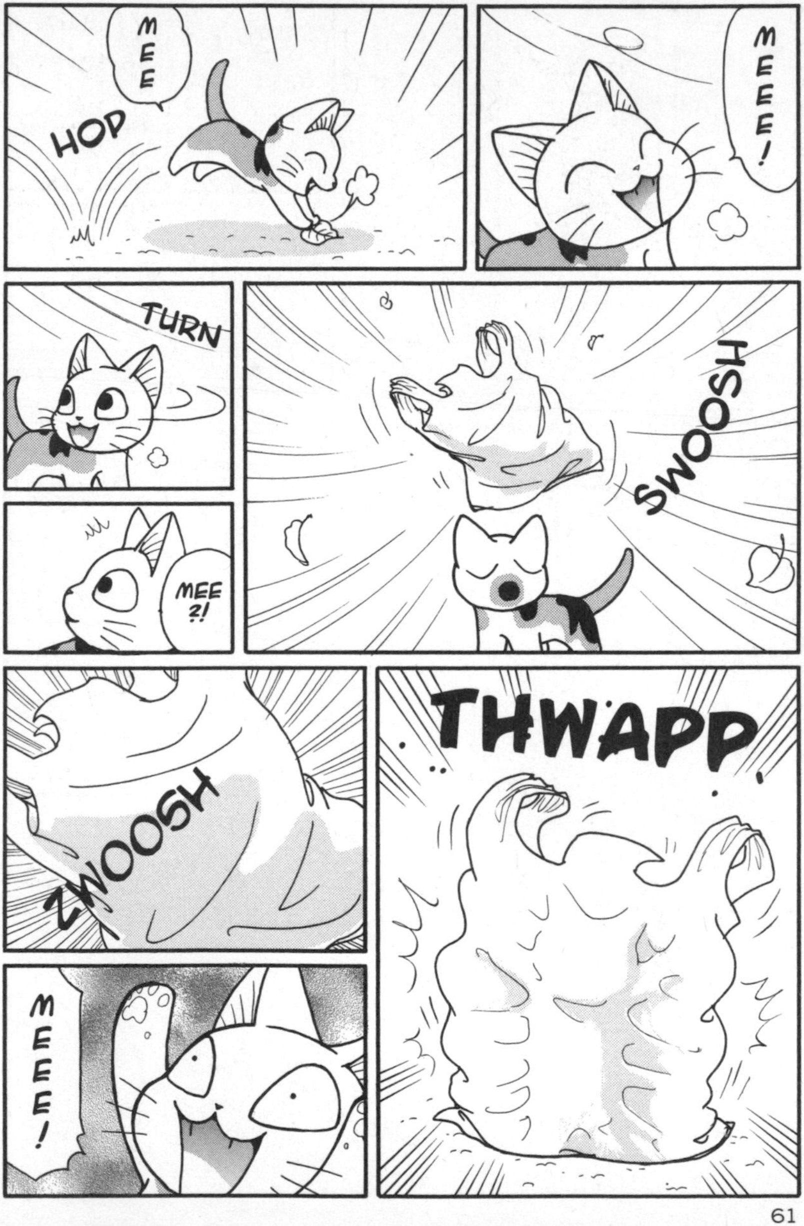
MEE
HOP
MEEE!
TURN
SWOOSH
MEE ?!
THWAPP
ZWOOSH
MEEE!

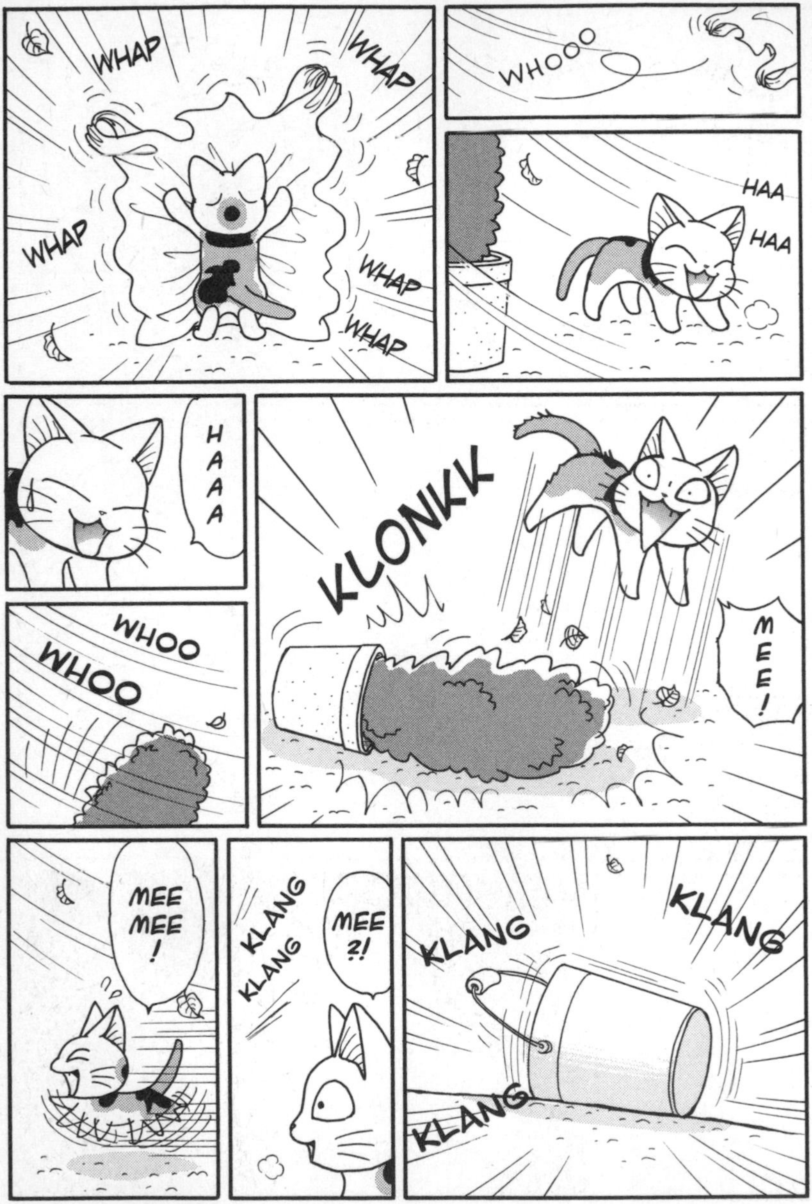
WHAP
WHAP
WHAP
WHAP
WHAP
WHOOO
HAA
HAA
HAAAA
WHOO
WHOO
KLONKK
MEE!
MEE MEE!
KLANG
KLANG
MEE?!
KLANG
KLANG
KLANG

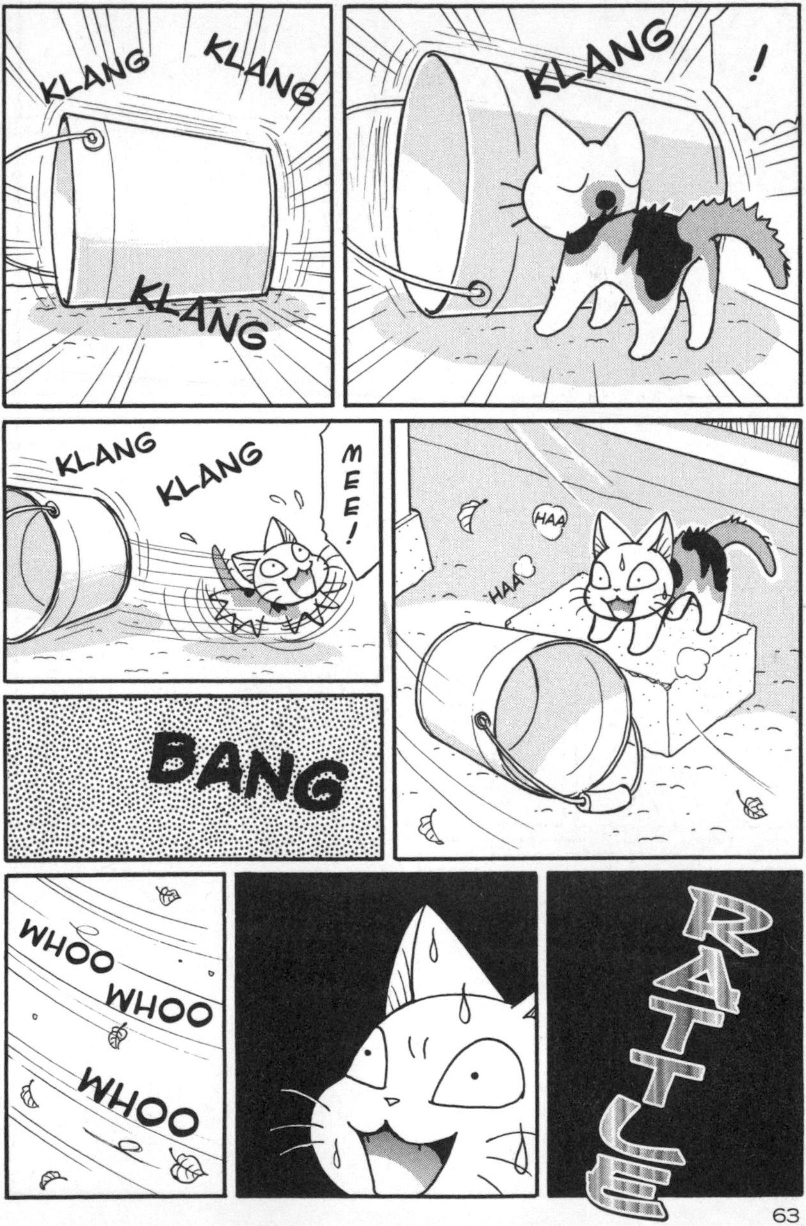
KLANG
KLANG
KLANG
KLANG
!
KLANG
KLANG
MEE!
HAA
HAA
BANG
WHOO
WHOO
WHOO
RATTLE

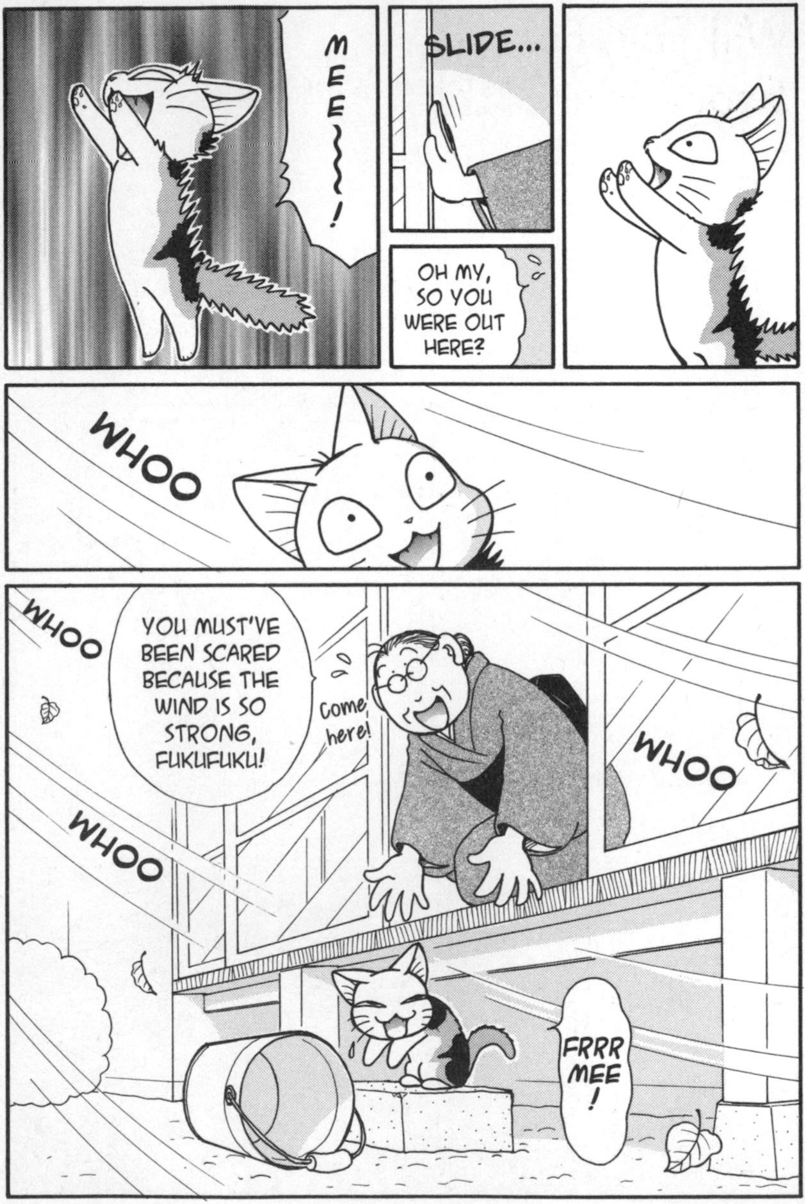
MEE~~~!
SLIDE...
OH MY, SO YOU WERE OUT HERE?
WHOO
WHOO
YOU MUST'VE BEEN SCARED BECAUSE THE WIND IS SO STRONG, FUKUFUKU!
Come here!
WHOO
WHOO
FRRR MEE!

the end

Will FukuFuku Be a Store Mascot?!

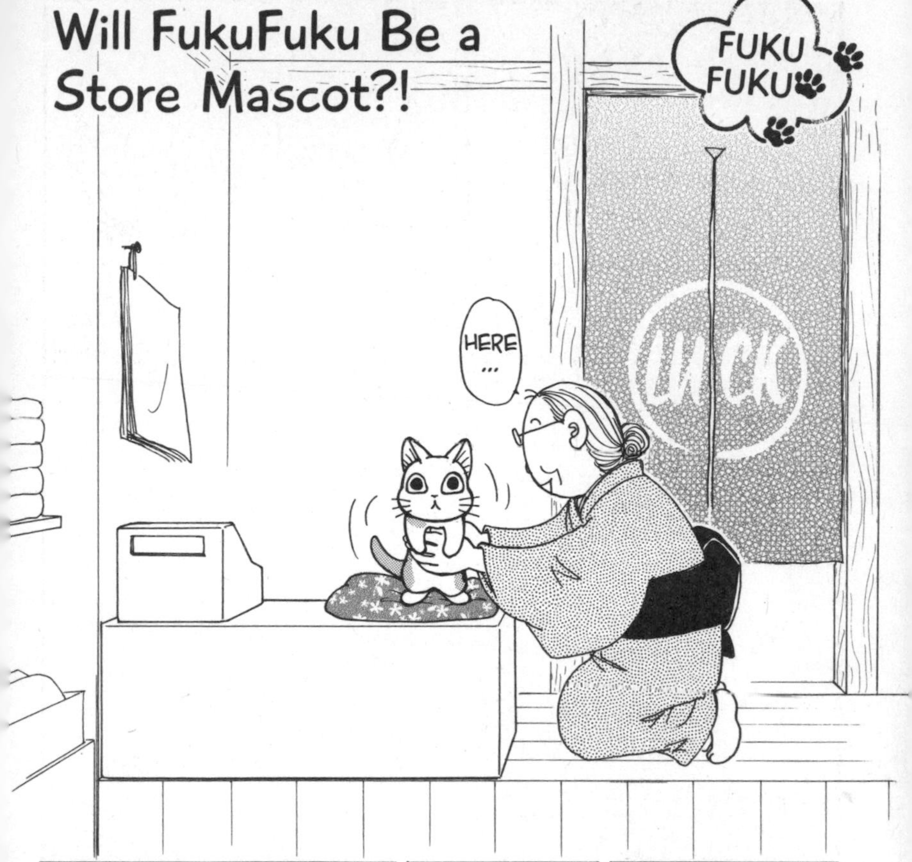
FUKU FUKU
LUCK
HERE ...

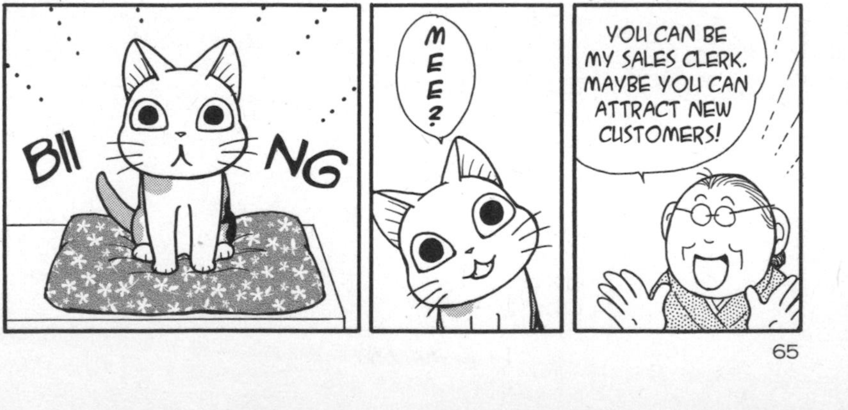
BIING
MEE?
YOU CAN BE MY SALES CLERK. MAYBE YOU CAN ATTRACT NEW CUSTOMERS!

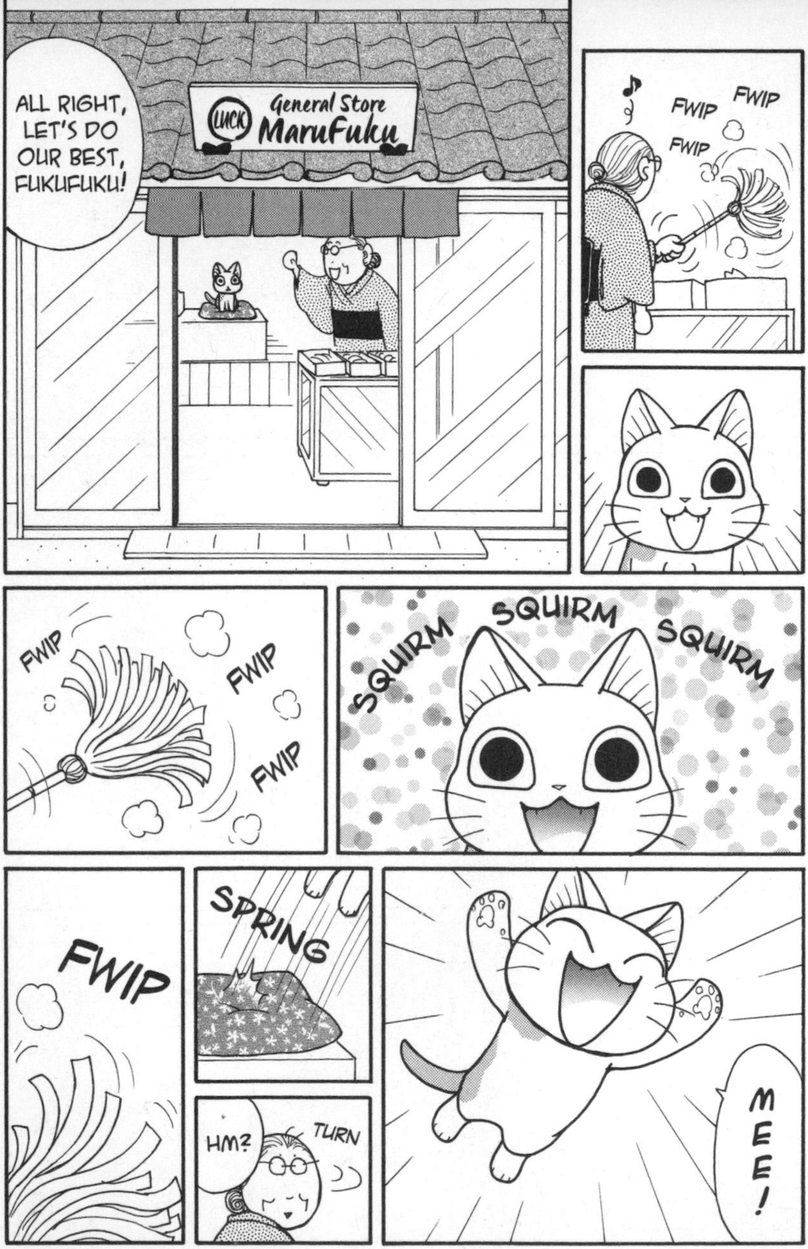
General Store MaruFuku
LUCK
ALL RIGHT, LET'S DO OUR BEST, FUKUFUKU!
FWIP
FWIP
FWIP
FWIP
FWIP
FWIP
SQUIRM
SQUIRM
SQUIRM
FWIP
SPRING
HM?
TURN
MEE!

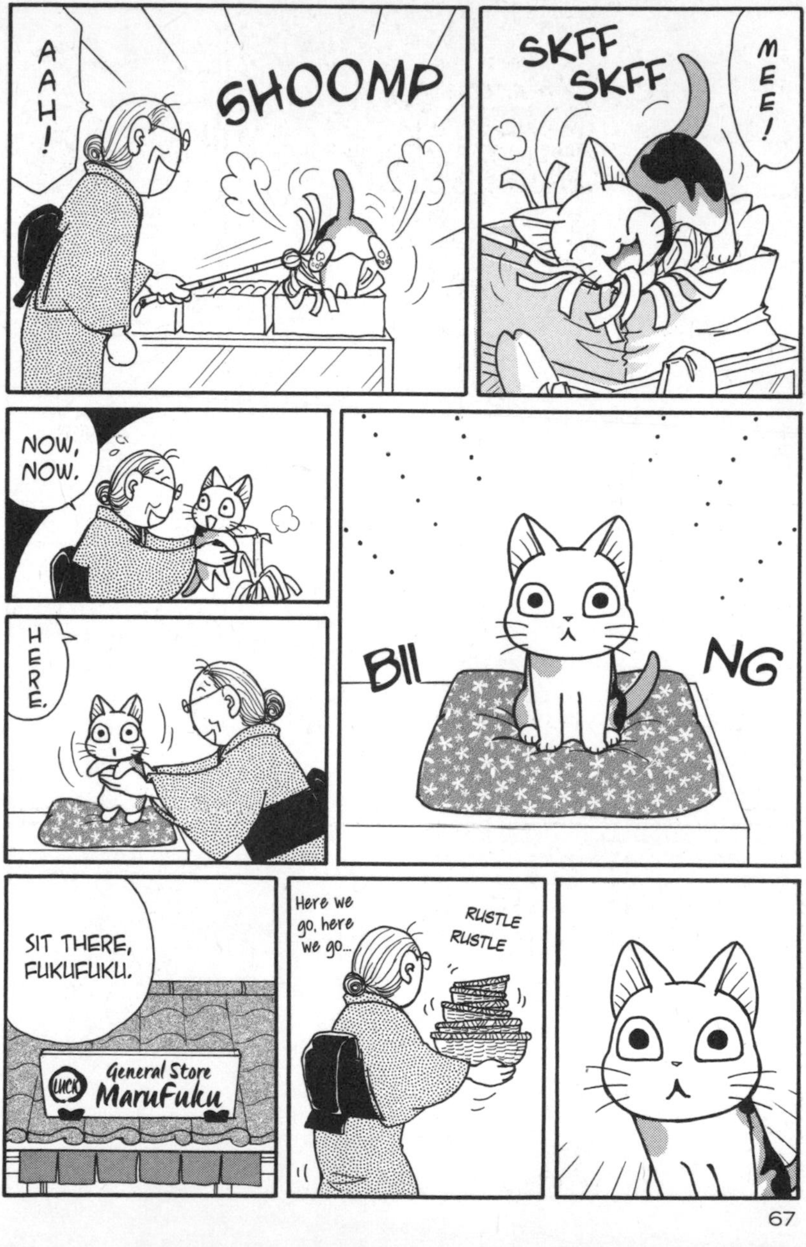
AAH!
SHOOMP
SKFF SKFF
MEE!
NOW, NOW.
HERE.
BII NG
SIT THERE, FUKUFUKU.
General Store MaruFuku
LUCK
Here we go, here we go...
RUSTLE RUSTLE

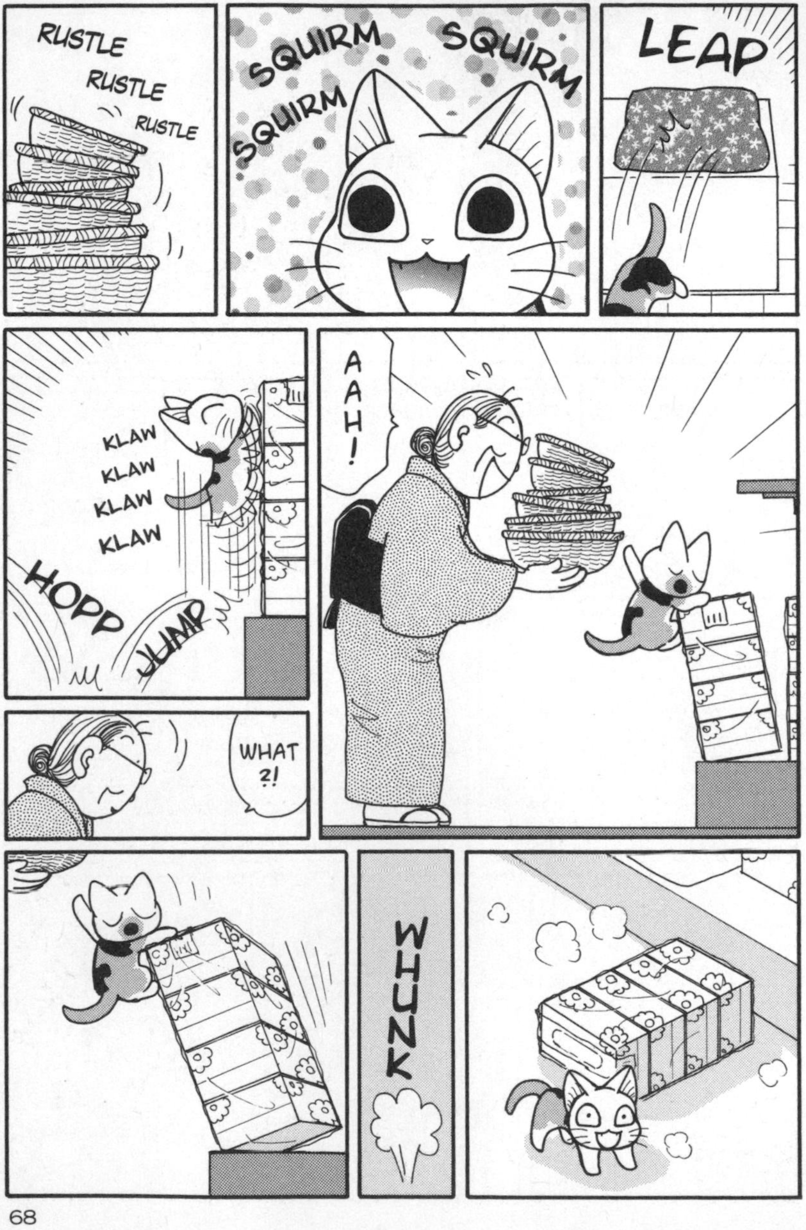
RUSTLE
RUSTLE
RUSTLE
SQUIRM
SQUIRM
SQUIRM
LEAP
KLAW
KLAW
KLAW
KLAW
HOPP
JUMP
AAH!
WHAT ?!
WHUNK

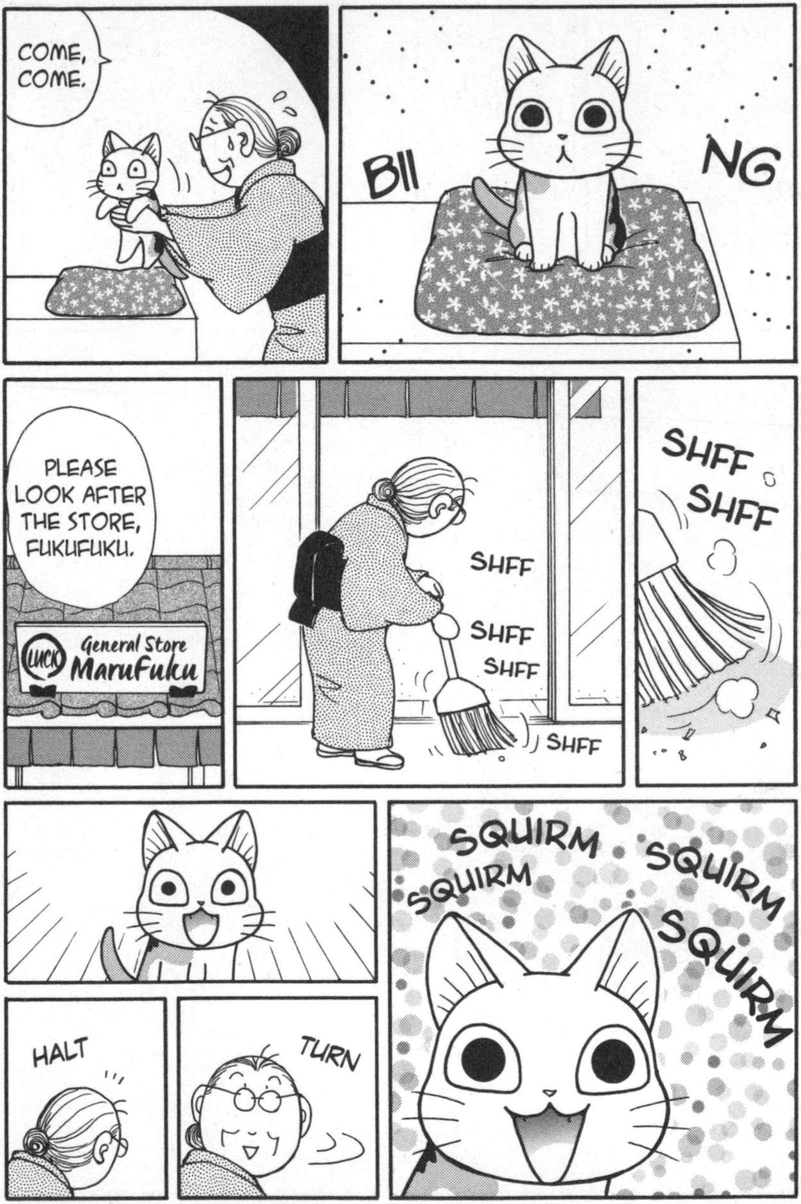
COME, COME.
BIING
PLEASE LOOK AFTER THE STORE, FUKUFUKU.
LUCK General Store MaruFuku
SHFF
SHFF
SHFF
SHFF
SHFF
SHFF
SQUIRM
SQUIRM
SQUIRM
SQUIRM
HALT
TURN

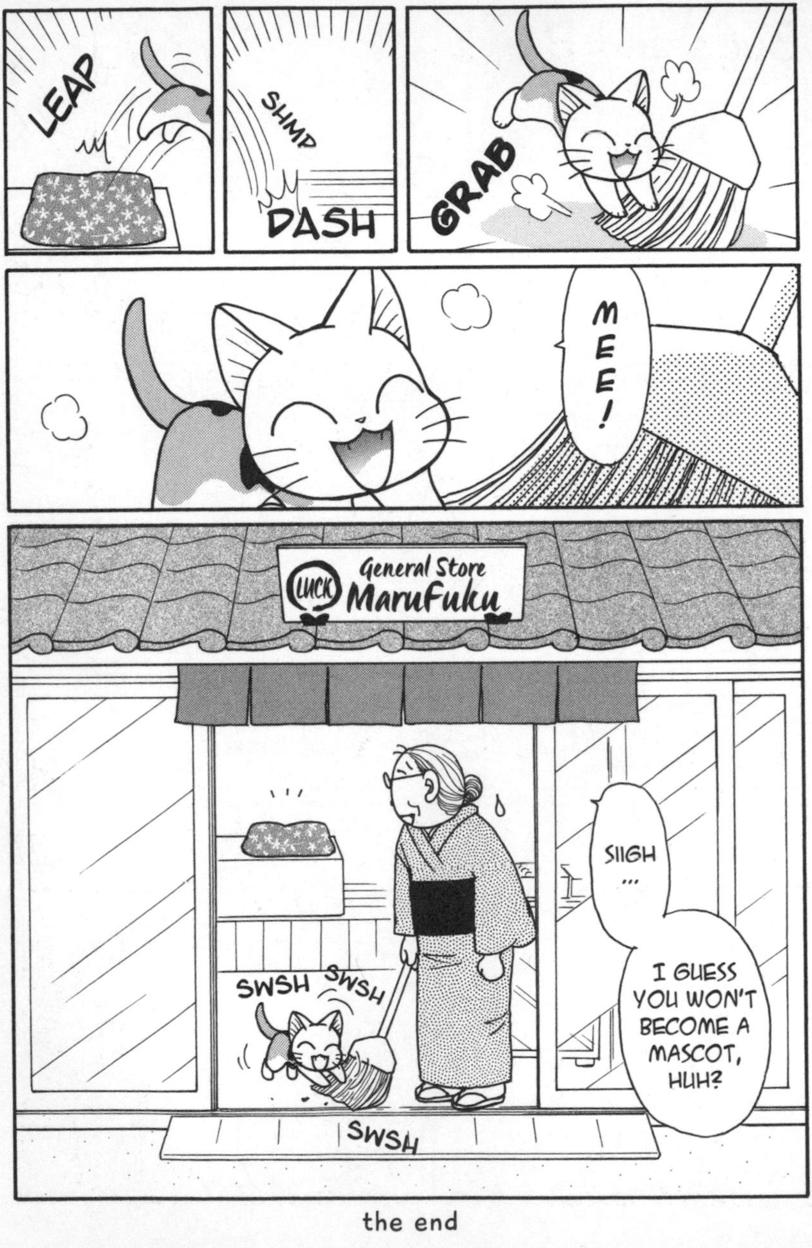
LEAP
SHMP
DASH
GRAB
MEE!
General Store
LUCK
MaruFuku
SIIGH ...
I GUESS YOU WON'T BECOME A MASCOT, HUH?
SWSH
SWSH
SWSH

the end

Bugs and Burrs

FUKU FUKU

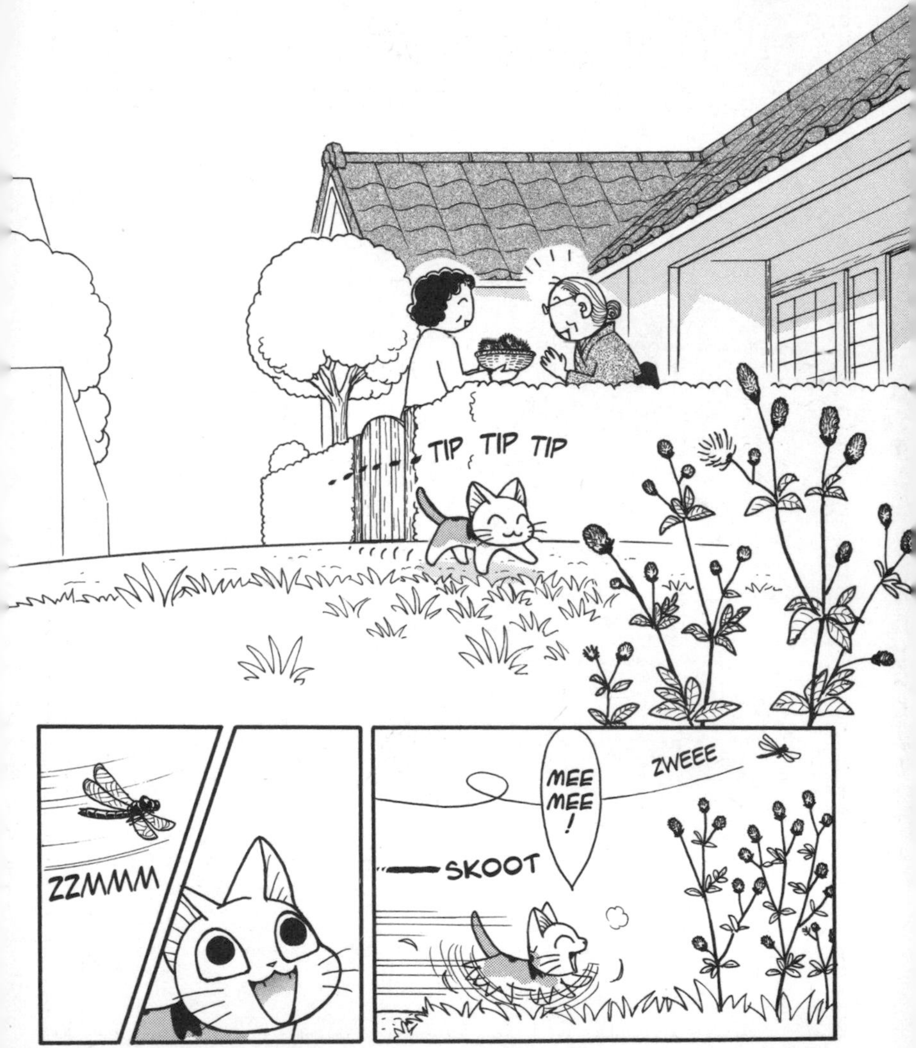
TIP TIP TIP
ZZMMMM
MEE MEE!
ZWEEE
SKOOT

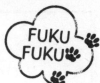

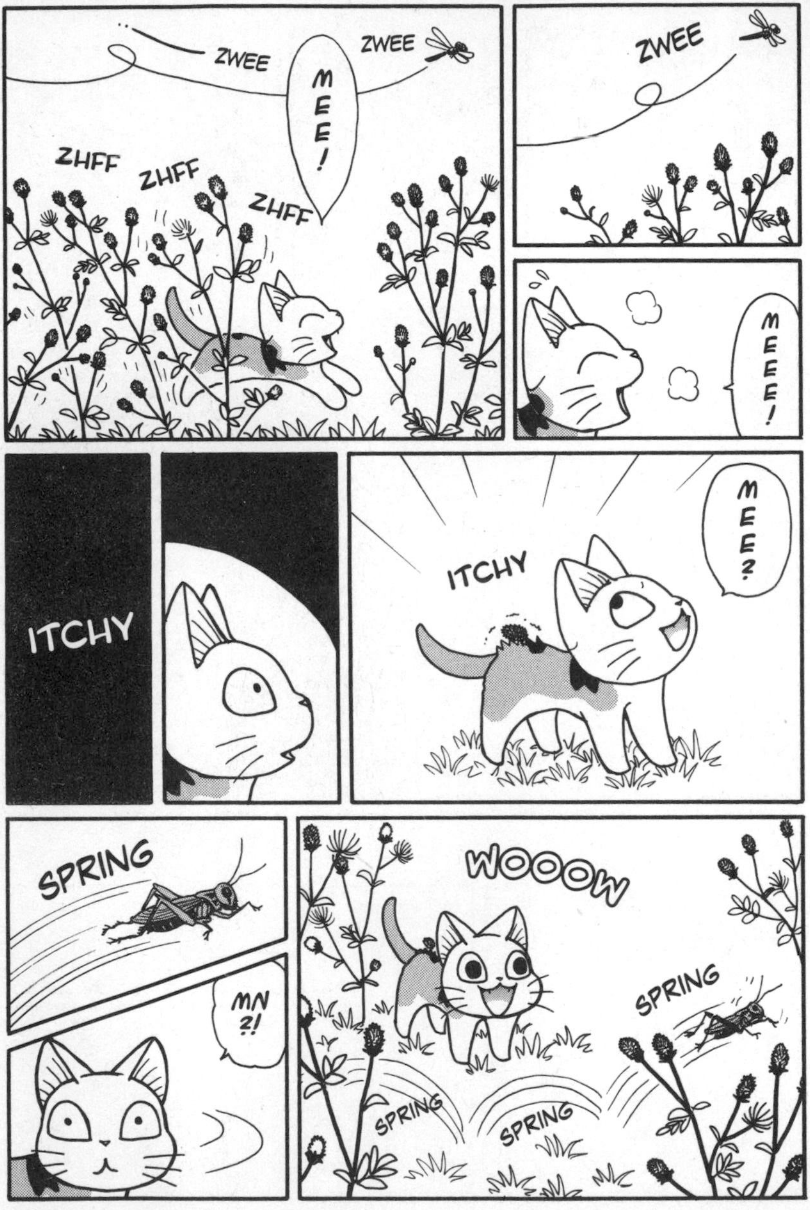
ZWEE
ZWEE
MEE!
ZHFF
ZHFF
ZHFF
ZWEE
MEEE!
ITCHY
ITCHY
MEE?
SPRING
MN?!
WOOOW
SPRING
SPRING
SPRING

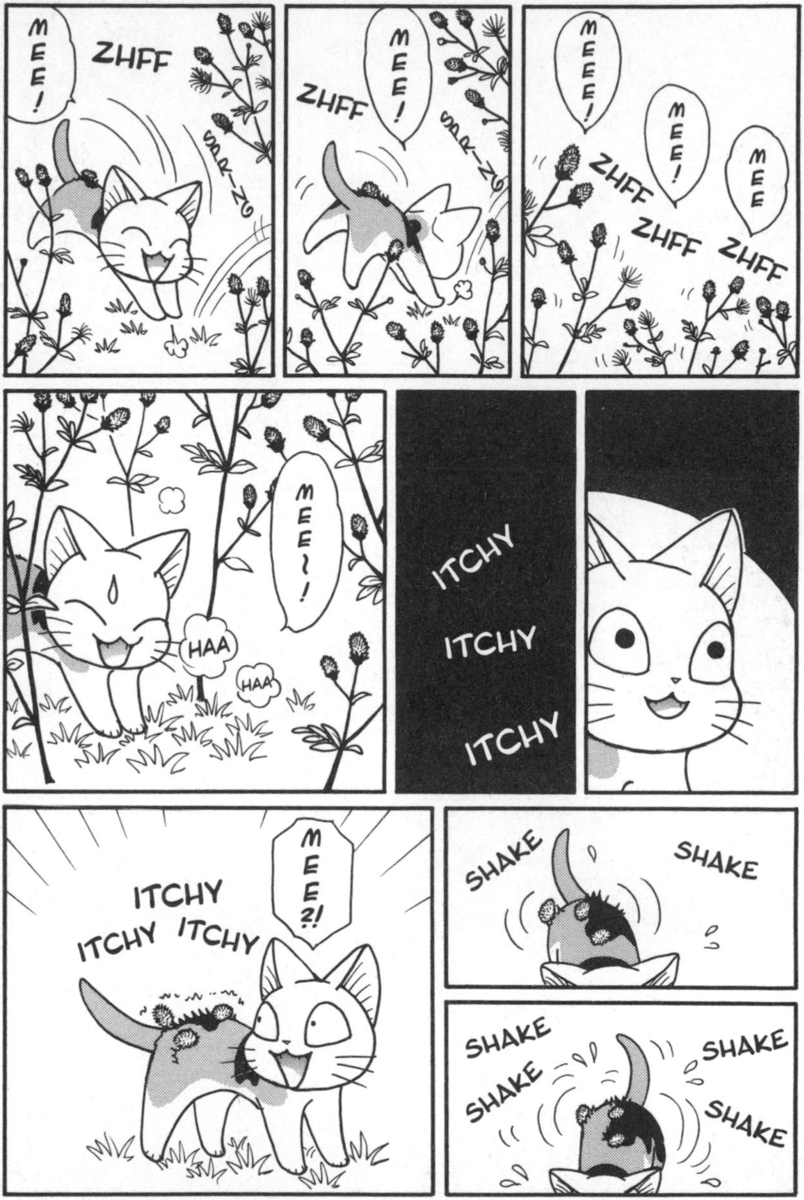
MEE!
ZHFF
SAR-ZG
MEE!
ZHFF
SAR-ZG
MEEE!
MEE!
MEE
ZHFF
ZHFF
ZHFF
MEE~!
HAA
HAA
ITCHY
ITCHY
ITCHY
ITCHY
ITCHY ITCHY
MEE?!
SHAKE
SHAKE
SHAKE
SHAKE
SHAKE
SHAKE

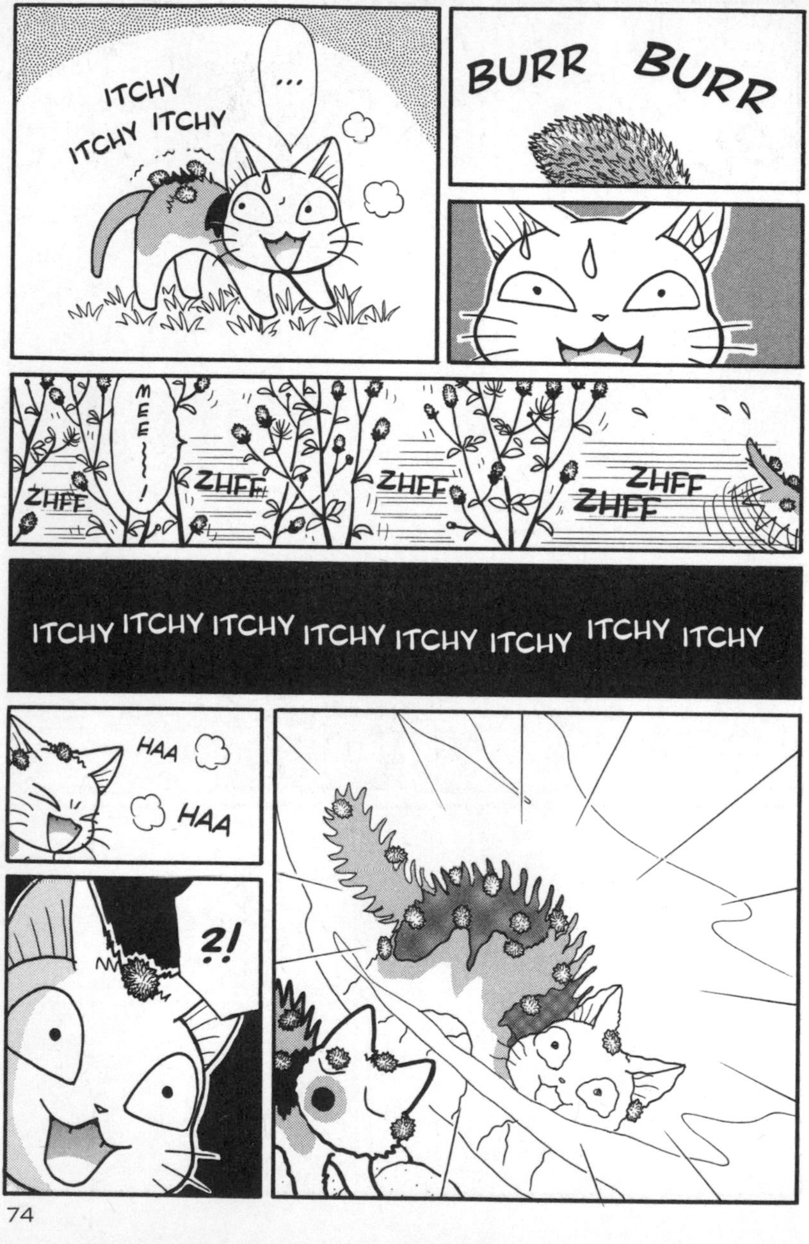
ITCHY ITCHY ITCHY
...
BURR BURR
ZHFF
MEE~~!
ZHFF
ZHFF
ZHFF
ZHFF
ITCHY ITCHY ITCHY ITCHY ITCHY ITCHY ITCHY ITCHY
HAA
HAA
?!

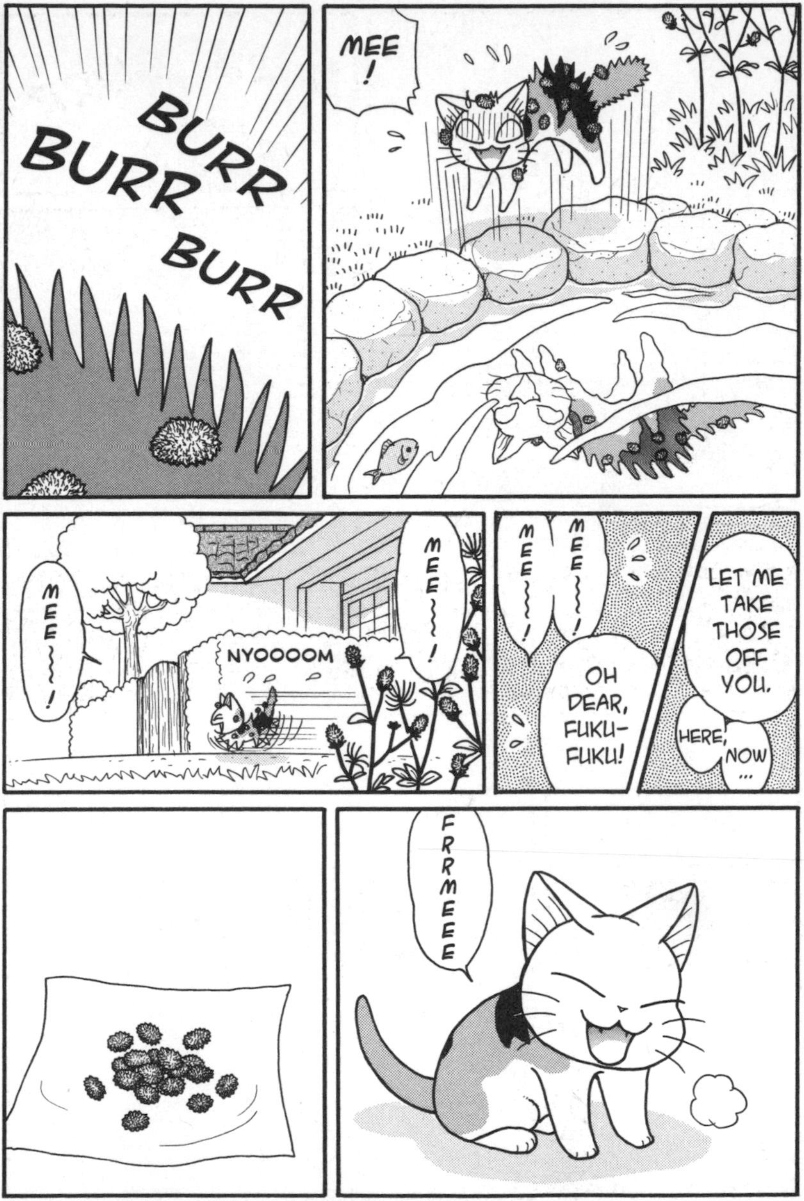
BURR
BURR
BURR
MEE!
MEE~~!
NYOOOOM
MEE~~!
MEE~~!
MEE~~!
OH DEAR, FUKU-FUKU!
LET ME TAKE THOSE OFF YOU.
HERE, NOW...
FRRMEEE

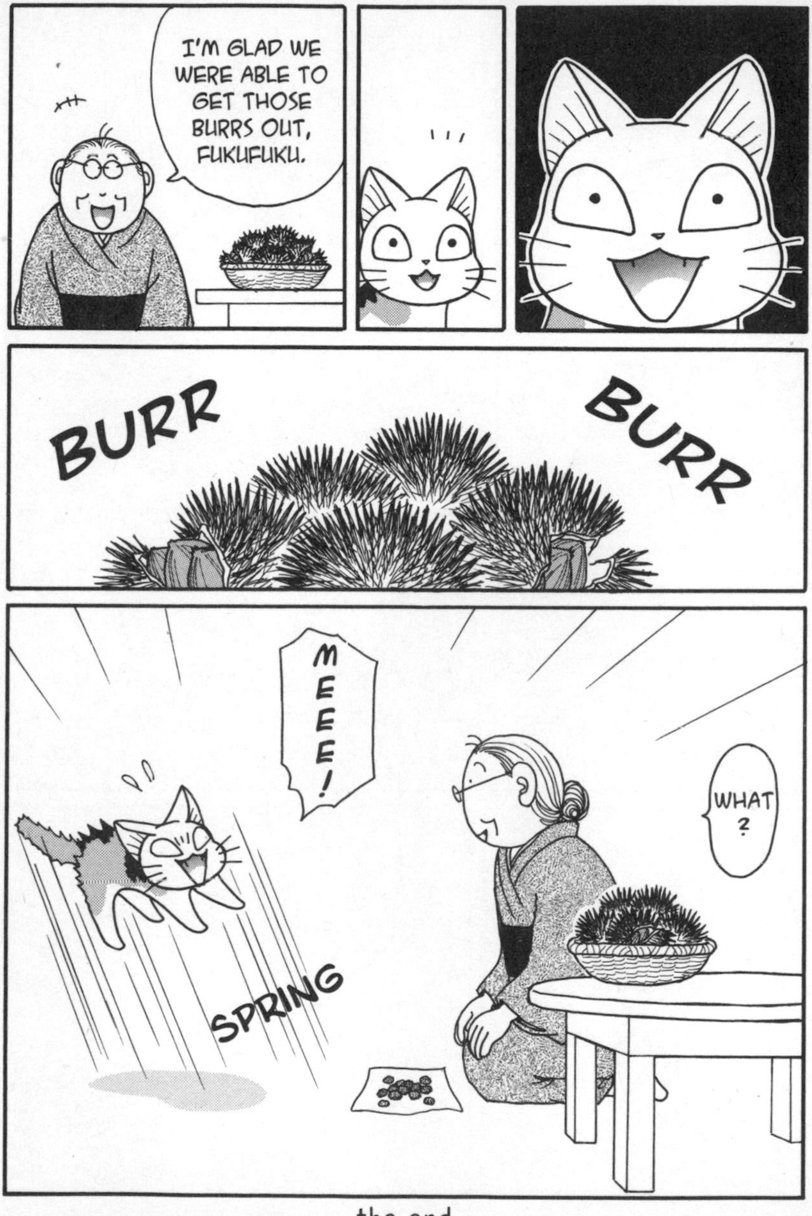
I'M GLAD WE WERE ABLE TO GET THOSE BURRS OUT, FUKUFUKU.
BURR
BURR
MEEE!
WHAT?
SPRING

the end

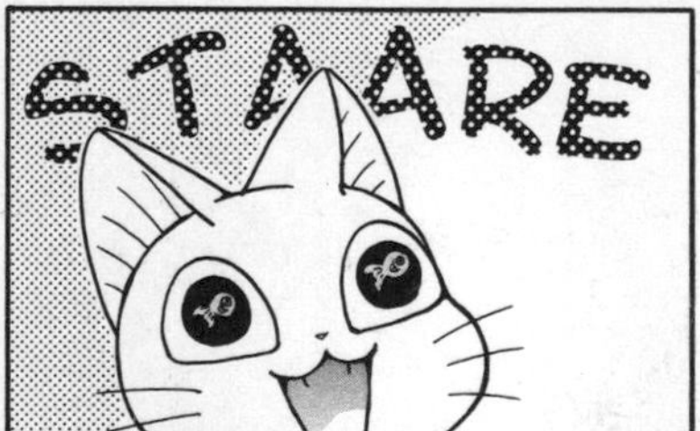
STAARE

FukuFuku, Master of the Kotatsu

FUKU FUKU

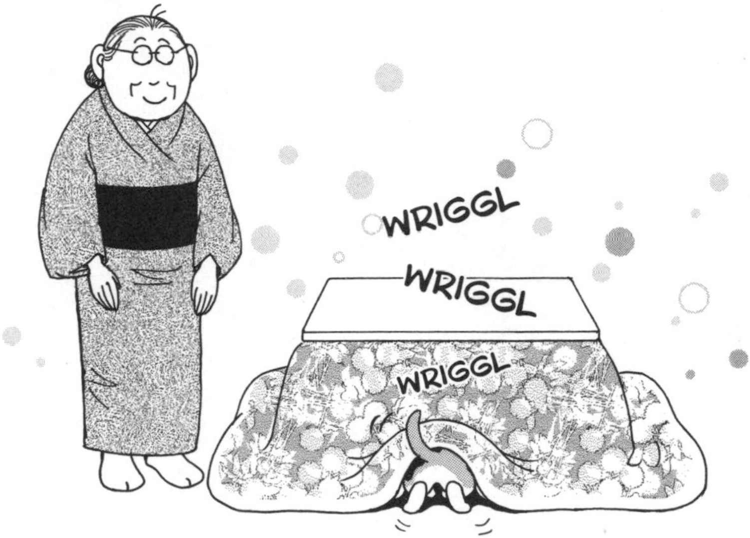
WRIGGL
WRIGGL
WRIGGL

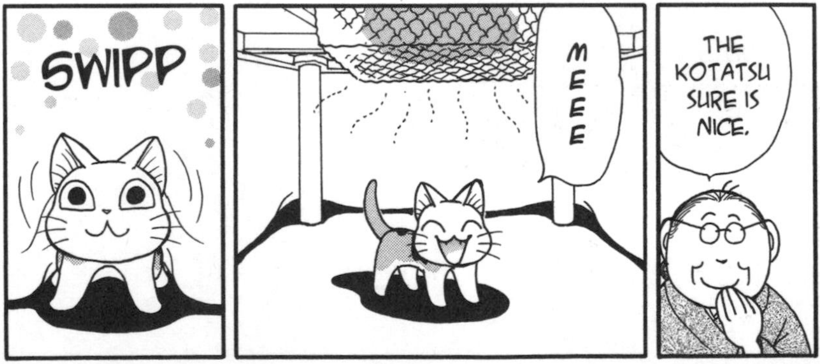
SWIPP
MEEE
THE KOTATSU SURE IS NICE.

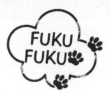

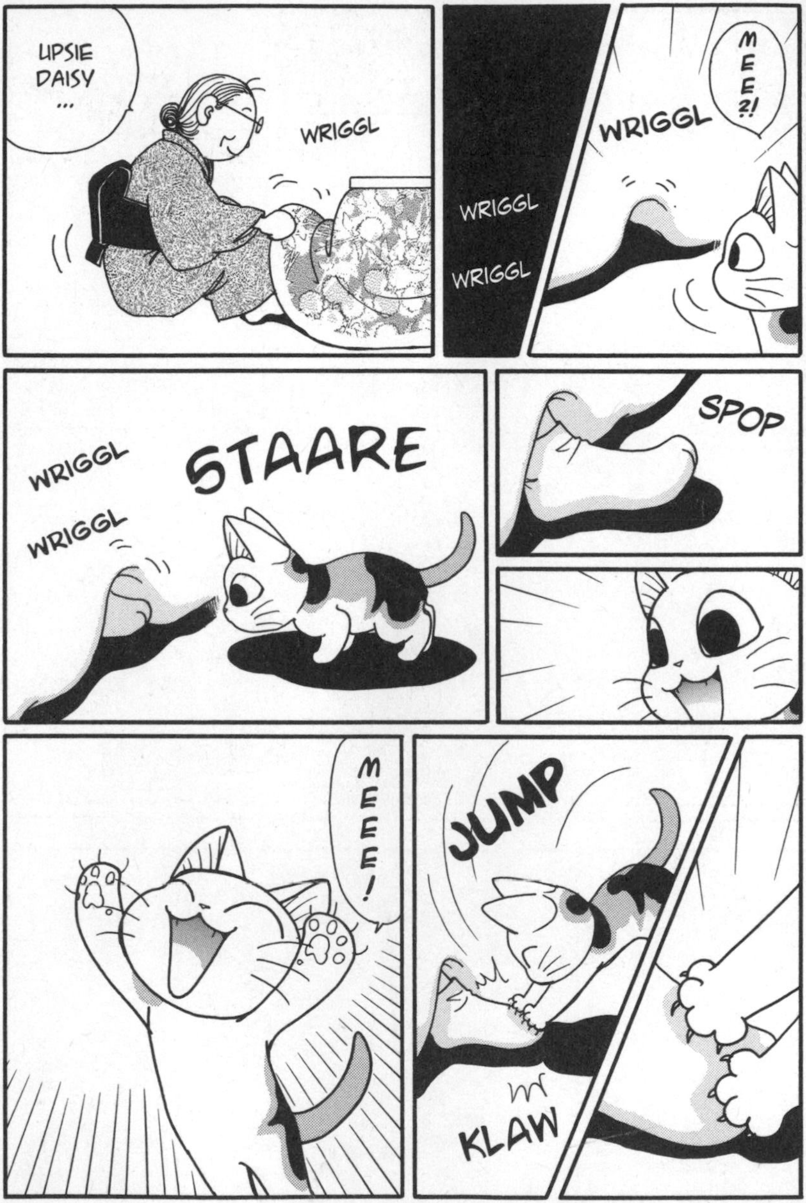
UPSIE DAISY ...
WRIGGL
WRIGGL
WRIGGL
WRIGGL
MEEE?!
WRIGGL
WRIGGL
STAARE
SPOP
MEEE!
JUMP
KLAW

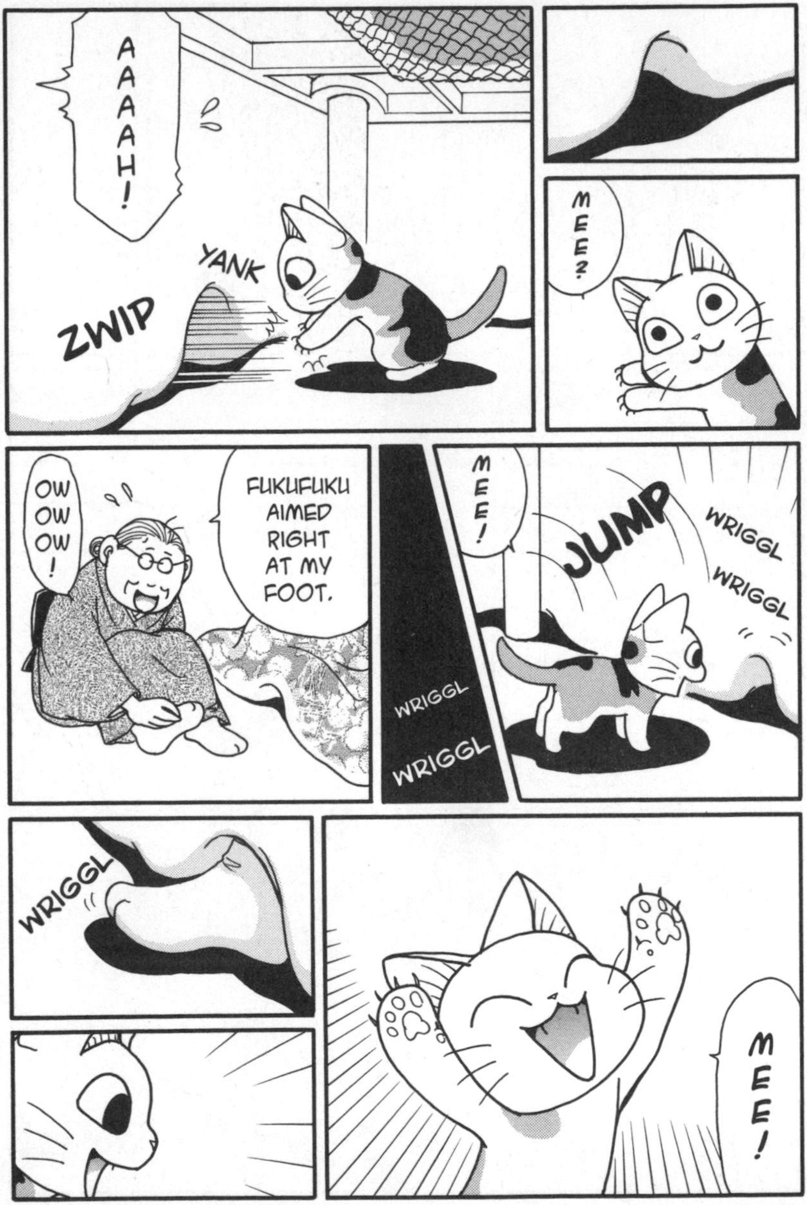
AAAAAH!
YANK
ZWIP
MEE?
OW OW OW!
FUKUFUKU AIMED RIGHT AT MY FOOT.
MEE!
JUMP
WRIGGL
WRIGGL
WRIGGL
WRIGGL
WRIGGL
MEE!

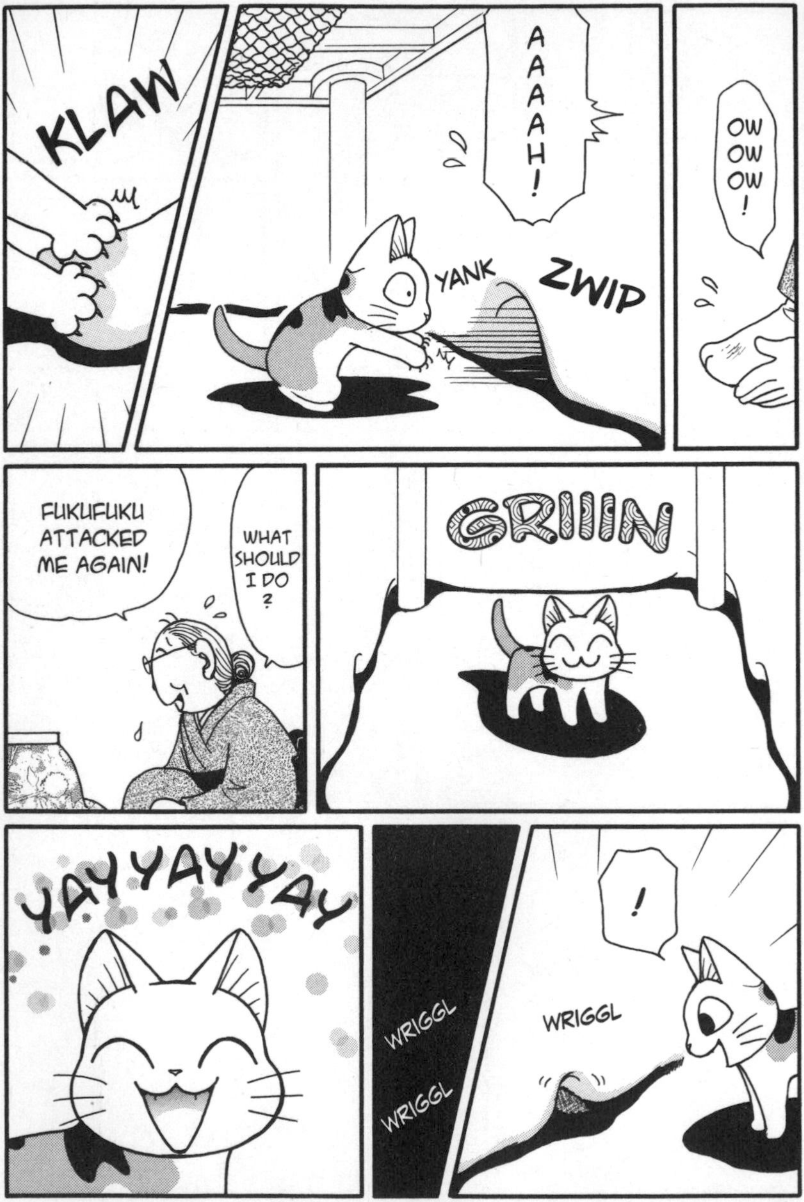
KLAW
AAAAAH!
YANK
ZWIP
OW OW OW!
FUKUFUKU ATTACKED ME AGAIN!
WHAT SHOULD I DO?
GRIIIN
YAYYAYYAY
WRIGGL
WRIGGL
!
WRIGGL

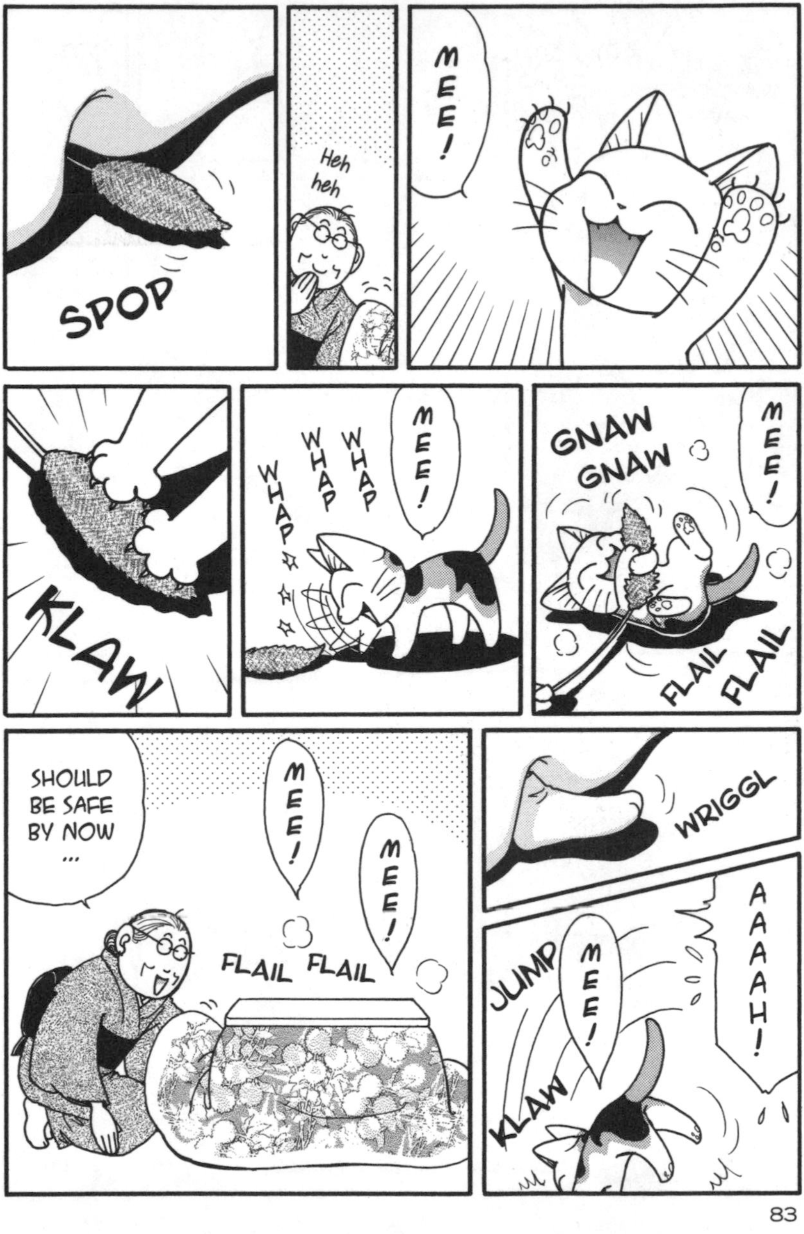
SPOP
Heh heh
MEE!
KLAW
WHAP WHAP WHAP
MEE!
GNAW GNAW
MEE!
FLAIL FLAIL
SHOULD BE SAFE BY NOW ...
MEE!
MEE!
FLAIL FLAIL
WRIGGL
JUMP
MEE!
AAAAAH!
KLAW

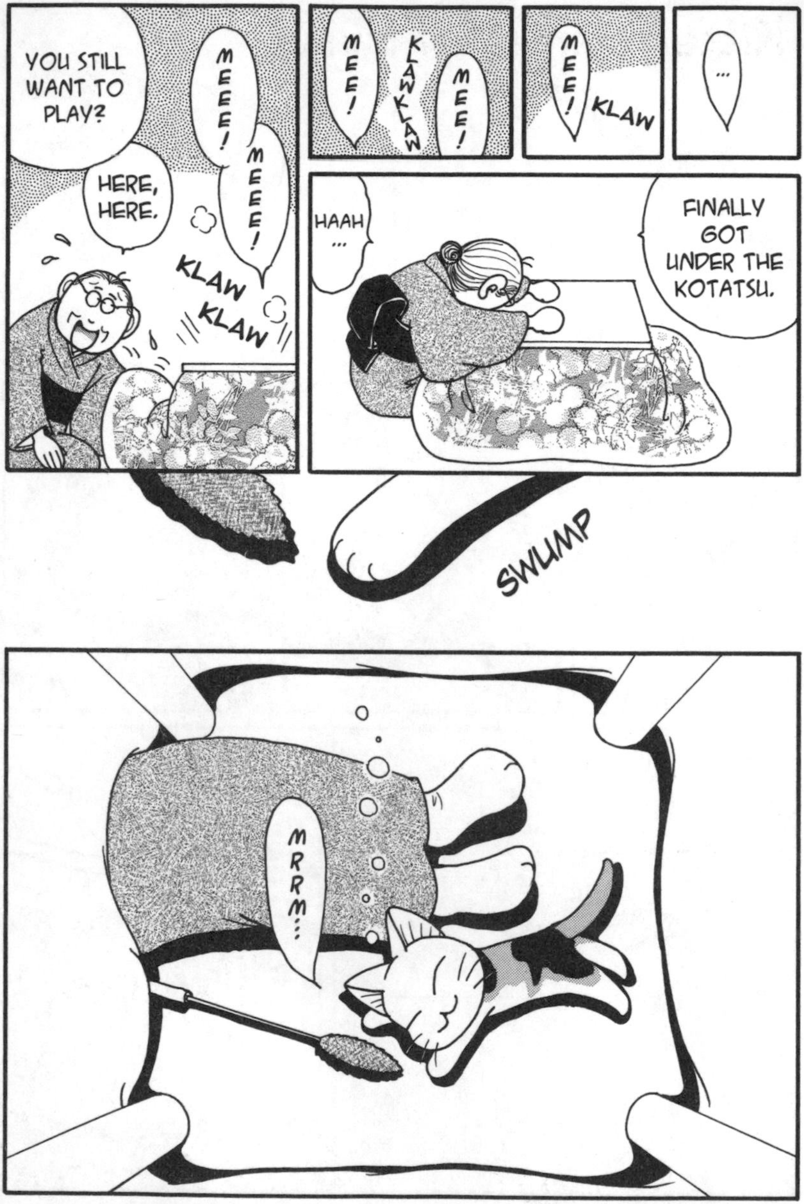
YOU STILL WANT TO PLAY?
MEEE!
MEEE!
HERE, HERE.
KLAW KLAW
MEE!
KLAWKLAW
MEE!
MEE!
KLAW
...
HAAH ...
FINALLY GOT UNDER THE KOTATSU.
SWUMP
MRRM...

the end

Kitten Santa FukuFuku

FUKU FUKU

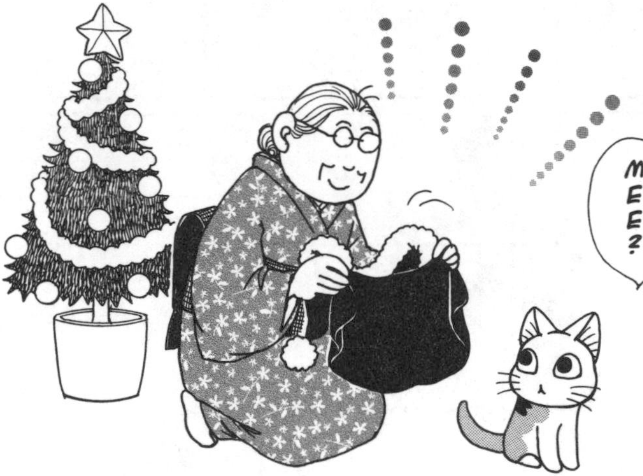

MEE?

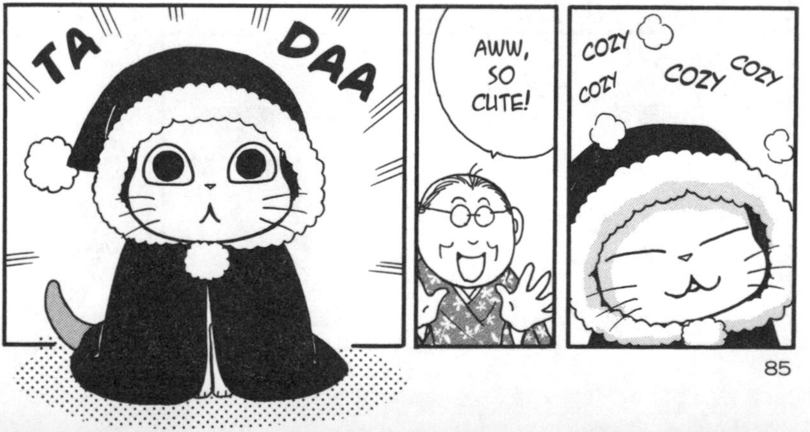

TA DAA
AWW, SO CUTE!
COZY COZY COZY COZY

MEE~

COZY

COZY

COZY

~DROWSY

COZY

YOU SEEM TO LIKE HOW WARM IT IS.

ALL RIGHT, TIME TO MAKE DINNER ...

KLINK

KLAK

KLINK

KLATCH
KLINK

ZHFF
ZHFF
ZHFF

RISE

NMEE?

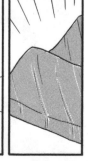

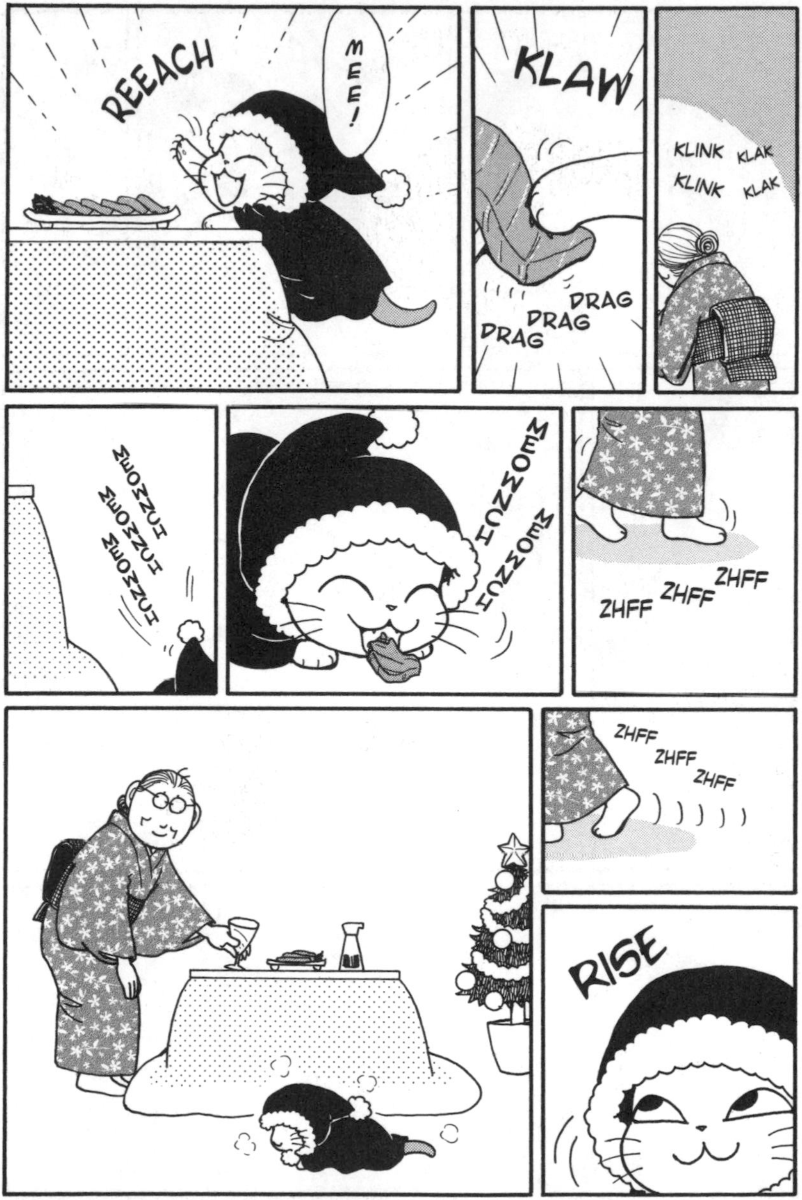
REEACH
MEE!
KLAW
DRAG DRAG DRAG
KLINK KLAK
KLINK KLAK
MEOWNCH
MEOWNCH
MEOWNCH
MEOWNCH
MEOWNCH
ZHFF ZHFF ZHFF
ZHFF
ZHFF
ZHFF
RISE

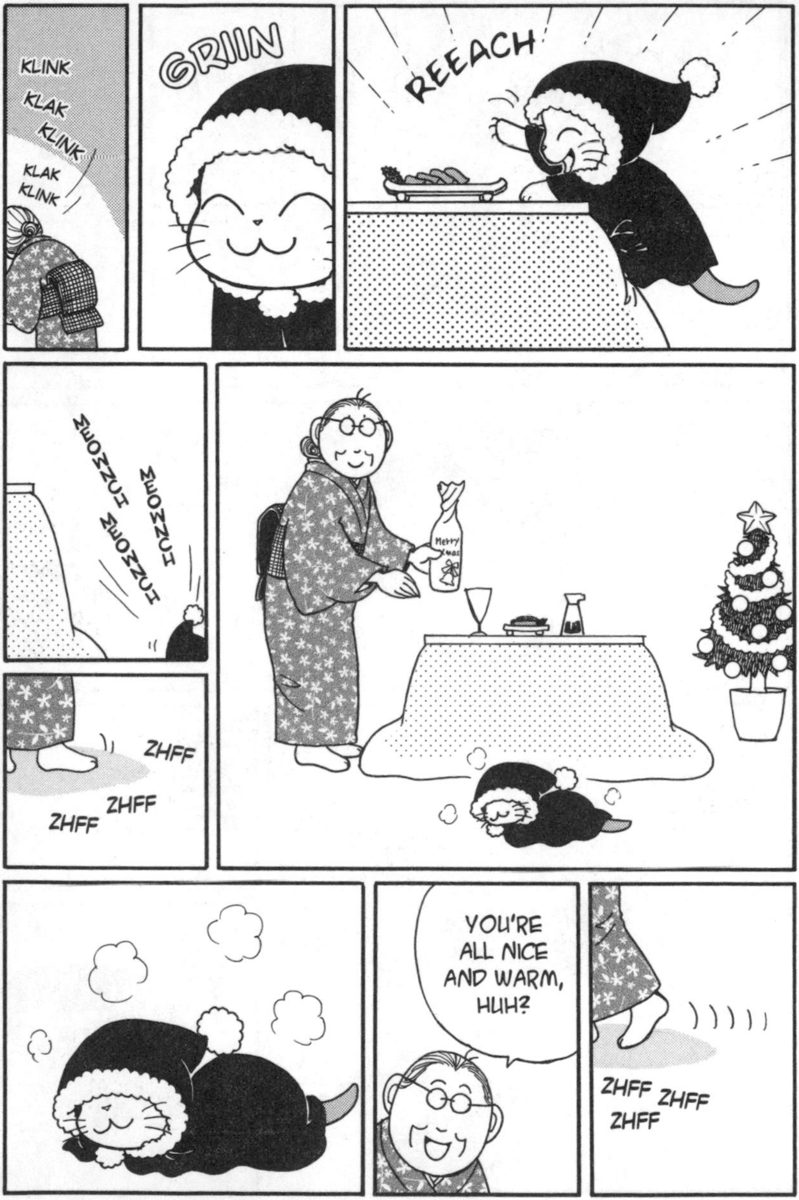
KLINK
KLAK
KLINK
KLAK
KLINK
GRIIN
REEACH
MEOWNCH
MEOWNCH
MEOWNCH
ZHFF
ZHFF
ZHFF
Merry Xmas
YOU'RE ALL NICE AND WARM, HUH?
ZHFF ZHFF
ZHFF

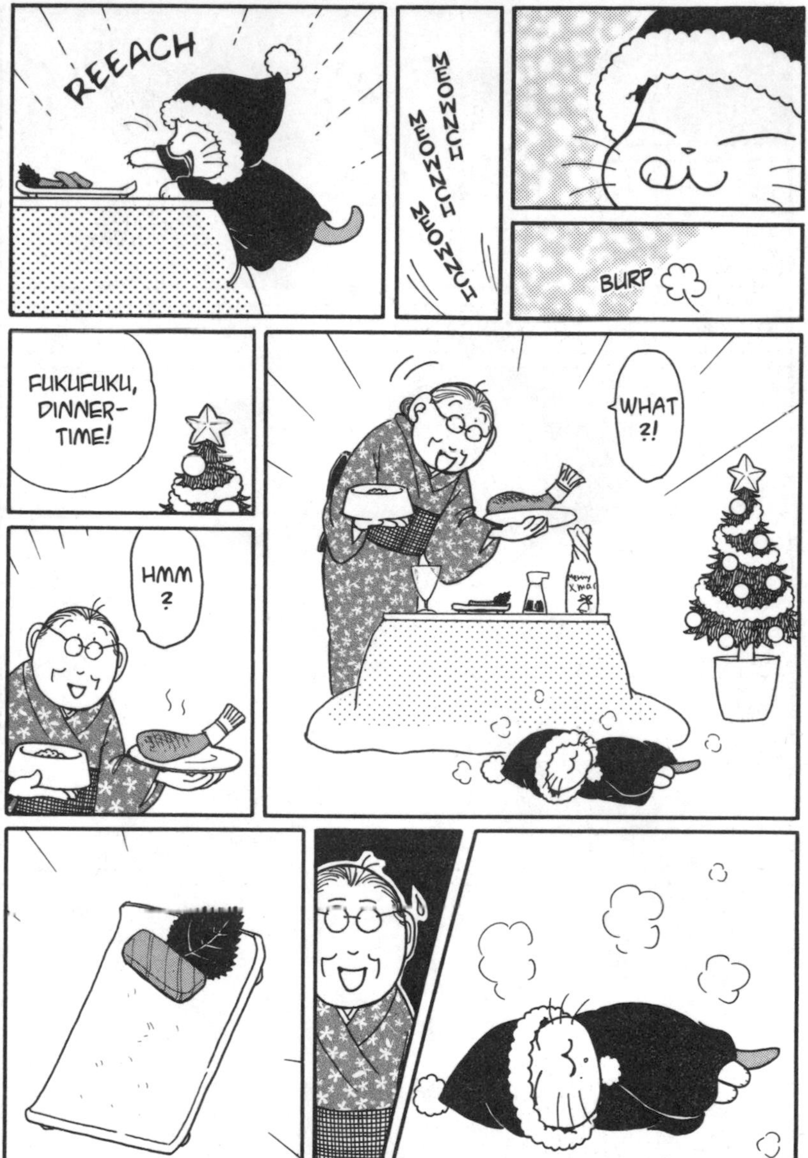
REEACH
MEOWNCH MEOWNCH MEOWNCH
BURP
FUKUFUKU, DINNER-TIME!
WHAT ?!
Merry Xmas
HMM ?

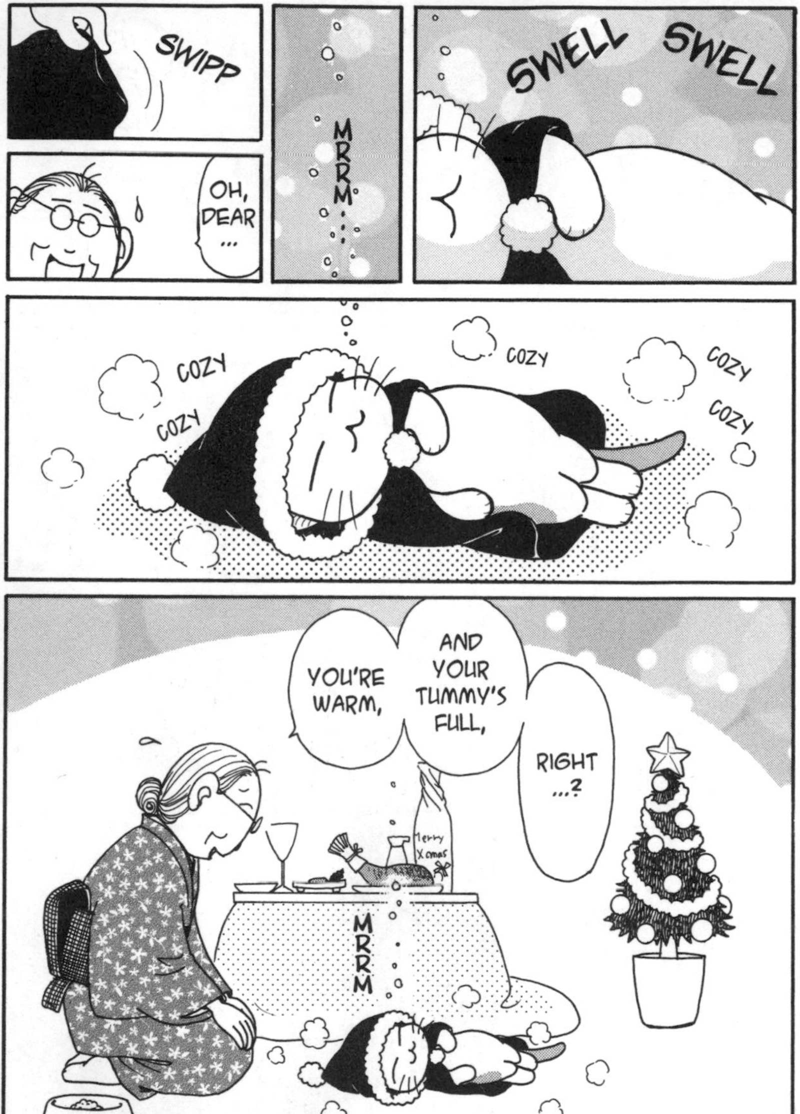
SWIPP
OH, DEAR ...
MRRM...
SWELL SWELL
COZY
COZY
COZY
COZY
COZY
YOU'RE WARM,
AND YOUR TUMMY'S FULL,
RIGHT ...?
Merry Xmas
MRRM

the end

Need This? Or That?

FUKU FUKU

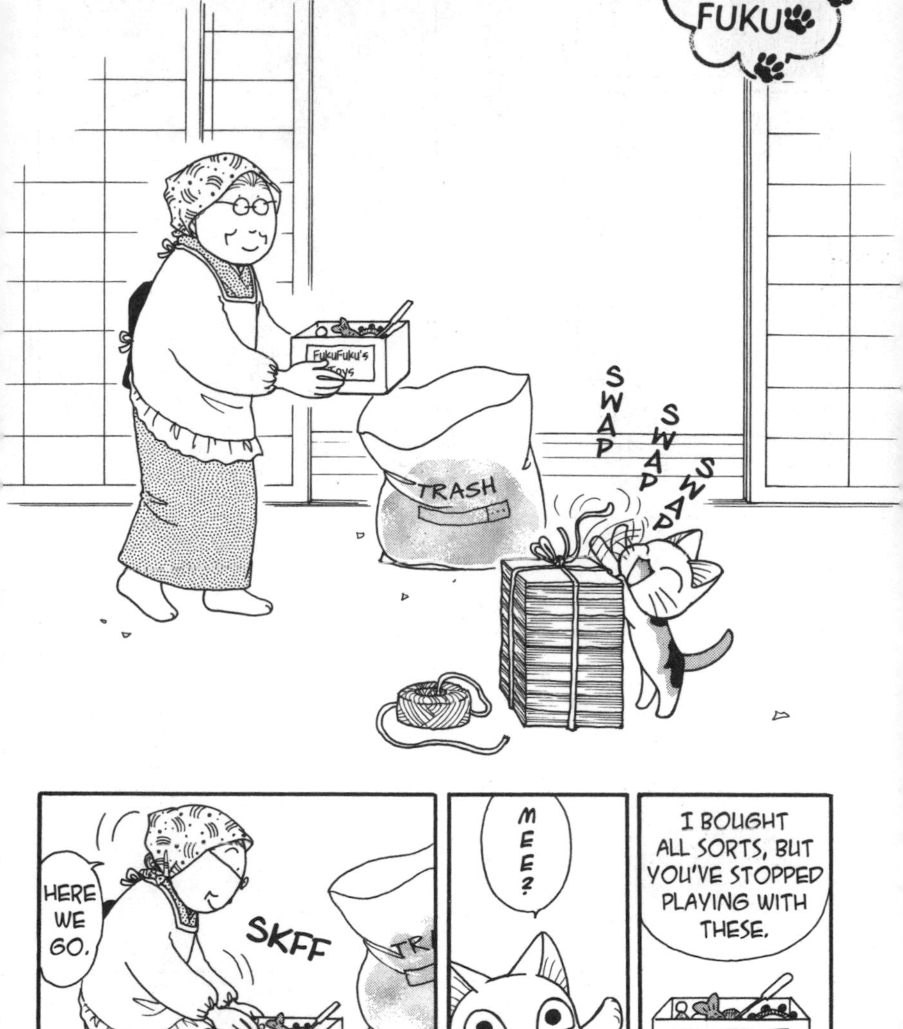

FukuFuku's Toys
TRASH
SWAP
SWAP
SWAP
HERE WE GO.
SKFF
FukuFuku's Toys
MEE?
I BOUGHT ALL SORTS, BUT YOU'VE STOPPED PLAYING WITH THESE.
FukuFuku's Toys

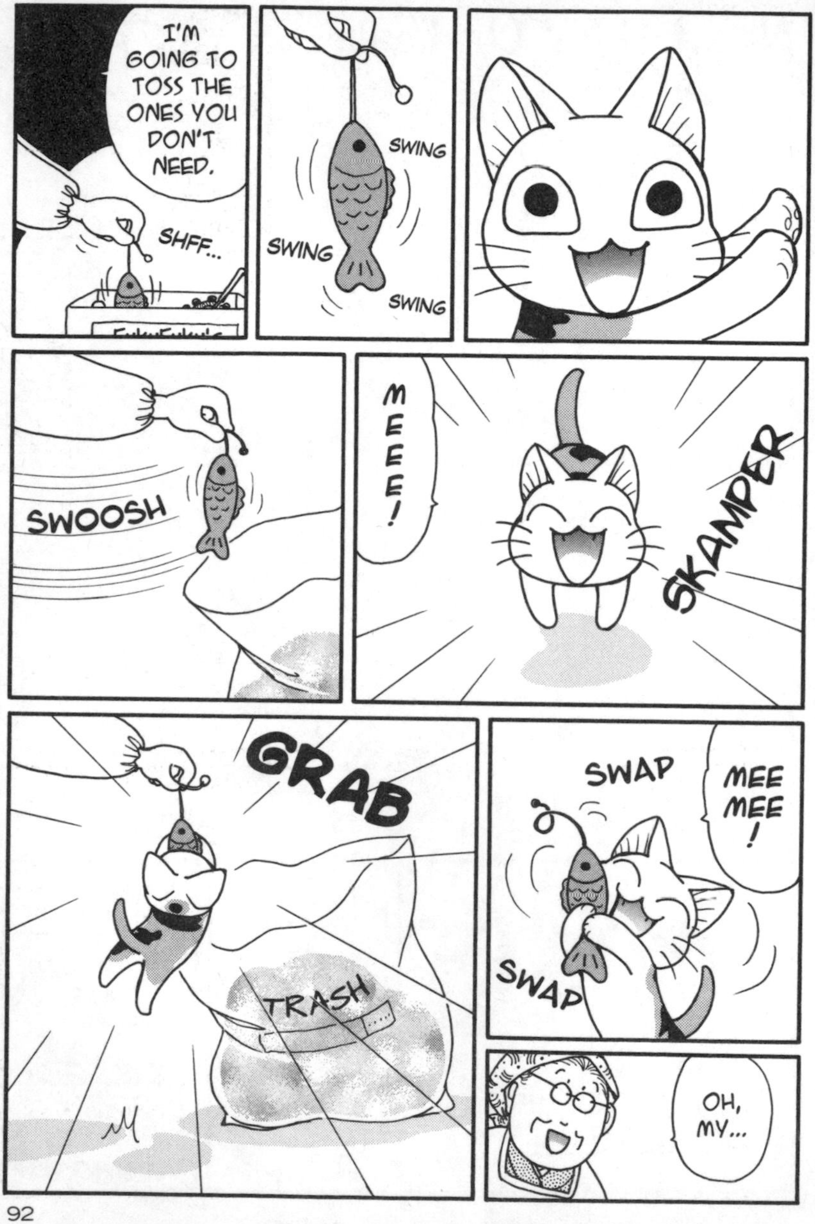
I'M GOING TO TOSS THE ONES YOU DON'T NEED.
SHFF...
SWING
SWING
SWING
SWOOSH
MEEEE!
SKAMPER
GRAB
TRASH
SWAP
MEE MEE!
SWAP
OH, MY...

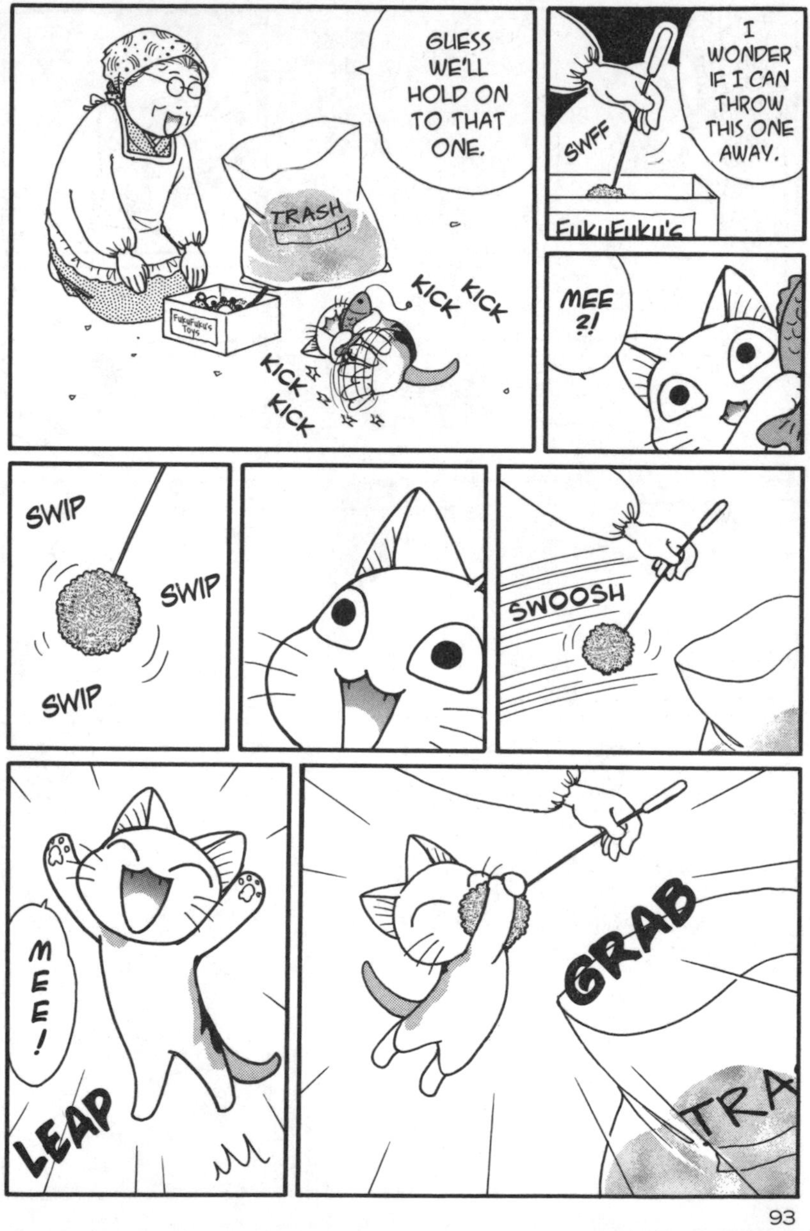
GUESS WE'LL HOLD ON TO THAT ONE.
TRASH
FukuFuku's Toys
KICK KICK
KICK KICK
SWFF
I WONDER IF I CAN THROW THIS ONE AWAY.
FukuFuku's
MEE ?!
SWIP
SWIP
SWIP
SWOOSH
MEE!
LEAP
GRAB
TRA

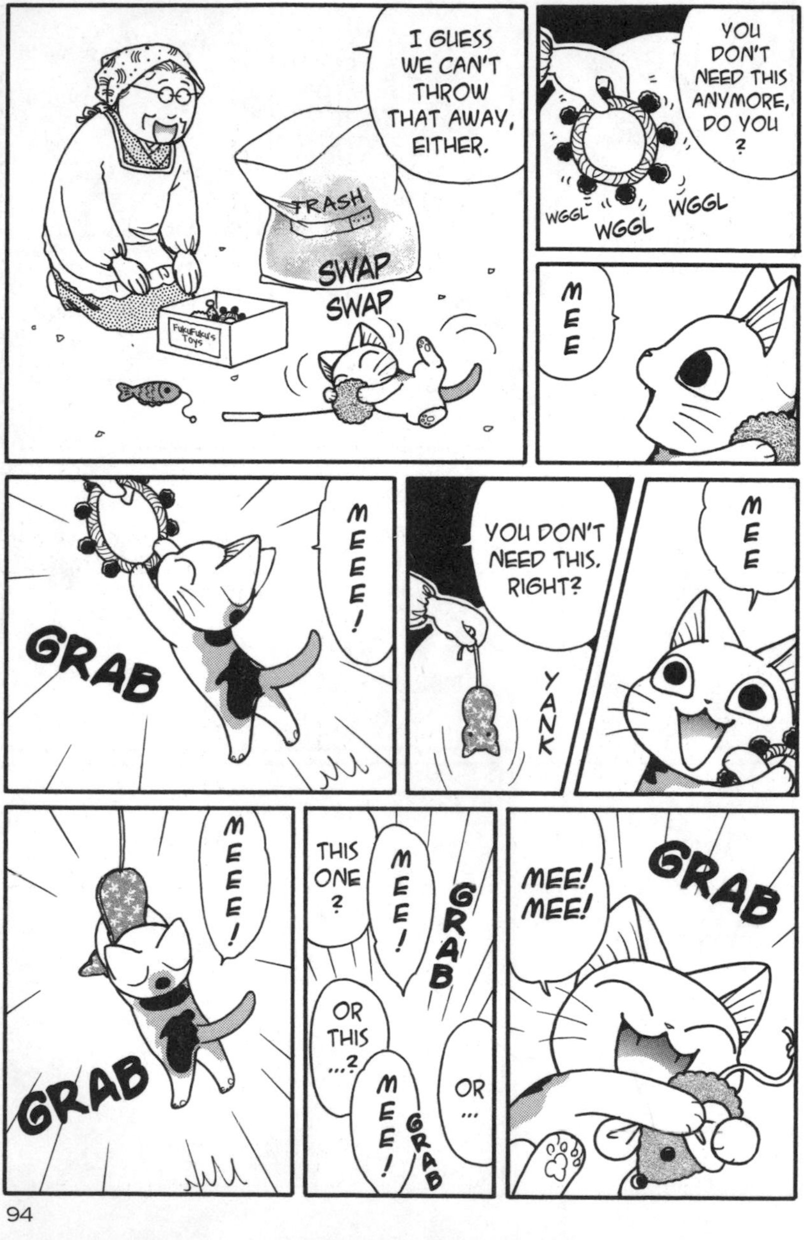
I GUESS WE CAN'T THROW THAT AWAY, EITHER.
TRASH
FukuFuku's Toys
SWAP SWAP
YOU DON'T NEED THIS ANYMORE, DO YOU?
WGGL WGGL WGGL
MEE
MEEE!
GRAB
YOU DON'T NEED THIS, RIGHT?
YANK
MEE
MEEE!
GRAB
THIS ONE?
MEE!
GRAB
OR THIS ...?
MEE!
GRAB
OR ...
MEE! MEE!
GRAB

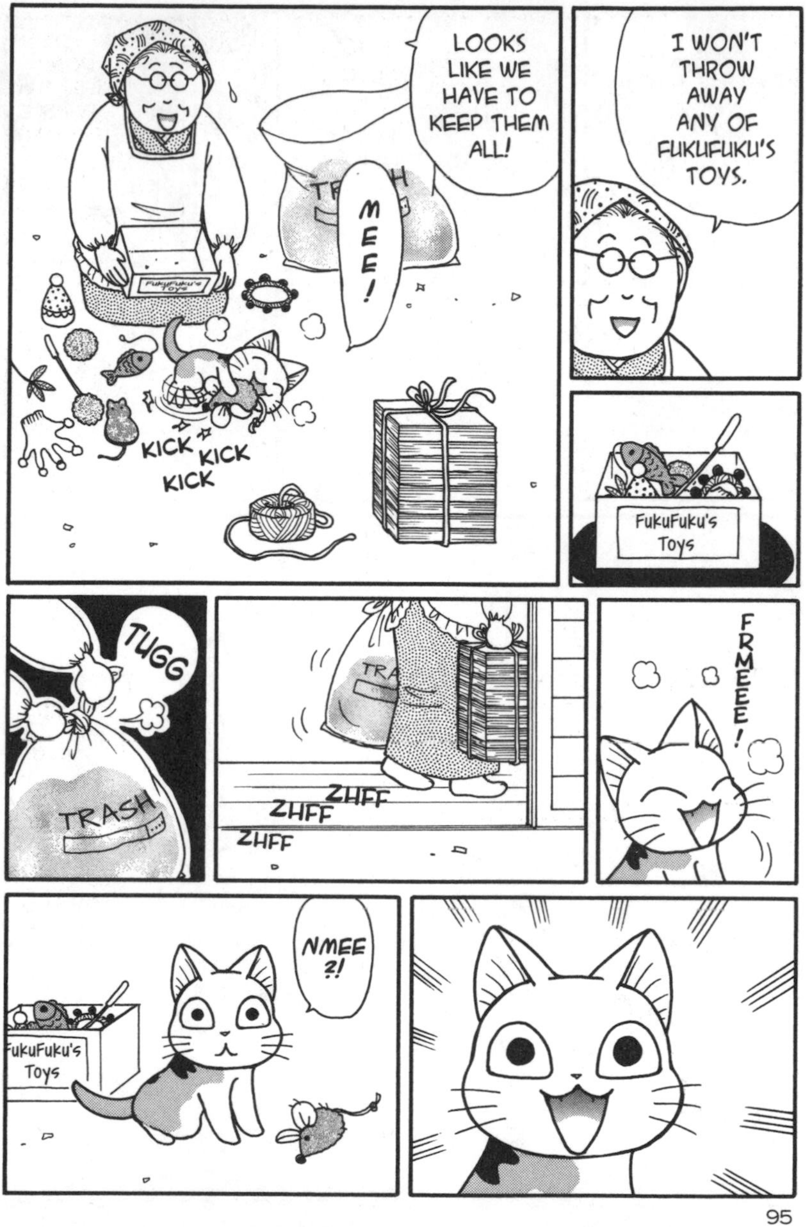
MEE!
LOOKS LIKE WE HAVE TO KEEP THEM ALL!
TRASH
FukuFuku's Toys
KICK KICK KICK
I WON'T THROW AWAY ANY OF FUKUFUKU'S TOYS.
FukuFuku's Toys
TUGG
TRASH
TRASH
ZHFF ZHFF ZHFF
FRMEEE!
NMEE ?!
FukuFuku's Toys

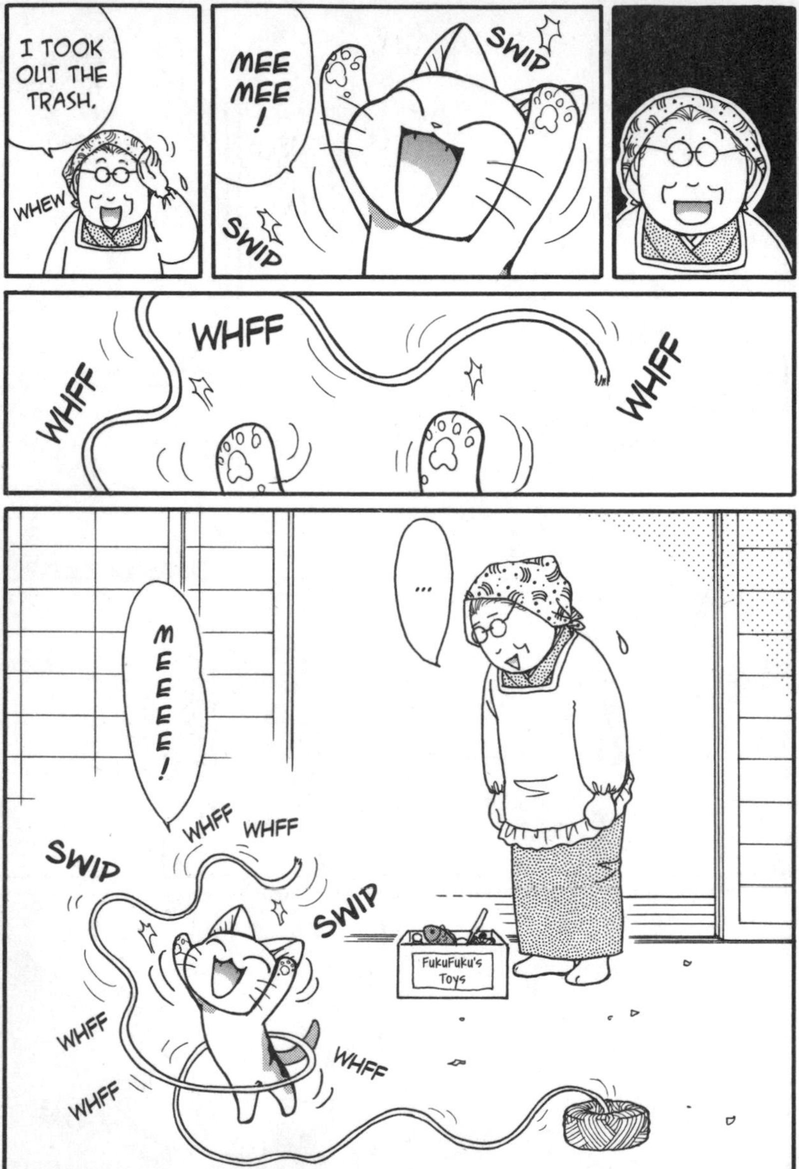
I TOOK OUT THE TRASH.
WHEW
MEE MEE!
SWIP
SWIP
WHFF
WHFF
WHFF
...
MEEEEE!
WHFF
WHFF
SWIP
SWIP
FukuFuku's Toys
WHFF
WHFF
WHFF

the end

First Games of the New Year

FUKU FUKU

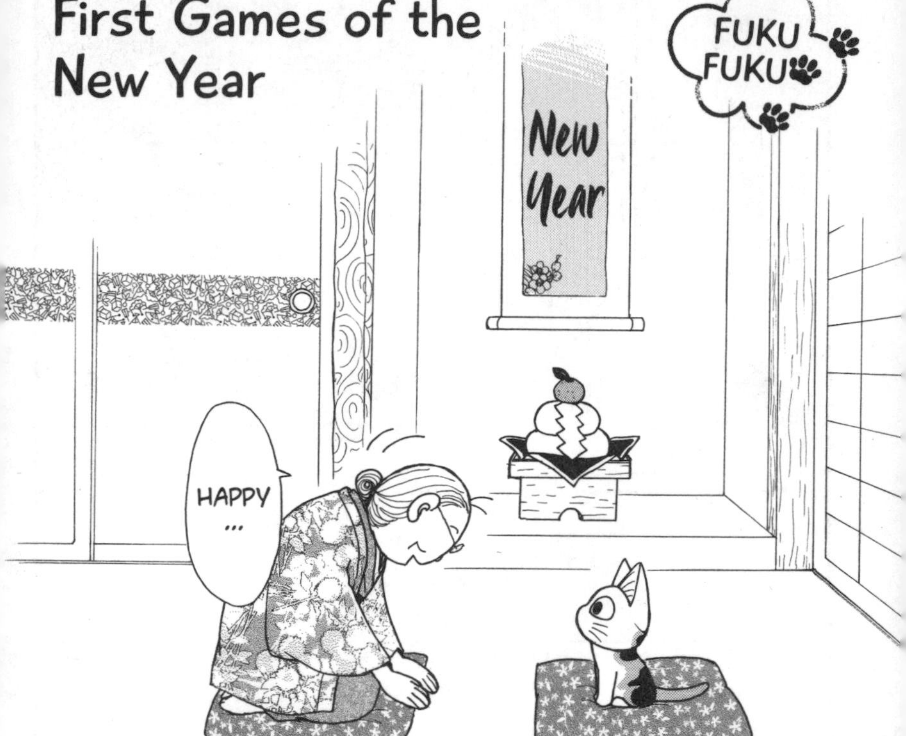
New Year
HAPPY ...

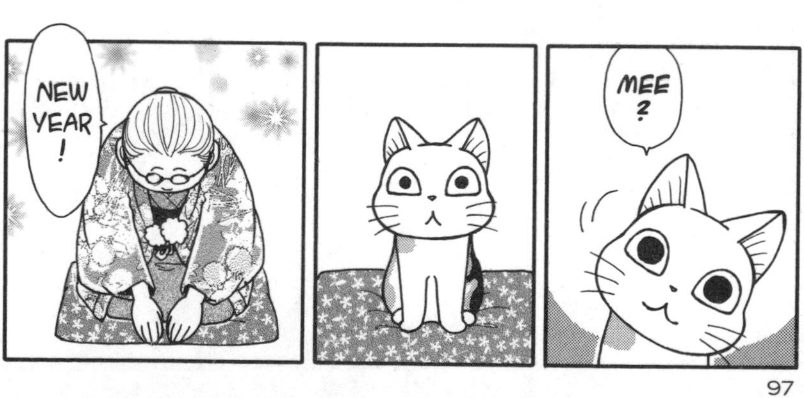
NEW YEAR !
MEE ?

KAPOW   POW

Happy New Year

PREE
PRITA
PREE

FUKUFUKU, YOU PROBABLY DON'T UNDERSTAND NEW YEAR'S...

YAWN

I KNOW, LET'S PLAY SOME NEW YEAR'S GAMES!

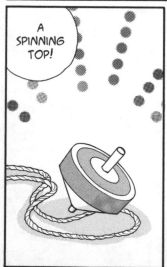

A SPINNING TOP!

MEE?

WRAP
WRAP
WRAP

READY?

ZWIP

98

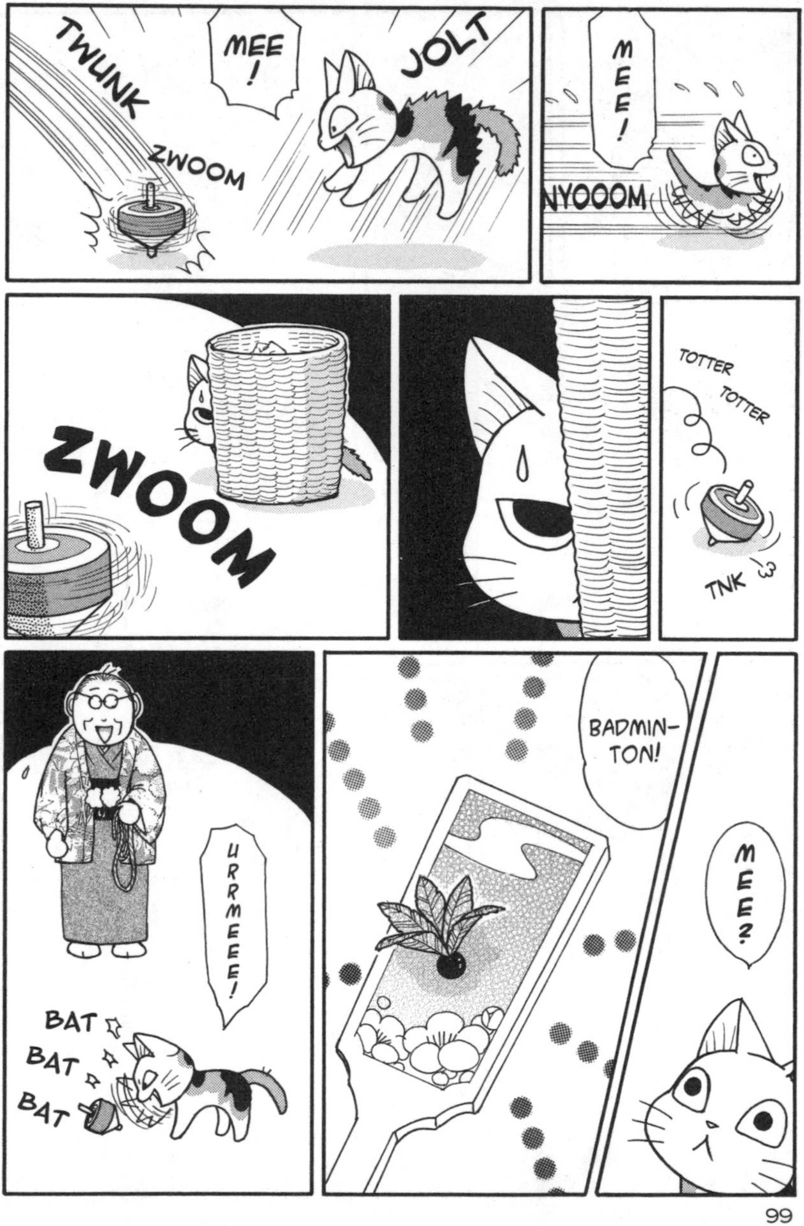

TWUNK
ZWOOM
MEE!
JOLT
MEE!
NYOOOM
ZWOOM
TOTTER
TOTTER
TNK
URRMEEE!
BAT
BAT
BAT
BADMINTON!
MEE?

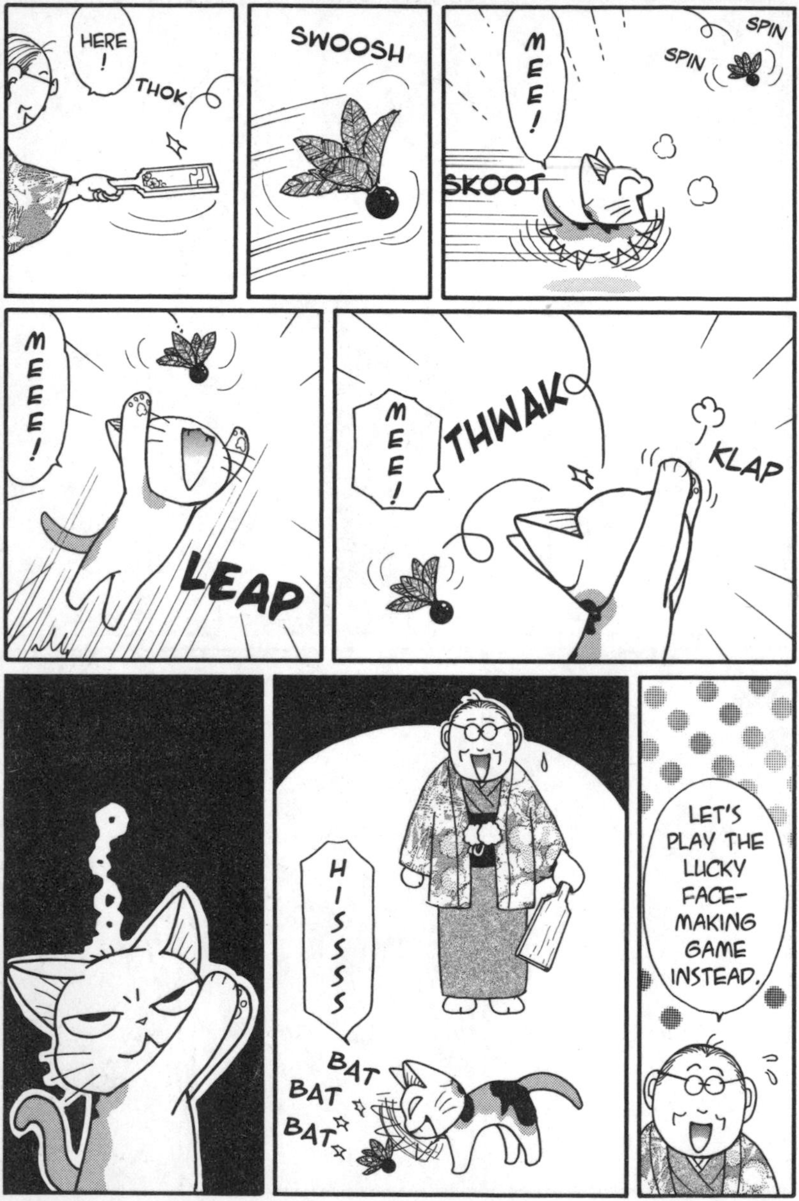
HERE!
THOK
SWOOSH
MEE!
SPIN
SPIN
SKOOT
MEEE!
LEAP
MEE!
THWAK
KLAP
HISSSS
BAT
BAT
BAT
LET'S PLAY THE LUCKY FACE-MAKING GAME INSTEAD.

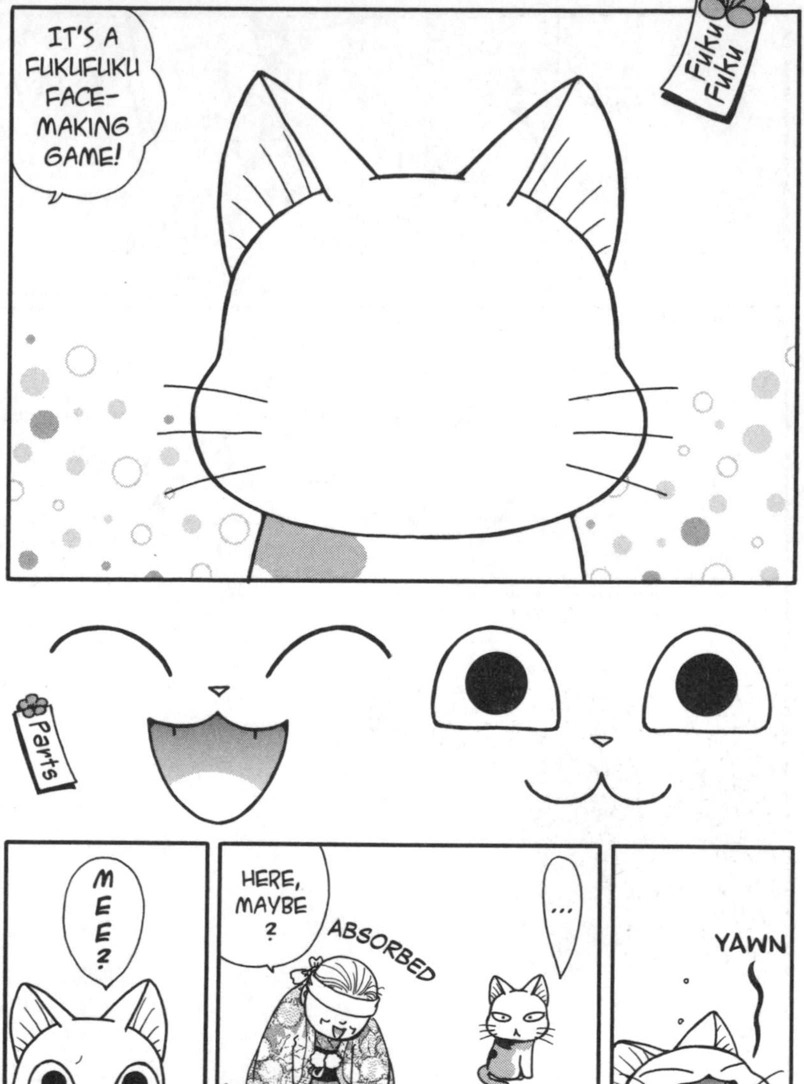
IT'S A FUKUFUKU FACE-MAKING GAME!
Fuku Fuku
Parts
MEE?
HERE, MAYBE?
ABSORBED
...
YAWN

If you copy this page, then cut out the parts, you can play the "FukuFuku Face-Making Game," too!

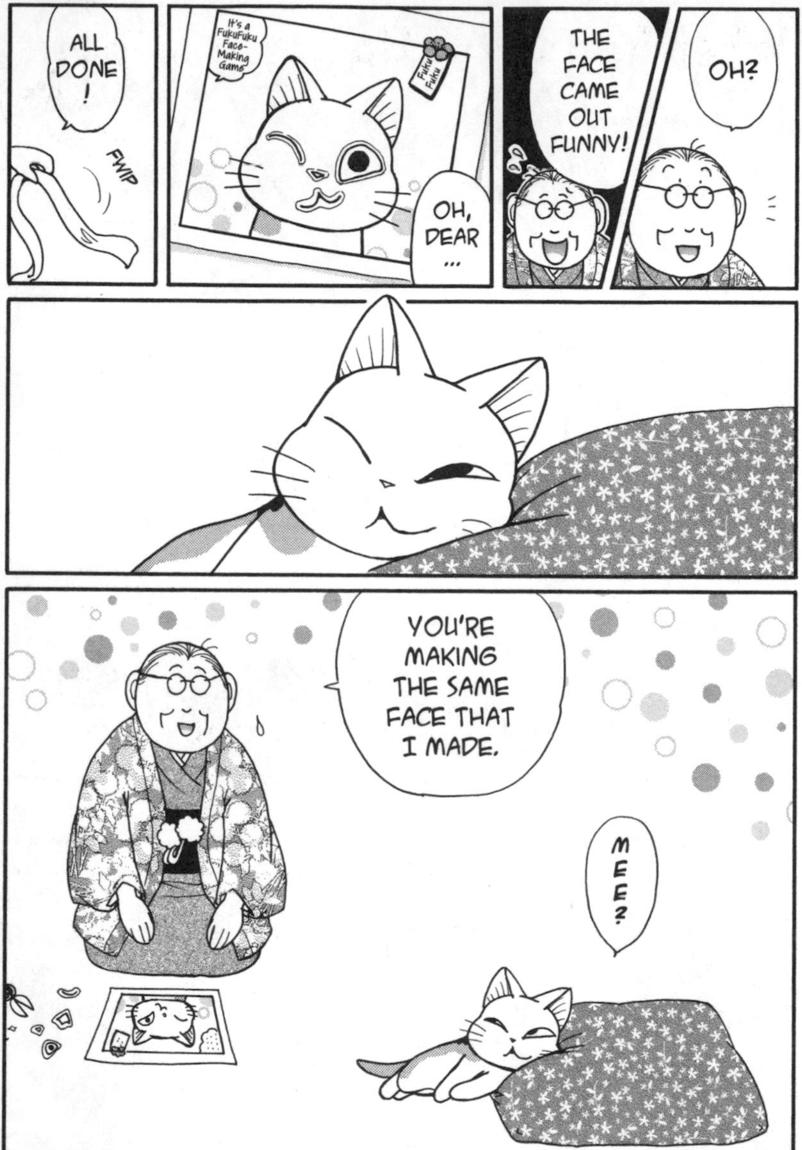
ALL DONE!
FWIP
It's a FukuFuku Face-Making Game
Fuku Fuku
OH, DEAR...
THE FACE CAME OUT FUNNY!
OH?
YOU'RE MAKING THE SAME FACE THAT I MADE.
MEE?

the end

When You Grow Up....

FUKU FUKU

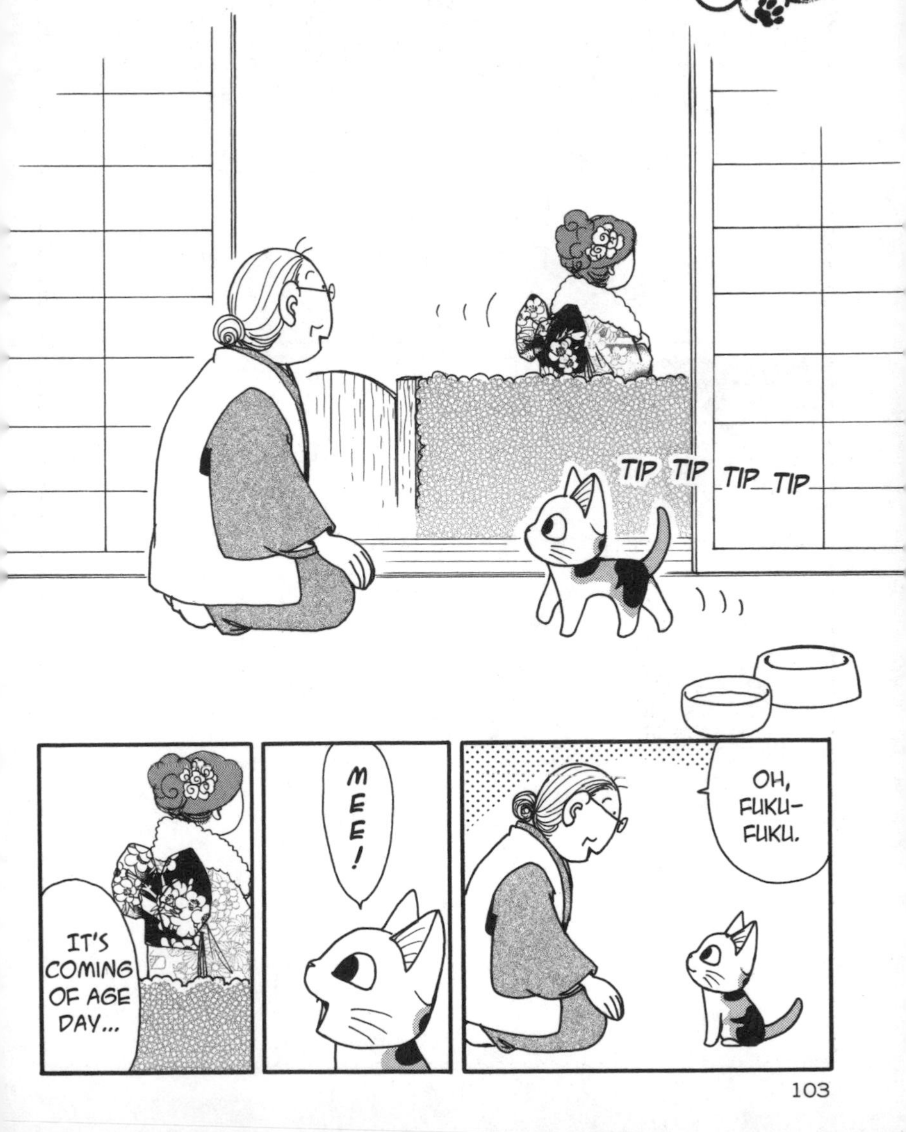
TIP TIP TIP TIP
IT'S COMING OF AGE DAY...
MEE!
OH, FUKU-FUKU.

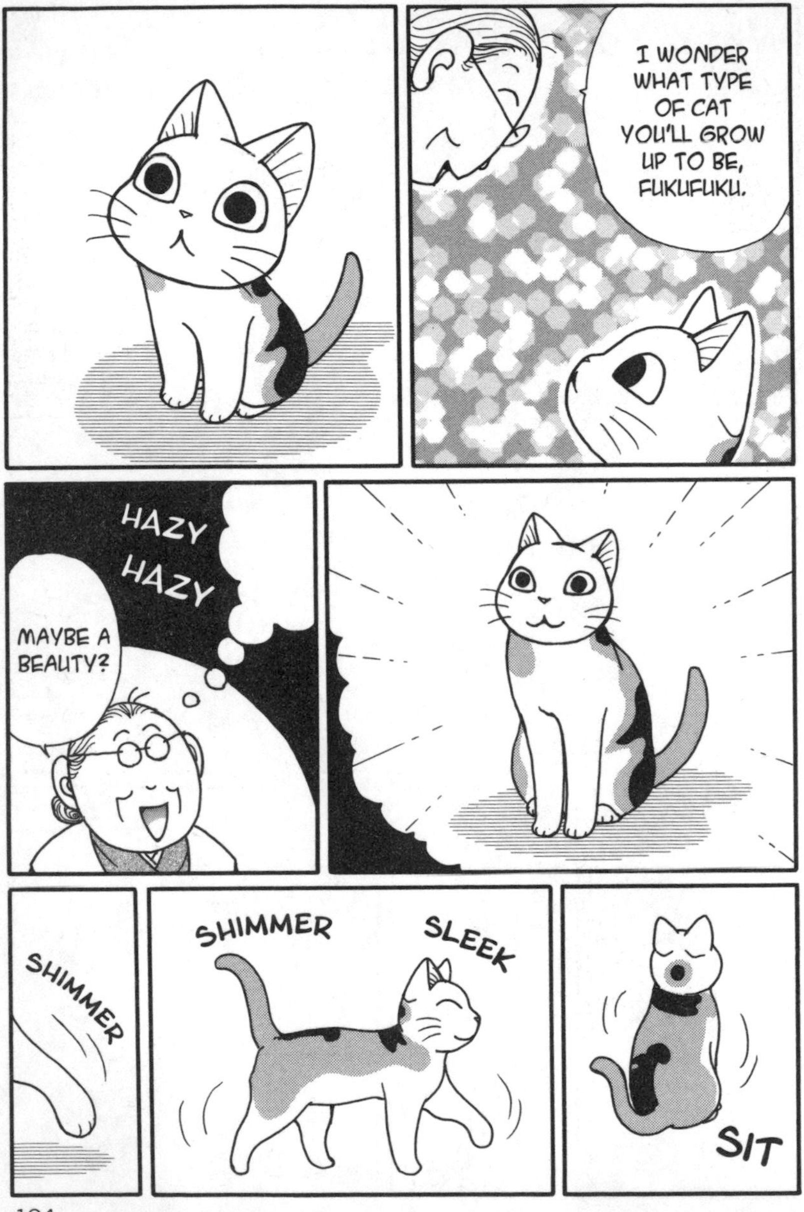
I WONDER WHAT TYPE OF CAT YOU'LL GROW UP TO BE, FUKUFUKU.
HAZY HAZY
MAYBE A BEAUTY?
SHIMMER
SHIMMER
SLEEK
SIT

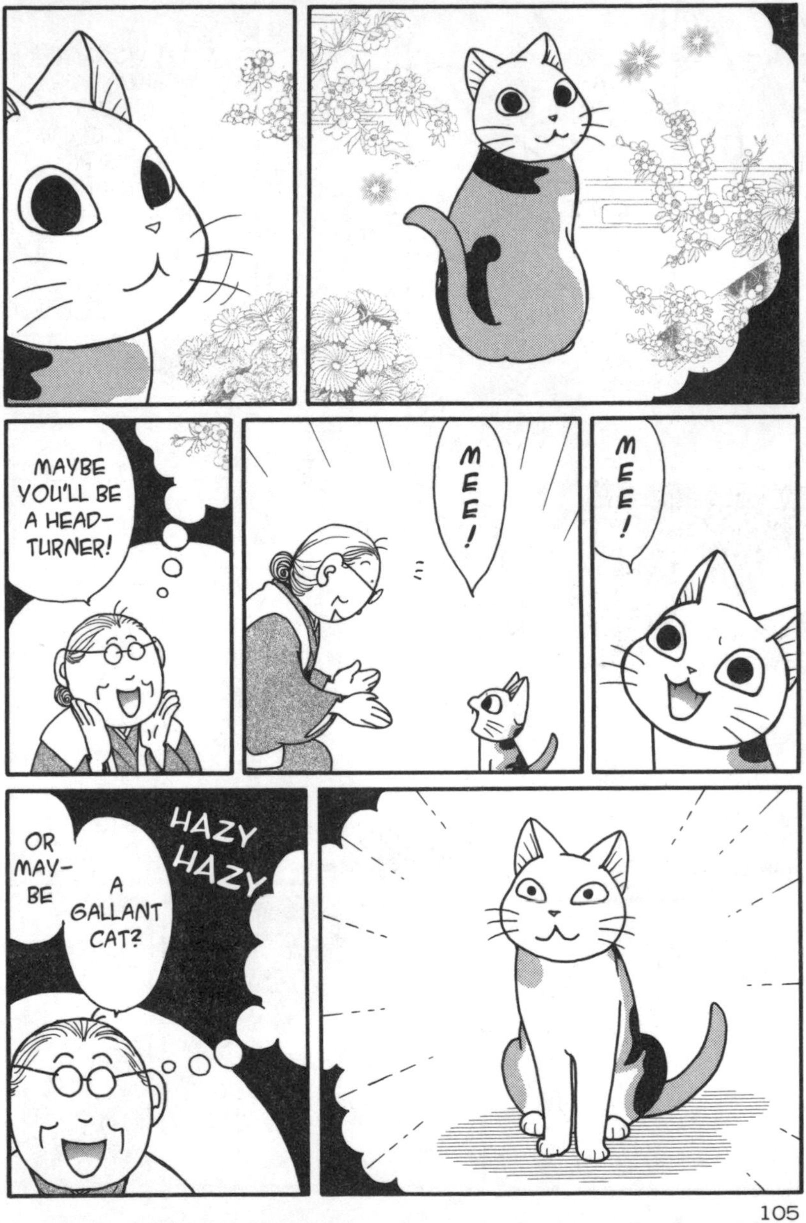
MAYBE YOU'LL BE A HEAD-TURNER!
MEE!
MEE!
OR MAY-BE
A GALLANT CAT?
HAZY HAZY

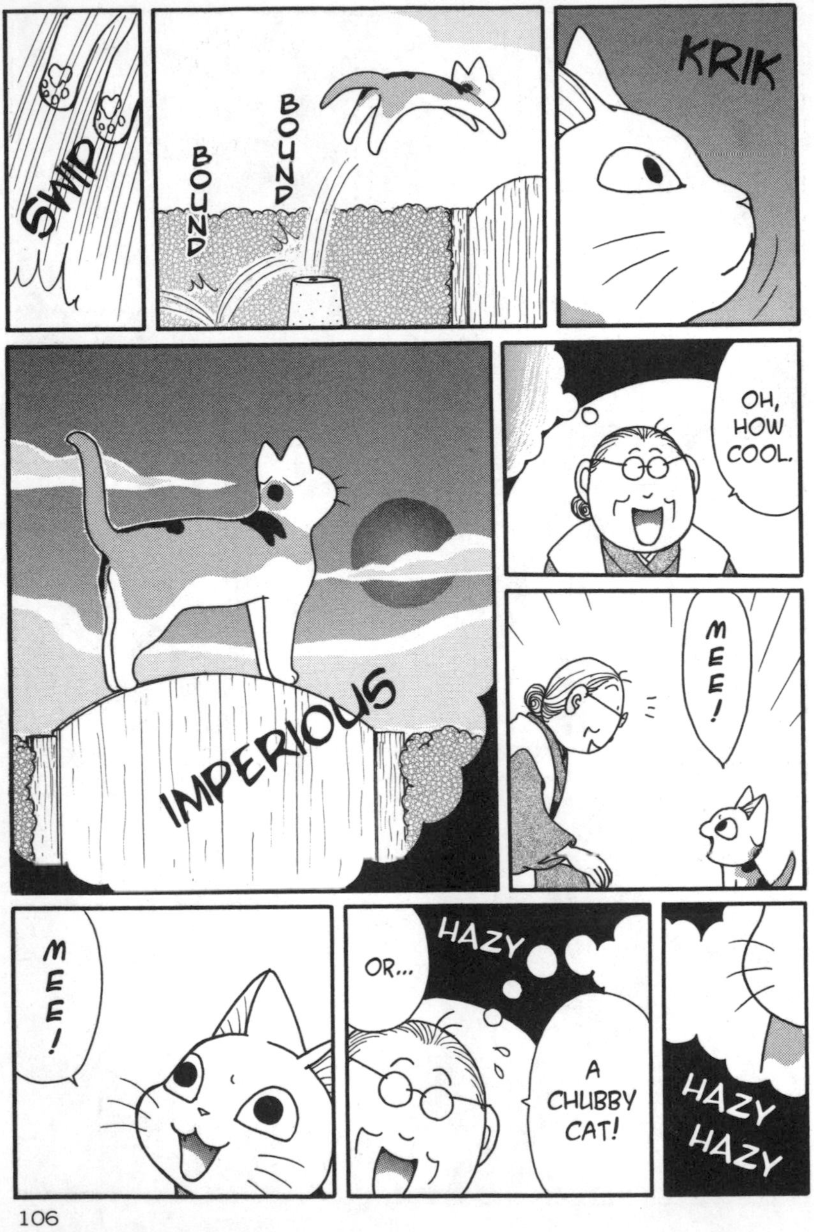
SWIP
BOUND
BOUND
KRIK
IMPERIOUS
OH, HOW COOL.
MEE!
MEE!
OR...
HAZY
A CHUBBY CAT!
HAZY HAZY

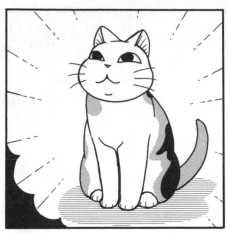

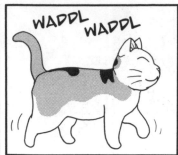

WADDL WADDL
KRUNCH KRUNCH KRUNCH KRUNCH KRUNCH
NYA!!
NYA!!
KRUNCH KRUNCH KRUNCH KRUNCH KRUNCH KRUNCH
SMAK
WHOMP

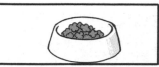

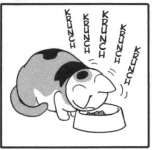

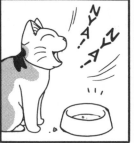

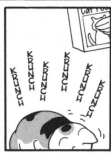

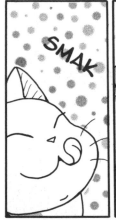

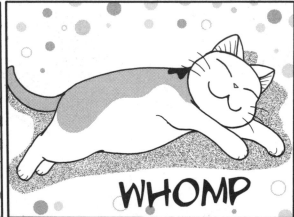

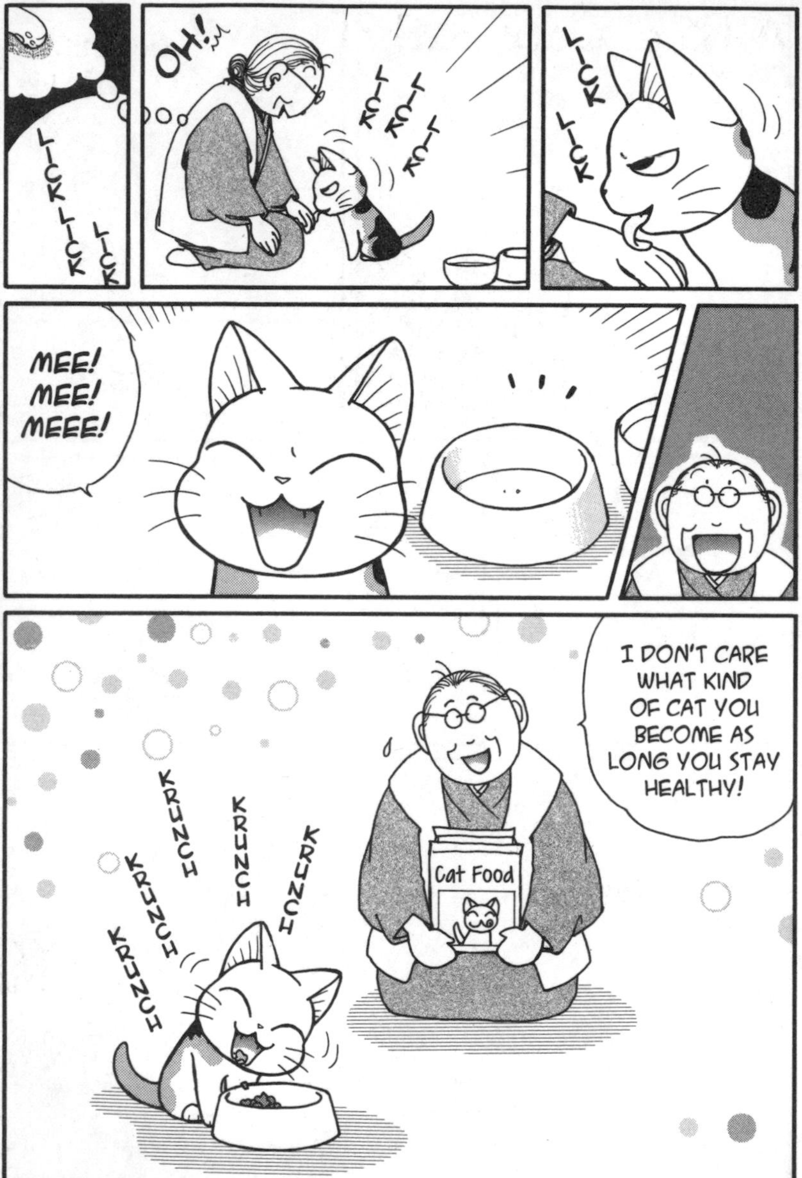
LICKLICK LICK
OH!
LICK LICK LICK
LICK LICK
MEE! MEE! MEEE!
KRUNCH KRUNCH KRUNCH KRUNCH KRUNCH
Cat Food
I DON'T CARE WHAT KIND OF CAT YOU BECOME AS LONG YOU STAY HEALTHY!

the end

A Nice, Cool Bath?!

FUKU FUKU

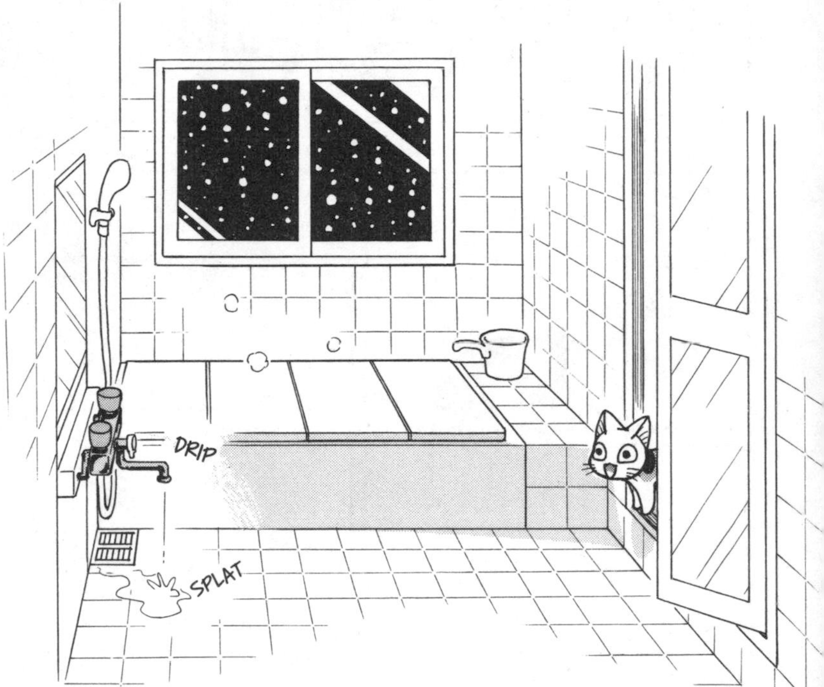
DRIP
SPLAT

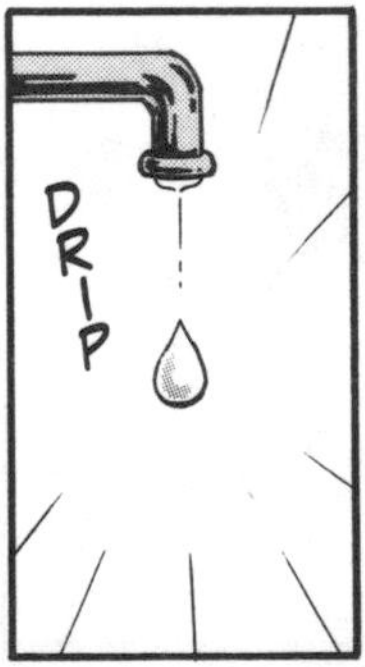
DRIP

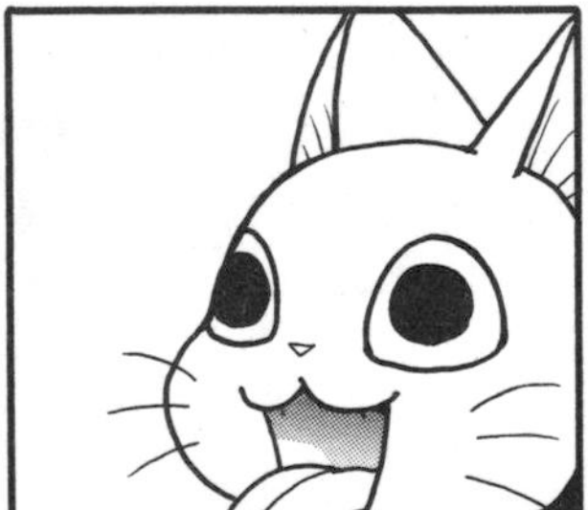

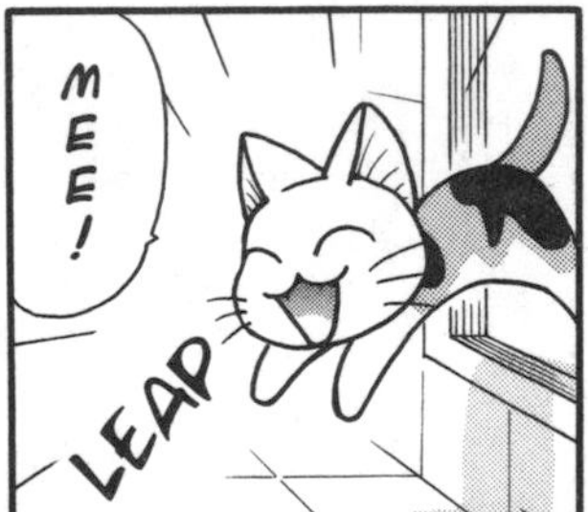
MEE!
LEAP

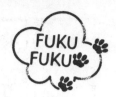

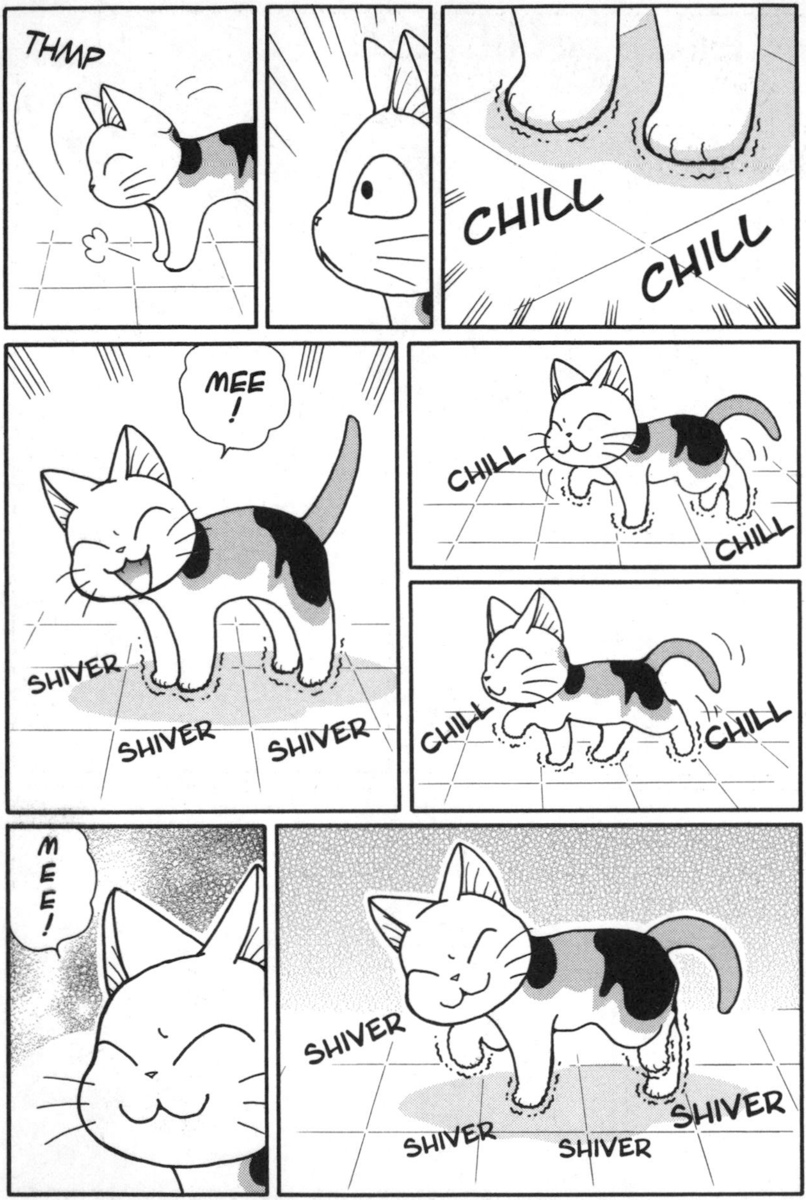
THMP
CHILL
CHILL
MEE!
SHIVER
SHIVER
SHIVER
CHILL
CHILL
CHILL
CHILL
MEE!
SHIVER
SHIVER
SHIVER
SHIVER

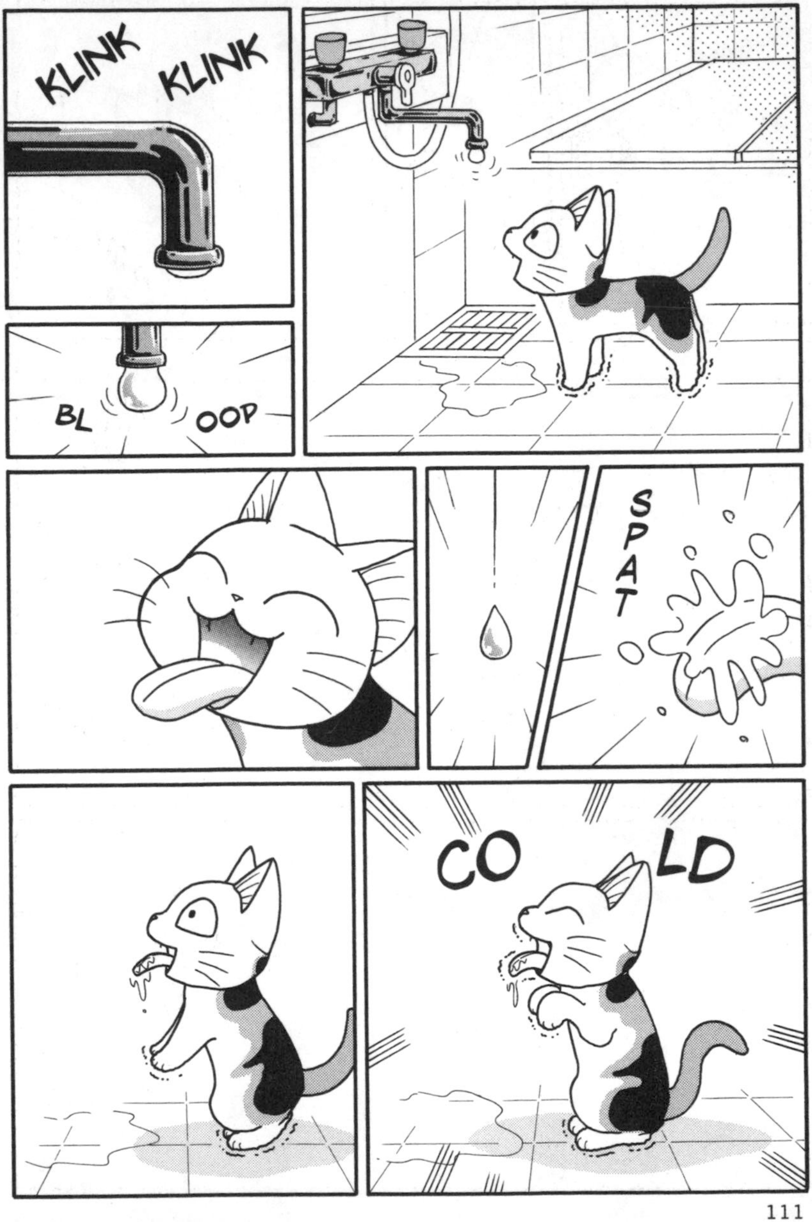
KLINK KLINK
BL OOP
SPAT
CO LD

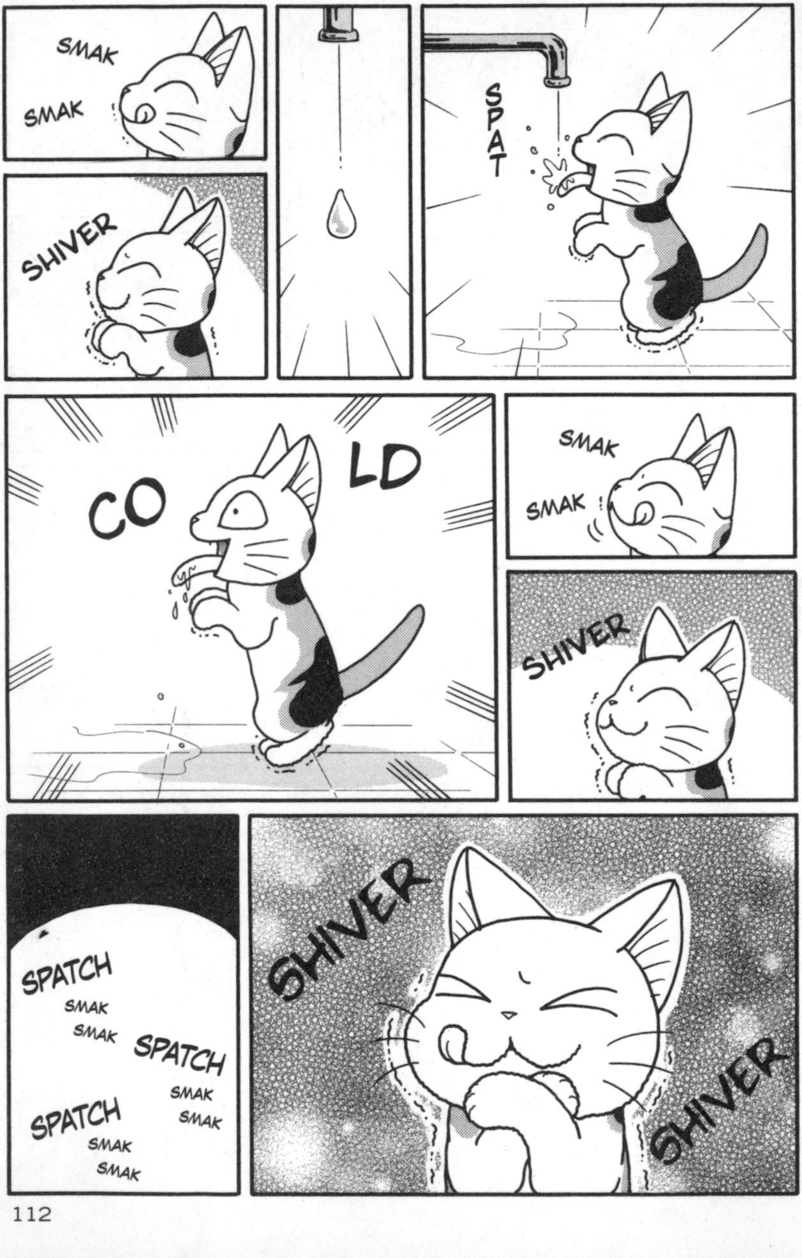
SMAK
SMAK
SHIVER
SPAT
CO
LD
SMAK
SMAK
SHIVER
SPATCH
SMAK
SMAK
SPATCH
SMAK
SMAK
SPATCH
SMAK
SMAK
SHIVER
SHIVER

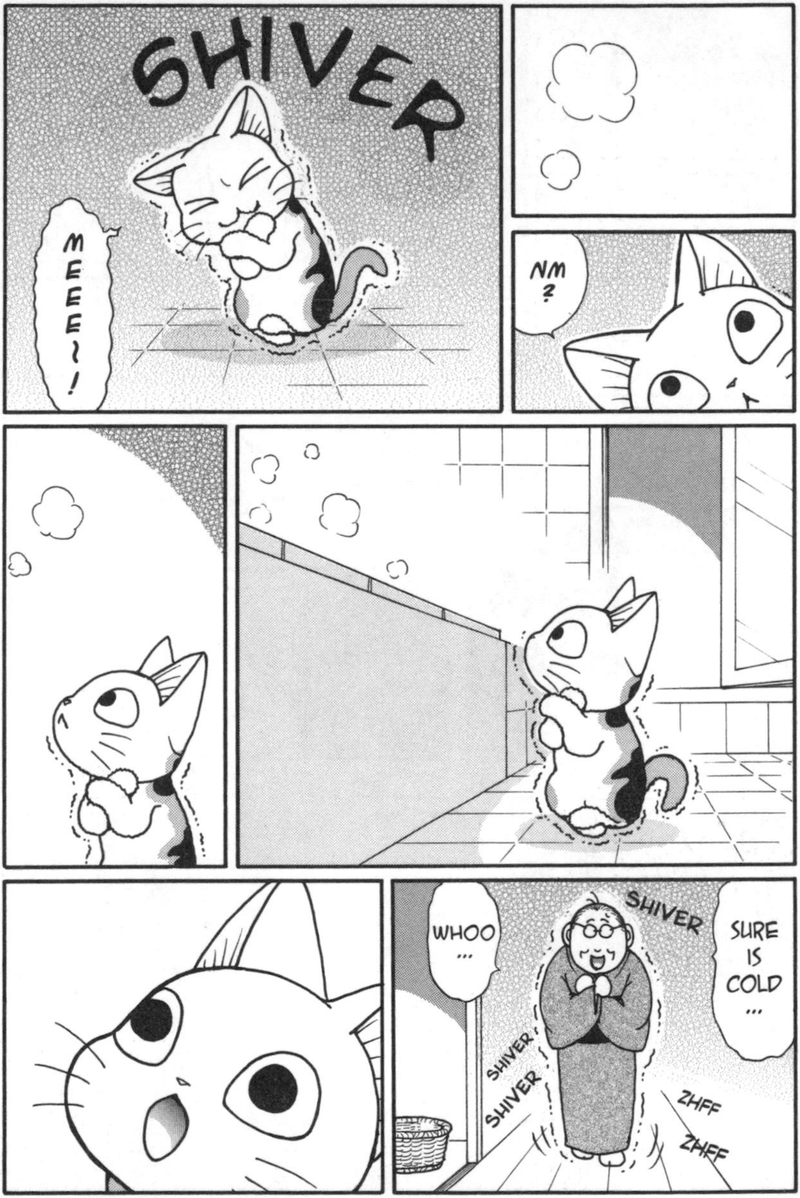
SHIVER
MEEE~!
NM?
WHOO...
SHIVER
SURE IS COLD...
SHIVER
SHIVER
ZHFF
ZHFF

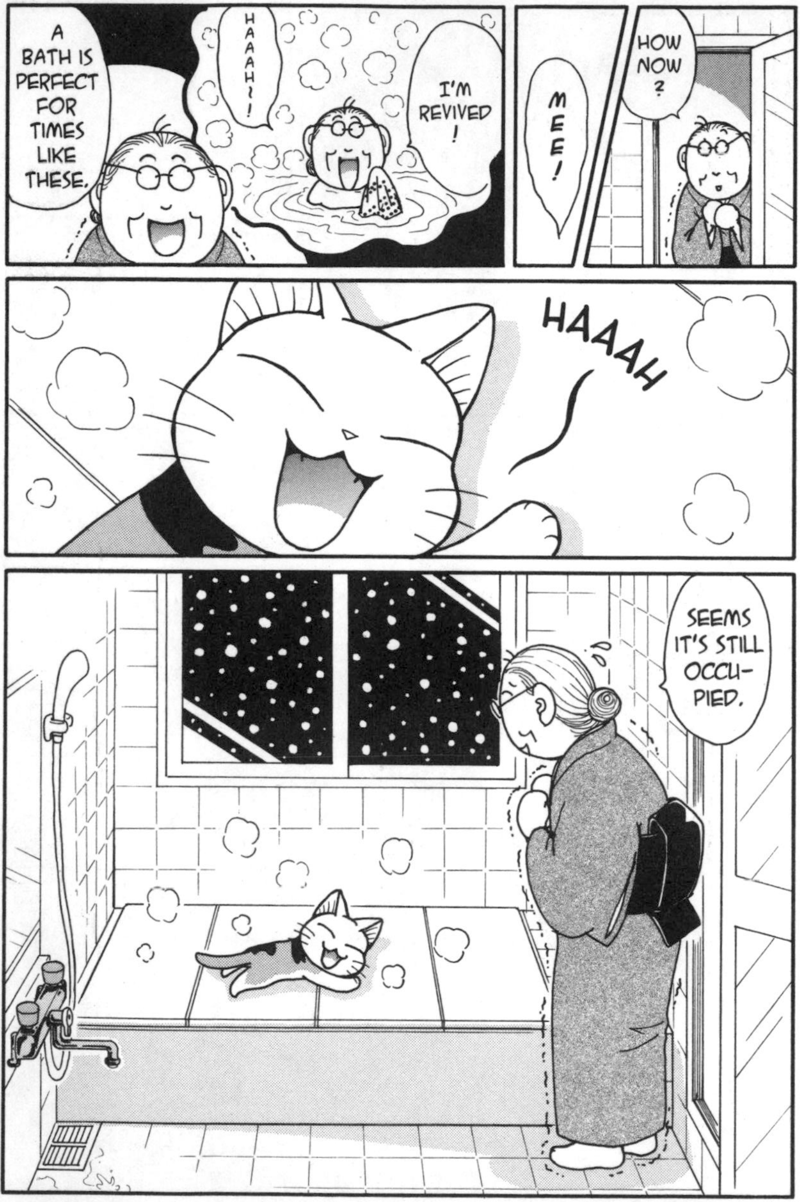
A BATH IS PERFECT FOR TIMES LIKE THESE.
HAAAH~!
I'M REVIVED!
MEE!
HOW NOW?
HAAAAH
SEEMS IT'S STILL OCCU-PIED.

the end

FUKU
FUKU

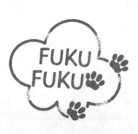

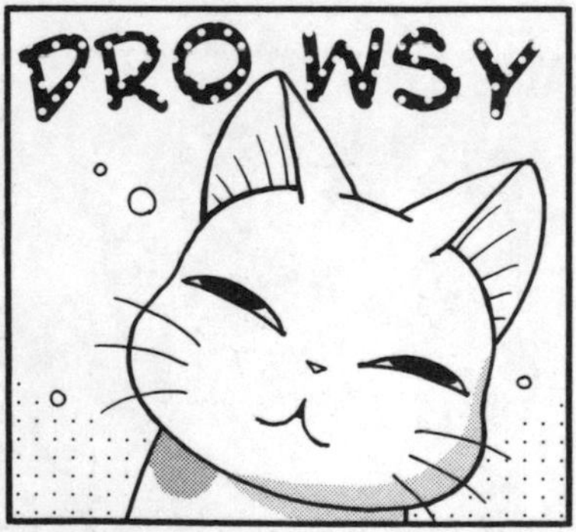
DROWSY

FukuFuku's Wild Side?!

FUKU FUKU

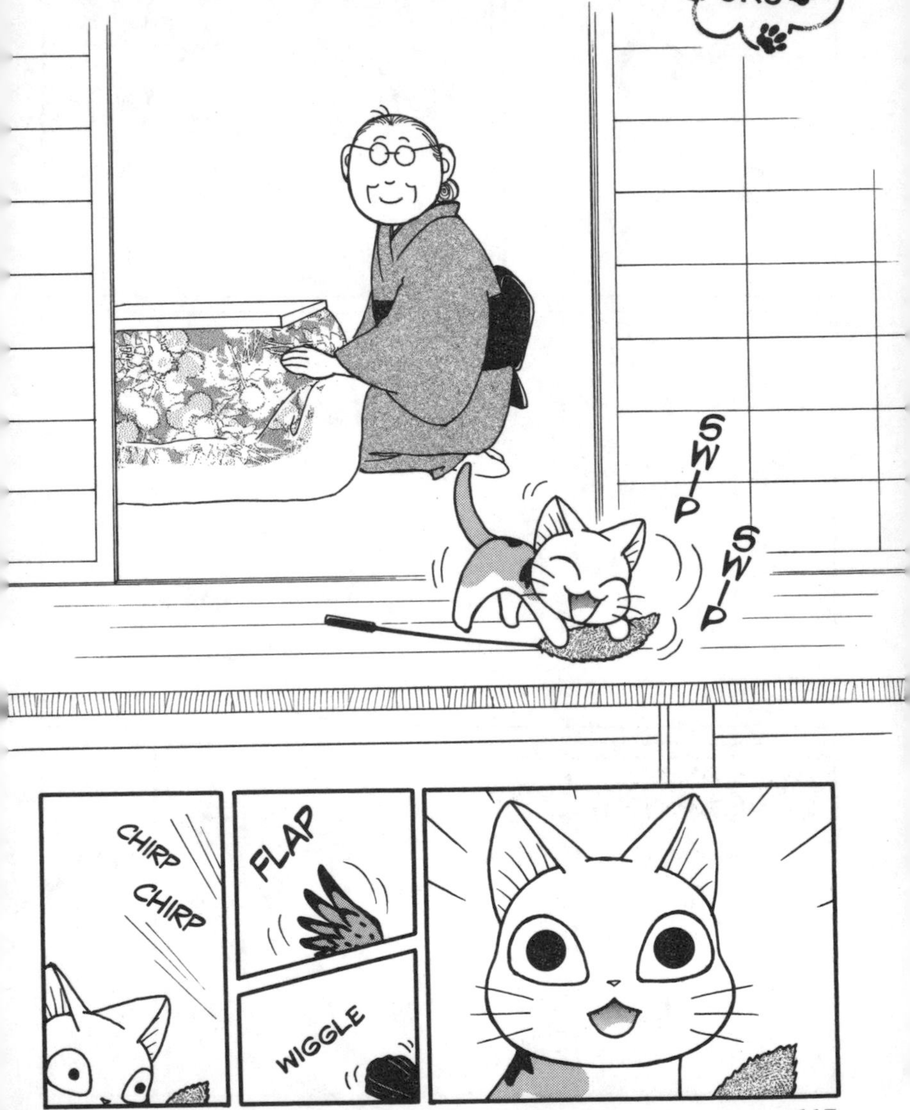
SWIP
SWIP
CHIRP
CHIRP
FLAP
WIGGLE

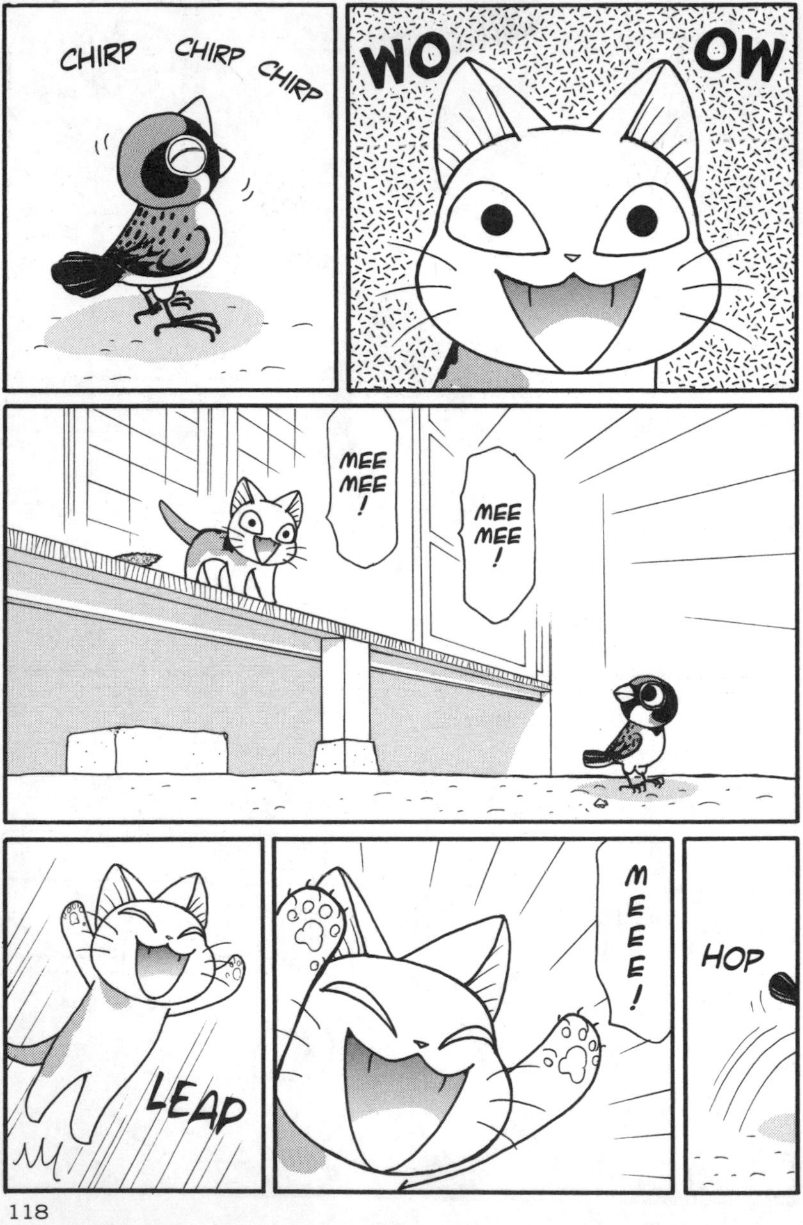
CHIRP CHIRP CHIRP
WO OW
MEE MEE!
MEE MEE!
LEAP
MEEE!
HOP

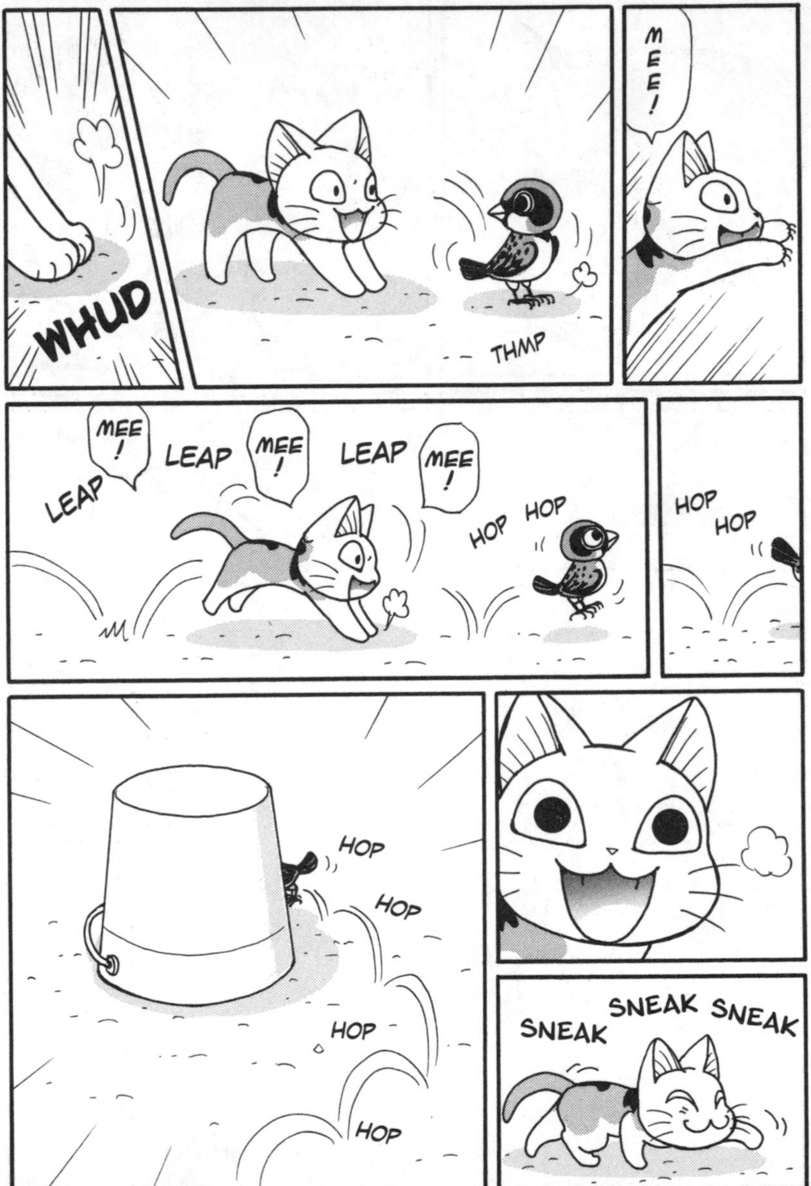
WHUD
THMP
MEE!
LEAP
MEE!
LEAP
MEE!
LEAP
MEE!
HOP HOP
HOP
HOP
HOP
HOP
HOP
HOP
SNEAK
SNEAK
SNEAK

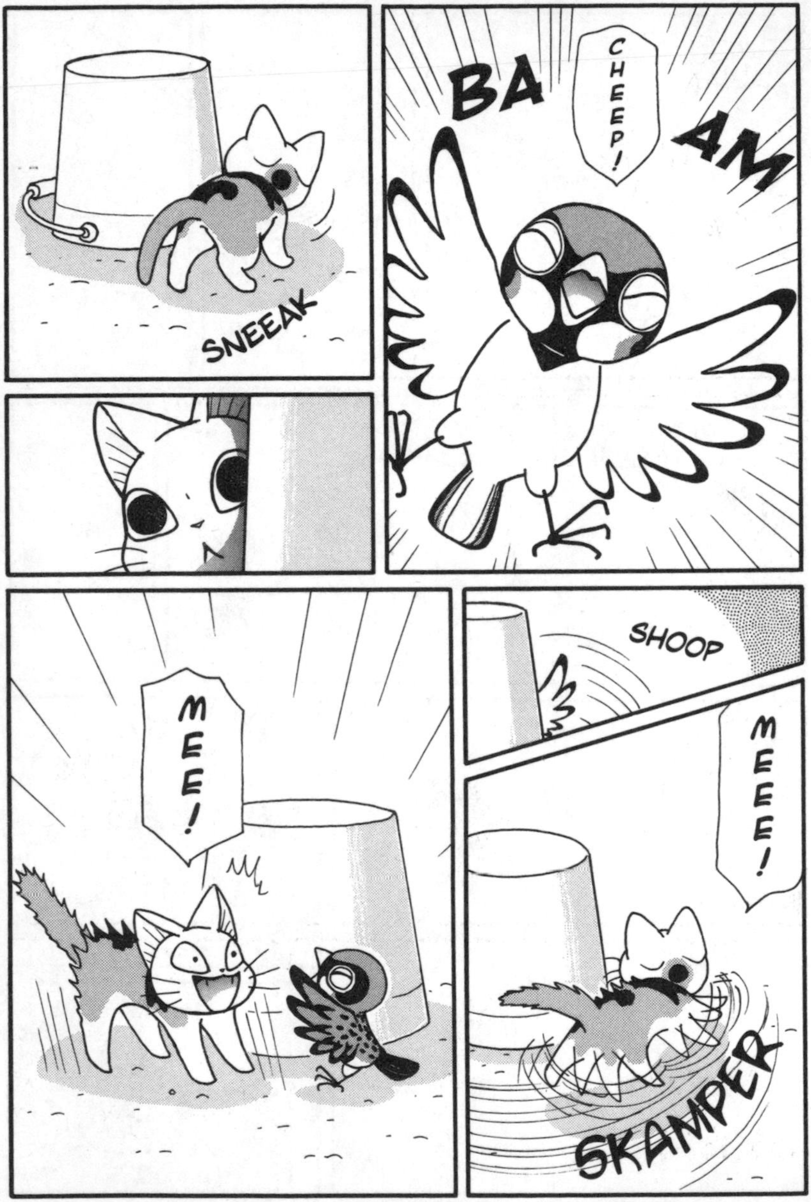
SNEEAK
BA
CHEEP!
AM
MEE!
SHOOP
MEEEE!
SKAMPER

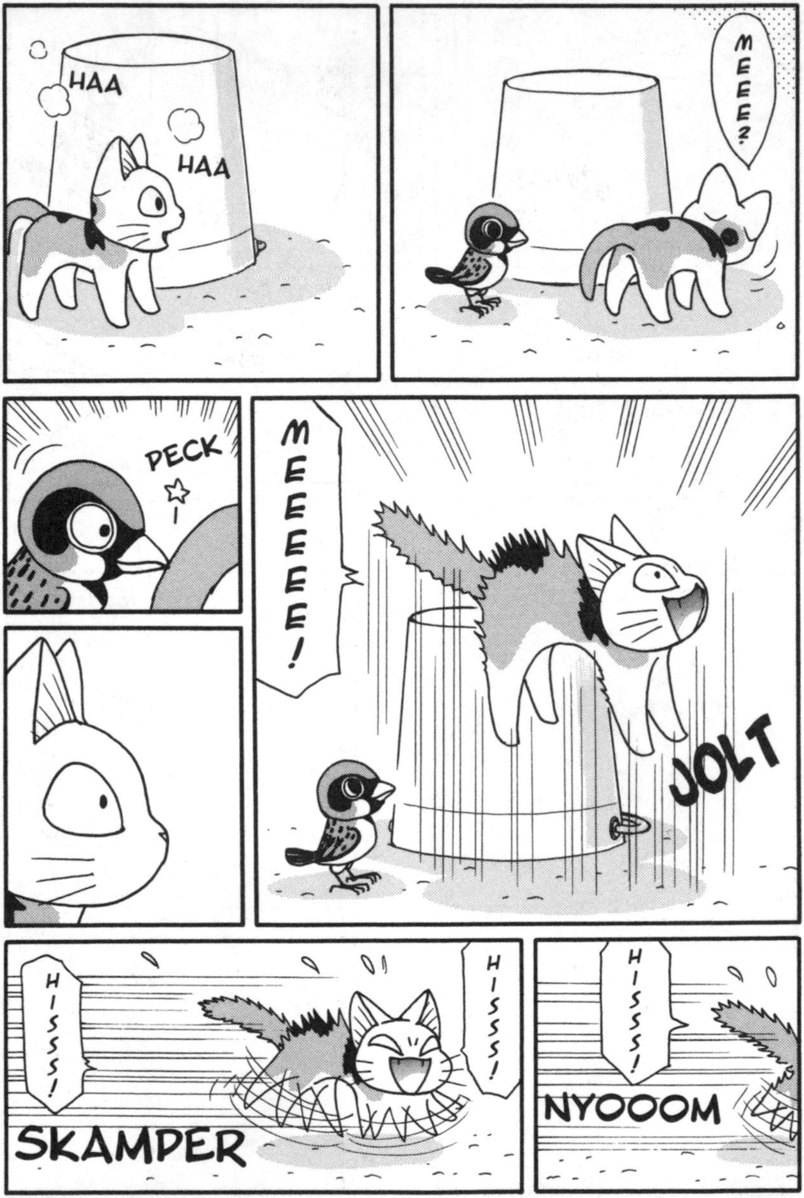
HAA
HAA
MEEE?
PECK
MEEEEEE!
JOLT
HISSS!
HISSS!
SKAMPER
HISSS!
NYOOOM

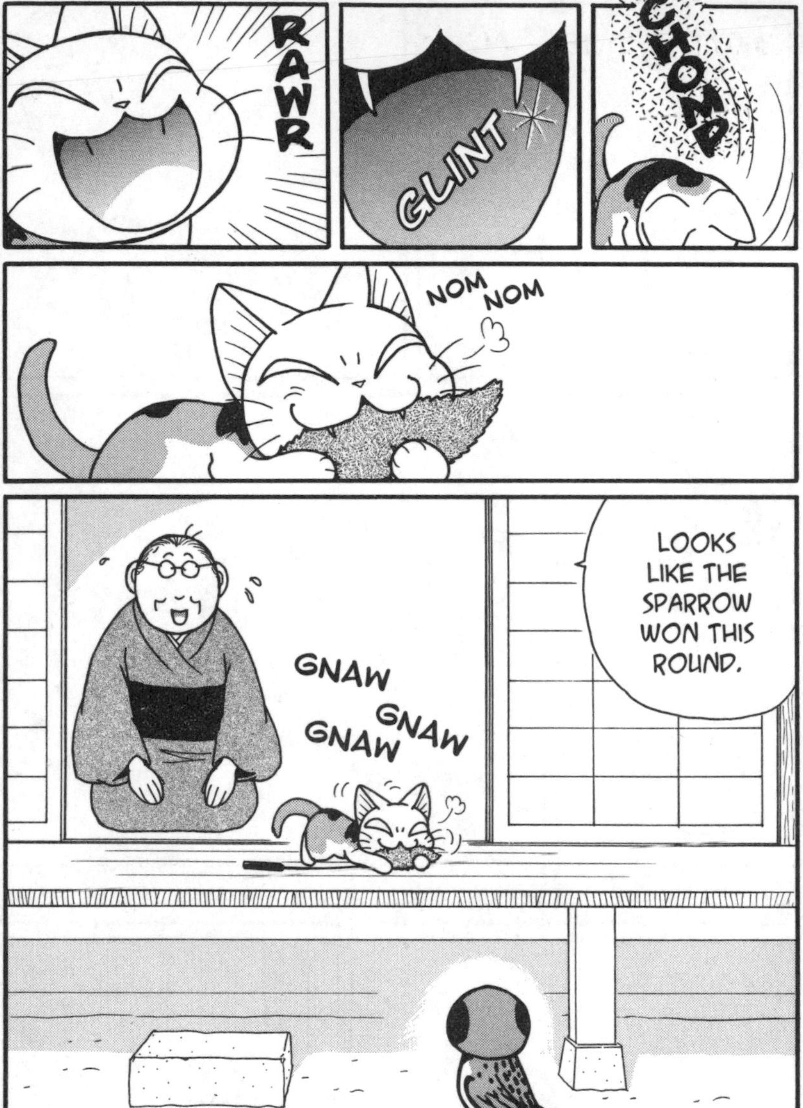
RAWR
GLINT
CHOMP
NOM NOM
LOOKS LIKE THE SPARROW WON THIS ROUND.
GNAW GNAW GNAW

the end

Springtime Walk

FUKU FUKU

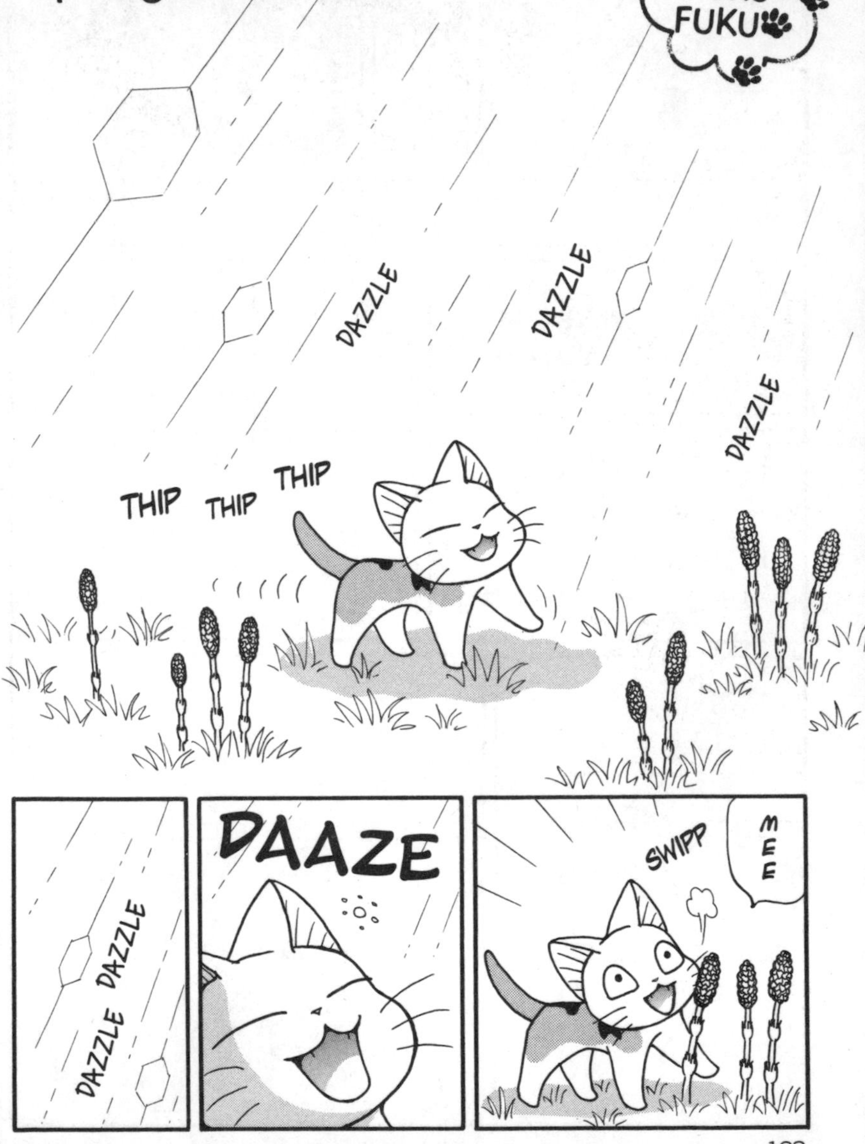
DAZZLE
DAZZLE
DAZZLE
THIP THIP THIP
DAZZLE DAZZLE
DAAZE
SWIPP
MEE

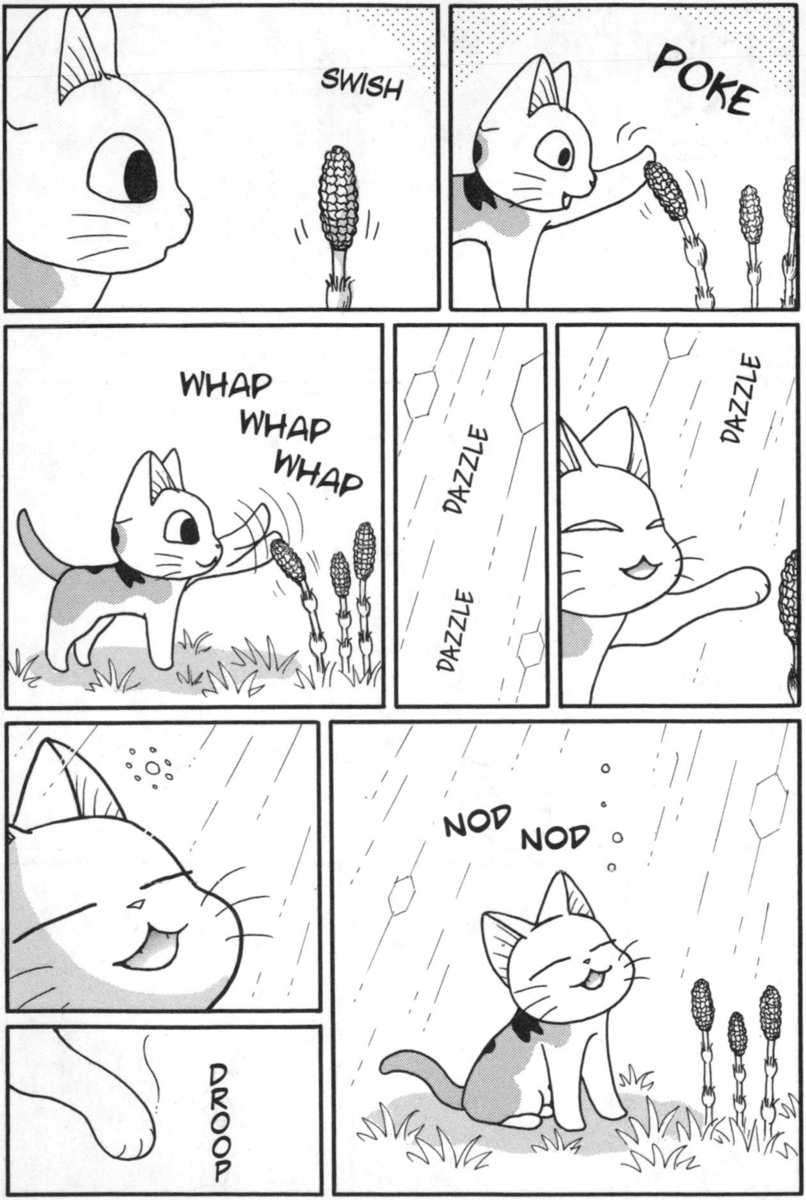
SWISH
POKE
WHAP
WHAP
WHAP
DAZZLE
DAZZLE
DAZZLE
DROOP
NOD
NOD

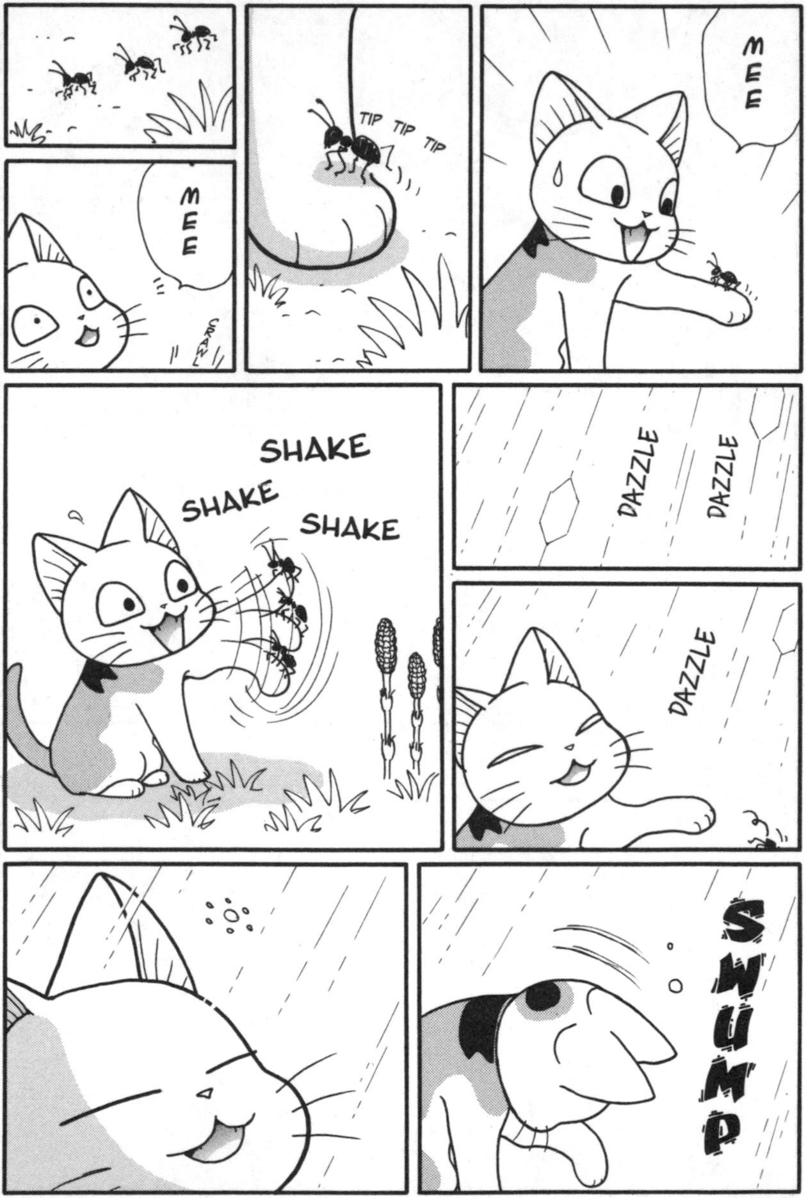
MEE
CRAWL
TIP TIP TIP
MEE
SHAKE
SHAKE
SHAKE
DAZZLE
DAZZLE
DAZZLE
SWUMP

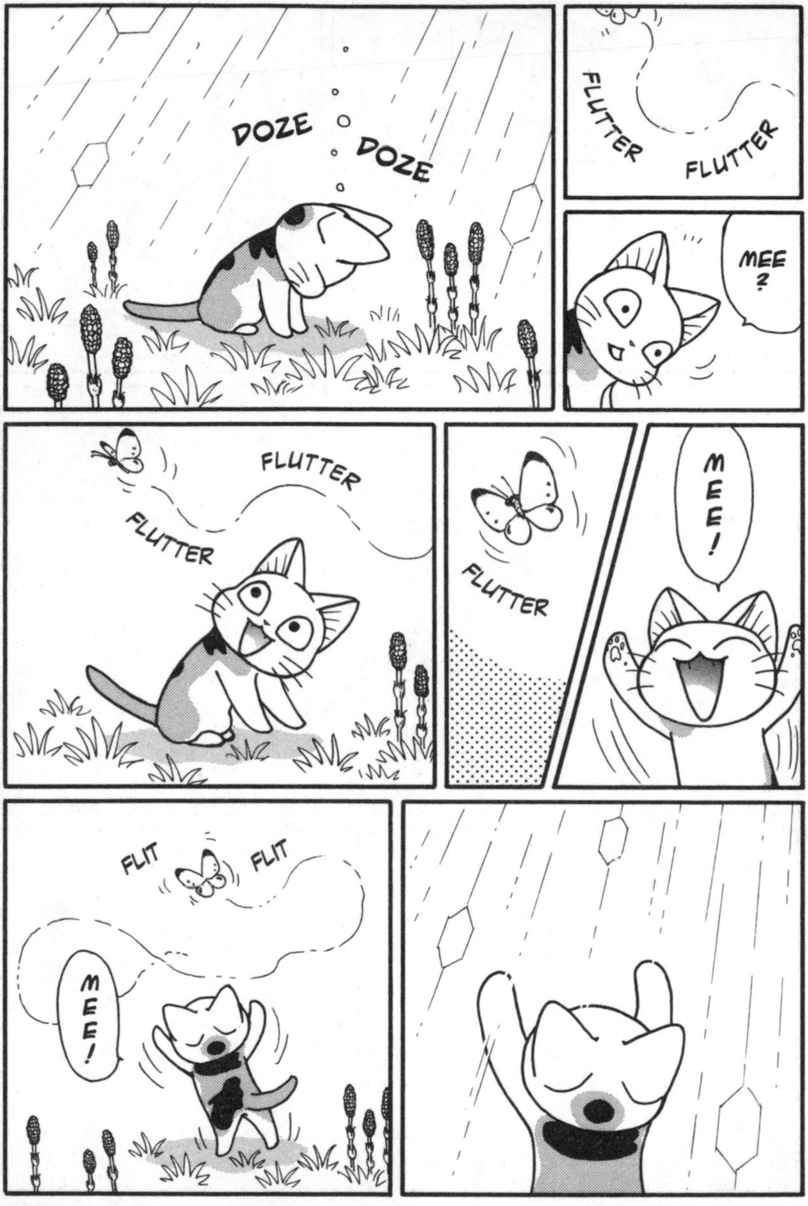
DOZE DOZE
FLUTTER
FLUTTER
MEE?
FLUTTER
FLUTTER
FLUTTER
MEE!
FLIT
FLIT
MEE!

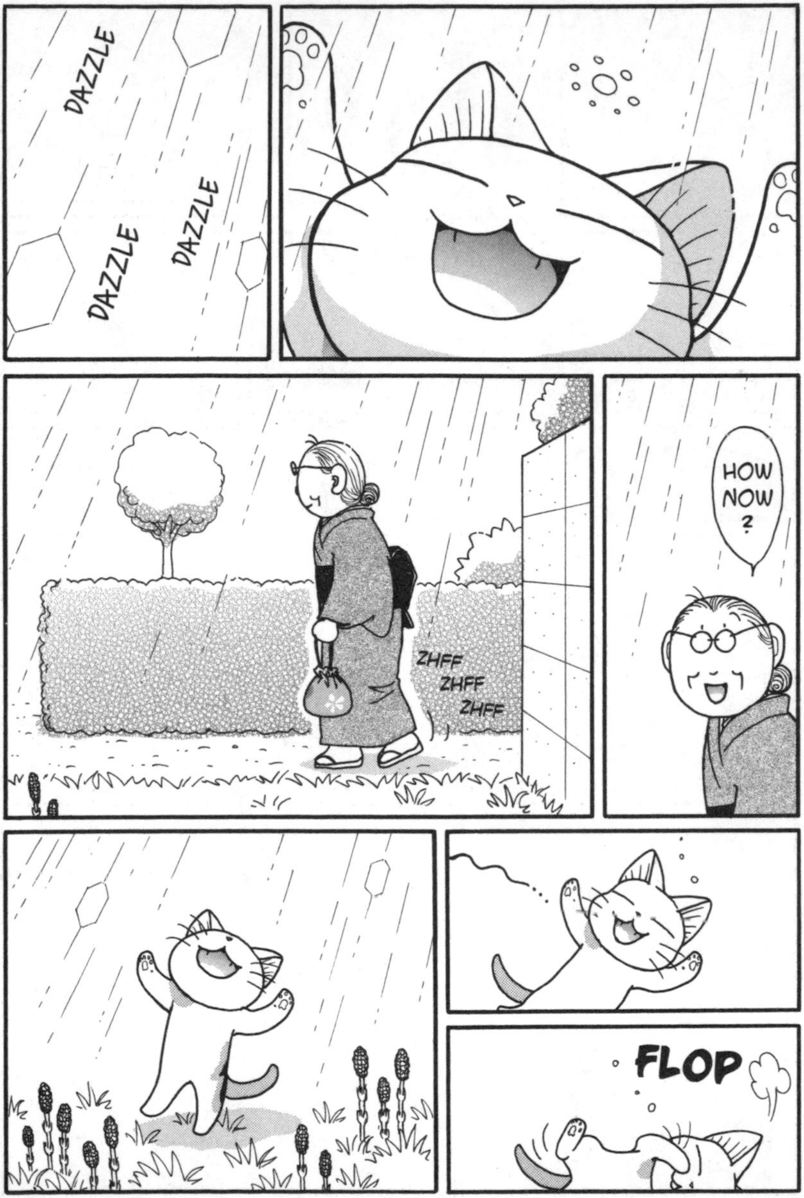
DAZZLE
DAZZLE
DAZZLE
ZHFF
ZHFF
ZHFF
HOW NOW?
FLOP

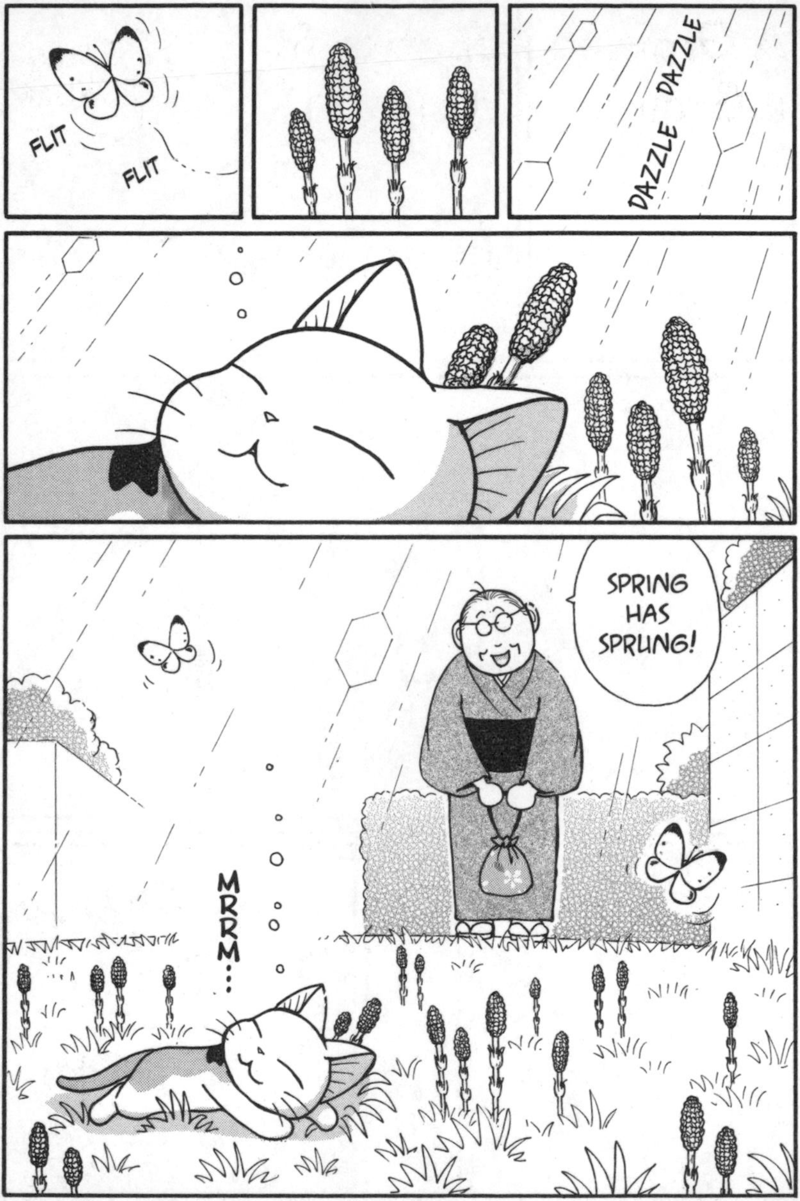
FLIT
FLIT
DAZZLE DAZZLE
SPRING HAS SPRUNG!
MRRM...

the end

A Growing Appetite for a Growing Kitten

FUKU FUKU

WIGGL
WIGGL
SPRING

SPRING
SPRING
HAAH
SWUMP

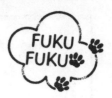

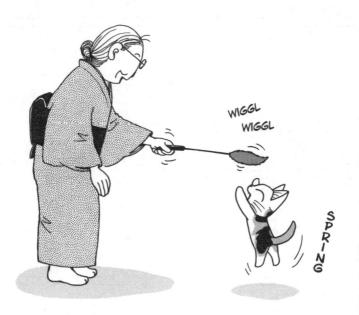

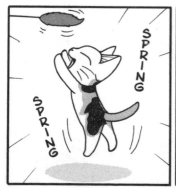

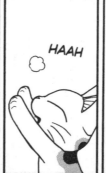

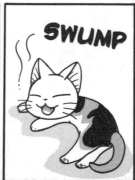

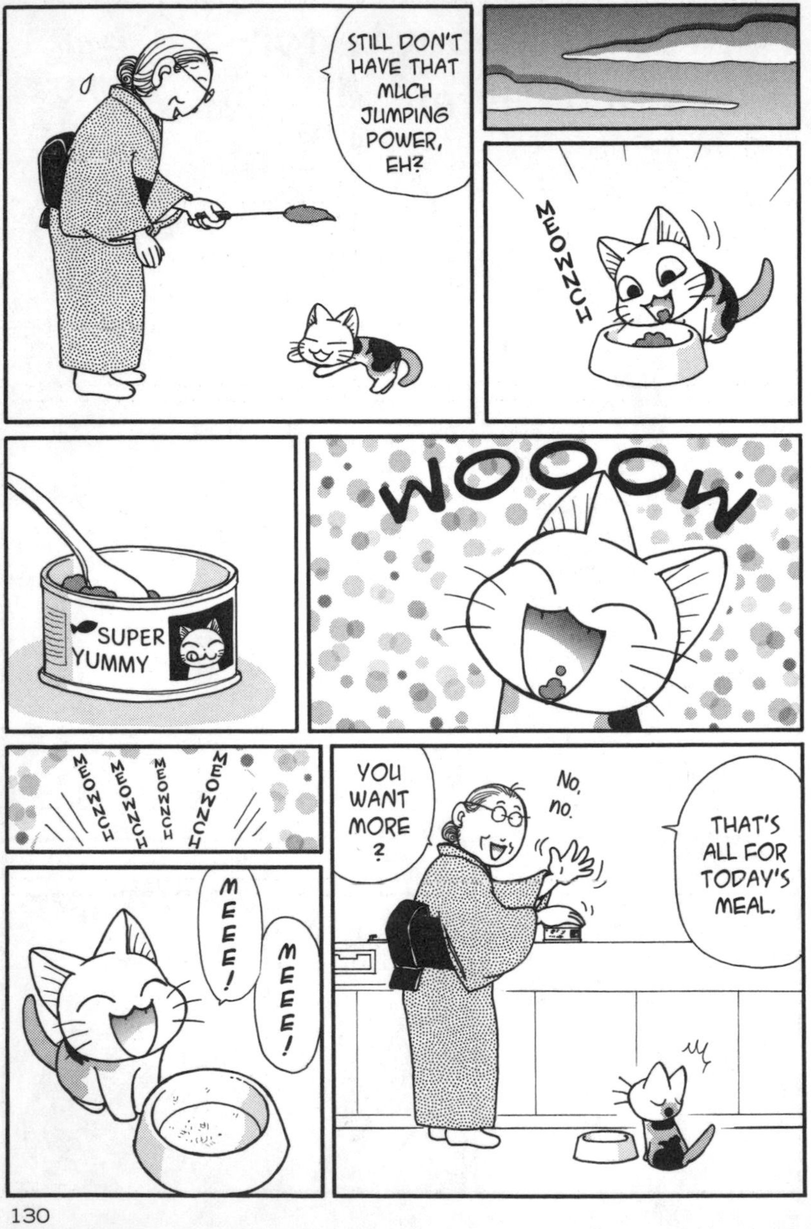
STILL DON'T HAVE THAT MUCH JUMPING POWER, EH?
MEOWNCH
SUPER YUMMY
WOOOW
MEOWNCH
MEOWNCH
MEOWNCH
MEOWNCH
MEEE!
MEEE!
YOU WANT MORE?
No, no.
THAT'S ALL FOR TODAY'S MEAL.

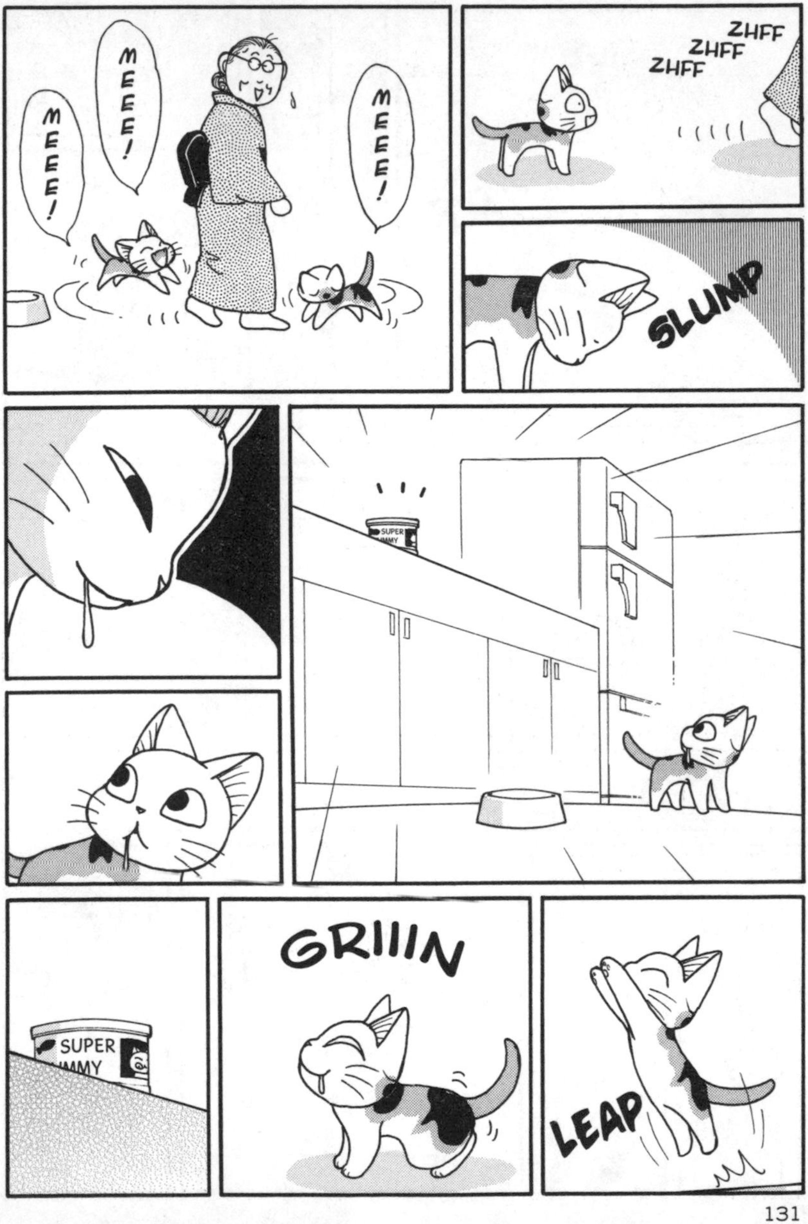
MEEE!
MEEE!
MEEE!
ZHFF
ZHFF
ZHFF
SLUMP
SUPER
MMY
SUPER
MMY
GRIIIN
LEAP

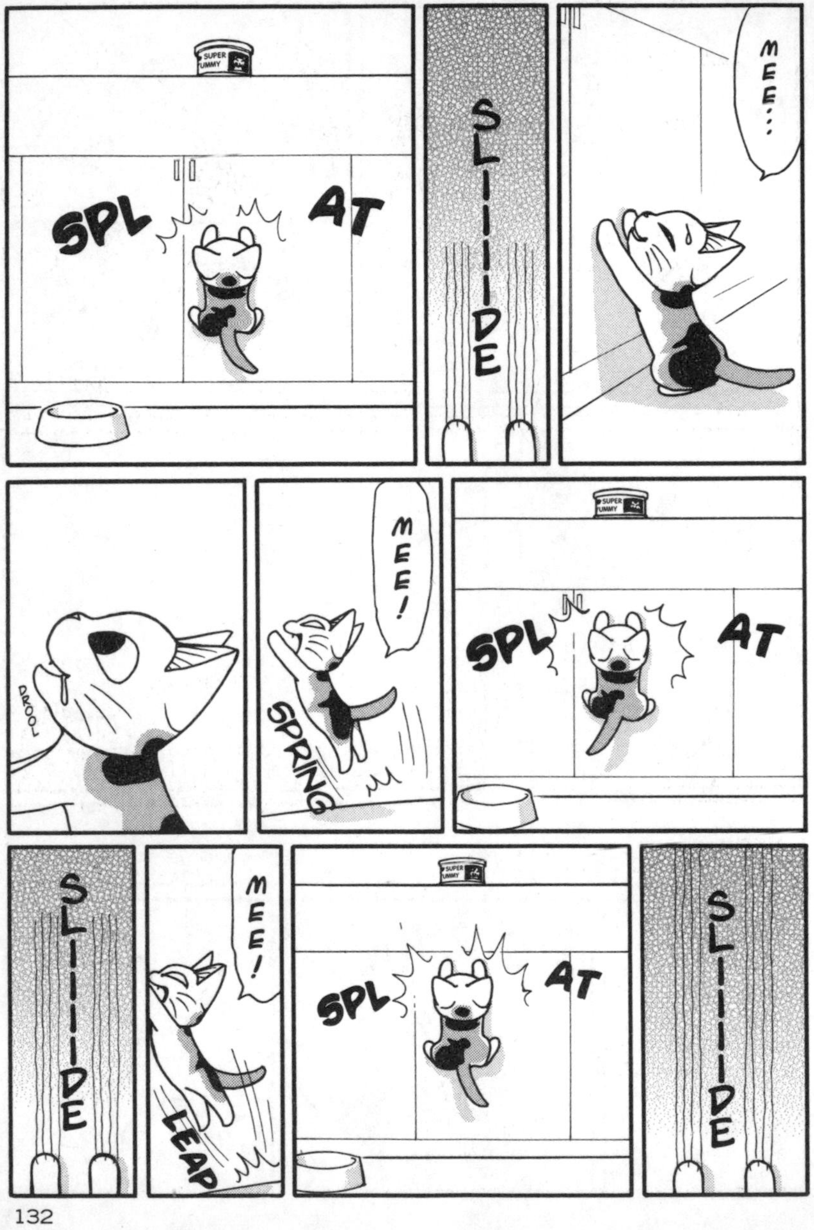
SUPER YUMMY
SPL AT
SLIIIDE
MEE...
DROOL
MEE!
SPRING
SUPER YUMMY
SPL AT
SLIIIDE
MEE!
LEAP
SUPER YUMMY
SPL AT
SLIIIIDE

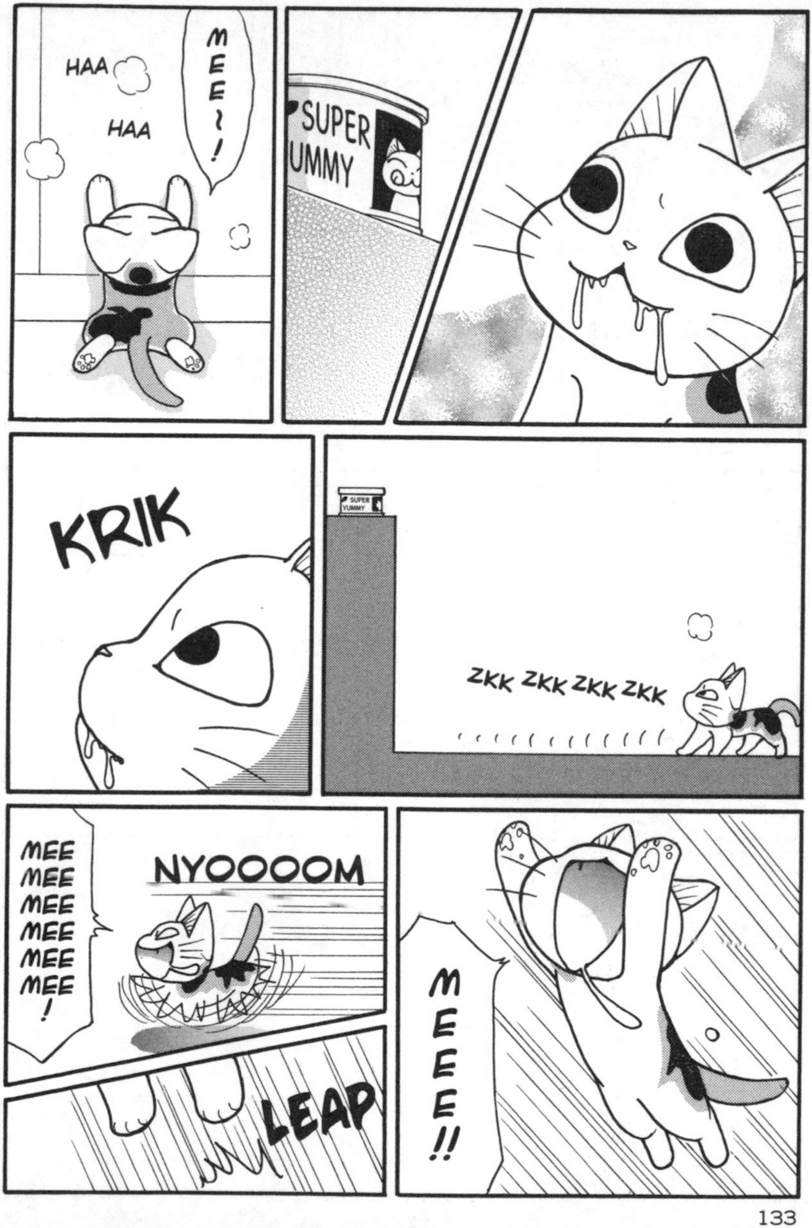
HAA
HAA
MEE~!
SUPER
UMMY
KRIK
SUPER
YUMMY
ZKK ZKK ZKK ZKK
MEE MEE MEE MEE MEE MEE!
NYOOOOM
LEAP
MEEE!!

GRAB
SUPER YUMMY
MEE!
Special Lid
SUPER
...
DNK DNK DNK
Special Lid
SUPER YUMMY

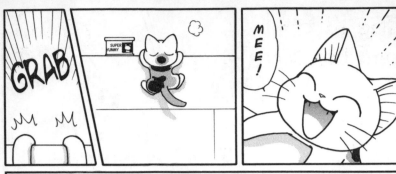

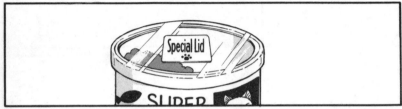

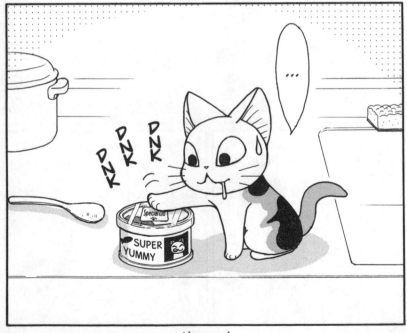

the end

The Kitten and the Mole

FUKU FUKU

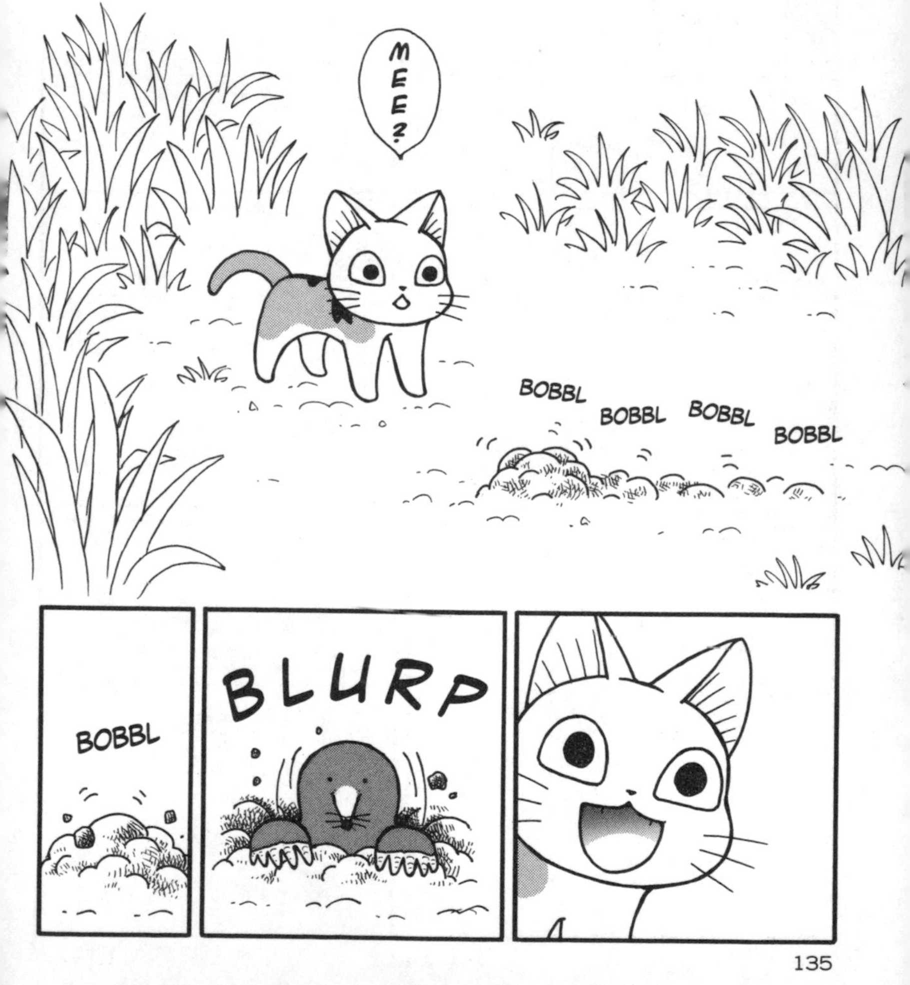

MEE?
BOBBL
BOBBL
BOBBL
BOBBL
BOBBL
BLURP

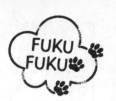

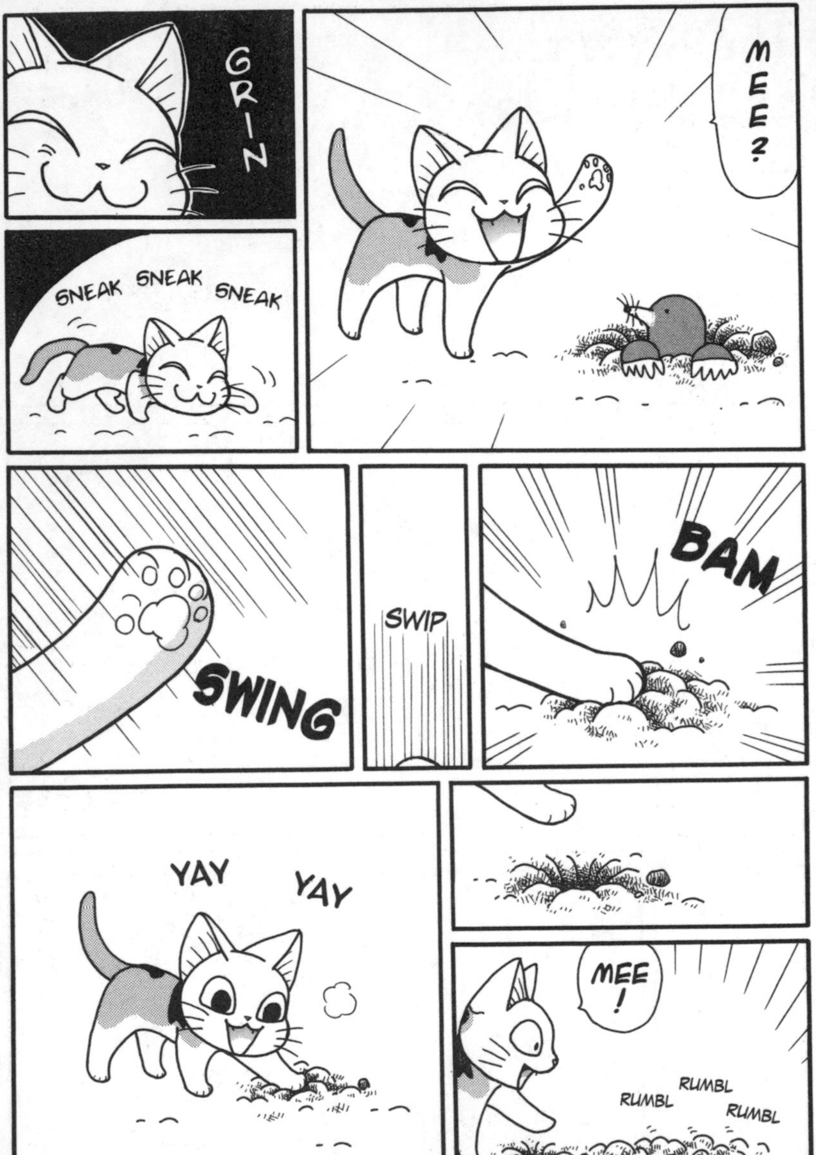
GRIN
SNEAK SNEAK SNEAK
MEE?
SWING
SWIP
BAM
YAY YAY
MEE!
RUMBL RUMBL RUMBL

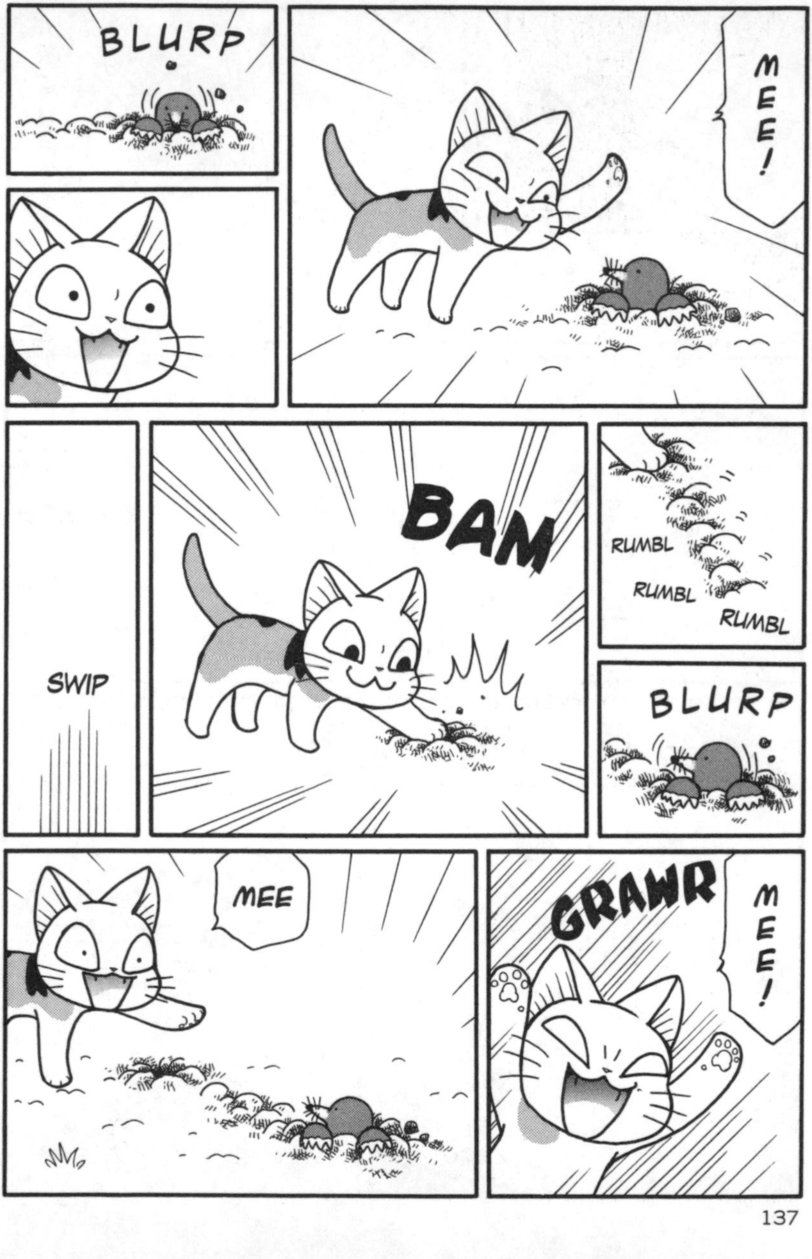

BLURP
MEE!
BAM
RUMBL
RUMBL
RUMBL
SWIP
BLURP
MEE
GRAWR
MEE!

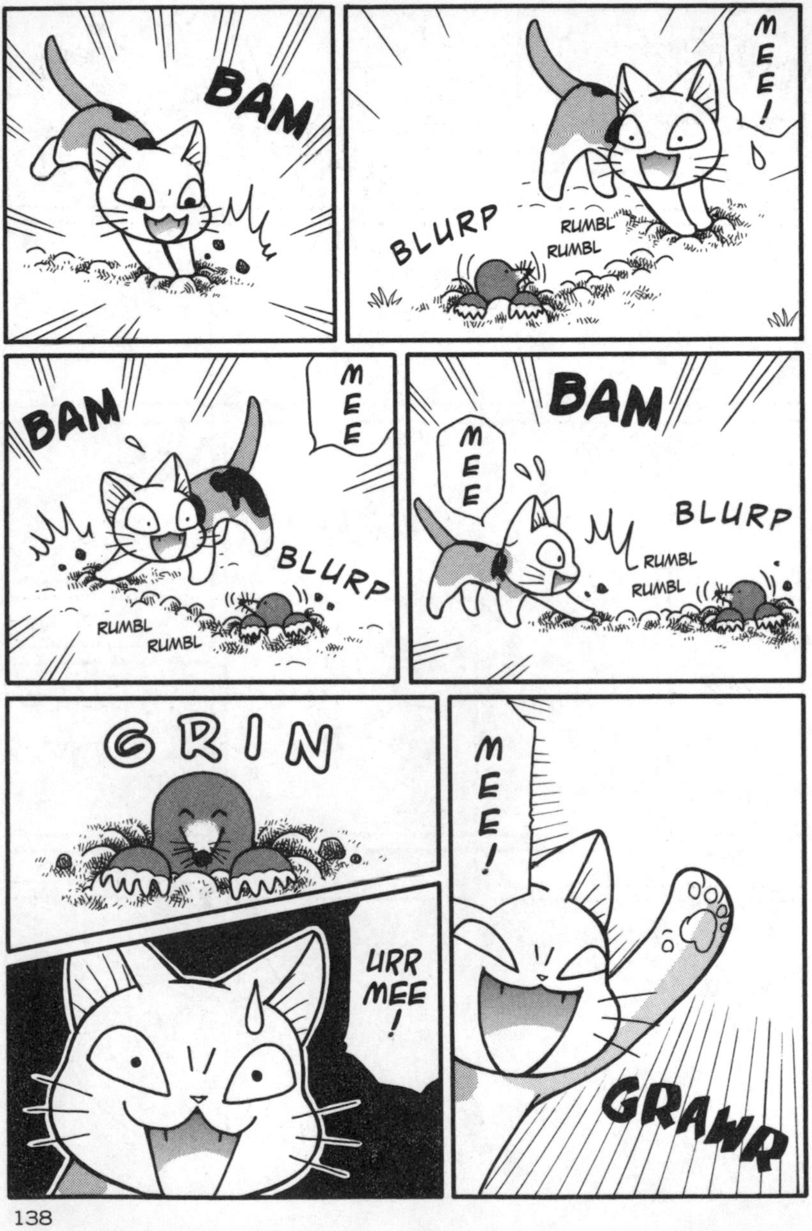
BAM
MEE!
BLURP
RUMBL
RUMBL
BAM
MEE
BLURP
RUMBL
RUMBL
BAM
MEE
BLURP
RUMBL
RUMBL
GRIN
URR MEE!
MEE!
GRAWR

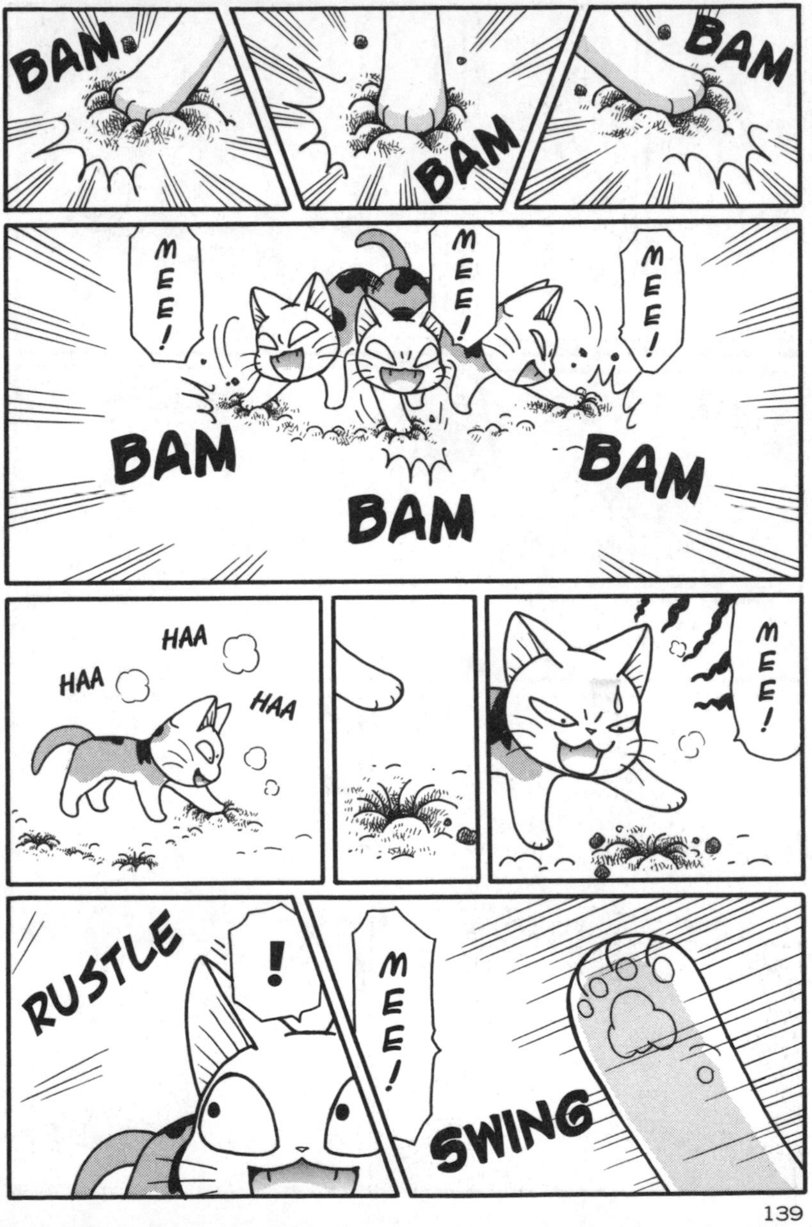
BAM
BAM
BAM
MEE!
MEE!
MEE!
BAM
BAM
BAM
HAA
HAA
HAA
MEE!
RUSTLE
!
MEE!
SWING

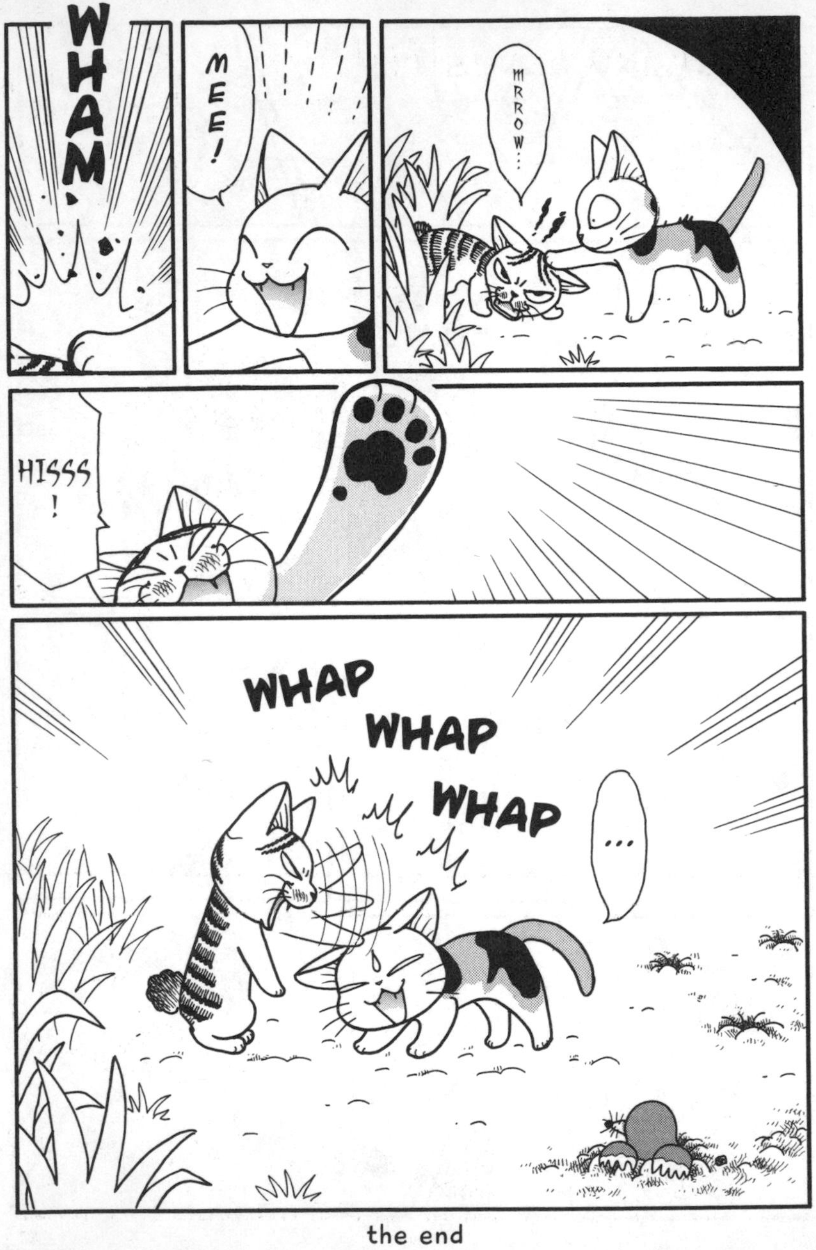
WHAM!
MEE!
MRROW...
!!
HISSS!
WHAP
WHAP
WHAP
...

the end

FukuFuku Loves Fish

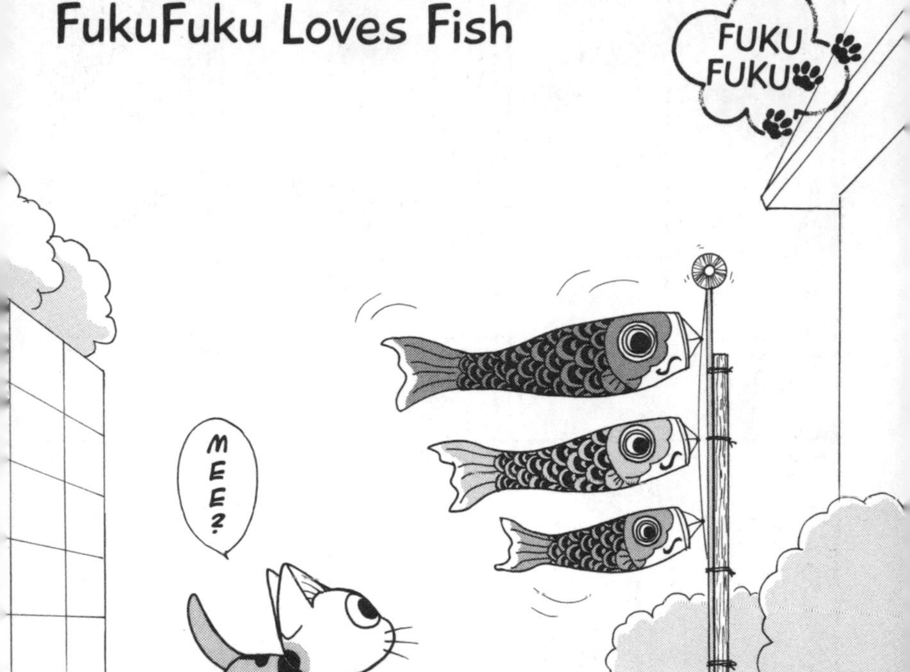
FUKU FUKU
MEE?

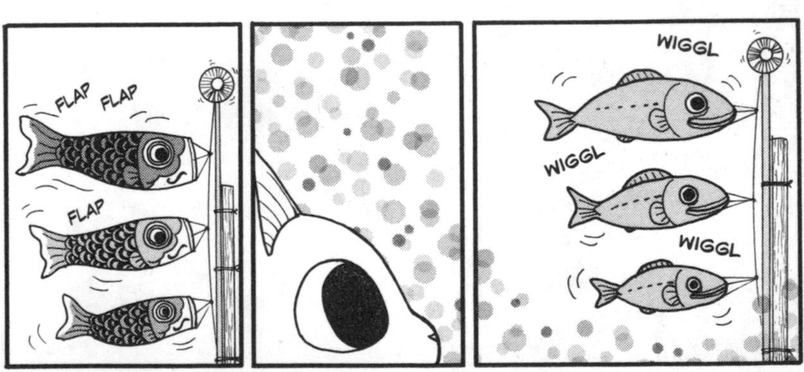
FLAP FLAP
FLAP
WIGGL
WIGGL
WIGGL

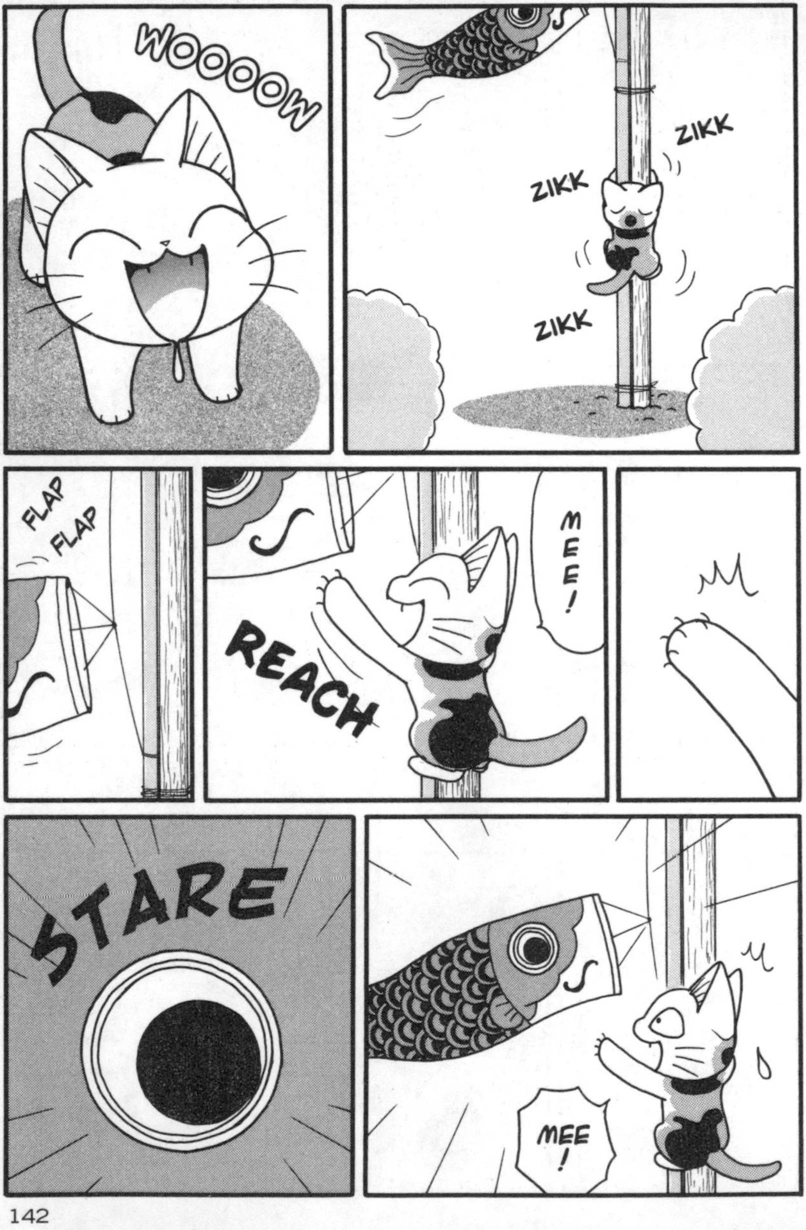
WOOOOOW
ZIKK
ZIKK
ZIKK
FLAP
FLAP
MEE!
REACH
STARE
MEE!

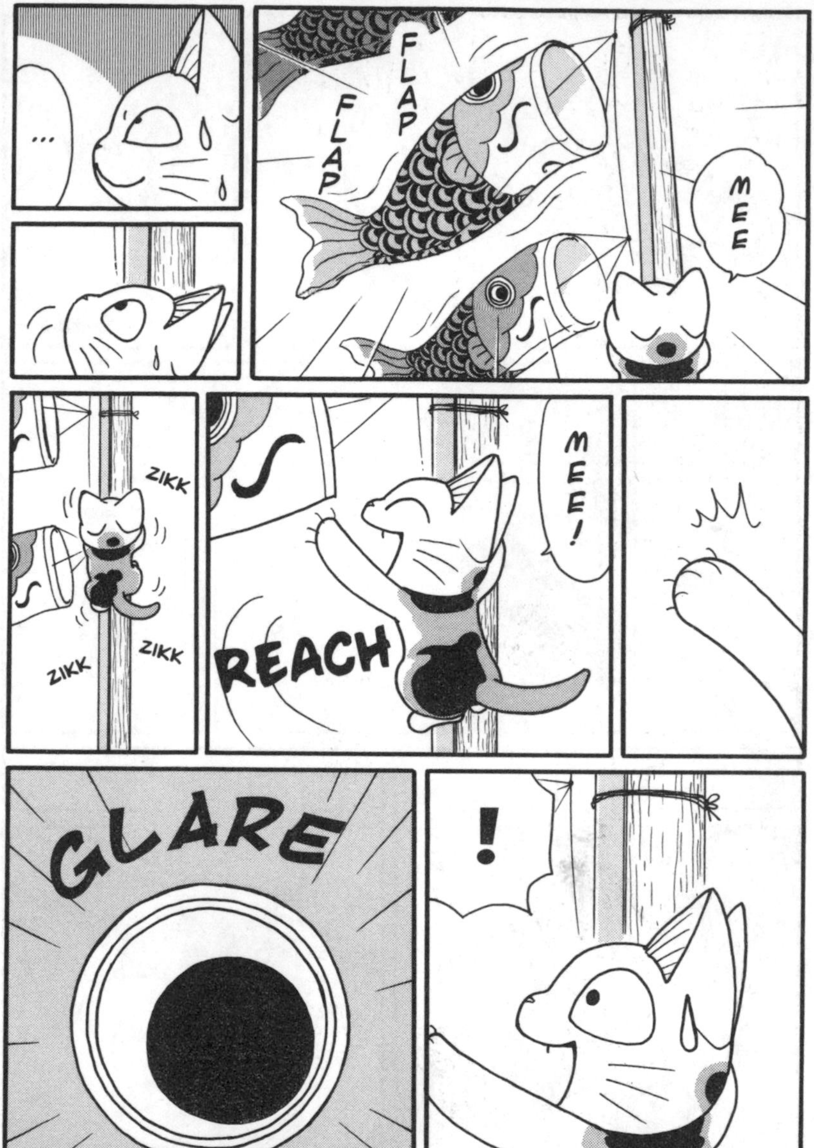
...
FLAP
FLAP
MEE
ZIKK
ZIKK
ZIKK
MEE!
REACH
GLARE
!

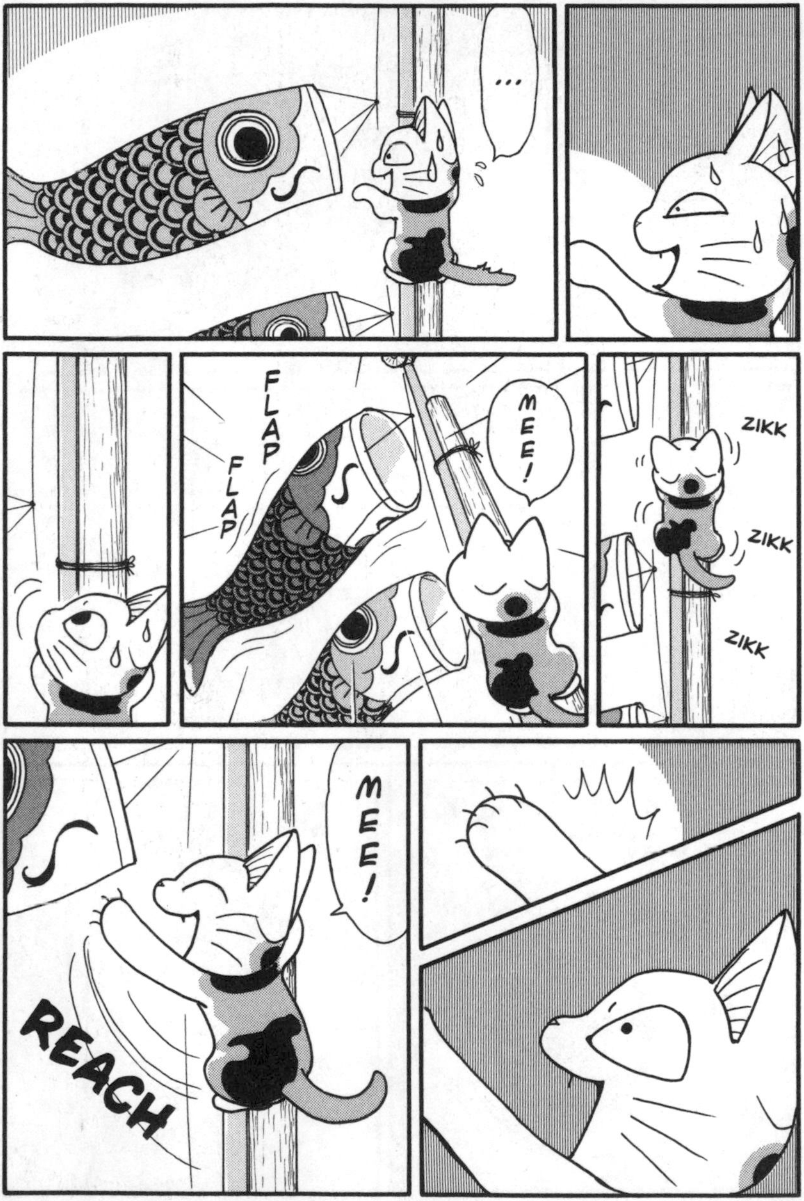
...
FLAP
FLAP
MEE!
ZIKK
ZIKK
ZIKK
MEE!
REACH

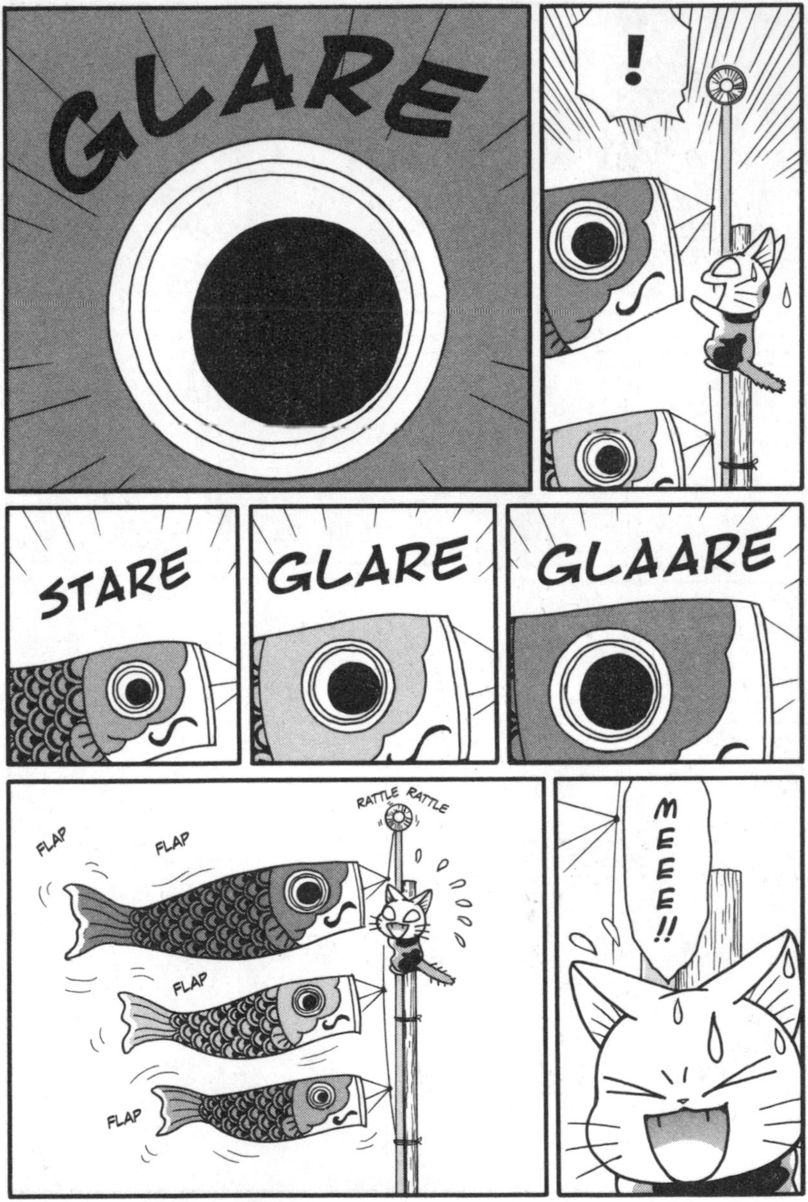
GLARE
!
STARE
GLARE
GLAARE
FLAP
FLAP
RATTLE RATTLE
FLAP
FLAP
MEEE!!

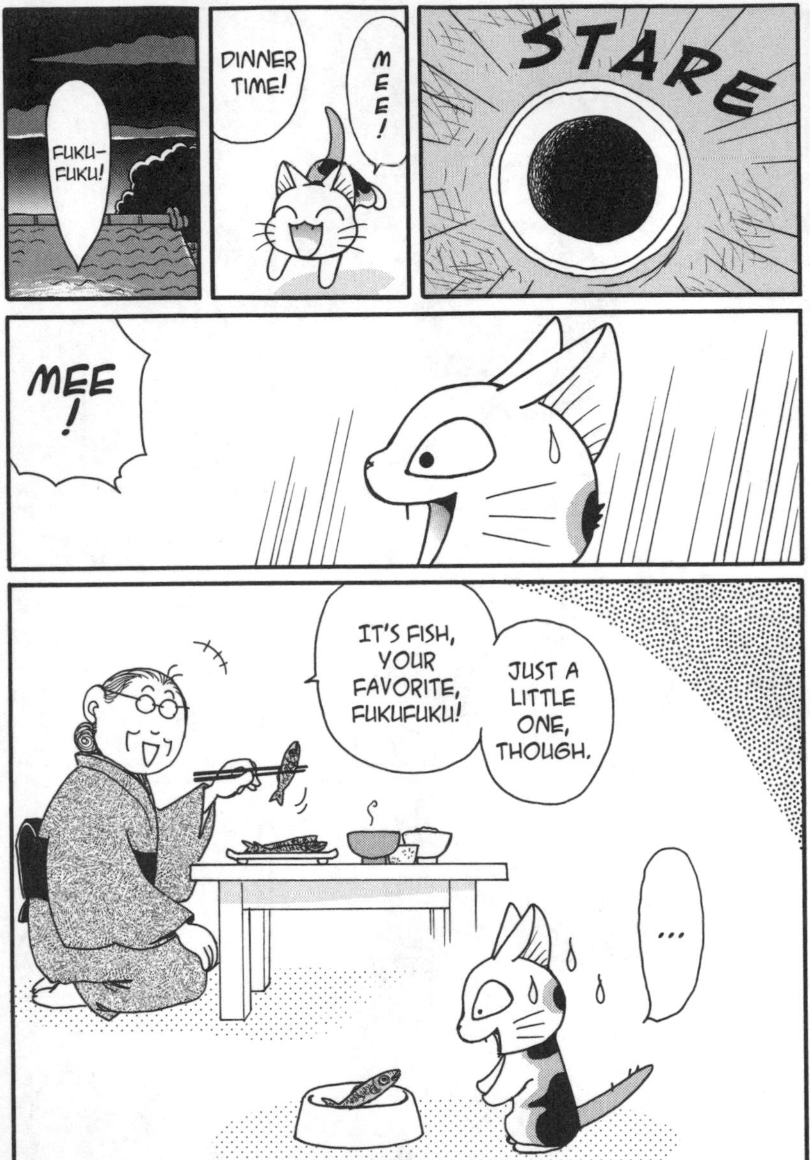
FUKU-
FUKU!
DINNER TIME!
MEE!
STARE
MEE!
IT'S FISH, YOUR FAVORITE, FUKUFUKU!
JUST A LITTLE ONE, THOUGH.
...

the end

FUKU
FUKU

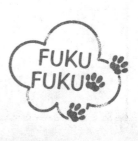

FukuFuku Grows Up

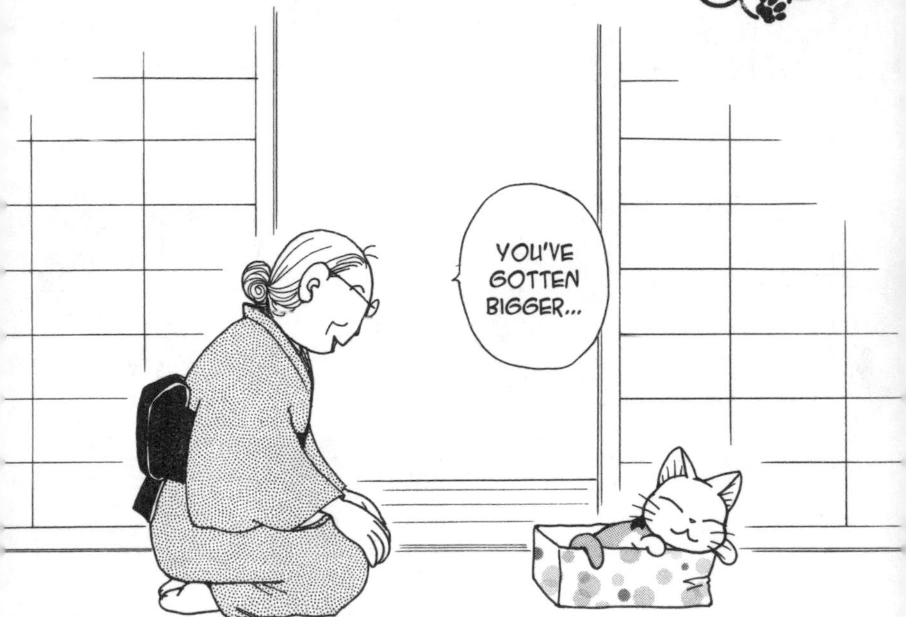
YOU'VE GOTTEN BIGGER...

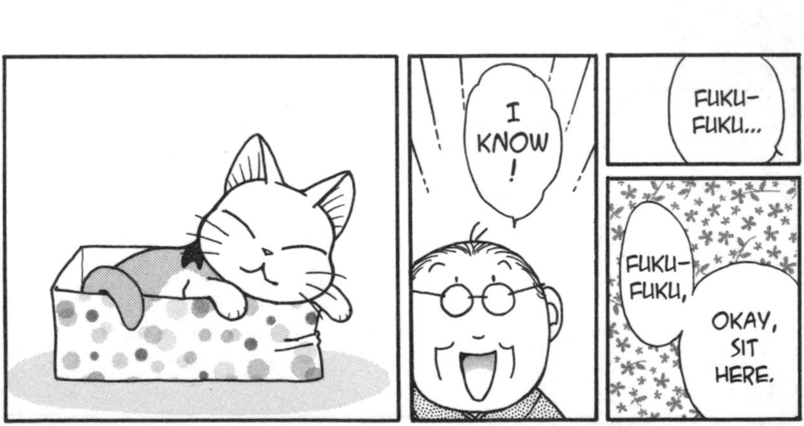
I KNOW!
FUKU-FUKU...
FUKU-FUKU,
OKAY, SIT HERE.

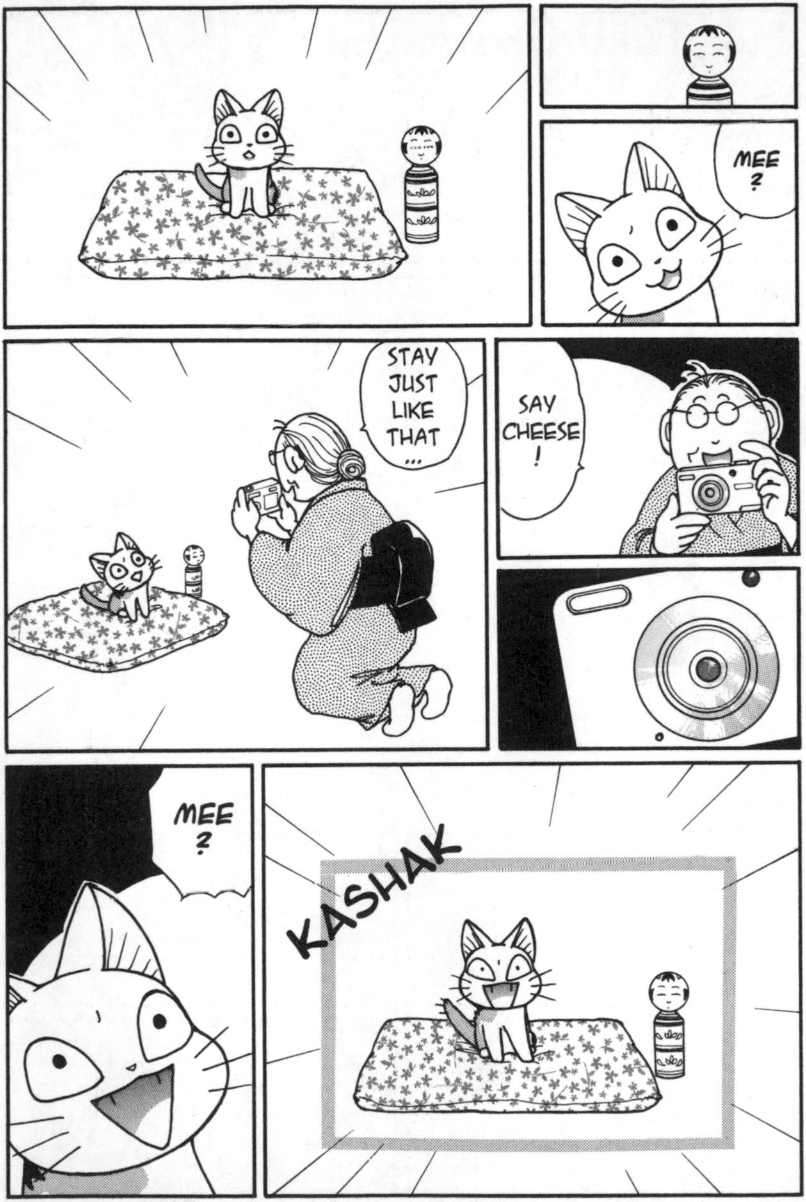
MEE ?
STAY JUST LIKE THAT ...
SAY CHEESE !
MEE ?
KASHAK

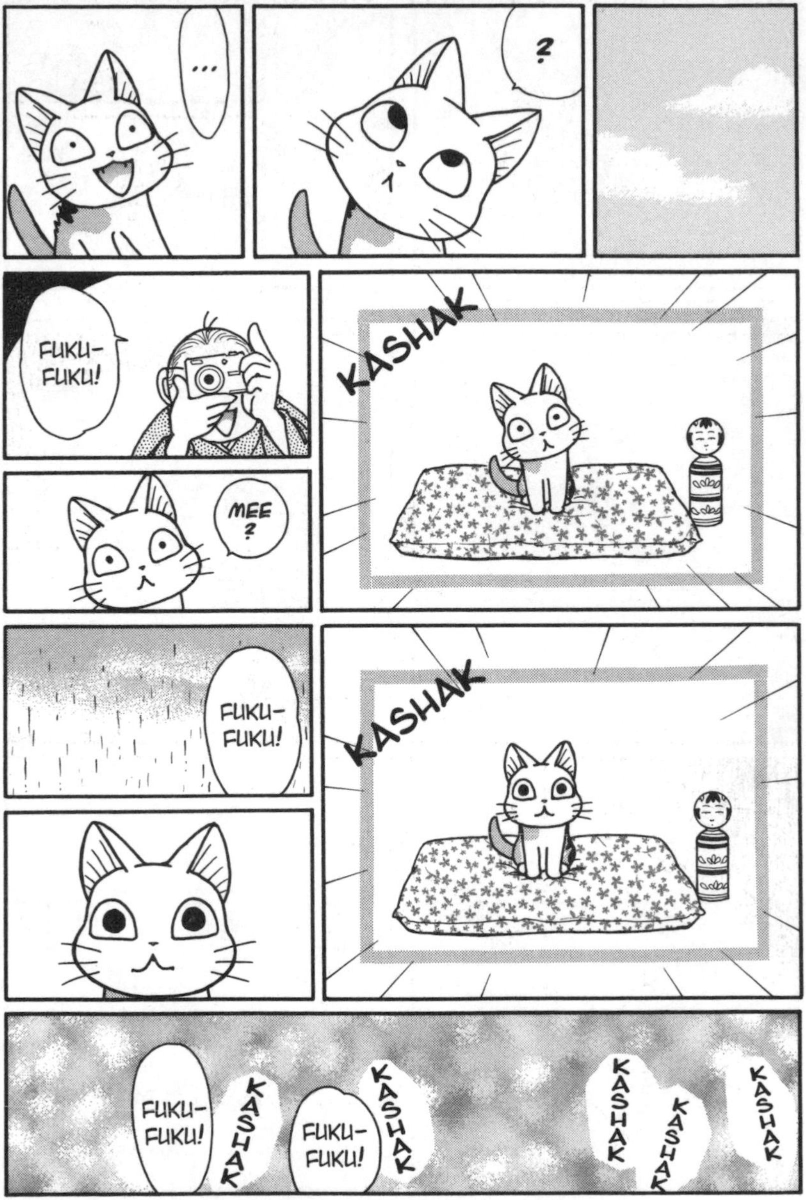
...
?
FUKU-FUKU!
MEE ?
KASHAK
FUKU-FUKU!
KASHAK
FUKU-FUKU!
KASHAK
FUKU-FUKU!
KASHAK
KASHAK
KASHAK
KASHAK

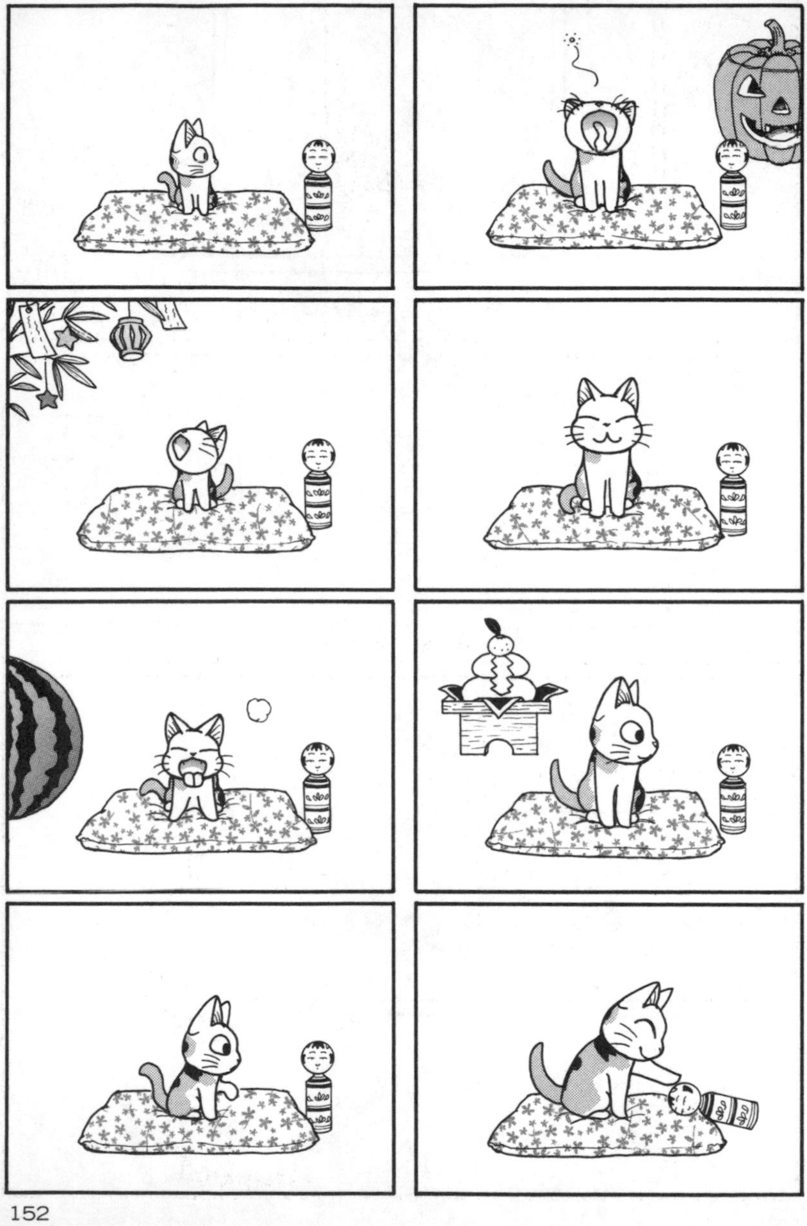

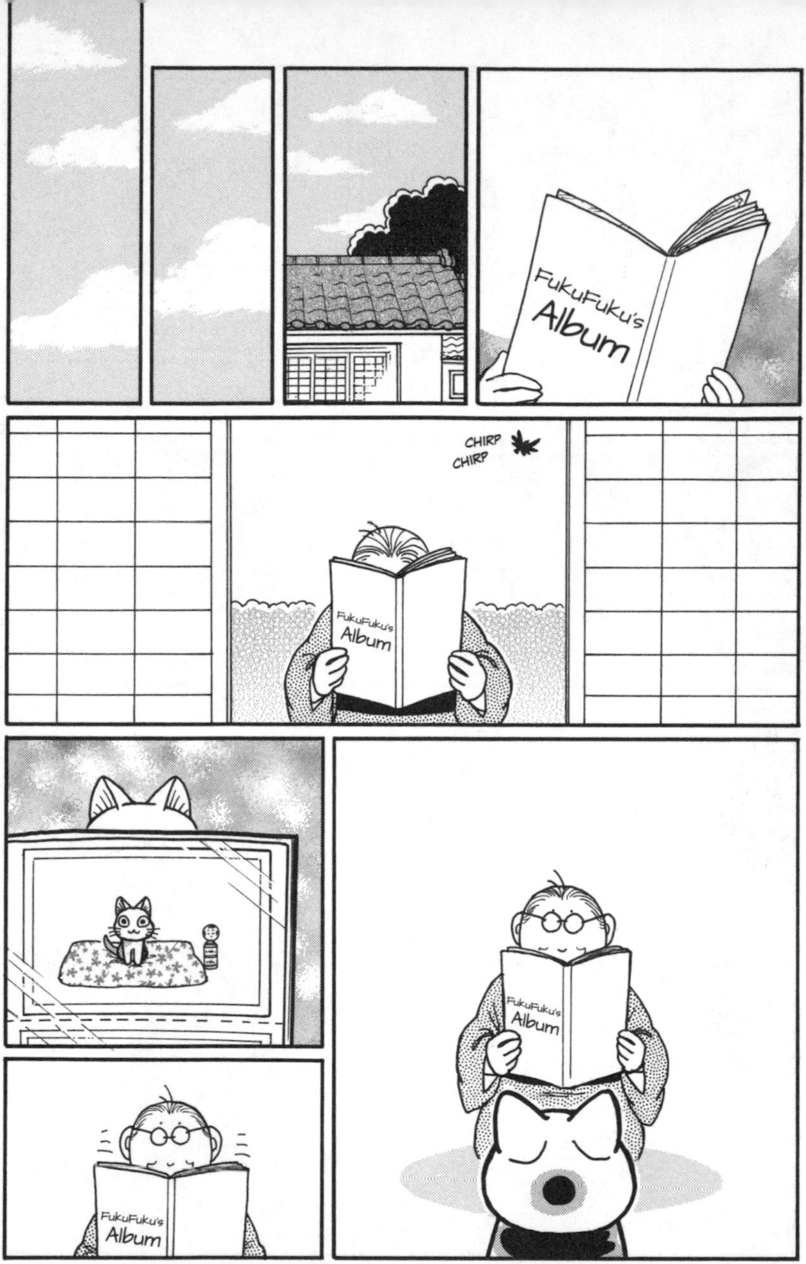
FukuFuku's Album
CHIRP
CHIRP
FukuFuku's Album
FukuFuku's Album
FukuFuku's Album

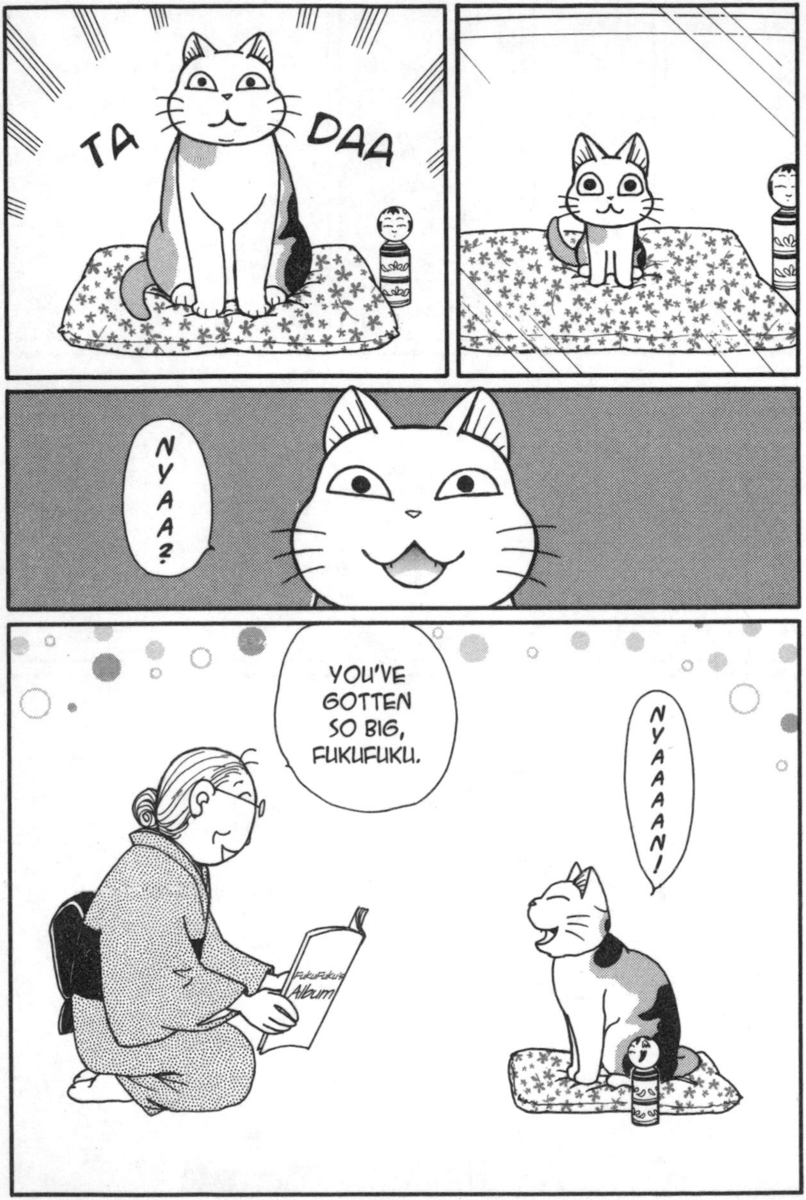
TA DAA
NYAA?
YOU'VE GOTTEN SO BIG, FUKUFUKU.
NYAAAAN!
FukuFuku's Album

the end

FUKU
FUKU

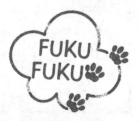

This Book is the Cat's Meow

Celebrating the conclusion of Konami Kanata's international megahit *Chi's Sweet Home*, **The Complete Chi** is a new edition that honors some of the best Japan has ever offered in the field of cat comics. A multiple *New York Times* Best Seller and two-time winner of the *Manga.Ask.com* Awards for Best Children's Manga, Konami Kanata's tale of a lost kitten has been acclaimed by readers worldwide as an excellent example of a comic that has truly been accepted by readers of all ages.

Presented in a brand new larger omnibus format each edition compiles three volumes of kitty cartoon tales, including two bonus cat comics from Konami Kanata's **FukuFuku** franchise, making **The Complete Chi's Sweet Home** a must have for every cat lover out there.

"*Chi's Sweet Home* made me smile throughout... It's utterly endearing. This is the first manga I've read in several years where I'm looking forward to the [next] volume."

—Chris Beveridge, *Mania.com*

"Konami Kanata does some pretty things with watercolor, and paces each of the little vignettes chronicling Chi's new life to highlight just the right moments for maximum effect... This is truly a visual treat." **—*Comics and More***

Part 1 contains volumes 1-2-3
Part 2 contains volumes 4-5-6
Part 3 contains volumes 7-8-9
Part 4 contains volumes 10-11-12

All Parts Available Now!

The Complete Chi's Sweet Home

Konami Kanata

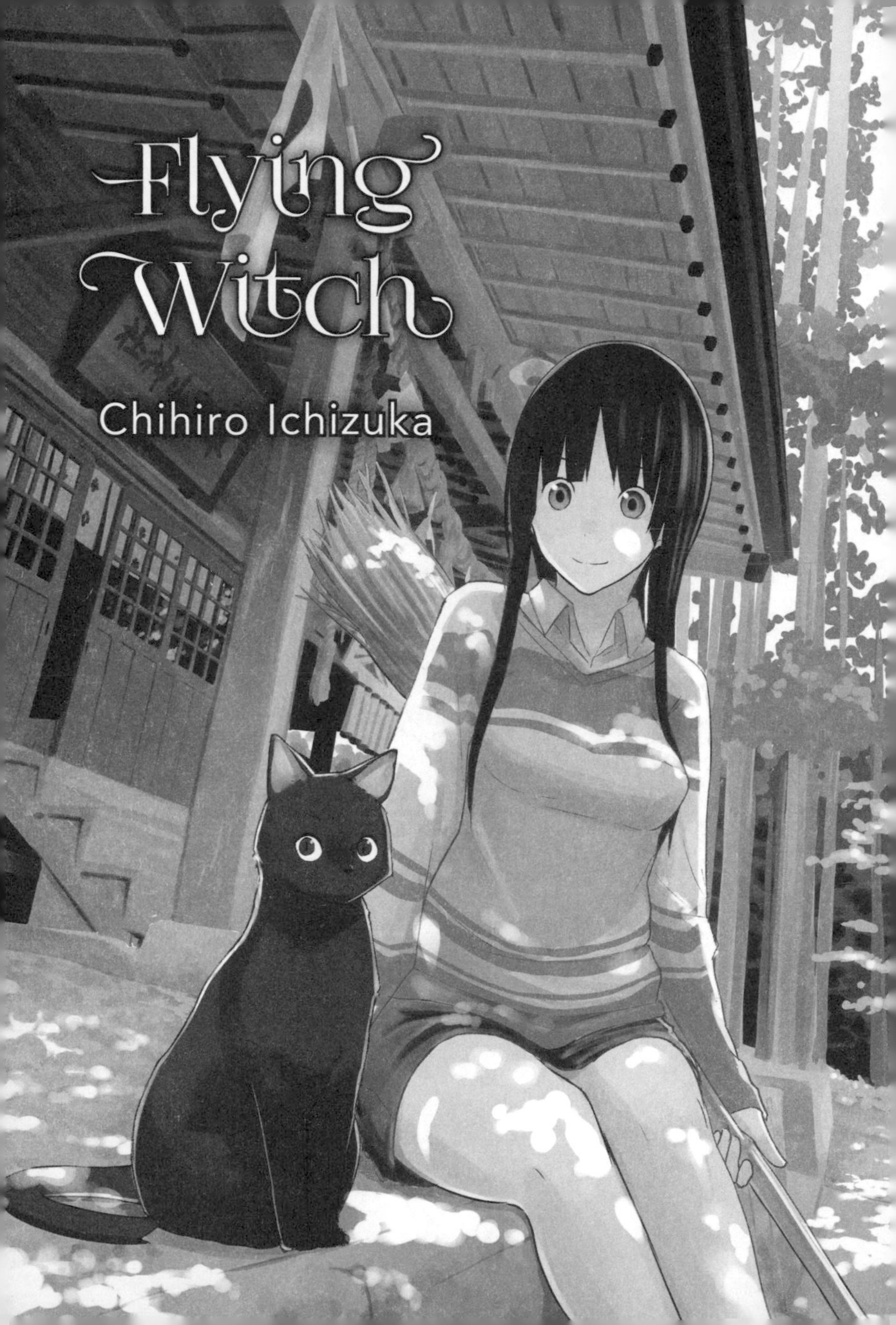
Flying Witch
Chihiro Ichizuka

Prepare to be Bewitched!

Makoto Kowata, a novice witch, packs up her belongings (including a black cat familiar) and moves in with her distant cousins in rural Aomori to complete her training and become a full-fledged witch.

"*Flying Witch* emphasizes that while actual magic is nice, there is ultimately magic in everything." —*Anime News Network*

The Basis for the Hit Anime from Sentai Filmworks!

Volume 1 On Sale Spring 2017!

My Neighbor Seki

Tonari no Seki-kun

Takuma Morishige

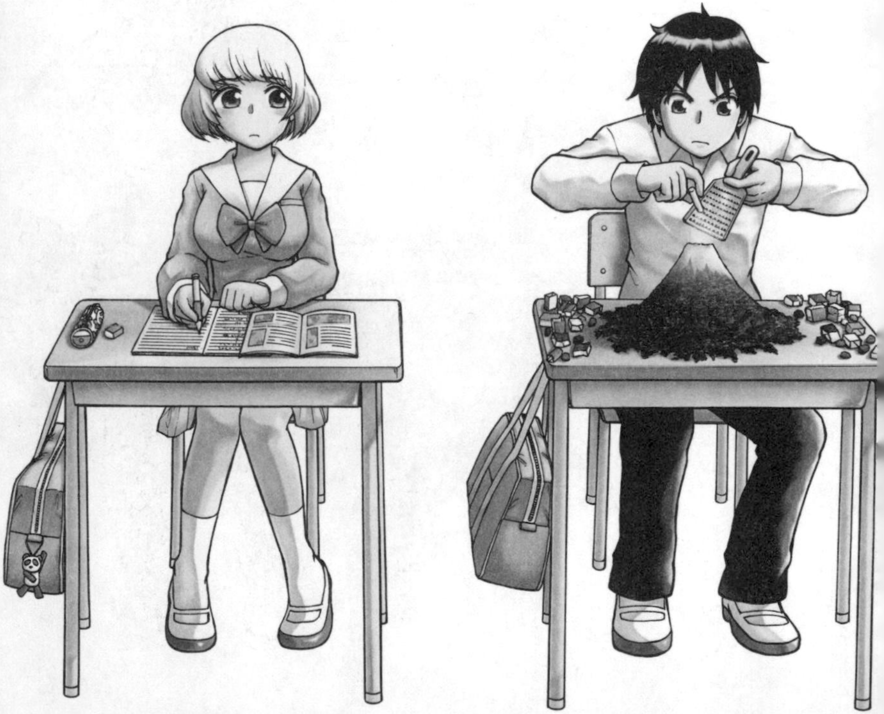

The Master of Killing Time

Toshinari Seki takes goofing off to new heights. Every day, on or around his school desk, he masterfully creates his own little worlds of wonder, often hidden to most of his classmates. Unfortunately for Rumi Yokoi, his neighbor at the back of the room, his many games, dioramas, and projects are often way too interesting to ignore; even when they are hurting her grades.

Volumes 1-8 available now!

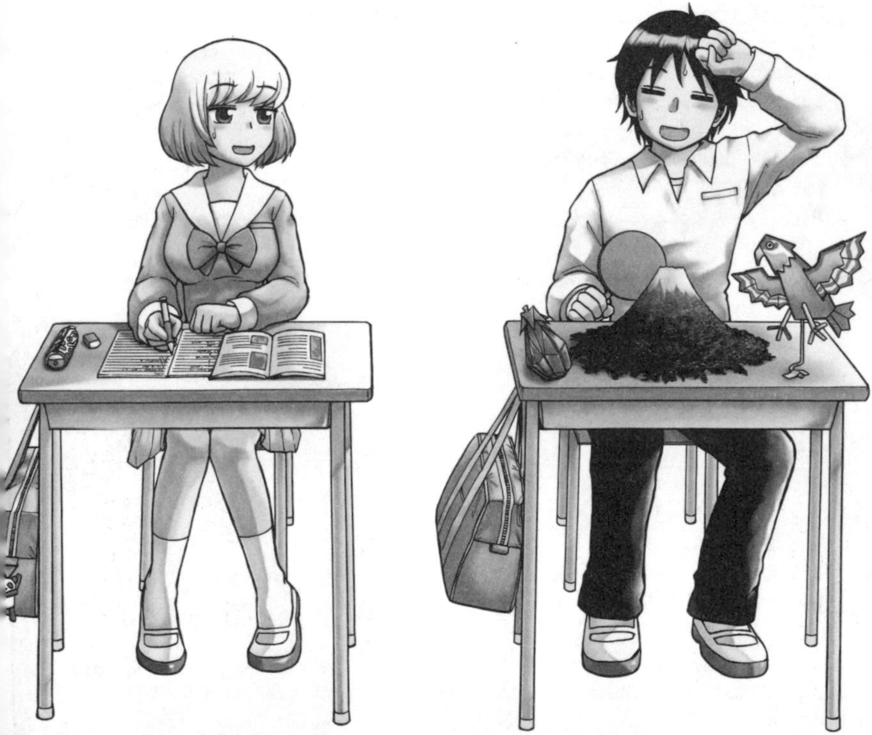

FukuFuku: Kitten Tales 2

Translation - Marlaina McElheny
Production - Grace Lu
Anthony Quintessenza

First published in Japan in 2015 by Kodansha, Ltd., Tokyo
Publication for this English edition arranged through Kodansha, Ltd., Tokyo

Translation provided by Vertical Comics, 2017
Published by Vertical Comics, an imprint of Vertical, Inc., New York

Originally published in Japanese as *FukuFuku Funya~n Ko-neko da Nyan 2* by Kodansha, Ltd., 2015
FukuFuku Funya~n Ko-neko da Nyan first serialized in *Be Love*, Kodansha, Ltd., 2013-2015

This is a work of fiction.

ISBN: 978-1-942993-63-6

Manufactured in Canada

First Edition

Vertical, Inc.
451 Park Avenue South, 7th Floor
New York, NY 10016
www.vertical-comics.com

Vertical books are distributed through Penguin-Random House Publisher Services.